A Dopeboy's Prayer

Eddie "Wolf" Lee

**Lock Down Publications
& Ca$h Presents
A Dopeboy's Prayer
A Novel by *Eddie "Wolf" Lee***

Eddie "Wolf" Lee

Lock Down Publications
P.O. Box 870494
Mesquite, Tx 75187

Visit our website at **www.lockdownpublications.com**

Cover design and layout by: Dynasty's Cover Me
Book interior design by: Shawn Walker
Edited by: Cassandra Barret-Sims

Stay Connected with Us!

Text **LOCKDOWN** to 22828 to stay up-to-date with new releases, sneak peaks, contests and more...

Thank you.

Submission Guideline

Submit the first three chapters of your completed manuscript to ldpsubmissions@gmail.com, subject line: Your book's title. The manuscript must be in a .doc file and sent as an attachment. Document should be in Times New Roman, double spaced and in size 12 font. Also, provide your synopsis and full contact information. If sending multiple submissions, they must each be in a separate email.

Have a story but no way to send it electronically? You can still submit to LDP/Ca$h Presents. Send in the first three chapters, written or typed, of your completed manuscript to:

LDP: Submissions Dept
Po Box 1482
Pine Lake, Ga 30072

DO NOT send original manuscript. Must be a duplicate.

Provide your synopsis and a cover letter containing your full contact information.

Thanks for considering LDP and Ca$h Presents.

Acknowledgments

First and foremost, all praises and glory to THE MOST HIGH YAH. It's only because of HIS chastisement, love and mercy that I'm alive, healthy and able to share my talents with the world.

To my mother, Judy Lee: You're a remarkable woman. You've loved, supported and made sacrifices for me even when I didn't deserve it. I am forever grateful. My life's mission is to make you proud to have me as your son as I'm proud to have you as my mother. I love you to death.

To my Queen and the Givan family: Vanessa, words cannot express the magnitude of love I have for you. Despite life's hardships, my demanding ways and the many haters, you've remained steadfast in your level of commitment and loyalty to me. It don't get no realer than that! You're a true Hebrew Israelite Queen...my Queen. And to everybody, Terrance, T.J., Angie, Quita, Moe-Moe, Te'Onnie, Fat Daddy, Tyrone, Tracey, Aljean (my mother) and Madea—I love y'all and appreciate the support.

To my siblings, Sharain, Dwayne Jr., Dawana and Keith Sr: I take pride when I say that each one of you have grown up to be exceptional adults. The fact that we all grew up on the south side of Chicago and none of you took the street route as I did is commendable. I apologize for letting y'all down, but I promise I'ma make it up. Kiss my nieces and nephews and tell em' I love em'. And to my youngest sister, Dawana, I can't thank you enough for all that you've done and continue to do to ensure your big bro lives as comfortable as possible behind these walls.

To a few good men who served the time and stayed true: Tornado a.k.a. Karo (Springfield, Illinois Finest. On behalf of everybody you've looked out for...we appreciate), Victor a.k.a. Juice (good lookin' out wit the lawyer), Forrest a.k.a. FuFu (told you I'd name a character after you) Marcus a.k.a. Taz (it's time to shake' Bama...you startin' to sound country! LOL), Marcus a.k.a. Blink (the pride of Rockford, Illinois) , Real El (you doing big thangs as the CEO of Hood Hope), Brad T. (the

L.E.G. fantasy football league, still going strong), Larnzell a.k.a. Cytee, Dione, Kenny a.k.a. Unc, Vincent a.k.a. Vino, Ryan a.k.a. Munchy, and last but certainly not least, Memphis Tennessee's very own Brian a.k.a. A'jamu (be patient, bruh. Any and every goal you wish to accomplish will come to pass. Remember we was cellie's in seg when I read a novel you wrote which inspired me to pick up the pen. Quit sittin' on them page turners and publish them. I know writing ain't ya thang, but them joints bangin'.

To my sandbox brothers, Arthur and Delmar: I try not to live with any regrets but sometimes I wonder how life would've turned out had I went to the same high school as y'all, like I was supposed to. Arthur, you told me is I needed you, don't hesitate to call. And you've answered every one of my phone calls. Delmar, what can I say? You named your first-born son after me. I love you guys and we gon' do it BIG when I touch.

To the Lockdown Publications family: Much love and respect to the C.E.O. of LDP, CA$H. Real recognize real and you lookin' real familiar…not only is your pen game official, so is your business mind. I appreciate the opportunity, bruh. Coffee, you're an amazing woman and writer. Royal Nicole, Bossn' Up—off the chain! Frank Gresham, The King's Cartel—great read! Jerry Jackson, The Streets Bleed Murder—read the series in two days! Askari, Blood of a Boss series—one word: Classic. To the rest of the LDP family, Kameelah Parker, CATO, ASAD, Aryanna, Jamaica, Destiny Skai, Adrienne Johnson, Qay Crockett, Misty Holt: Keep doin' what ya doin'. I plan to read at least one of each of y'all's novels.

To my editors: Dr. Maxine Thompson, you challenged me and made me a better writer. Cassandra Sims, you breathed more life into the story. Shawn Walker, I appreciate your patience. Because of your hard work and dedication, this book will be a success. And John, my typist, for a white dude, your critiques are priceless.

To my homies still on lock: It's way too many of y'all to name, but there's more hot joints to come I 'ma let y'all shine on the next one.

Special thanks to Melvin (I love you old man), and my cousin Gina for appearing at my clemency hearing and to all my family members and friends who signed the petition in support of my clemency.

And finally, shout out to the readers, book stores and book clubs that support urban authors.

Violence is second nature without y'all, none of this would be possible.

A Message from the Author

It is common knowledge that Chicago has a track record for producing some of the most notorious gangsters and corrupt politicians known in American history.

Today, you can't turn on your television without hearing how unsafe urban neighborhoods and public school systems have become due to gang violence.

Or, you will find out how an investigation has led to the arrest of crooked judges, police officers, aldermen, or even the sitting governor of the state. Corruption by police officers and elected officials is the engine that powers the criminal activity in the Chicago underworld.

Abuse of power by these so-called leaders has the greatest, negative impact on the African-American communities. These leaders not only steal money from government-funded programs aimed to provide assistance for the less fortunate, they accept bribes from special interest groups and drug traffickers, whose sole purpose is to exploit the black community. And, to add insult to injury, pass unfair drug laws with lengthy prison sentences, targeted exclusively at blacks.

These, and other governmental practices, are the direct cause behind the deplorable social conditions millions of poverty-stricken Americans, mostly black, residing in segregated urban communities, are forced to live under.

The most common social factors that plague urban neighborhoods, strategically, created by these corrupt individuals is the easy accessibility of highly addictive and cheap drugs such as crack cocaine and heroin, sub-par housing developments, menial job opportunities, and under-funded educational institutions.

These, and other racist government practices of a similar nature, began during the civil rights movement, but got its roots from the days of physical slavery. The goal was to discourage black pride, turn the family against itself, and keep their modern-day slave plantations, known as correctional centers, filled to capacity.

A by-product of these social injustices was the formation of multiple organizations launched by black men to serve and defend their families from these evil forces.

One of the more prominent and nationally known organizations was the Black Panther Party. Many lesser known groups with the same agenda were formed throughout the Chicagoland area. However, as time went on, and the fate of black people worsened, some leaders of these organizations began to view the drug trade as a means to end their poor quality of life. Within the blink of an eye, what was once a solution to the plight of the people became its biggest cancer; the leaders of those organizations took control of the illegal narcotics distribution overnight, transforming the organization in which they represented into the street gangs that still exist today.

As the demands for drugs increased and the cash piled up, so did the need for more territory and recruits. Gang leaders learned that drug and gun laws were lenient towards juveniles, and, quickly began recruiting black youths to do their bidding.

With their parents strung-out on drugs, or working two jobs to make ends meet, placed on a slave plantation or dead, recruiting their children into this deadly underworld was easier than taking candy from a baby. This created a hellish environment steaming with black-on-black crime where murder, rape, robbery and vandalism committed by young black males became the norm in society.

The purpose of this book is not to glorify gang culture, drug activity or underage sex. It was written with the intentions of, accurately, depicting the environment and life-altering decisions that adolescents are forced to make on a daily basis, living in Chicago.

Without further ado, meet ZEPHANIYAH and TISO, best friends born and raised on the south side of Chicago, whose love interests just happen to be cousins, CAPRIA and MIMI.

Follow their journey as they navigate through the perilous streets.

The question is will they spread their wings and soar the heavens above the pitfalls set before them, or will they fall victim and be blown into the pits of damnation by the City of Wind?

PROLOGUE

September 6, 1999
Chicago, IL
12:36 p.m.

"Pull Over!" the narcotic's detective bellowed over the loud speaker.

"Shit!" Zep shouted, looking at the unmarked detective car, through the passenger door mirror. He was trying his best to remain calm and refrain from looking back. "It's the muthafuckin' dick boys, Tiso, you ain't got no guns or work in here, do you?"

"Nope," Tiso replied, with a devilish smirk.

"Cool, pull the fuck over 'cause they ain't gon' trip 'bout this dro or you not havin' no license," Zep said. He knew that unlike uniformed officers, the narcotics detectives wouldn't bother arresting two thirteen-year-old boys for being in possession of a user's amount of high-grade marijuana and joy riding in a brand-new Escalade. They only made arrests for guns, large sums of marijuana and hard drugs such as cocaine, heroin and PCP.

Suddenly, over the loud speaker, the detective ordered, "Make a right at the corner, pull over to the curb and turn off the car."

Once they reached the corner, Tiso made the right turn and brought the Escalade to a stop at the curb. Despite their ages, this wasn't their first run-in with the law. On six separate ocassions, over the past three years, the police suspected and questioned them for vandalism, theft and assault and battery.

Luckily, Zep was able to talk their way out of getting arrested each time. But for some reason, he had a funny feeling in his gut that today he wouldn't be so lucky.

The fact that he wasn't in complete control of the situation, coupled with the condescending vibe he was getting from Tiso, had Zep feeling edgy. His heart began to beat rapidly and loudly, so loud, he could hear it. His face, upper body and palms were covered in sweat.

"Turn off the car!" the cop repeated.

"Kill the engine," Zep said. Curiosity got the best of him.

He turned and looked, as the passenger side door of the unmarked car swung open. "They gettin' out the car," Zep blurted, in distress.

For reasons unknown to Zep, Tiso gripped both hands on the steering wheel, braced his body up, and like a villain in a horror movie, let out a sinister laugh. And, just as the detective approached the driver's side door, he leaned back in his seat and faced Zep. "Fuck these bitches. They gon' hafta catch us," he said. He turned up the sound system and hit the gas.

And, just like that, a high-speed chase was now in progress.

CHAPTER ONE

Thursday, September 2, 1999
7:15 a.m.

The aroma of Bob Evan's sausages, homemade bisuits, cheese omelets and hash browns brought Zep to a stir in his sleep. He had spent the summer in Atlanta with his eleven-year- old sister, Sharmaine, and nine-year-old brother, Kevin, and he was happy to be back at home. It was the first meaningful time Zep and his siblings experienced away from home with members of their deceased father's side of the family.

The vacation had been planned three months earlier, when a lady appeared at the front door of the two-flat apartment building Zep lived in.

Friday, June 11, 1999
3:36 p.m.

"Who is it?" Zep answered the door.

"Beverly," a feminine voice replied,

"Beverly who?" he asked, looking through the peep-hole.

"Does Diane live here?"

"Yes, that's my mama, but she ain't here," Zep replied.

"Is that Zephanlyah?" the lady asked.

"Yeah, who is you?" Zep asked, beginning to get agitated.

"Baby, I'm your grandmother. Is Mrs. Berry home?" she asked again.

"Yeah, hold on lady," Zep said as he turned away from the peep-hole.

"Grandma!" he yelled. His maternal grandmother, Mrs. Berry, was in the kitchen. "Some lady at the door named Beverly talkin' 'bout she my grandma."

"Boy, watch yo mouth. That's your daddy mama," Mrs. Berry said to Zep's surprise. "Let her in.

Zep opened the door and before his eyes stood his paternal grand-mother. Up until this point, and all throughout his thirteen years of existence, he'd never heard a word from her, nor had anyone said a word about her. He'd never even wondered if there was such a person. But, here she was, and a sight to behold at that.

Beverly stood five-eight, 135 pounds, in a two-piece, creme-colored Hermes skirt and jacket, which fit her hourglass figure to perfection. She wore a light pink blouse which had left her neckline, and a peep of cleavage exposed, to show off her platinum diamond tennis necklace. Her skin was a deep rich dark brown, her lips were full, covered with a light coat of pink lipstick, and her hair was straight, hanging an inch or two below her shoulders. Each hand was adorned with a diamond ring. The one on her left ring finger was the biggest. It was a huge, flawless, 6 carat, canary yellow princess cut diamond, centered around an additional 3 carats of pink diamond on a platinum band.

In Zep's eyes she couldn't be his grandmother. First, she didn't look a day older than thirty-five. Second, she talked with proper English. And, last but not least, to top it all off, she appeared to be rich.

"Boy, you've grown since the last time I saw you. Last I remember you were just a toddler about knee-high. Where are your brother and sister?" Beverly asked, placing both her hands on Zep's face, tilting his head up to face her.

"They on the back porch," Zep told her.

"Boy, hurry and get your brother and sister," Mrs. Berry shouted out.

Upon returning with them, hugs and kisses were planted on their cheeks by the foreign woman. Beverly sat and chatted with them for about forty-five minutes. They learned she used to live in Chicago but had moved to Georgia in 1980, and this was the second time she'd been back to Chicago since then. The only other time she'd come back was when she had to identify her son's remains and attend his funeral after he was killed in a car accident. At the time, Zep was four, Sharmaine was two and Kevin was only six months.

Beverly explained why she had moved down south, informing them she had been hired by a Fortune 500 company to be Senior V.P.

After being with the company for ten years, she resigned and started her own marketing and consulting firm.

After catching them up on her life, she assured them she would return the next day to take them out for lunch, and to the movies.

***

The next day came and she made good on her promise. She bought the children clothes, toys, video games, and whatever else their hearts desired.

She was really enjoying her time with them and she suddenly got an idea.

"Would you all like to go home with me and stay in Atlanta for the summer?" she asked, looking from one child to the other.

Frantically, all three or them shouted, "Yes!"

Zep and his siblings couldn't wait to get back to their house. They rushed inside hoping their mother was home to grant them permission to go to Atlanta. Unfortunately, she wasn't.

As usual, Diane was out running the streets doing God knows what, with God knows who, to feed her nine-year crack cocaine addiction. She had been battling her addiction since the age of twenty-two. The sudden death of her fiancé, also the father to her three children, had left her heartbroken with a severe case of bereavement and depression. The day of the burial Diane had become distraught and confused as she was leaving the cemetery. Walking the streets, aimlessly, crying and cursing God, she bumped into Orlando, an old childhood friend. Orlando convinced her that taking a hit of crack would ease her pain. He'd told her not to worry about becoming addicted because it was impossible with only one hit.

Orlando's words couldn't have been more wrong, Diane's urge to chase the euphoric feeling she experienced from that first hit was so strong, she immediately quit going to work and began to neglect her children.

Mrs. Berry couldn't help but notice the drastic changes in her daughter's behavior. She felt she had no other choice but to assume the responsibility as the main caretaker for her three grandchildren. She

17

clothed, fed and provided a roof over their heads with very little financial, or hands-on, support from Diane. Mrs. Berry still made it a point to consult with Diane about any major issues regarding her children. However, she knew Diane wouldn't disagree with whatever decision she made, so she gave them permission to go to Atlanta.

For the next two weeks, the only thing Zep discussed with his brother and sister was their rich grandmother and the upcoming summer in Atlanta.

The same day school dismissed for summer break, Beverly was back in Chicago. She told them to pack lightly because she would purchase them clothes once they arrived in Georgia.

For the most part, Zep enjoyed the time he spent in Georgia, but as the days went by he began to miss his grandmother, Mrs. Berry, more and more. She had been raising him and his siblings for nine years. He had become accustomed to her ways, which he noticed were quite different from his paternal grandmother's. As far as he could see, the only thing they had in common was their devotion to Christianity. Both women were deeply involved with their churches.

His grandmother, Beverly, sat on some sort of financial committee for her church, which consisted of over five-thousand members. In contrast, Mrs. Berry was head of the mother board at her church, which had maybe seventy-five members.

She was in her sixties and stopped working before Zep was born. Her source of income came from a monthly retirement check from her deceased husband, and rent she collected from her two tenants. She owned a two-flat brick building which had a furnished, live-in basement. They lived on the first floor. Like most southern women who migrated from the south to the big cities, she stayed true to her old-fashioned roots.

Mrs. Berry believed taking care of the household was a duty given to all women by God. She took pride in cooking, cleaning and instilling Christian values in her grandhcildren.

The only other activities she was passionate about was gardening and sewing. Every spring she planted flowers and bushes in the front yard and tomatoes, collard greens, cucumbers, bell peppers and herbs in the backyard. She would cook a full course meal at least twice a day, mostly breakfast and dinner. She rarely left her house and didn't own a car because she never learned to drive.

On the other hand, Zep noticed his paternal grandmother, Beverly, wasn't much of a cook, but instead, a work-a-holic. She wore designer clothes and diamonds of all colors, shapes and sizes. She upgraded her Mercedes Benz yearly. She watched her diet closely and attended aerobics class three to four times a week. Nobody really knew her exact age, but Zep guessed she had to be at least in her mid to late fifties because he overheard her telling some one her oldest son was thirty-six.

Zep appreciated the gifts and love his grandmother gave him and his siblings while they were in Atlanta. He met several other members of their estranged family, and they too, opened up their loving arms to the trio. They went on family outings to places like the Underground Railroad Mall, Six Flags Georgia, bowling alleys, movie theaters, and most importantly, The Dr. Martin Luther King Jr. Center.

Zep's fondest memory was attending a laser show in Stone Mountain, Georgia. He was amazed at the colorful display of laser figures presented on the huge mountain, the music and southern hospitality of the thousands of people in attendance.

Even though Zep managed to enjoy his time there, he did begin to become homesick. Not only did he miss his grandmother, he also missed his best friend, Tiso, and the never-ending drama and action in the streets of Chicago. He demanded to be taken home, so the vacation was cut short by a few days.

***

Man, that food smells good, Zep thought, as he woke up to the mouth-watering aroma of his grandmother's cooking.

Quickly, he rose to his feet. Stretching, he let out a yawn then sat down on his bottom bunk. He reached into his underwear, freed his rock-hard erection and began to stroke himself.

Ten seconds later, and without busting a nut, something compelled him to stop and look around his bedroom. Everything was exactly how he left it before he'd gone to Atlanta. But, for the first time, he realized he didn't like what he was seeing.

Zep had to share his bedroom with his brother. The room was located in the rear of the house and was the smallest room in the apartment. It should have been an office or storage room, but the family of five needed the space for living quarters. The room had brown carpet, a bunk bed, a chest of drawers and a radiator.

"This little ass room," Zep mumbled, as he glanced around in disgust. He closed his eyes and began to take a mental walk through his entire house.

When leaving or entering his room, Zep had to pass through his mother's bedroom which she shared with his sister. His mother and sister's bedroom was twice the size of his but they only had one bed, and since Diane was hardly home, Sharmaine slept in the bed alone most nights. Unlike his room, they had a matching three-piece bedroom set that consisted of a dresser with a big mirror, a chest of drawers, and a queen sized bed. A chair and small desk that held a thirteen-inch TV were the only other pieces of furniture in the room. The TV was what Zep played his Playstation on, which he shared with his brother and sister. Mrs. Berry believed video game systems caused damage to TVs, and thereby forbade him from hooking it up to the thirty-two-inch family television in the living room. The biggest and only other bedroom in the house belonged to Mrs. Berry.

The rest of the house consisted of a small living room, an even smaller dining room, and a tiny kitchen. At all times, the house was kept clean and orderly, but all the furniture and appliances were dated. Zep couldn't deny the fact that the house he lived in was a far cry from the 8,000 square foot mansion his paternal grandmother owned in the Buckhead section of Atlanta.

Suddenly, Zep's room door opened and Kevin stuck his head in. "Grandma said wash up, breakfast ready," he said.

"A'ight," Zep replied, as he quickly stuffed his flacid penis back in his underwear. "Tell her I'll be there in a minute."

Instead of getting ready for breakfast, Zep went over to his bedroom window. He opened up the aluminum venetian blind and allowed the sunrays to brighten up the room.   As he stared out of the window into the alley, his mind began to ponder some unresolved issues, as well as a couple of completely new ones.

The summer vacation in Atlanta had provided him with a temporary escape from the harsh realities of Chicago. While there, he had been exposed to a way of living he previously believed only existed on TV, or in rap lyrics. Now that he was back in Chicago, the trip was impacting him in ways his undeveloped pubescent mind couldn't fully comprehend.

Staring out into the decrepit alley, Zep's mind was on overload. He was consumed with thoughts of his mother's crack addiction, and the fact that he was fatherless— two issues he had been internally dealing with for some years. The fact that he was living in poverty, and his grandmother Berry's old age and multiple health problems, was something he'd never given thought to in the past. It wasn't until he returned from Atlanta did he notice the two additional facts. No matter how hard he tried to shake the thoughts, they refused to go away. Tears began to fall from his eyes as he focused all his thoughts on his father.

Up until his father's death, Zep had lived in the house with both his parents and two siblings. At the funeral, he viewed his father's body in the casket, but for some reason, he had no memory of his facial features. The only recollection he had of his father was that he was buried in a gray-colored casket.

Zep had never seen any videos or pictures of his father before visiting Atlanta. Photos of his father were spread throughout his grandmother's mansion, and every other relative's house he'd visited in Georgia. He looked through several photo albums that had hundreds of pictures detailing his father's life from the day he was born until the week before he died. Much to Zep's surprise, one photo album contained several sets of professional studio taken photos of his father, mother, brother, sister, and himself.

The first five nights after seeing those pictures, Zep cried himself to sleep. Nobody knew he had always wondered what his father looked like. Nobody knew he didn't watch TV shows or movies that depicted a strong father and son relationship. Nobody knew he envied other boys he saw interacting with their fathers and refused to befriend them. Zep never shared these thoughts with anyone, and seemingly, no one cared.

"Fuck a daddy!" Zep grumbled, like he always did when thoughts of his father, or the fact he didn't have one came to the surface. *"You're the oldest, you're the man of the house. You have to set the example. You have to be responsible for yourself, Sharmaine and Kevin."* He repeated the words his grandmother had been telling him since the day she'd taken them in.

"What you say?" Kevin stuck his head in the room for a second time. "What's wrong, why you cryin'?"

"Shut up!" Zep snapped, as he turned his face away from his brother. "Ain't nobody cryin'."

"Yes you is, you wanna go back to Atlanta?" his brother asked.

"Fuck Atlanta! I ain't never goin' back down there. Now, get outta here and close the door!" Zep yelled.

"Grandma said come in the kitchen," Kevin added, making sure to deliver Mrs. Berry's message before leaving.

Zep closed his bedroom door then went over to the chest of drawers. He picked up a small mirror and stared at his reflection. He wiped away his tears and began rubbing his fingers across the peach fuzz growing on his chin.

"I'ma grown-ass man," he smirked at himself. "I'ma buy my family a house just like the one in Atlanta. Naw, fuck that! I'ma get us a bigger one. Fuckin' watch," he said, trying to convince himself of the pipe dream.

He tossed the mirror on his bed and took a sock out of the dirty clothes hamper. His hormones were raging. He pulled out his rock hard penis and jacked off until he spilled his seed into the dirty sock. After wiping his penis dry, he tossed the cum soiled sock back into the hamper, went into the bathroom and urinated. He left the bathroom without taking care of his hygiene and went into the kitchen.

"Boy, did you wash your face and brush your teeth?" his grandmother asked, suspiciously.

"Yeah, Grandma," Zep lied in a low whisper.

"Chile, don't lie to me. I see cold in the corners of your eyes. Now go clean yourself up and put on some pants, and a shirt too. You know better than that. I pray you wasn't down south behaving like I didn't teach you no manners," she said, agitated.

Zep walked off to do as he was told and returned back minutes later.

"Grandma made your favorite, fried green tomatoes," Mrs. Berry said, fixing him a plate.

"Sounds and smells good to me," Zep replied, rubbing his belly.

"So, tell me, how was y'all's trip to Georgia?" she probed.

"It was a'ight," Zep said. "I'm glad to be back doe."

"Chile, from listening to y'all talk on the phone and looking at them pictures y'all took, if I had it my way, I'd take all three of y'all and move down there," she said, while giving Zep his plate of food.

"Why?" Zep asked, as he stuffed two fried tomatoes in his mouth.

"'Cause, Chicago just ain't the same no more. All night it's gunfire and police sirens. I can't even get a good night's sleep 'round here no more. It's just sad, I tell you. This neighborhood was peaceful when me an y'all grandpa moved here. Diane was only five then. Now, the whole Englewood area done went to the dogs! Some boy got shot dead three nights ago at the end of the block," Mrs. Berry said, shaking her head.

"That's messed up," Zep replied, coughing and choking as he talked. "Who got shot?"

"Boy, like I know! And why you eatin' so fast and talkin' with a mouth full of food? Was you down there embarrassin' me like I don't feed you?" she asked, staring at Zep, intensely.

Zep washed the food down with a gulp of orange juice and cleared his throat. "I gotta go down Tiso's house," he said, preparing to remove himself from the table.

"No, you ain't!" Mrs. Berry pointed her finger in his face. "I don't want you hanging 'round him no more!" she said, with the look and seriousness of a raging bull.

"Why?" Zep asked, baffled by her body language and remark. "He's my best friend."

She took a deep breath and exhaled. "I'ma let Diane tell you," she paused in agitation, "whenever she get herself here. In the meantime, stay your butt right here in this house!" his grandmother said with finality in her tone.

Zep wasn't about to wait for his mother to get home. There was no telling when that would be. He knew as soon as breakfast was over, and the dishes were washed and put away, his grandmother would go to sleep. Then, he'd go straight to Tiso's crib just as he'd planned.

CHAPTER TWO

Three long hours passed before Mrs. Berry finally retired to her bedroom. Zep hurried out the door en route to Tiso's house which was only a few doors down. As he approached the first step leading to the front door, Tiso came out.

"Aww, hell naw, my nigga back," Tiso shouted. He hurried over towards him with both arms spread wide for an embrace.

Before Zep could speak a word, Tiso lifted him off his feet into a bear hug, squeezing him to death. Tiso was a few inches shorter than Zep, but he was stocky and outweighed Zep's lanky frame by at least twenty-five pounds.

"Nigga, I can't breathe, put me down," Zep managed to muffle, between deep breaths.

"Man, quit whinnin'. I'm just glad you made it back. Shit been real fucked up since you left," Tiso said, loosening the grip of his bear hug.

"Whatchu' talkin' 'bout shit been fucked up?" Zep asked.

"First off, we ain't shorty's no more. Me, Terrence, Shit-Shit, Psycho, Krazy, Yatta and Poopa got plugged," Tiso explained.

"Got plugged?" Zep repeated, not understanding Tiso's choice of words.

Since the age of six, he had been throwing up gang signs and performing the handshake with the older gang members in the hood. To the best of his knowledge, that made him an active member plugged into the gang. "Nigga, we been plugged," he asserted.

"Naw, my dude we was just shorty's BD's," Tiso said, shaking his head from side to side. "Them niggas kept comin' through the land shootin' up shit and ended up killing Lil' Greg."

"What, Lil' Greg dead?" Zep couldn't believe his ears. "Nigga, you lyin'!"

"I ain't lyin'. They hit fam up right on Halsted comin' out the liquor store. He had went in to buy me and Poopa a Snickers," he told him.

Scanning his face for signs of deceit, Zep's jaw dropped as he shook his head in disbelief. "Nigga, put it on sump'n Lil' Greg dead!" he demanded.

"On BD, he graveyard dead, my nigga," he said. Tiso went on, "Later that night, the rest of the clique decided we was gonna get at them bitch-niggas who killed 'im. Since we knew Lil' Greg's big brother, Fatz, was plugged and kept guns, we went to his house. Fatz was sittin' on his front porch talkin' to Chop when we walked up. I asked Fatz to give us a few bangers so we could go put in some work on the GD's. He told us naw 'cause we was just shorty's. He said he was gon' handle the shit hisself. But, Chop told Fatz we hung out with Lil' Greg every day, all day, and one of us could be dead right now too. He was lettin' Fatz know shit had just got real fo' us. Then Chop told all of us to be at Ryan Harris Park the next day at one o'clock. He was gonna get Rome to make it official and bless all of us Black Disciple."

Twenty-seven-year-old Rome was the most loved, respected and feared Black Disciple in the neighborhood. He held the title of Minister, which made him the highest ranking BD over the set. Many responsibilities came with having the Minister title. One of them was to decide who got initiated, or *blessed*, into the gang.

Chop was Rome's cousin and junior by six years. He also served as Rome's personal security and most trusted henchman.

"So, we ain't never been blessed?" Zep asked.

"*You* ain't never been blessed," Tiso corrected. "Chop got Rome to bless me and everybody else in the clique the day after Lil' Greg got killed."

"How he bless y'all?" Zep inquired.

"That's for me to know and you to find out. All I can tell you is once you get blessed, you gon' hav'ta go to meetings once a week, and to Rome's crib for lit class afterwards."

"What's lit class?" Zep asked, trying to gather as much new inside information about the gang as possible.

"Lit class is where they teach all the new niggas the laws and prayers."

"Did y'all kill them niggas that shot Lil' Greg?" Zep asked, changing the subject.

"Fatz and Chop did a drive-by on 69th and Carpenter and shot two niggas, one in the ass and the other one in the neck. The one that got hit in the neck died." Tiso paused and smiled for a second. "I'm tellin' you, Zep, shit fucked up fo' real. Lil' Greg ain't the only nigga that got slumped."

"Somebody else got changed too?" Zep questioned, in a high-pitched voice.

"Yeah, man, two days ago them niggas came through the block and caught Slickem snoozin', comin' out of Big Tittie Tina crib. Shot fam ten times, close range." Tiso was animated as he explained Slickem not being attentive to his surroundings and getting shot up. He fixed his fingers to resemble a gun and made ten, rapid-fire, popping sounds before clutching his torso.

"But Slickem wasn't no weak-ass Black Disciple. He still had the strength to walk a half a block to his car. He managed to open the door and get his banger out the glove compartment before he dropped dead," Tiso said.

And with that revelation, Zep had to take a seat on the concrete step, leading up to Tiso's front door. Hearing about Lil' Greg and Slickem's deaths impacted him, greatly. After Tiso, he had considered Lil' Greg his best friend and he'd viewed Slickem as the big brother he never had. Unconsciously, Zep's mind blocked out everything taking place around him, as he reminisced about Lil' Greg and Slickem.

Lil' Greg was the newest member to their clique. He had just moved to the neighborhood two summers ago. Zep, Tiso and the rest of the boys in their clique used to jump on him all the time because he was the new kid on the block. But, he never ran or backed down, and he always fought back. They knew Lil' Greg came from the Robert Taylor Housing Projects, and jumping on him was their way of showing him that E-dub niggas go hard too.

One day, they were putting hands and feet on this boy named Marco. He had been a part of their clique until his mother moved from 68th and Emerald to 67th and Carpenter. It was only a few blocks away, but it was territory of the Gangster Disciples.

Marco's grandparents still lived on Emerald and he'd come to visit them wearing a Duke Blue Devil's shirt and fitted cap with the pitchforks hoisted up. Instantly, Zep, Tiso and everybody else in the clique knew he had flipped, so they chased him down and administered a beat down. Out of nowhere, Lil' Greg came and joined in. Soon after, a few adults who knew them walked up and stopped them.

Once everybody got to safety, Lil' Greg threw up the tray. "Fuck that nigga," he shouted, "it's BD or nothin'!" And, ever since that day he'd been a part of the clique and deemed a shorty BD by the older gang members in the hood.

Slickem had just turned twenty years old. He lived on 69ᵗʰ and Union, the next block over from where Zep lived. Zep looked up to Slickem. He loved the legendary hood story of how Slickem ended up in Englewood and got the nickname Slickem.

Slickem had gone to The Juvenile Detention Center when he was just eleven years old, for robbing a man who was leaving the currency exchange. The police caught him red-handed, two blocks away, armed with a rusty .38 special, and the man's wallet. Since he'd worn a ski mask, the man couldn't positively identify him, but he'd remembered what the pint-sized robber had said before robbing him, 'Slick 'em up' instead of 'Stick 'em up'.

For some reason, Slickem had a strange speech impediment which prevented him from correctly pronouncing some words. So, when the police told him to say 'Stick 'em up', he said 'slick 'em up'. From that day forward, he was known as Slickem on the streets.

Slickem was a thoroughbred gang banger and stick-up artist, but showed love to the people in his hood. He used to buy all the young kids in the neighborhood ice cream and candy when they didn't have money. He didn't have a family. His mother had overdosed on heroin when he was three, and he'd been taken into custody by the Department of Children and Family Services. Since nobody came forth to claim his mother's remains, he was shuffled around from foster home to foster home.

At the age of ten, he ran away from the, physically and sexually abusive, foster parents and started living on the streets. From hopping on trains and riding on the outisde of C.T.A. buses, Slickem ended up in Englewood, where a prostitute named, Cremey, took him in.

He was sleeping in an abandoned courtway building when Cremey spotted him while giving a trick a blow job. Cremey, not having any children of her own, felt all alone and un-loved by anyone, and had compassion for the boy. So, she figured she would adopt him, not legally, of course.

Cremey was addicted to crack. She really just provided a roof over his head. Slickem still had to feed and clothe himself. He started stealing out of stores and eventually graduated to armed robbery. He was a fearless stick-up kid, and the older wolves in the hood took notice. They recruited him and he was eager to sign on the dotted line. Slickem was blessed a Black Disciple at the tender age of twelve.

Slickem always wanted to have some brothers and sisters, so he embraced me and Tiso. He would look after us as if he were our big brother. Whenever we needed help or a couple dollars we would call on him and he never failed to answer. Between the two of them, Slickem had a tighter bond with Zep, which was why he would give and do a little more for him than he did for anybody else.

On Zep's tenth birthday, Slickem stood by and listened to Zep tell Tiso how if he was older he would make Big Tittie Tina his woman. Slickem waited until he was finished talking about how thick and sexy she was to pull him off to the side. He told Zep he had thirty minutes to lose Tiso, come inside Big Tittie Tina's back door and into her bedroom if he wanted the birthday present he had for him.

Zep shook Tiso, entered her house, walked into her bedroom and couldn't believe his eyes. Big Tittie Tina was butt naked, bent over, getting hit from the back by Slickem.

As soon as Big Tittie Tina realized Zep was in the room, she pulled herself away from Slickem and asked him to leave the bedroom. She took Zep by the hand and made him promise to keep the secret, before pulling out his dick and giving him his first sexual experience, a blow job.

"Zep, Zep," Tiso called out, pulling him out of his reverie. "Fuck wrong with you, nigga? You day dreamin' or sump'n?" he asked, annoyed.

"Naw B, I'm just thinkin' 'bout Lil' Greg and Slickem, that's all. Slickem used to look out for us," Zep added as an after-thought.

"Fam, them niggas fuckin' dead, out the game, dick in the dirt and ain't never comin' back, so fuck 'em! The only thing we can do is kill every GD in the city," Tiso demanded.

Zep was shocked by Tiso's murderous intentions and dismissive attitude towards the deaths of two people they considered to be family.

Tiso stepped closer to Zep, bent down and made eye to eye contact. He was so close Zep could feel his breath on his nose. "You ain't heard shit I said!" he uttered, in an authoritative tone.

Zep's mind was racing in a million different directions. Part of him wanted to check Tiso for invading his personal space and trying to son him. However, another part of him felt the two months he'd spent in Atlanta had him off balance and game conscious.

"Gimme three feet, fam," Zep warned. "I was just sayin' it's fucked up what happened to folks n'em. But, like you said, it is what it is," he said, reluctantly.

Tiso backed away and sat down next to him. "Listen, B, I was just tryna say you gotta get blessed. All the folks finna be at the meeting in Ryan Harris Park. So, come on, let's go. Plus, this meeting gon' be about gettin' revenge fo' Slickem," Tiso said, as he stood up and began walking towards the park.

***

Ryan Harris Park was located on 68th and 67th and Lowe Avenue. Previously named Lowe Park, the city decided to rename the park after eleven-year-old Ryan Harris went missing for a day; her body was found in the park on July 28, 1998. Tragically, she was found with her face covered in blood, panties stuffed in her mouth, and a leaf in each nostril. Two weeks later, the murder received national headlines when Chicago police charged two boys, ages seven and eight, with her rape and murder. Weeks after their arrests, the crime lab found semen stains on her panties, and it was determined boys so young couldn't produce semen. So, the states attorney's office dropped the charges. Further DNA analysis indicated that the semen belonged to a twenty-nine-year-old man who was suspected of raping three other young girls in the Englewood area earlier that year.

Before, and after the horrific events of Ryan Harris, Rome held gang meetings and sponsored barbeques at the park. He would pay for all the food and drinks. The music was provided from the trunk of one of his many cars. All the BDs from his set would be in attendance, along with teenage girls and women of all ages. The shorty BDs who the older gang members affectionately referred to as the lil' folks would be there too. Everyone would gather together eating barbeque, drinking alcohol, smoking weed, and collecting a few dollars.

What Zep and Tiso enjoyed the most was when the older members, whom they called the big folks, paid them money to feel on the grown women's titties and asses. The women would pretend to be upset and kick, punch and scream at them to stop. It was all in fun, except when the big folks would place bets on who could win a fight between the lil folks, making them fight one another. Regardless of who won, as long as you fought back, you were rewarded and given advice on how to win the next time. Zep's thoughts of the barbeques began to put his mind at ease until Tiso spoke up again.

"Come on, nigga, you walkin' slow as hell. The whole set gon' be there, plus, I can't be late. Last week Shit-Shit and Poopa showed up late and got a three-minute head-to-toe violation. Wait 'til you see them niggas, they still fucked up!" Tiso chuckled and shook his head.

Hearing him say this caused Zep to question himself, silently. *How the hell I'ma get outta goin' to this meetin'?* He pondered.

"Dig, I ain't gon' be able to go 'cause I just got back and I gotta wait fo' my mama to get home. I ain't seen her yet. Soon as the meeting over, stop by my crib and I'ma go to lit class with you," he blurted out, as soon as they got in front of his house. Zep tried to appear as calm as possible as not to raise any suspicions from Tiso.

Tiso turned towards him with a perplexed look on his face. "Come on, nigga, I know you ain't scared.   It's only gon' be 'bout thirty minutes."

Zep quickly responded by raising both his hands in the air. Using their index, middle and ring finger, each threw up the Black Disciple gang sign, aka the trays.

"Nigga, on King David I ain't scared," Zep shouted, aggressively, "when the meetin' over, come pick me up and I'ma go to lit class."

Zep knew swearing to something on King David would settle the matter. King David was David Barksdale. He had been deceased since the seventies but he was the founding father of the Black Gangster Disciple Nation. After his passing, the gang split into several different factions— two of the more prominent ones being the Black Disciple and Gangster Disciples. Although both gangs had new leadership, the Black Disciples still revered the deceased leader and paid homage to him. Zep could've put it on Jesus Christ and later been proven a liar and nothing would've come behind it. But swearing to something on the name of King David and not following through was a sin, a sin with dire consequences. Any lie told on King David would undoubtably result in a vicious beat-down.

Swearing on King David was all Tiso needed to see and hear to be assured Zep was going to lit class. "A'ight, B, I'ma holla at'cha," Tiso stated. They slapped hands, performed the gang's handshake, and Tiso headed to Ryan Harris Park.

Zep turned and went inside his house. Back in his bedroom, he sat on his bunk recapping everything Tiso had told him and pondered his next move.

How the fuck I'ma wiggle my way outta going to lit class, he thought. *I'll just tell Tiso my mama ain't made it back yet. Naw, that won't work. Anything I say he gon' be like, nigga, you put it on King David, you in violation. Fuck it,* he pondered, continuously. *I don't got shit to worry 'bout no ways. He said they bless niggas at the meetin's, not in lit class. I got a whole week to figure something out,* he concluded.

He laid down on his bed and fell asleep thinking about his life-long friendship with Tiso...

Zep and Tiso attended different schools. Tiso went to Henton Elementary School located on 70th and Lowe, while Zep attended Parker Community Academy, located on 68th and Stewart. However, that wasn't always the case.

Tiso had also attended Parker, and when he was there, the two were inseparable. Although they were just close friends, they had always told the other students they were cousins. All the kids believed them because their mothers would take turns bringing the boys to, and from, kindergarten. Even back then, the teachers and staff pegged Tiso as a troublemaker. Indeed, he was just that, and as strange as it may sound, he seemed to have come out of the womb ornery rotten to the core!

When the two-some entered the first grade, the yellow school bus used to pick them up. Tiso would try to convince the bus driver to let him get off the bus with Zep, instead of down the street where he lived. Finally fed up, one day, Tiso decided he was getting off at Zep's house no matter what the driver said. He waited until the bus came to a stop and quickly opened the emergency door located at the rear of the bus. He jumped out, landing flat on his face. And right on cue, Zep jumped out the emergency door behind him to make sure his buddy was okay. That episode resulted in the termination of government paid transportation for both of them. Not only had they endangered their lives, but they had also endangered the lives of the other children who were on the bus.

Tiso was extremely violent as well. He would throw books and chairs at his teachers whenever he didn't get his way. He would intimidate girls into being his girlfriend by pulling their hair. All the boys in his class were scared to buy cookies and donuts at lunch for fear of him taking their money. However, as a gesture to his ace-coon-boon, he'd give whatever he'd taken to Zep. In turn, Zep would split everything down the middle and tell the girls they were his girlfriends too.

None of the teachers understood their relationship. Anytime a student snitched on Tiso, they'd always mention the fact that Zep had been there and had seen it all. However, Zep would never directly participate or say a word then the parents of all the students involved would be summoned to the school.

The kids would be separated and questioned, at length, about what Tiso had done. Zep never told on Tiso, and his loyalty broke the teacher's hearts. Tiso's mother never saw any fault in her only child. She would always take his side, citing Zep as proof that her son was being falsely accused.

The school's principal, teachers, janitors and crossing guards constantly told Diane Tiso was a bad influence on her child. Zep was a model student, but for his frienship with Tiso. He did all his school work, got straight A's, and he was respectful to authority figures.

Tiso, on the other hand, did little work, got D's and F's, and he was disruptive and disrespectful. Teachers would pass him on to next grade because they didn't want to gamble at the chance of him being placed in their class for another semester. Finally, Tiso flunked the third grade and was kicked out of Parker. He was forced to attend the closest school to his residence which was Henton.

The next semester, Parker started a program called the Gifted Students. The school would select twenty to thirty students in each grade with the highest G.P.A.'s, and place them in a class together. They were given the most qualified teachers, along with new up-to-date textbooks. As an added perk, the gifted students were given two extra prepaid field trips per year. Those students were encouraged to do good by constantly being reminded they were the smartest in the school. Zep was selected to be in the gifted student's classroom.

No longer attending the same school, the duo still remained best friends. Every day after school they'd meet up and run the streets together. Just like in school, Tiso would terrorize other children and adults. He would do little mischievous criminal acts such as bust out car windows, steal out of stores, set abandoned buildings on fire, and break into people's houses. All the while, Zep would be at his side. Zep always told him not to do this or that, but Tiso would insist he needed to do it in order to get them money. Or, he'd do it simply because he considered it fun. All he required Zep to do was watch his back, so naturally, Zep would always oblige.

As the two got older, they began hanging with other boys from the neighborhood. Their petty crime sprees gradually began to escalate, and became more frequent. They upgraded to stealing cars, robbing the freight trains, and strong-arming kids and elderly people. For fun, they would go on the train tracks and throw rocks over the viaduct at passing cabs, C.T.A. buses and police cars.

These meaningless and unjustifiable acts were horrible but didn't compare to 'one hitter-quitter'. One hitter-quitter was a game Tiso had come up with in the summer of 1998 after his favorite sport and athelete, Mike Tyson. The group of boys would patrol the streets after dark and take turns trying to knock out the first person they'd encounter walking alone.

The only people given a pass were family members, friends, and well known people from the neighborhood. Everybody and anybody else was fair game — age, gender, race or even health didn't matter. A person could be blind, crippled or crazy, they could get it too.

If one of them succeeded in knocking someone out with one punch, everybody owed him a dollar. But, if somebody got scared, or for whatever reason reneged when it was his turn to knock somebody out, he'd receive a two-minute head-to-toe violation from the group. Even though Zep willingly participated in all these criminal acts, he never found pleasure in them as Tiso did.

Strange as it may seem, the two were the perfet couple. Tiso committed petty crimes to get them extra money, and sometimes for his own personal humor, while Zep watched his back to make sure he wouldn't get caught. What made this union even better was Zep's squeaky clean image and charisma. Zep would use that to their advantage. On occasions when Tiso would get caught or was suspected of doing something he had no business, Zep would concoct a story to either completely exonerate him, or cast doubts on his suspicion. Sometimes, he'd go so far as to admit he'd done it, but claim it had been an accident just because he knew it was unlikely for anyone to call the police on him.

Zep and Tiso were two peas in a pod, birds of a feather, friends to the end, and nothing or no one could ever come between them. Well, on second thought, nothing or no one, except for lying on King David.

Eddie "Wolf" Lee

CHAPTER THREE

In no time, Tiso was back at Zep's house, and he was animated about Zep joining the gang. "It's 'bout to be on," he shouted aloud. "Niggas ain't gon' be able to fuck with us," he said, excitedly.

Zep wasn't in a happy mood. But, Tiso was too wrapped up in his own glory to pick up on his bestfriend's vibe. Zep didn't think it was fear that had him down; he believed it was nervousness because he felt butterflies in his stomach. He had always believed he was a member of the gang, and he behaved as such. He was even received by known members as if he were a full-fledged member. So, in his mind, making his membership official would be a walk in the park, however, as logical as it seemed, he was still somewhat nervous.

Why the hell am I nervous? He began thinking over the situation. *'Cause once I get blessed ain't no turnin' back and I could easily get killed,* he reasoned. *Plus, I'ma hafta kill somebody and I don't wanna kill nobody.* He shook his head, unknowingy. *You go to hell fo' killin' people,* he surmised. Looking up at the sky, he tried to clear his mind for a second. Bringing his head back down, he started thinking again.

Lil' Greg didn't even get blessed and he dead, the Bible says an eye for an eye, so as long as I kill people who killed my friends first, I won't be in the wrong. Then, all I gotta do is pray and ask Jesus fo' forgiveness. Zep's mind was going in circles, but still he went ahead as planned.

The walk to Rome's building only took a few minutes. He lived two blocks east of Lowe in the 7000 building— a beige six story apartment building called the seven thousand building because its address was 7000 South Parnell.

As soon as they arrived at the entrance of the building, Tiso became so overjoyed he began to laugh, and bounce around like a hyper-active child. He opened his mouth to say something to Zep, but no words came out. Instead, he leaned toward his friend and gave him a hug.

"I'm tellin' you, niggas ain't gon' be able to fuck with us. Just wait 'til you see the faces on folks n'em when they see you," Tiso said, grinning from ear-to-ear. Zep just nodded in agreement.

They entered the building and rode the elevator to the sixth floor. The seven-thousand building was one of the few multi-unit apartment buildings in the area that wasn't run-down. No graffiti or gang insignia covered the freshly painted red walls. An on-site janitor kept the floors, stairways, hallways and elevator clean. At night, from 8:00 p.m. to 8:00 a.m. a uniformed security guard sat at the front desk in the lobby.

With the exception being Rome, eighty-percent of the tenants were middle-aged or older, and the other twenty-percent were young, single mothers on Section 8.

Everybody living and working in the building knew about Rome's affiliation with the Black Disciples, but his friendliness and generosity caused them to turn a blind eye to his criminal ways.

Exiting the elevator, Zep and Tiso could hear *Adrenaline Rush,* by Twista, blasting from a stereo system. The closer they got to Rome's door, the louder the music became.   They had to bang and kick on the door before somebody finally opened it.

"Look at what the bird flew in. 'Sup lil' folks, BD," Chop said, extending his right hand to shake-up with Zep, while clutching a .44 Desert Eagle in his other hand.

"Shit, nigga, I just got back from the A," Zep replied, shaking his hand.

Chop was known throughout the neighborhood and everybody knew he wasn't one to be fucked with. It was rumored he was the hit-man for the gang with a double-digit body count. Talk was he'd killed several rival gang members. He'd even off'ed a BD after he'd been served a death violation for snitching. He went on trial for that murder but was acquitted.

Chop's reputation as a killer was so immense, any time someone was murdered and the killer was unknown, everyone assumed it was him. For this reason, Rome appointed him as his personal security and right-hand man.

"Get yo' lil' ass up in here," Chop said, playfully grabbing Zep by the back of this neck.

The apartment was small. It had two bedrooms, a living room, bathroom and kitchen. The living room had a Bose stereo system, a big 50-inch screen TV, a black leather sectional sofa and several bar stools.

The apartment was stuffy because it was jam-packed with bodies and clouds of marijuana smoke. Dozens of empty beer and hard liquor bottles were strewn across the floor, along with empty boxes of Swisher Sweets.

No one noticed Zep and Tiso's arrival until Chop turned off the stereo.

"Y'all niggas don't see lil' folks," he said, pointing toward Zep.

All sixteen heads faced Zep, and immediately got excited.

"BD," a few of them said in unisom.

"What's up, B," two men shouted.

"Trays for days," the other men said, as they bum rushed Zep to show him love.

The jitters Zep previously felt began to fade. The attention he was receiving had him feeling himself.

"What the fuck is going on in here?" Rome shouted, as he emerged from his bedroom. The room fell into a dead silence.

"What the fuck you think going on? Zep just came up in this bitch," Zep boldly stated, with his arms folded across his chest, head slightly tilted back, ice-grillin' Rome.

Everybody burst into laughter. Rome strolled over and greeted Zep with the handshake and a hug. "I was wonderin' when my lil' nigga was comin' back." Rome raised his voice. "Everybody calm down, I got a couple questions only Zep can answer." He removed his arms from around Zep. "Are you ready or what?" he asked.

"I was born ready," Zep swiftly jabbed back.

"Okay, I hear you talkin' lil' nigga, but are you sure you ready to come home?" Rome asked with a stern expression on his face.

"Man, I'm already home," Zep proclaimed. He pounded his chest and threw up the trays.

"No doubt. I feel you on that, but you ain't a kid nomore. It's time to step up to the front line. I know you heard 'bout Lil' Greg and Slickem. Right now we at war, and play time is over. All y'all lil' niggas in this room is the future, and the reason why we gon' win this war, ya' feel me. So let's make sure we on the exact same page. Zep, are you sure you wanna get blessed?" Rome asked again. His voice had taken on a more serious tone, and he stared in Zep's eyes, never blinking.

"Yeah, I'm sure," Zep said, confidently.

"Why you wanna be BD?" Rome futher questioned him.

Before Zep could open his mouth to speak, Chop intervened on his behalf. "No disrespect, Rome, but what you on, B? That's not just anybody standin' in front of you, that's lil' Zep. We raised that nigga, he practically one of the guys already anyways. Gone 'head bless the lil' nigga," he insisted.

"Naw, I'm not lettin' him get off easy like the rest of them, he gon' hafta answer the question," he told Chop.   Focusing his attention back on Zep, he repeated himself. "Why you wanna be BD?"

It was a tense moment. Everybody was on pins and needles in anticipation of Zep's answer.

Feeling the pressure, Zep spoke up. "All my life I been reppin' BD. BD is all I know and all I'm about. I got love for this thang and I'll die for this thang. Plus, it's GDK," he said, letting it be known he was a Gangster Disciple Killer. "That's why I wannabe BD."

Cheers erupted throughout the house. Those few words Zep spoke sparked electrical currents in the veins of everybody. Zep was lovin' every moment too. Feeling like a proud father, Rome nodded his head in approval. He ordered everyone to form a circle, with him and Zep in the middle. Looking around the circle, Zep noticed everyone's hands were clasped together, and their fingers were interlocked, held high to the center of their chest.

"Tighten up this three-sixty and keep them gates clenched proudly up on y'all chest," Rome instructed, sounding like a drill sergeant. "Zep, repeat after me…"

Rome began reciting an oath comprised of sixteen lines that rhymed. He paused after each line, allowing Zep to repeat his words. The ritual lasted less than two minutes. It was just that simple. Zep was an official memeber of the Black Disciple Nation.

Tiso made it his business to shake up with him first. In his mind it was important for him to be the first person to show Zep love after his crowning moment.

The music was turned back on and what was supposed to be literature class ended up being a smoke session, and coming home celebration for Zep. Before Zep knew what was happening, he was puffing on a blunt and sipping on Remy. The dro stayed in heavy rotation, and cups of liquor was continously poured as the partying continued, for hours. Zep was getting reacquainted with his clique and every one of them was present. He kicked it with them as a whole and spent time talking with them individually. Most of them retold him the events of the summer and gave him props on how he'd answered Rome's questions. But, Poopa was the one who'd caught his attention with his words and actions.

Poopa was the oldest member of the clique. He was entering his first year of high school. He was short, and a little pudgy, with a Napoleon complex. He would huff and puff at the smallest of things, but his bark was louder than his bite. It was his belief that he should be the undisputed leader of the pack. However, nobody else shared his view except his sidekick, Shit-Shit. Poopa would get pissed whenever his ideas got overruled, which happened to be often.

Although he'd never admit it, he recognized Tiso as the most respected leader of the clique because his ideas always got accepted above everyone else's. And because of that, he figured Tiso would probably be the first to get promoted to a position of authority by Rome. This infuriated him and there was nothing he could do about it. Deep down, he wanted to fight Tiso, but he'd seen the way Tiso got down time and time again, and knew he didn't stand a chance. He constantly picked his brain, trying to figure out a way to be accepted and respected ahead of Tiso.

This summer his prayers had been answered. He peeped game and noticed Tiso wasn't the same without Zep by his side. Poopa noticed how Zep would immediately back up Tiso's ideas of which stores to steal from, where to go looking for fights, and what they should vandalize or set on fire. Tiso would also call out which member he felt should receive a violation for not carrying his weight. Zep had convinced everyone to follow Tiso's lead which caused Poopa to view Zep as the most respected in the crew, not Tiso.

This past summer had been different. Most of Tiso's ideas had fallen on deaf ears, and Poopa's ideas had been accepted. Poopa felt like he was in control of the group and he was hell bent on keeping it that way. Now, as Poopa watched the love everybody was showing Zep, he knew winning him over was the key to maintaining control. Poopa waited until he saw Tiso and Zep in deep conversation before approaching.

"Can I holla atcha', B? You done chopped it up wit' every nigga here 'cept ya' boy," he said, as he stood closest to Zep.

"My bad, B, you know I was gonna get around to you," Zep replied.

"It's too loud out here. Let's step in the bathroom for a sec," Poopa suggested.

Closing the door to the bathroom, Poopa started the conversation. "I'm glad you home. I'm serving for Rome now. He won't let y'all serve 'cause y'all still in grammar school, but the spot startin' to pick up and he need more workers. I'ma be sure to put a word in for you, ya feel me. Chop runs the spot for him and he gives me a jab with 120 bags in it. I turn in a G and keep $200 for myself. I move at least four jabs a day, sometimes more. All that stealin' out of stores and shit over with for me. I can get you in and we can leave that petty shit up to Tiso and n'em," he said, slyly.

Reaching in his pockets, Poopa pulled out a wad of cash. "Look, nigga, you ain't never had this much loot before." Spreading the money in his hand, he made sure Zep was able to see the bills. "Nigga, not one single in here, and since you my dude, this be you." He took a few bills and separated them from the rest of the money.

Zep's eyes lit up when Poopa handed him three-hundred dollars. "Man, this love," Zep said, accepting the money.

"Nigga, that ain't shit, me and you always been tight. You want me to put the word in with Rome fo' you or not?" Poopa reiterated.

"Hell, ma'fuckin yeah," Zep replied without a second thought.

'A'ight, fam. I got yo' back and from now on it's me and you."

"'Preciate it fa'real, B, but what happened to your lip?" Zep asked, messing with him because he already knew.

"I'm cool, Rome got on some bullshit with me 'cause I was late to a meetin' and shit." He shook his head in dismay.

"Bet, yo' ass won't be late again," Zep said, laughing.

"I bet you better not be late either," Poopa countered.

"Oh, best believe I won't," Zep said, laughing as they exited the bathroom.

When Zep and Poopa returned to the living room, Rome was just about to make an announcement. "Today was s'pose to be lit class, but instead, it turned into a get-together which was cool.   So, here's the plan," he paused, "lit class on hold for the next month.

I'ma give each of y'all a copy of the three essential pieces you need to know, which includes King David's prayer, laws one thru sixteen, and prayers one thru nine. Learn them and don't lose the papers I give you. Next month I'ma collect the papers back and have y'all recite the prayer and laws. Whoever don't know all these laws is gettin' a violation. A'ight, lil' niggas, I gotta take care of some bidness. I'ma holla at y'all later. But be sure to pay close attention to your surroundings, and any cars, speeding, or slowly driving by, 'cause one of them niggas might try to catch you slippin'," he concluded.

Tiso quickly responded, "Them niggas got guns, so where our guns at?"

"We got plenty guns and when the time's right, you'll get one," Rome said.

"What you mean when the time's right?" Chop cut in. "No disrespect, but when you think about it, the time is right now. How we gon' bless these lil' niggas in the midst of a war, send 'em out there on the streets, and not provide 'em with shit to protect they self wit'? Tiso right, them niggas got guns and they usin' them," Chop added.

"You know what, you got a point," Rome agreed.

Chop reached behind the sofa and came up with a loaded, chrome .380, semi-automatic pistol and gave it to Tiso. "Don't do nothin' stupid, Tiso, I'm personally holdin' you responsible for that banger," Rome said to Tiso, but stared at Zep as he spoke each word.

CHAPTER FOUR

Capria's alarm clock woke her up at 6:30 a.m. She frantically jumped out of her bed to begin her morning routine. She lived with her mother, Cynthia Jackson, in Hoffman Estates, Illinois, an affluent suburb on the outskirts of Chicago. They had moved there three years ago from the gang infested housing projects known as the Village, located on Chicago's west side. It was there the poverty-stricken family stumbled across a fortune, unexpectedly.

Summer of 1996

Cynthia's first born, Dominique aka Niq, began dating a well-known, high-ranking member of the New Breeds, known as Bull. He ran the gang which dominated the Village with an iron fist. He controlled all the heroin and cocaine distribution in the projects. No one was allowed to sell heroin, except him, but he allowed anyone to sell cocaine as long as they purchased it from him. On average, he got rid of twenty-five kilos of coke and six kilos of heroin per month. The coke was sold in weight, but the heroin was packaged in ten dollar bags for street sale.

The thought of wifeing a woman had been absurd to him until he caught a glimpse of eighteen-year-old Niq. He was in awe of her petite frame, big eyes and natural beauty. Niq could've been a body-double for the actress Meagan Good. Bull had fallen head over heels in love with the much younger and seemingly naïve girl. He moved her out of the projects and into his Gold Coast condo on the city's North Side.

Bull lived up to his name as a bully. So, he couldn't trust anyone. The only person he halfway trusted was his brother, Dante. Dante was his business partner in all his endeavors and would kill per his orders at the drop of a dime. Dante was shocked at Bull's instant trust in Niq.

Within the first week of their relationship, he showed her where he kept damn near everything. He figured since help needed was long overdue, he might as well groom his future wife to the game. He taught her how to shake and bag dope, and how to cook and weight crack; she was a natural. Never missing a beat, she mixed, cooked, packaged, and made runs with the men when they sold weight. For three months straight, she assisted in making drop-offs and pick-ups to various heroin spots.

When she finally decided to take a day off to spend time shopping with her little sister, Capria, both, Bull and Dante were murdered in a drug deal gone wrong. Fate must have been on her side, because Niq became the sole beneficiary of twenty-one bricks of coke, nine thousand grams of China White, and a little over $100,000 in cash.

Niq knew there was plenty more money but she didn't know where Bull had it hidden. She went back to the projects and began putting together a team of her own. In all she recruited six females, along with the few men she felt she could trust. Her newfound team began moving the drugs, but strictly in weight.

The projects were no longer safe for her family so she purchased the Hoffman Estates Home which also served as a safe house for her.

Capria transferred to a private school, and she was the family's pride and joy. They anticipated on providing her with the best education money could buy. Their goal was to ensure she be the first in their family to graduate college. Thirteen-year-old Capria didn't share in her family's dreams for her future. She wanted to live in the hood and attend a public school. She hated the goody-two-shoes, proper English talking kids at her school, and chose not to associate with them. Capria's only friend was her cousin, MiMi. They constantly talked on the phone and hung out together on weekends during the school year.

Cynthia and Niq would often talk about Capria becoming a doctor, but Capria was well aware of what Niq did for a living and wanted nothing more than to be her sister's right-hand woman. Not wanting to disappoint her mother or sister, she went along with their plans and never spoke a word of her true wishes.

***

Several days prior, Niq promised Capria and MiMi she would take them shopping over the weekend. Capria was so excited to be getting new clothes she set her alarm clock thirty minutes earlier than usual. She knew the sooner she got to school and got the day over with, the sooner she'd be able to fill her closet with more Nautica, Hilfiger, Baby Phat and Coogi.

The next morning, she showered and dressed in record-breaking time. She did a final check of her appearance in the mirror, grabbed her bookbag and ran down the stairs, straight to the front door. She was in such a hurry to get to school and back, she failed to notice her mother sitting on the couch.

"Slow down, 'Pria, it's only five minutes to seven, baby, and school don't start 'til eight. So sit down and have some breakfast. I bought some more Fruity Pebbles," Cynthia said, stopping Capria in her tracks.

"I'ma eat breakfast at school today," Capria said, twisting the front door knob.

"Well, good morning, good-bye and have a nice day to you too," Cynthia said, sarcastically.

Capria walked over to her mother and gave her a hug and kissed her on the cheek. "Excuse me, Ma, I don't mean to be rude and just bounce out the house without speaking. I love you and you have a nice day too, Ma."

"Now, that's my baby," Cynthia gushed.

***

For the past three weeks, the two stick-up kids had been watching Niq's house at various hours of the day. The two had been copping work for four months, basically stalking her. Then finally she was caught slipping, and her carelessness allowed them to tail her, leading them to her safe house.

"There go her lil' sista right there!"

"Yeah, I see her, ain't it a little early for her to be headin' out to school?"

"You right, it is early, but she probably goin' to cheerleadin' practice or sump'n."

"Well, let's just sit tight. We still got forty-five minutes, an hour at the most, before that nosy-ass couple that live across the street leave fo' breakfast."

Friday, May 28, 1999

For the past three years, Niq had been running her operation to perfection. With no major arrests and only minor losses, she decided it was time to expand her business. While searching for new clientele she began to frequent night clubs. She knew most individuals weren't who they appeared to be in the clubs, which was why she went club hopping with the top five, baddest, gold digging chicks she knew. Along with their help, she could easily decipher the fake, broke wannabe-ballers and gangsters, from the true thugs and hustlers.

One night, while at a strip club in Harvey, Illinois, she set her eyes on someone who appeared to be perfect for what she was looking for—

someone who wasn't a seasoned vet, yet far from being young and dumb— someone grinding and paper chasing, yet not pushing serious

weight. Her perceptiveness of this particular prospect was simple, but with logical reasonings'. For one, she didn't want to be dealing with someone who thought he knew more about the game than she did. And two, she didn't want to involve herself with someone who'd been in the game for a long period of time, moving lots of weight. She surmised that a person with his status may very well be on the feds' radar already, and she definitely didn't want somebody else's heat brought down on her.

She summarized this particular dude as a prospect who fit her criteria to a tee. She was observant of his attire, the company he kept, and his overall demeanor. He was seated in the V.I.P. with six other thugged-out goons. There was seven bottles of Móet, and three fifths of Hennessy sitting on their tables. He was dressed casual in a pair of Sean John denim jeans, a Cashmere Sean John fleece long-sleeve shirt, and a pair of Havanna Joes. He wore two modest-sized diamond studs in each ear, a white gold chain with a diamond Jesus piece, and a big face Jacob and Company watch. That was only the half of it. What made him an official target was the poise and command he demonstrated over the group of thugs that accompanied him.

Once Niq and her girls appeared in eyesight of the V.I.P. section, everyone started pushing the strippers away, trying to spit game at the six dime pieces.

During the melee, tons of money had fallen to floor, and the strippers were falling down, while bumping and clawing one another in an effort to get as much of it as possible. The situation was getting out of hand, so security attempted to calm the thugs down, but to no avail.

Out of nowhere, the guy in the Sean John outfit stood up and, quickly, took control of the situation. He ordered his guys to sit down, which caused the other people to calm down. When things seemed to quite down, security proceeded to seat the women in the V.I.P. section, along with the anonymous dude and his thugs. Of course, that was exactly what Niq wanted.

After they were seated the waitress approached. "May I take your orders?" she asked Niq.

"Yes, we'll have three bottles of Cristal and a fifth of Louis XIII," she ordered.

"Comin' right up and will that be all?" the waitress asked, politely.

Digging into her Gucci clutch, Niq pulled out a pen and napkin. She quickly jotted down the word 'thanks', along with her name and number. She kissed the napkin, leaving a red impression of her lips. "Would you please give this and the fifth of Louis to the fine gentleman in the first section of VIP?" she asked. She discreetly turned towards the gentlemen as the waitress followed her eyes. "The one rocking the Sean John cashmere and chain with the diamond Jesus piece," she added.

"Yes, ma'am," the waitress responded, smiling.

***

The following day, Niq received a phone call from her new prospect. However, she didn't reveal her true intentions. Instead, she pretended to be interested in him romantically.

During their hour of conversing, he'd told her his nickname, and the area of the city he was from. She planned to use the information to check his street-cred. Nevertheless, she had to manipulate him in to divulging his government name and date-of-birth, the information she'd need to pass along to her well-connected attorney so he could run a criminal background check on him.

After getting the info, she gave it to her attorney as planned, and just as she'd thought, he came back clean. The propect had no felony convictions, no cases pending, he wasn't an informant, and word on the street was his hustle and murder game was official.

Two days later, Niq and the gentlemen from the club ended up going on a dinner date. What he assumed would be a night ending in hot, steamy sex, turned out to be an introduction to the kind of Connect he'd always dreamed of having. The deal she offered him was too good to be true. He'd been paying $21,000 for a key of coke. Niq offered him a deal of $18,000 per key, plus, whatever he'd purchase would be fronted on consignment. It didn't take him long to give her an answer, for sure, the offer was a no brainer.

***

The two stick-up kids exchanged pounds. "A'ight, nigga, let's check this paper!"

They slipped on their F.B.I. jackets and hats and drove the rented Crown Victoria up to Cynthia's house. Exiting the car, they walked up to the huge wood and glass door, and rang the doorbell.

Just as he was about to ring the doorbell a second time, Cynthia appeared at the front door. "May I help you?" she asked, looking through the glass door.

Both men held their fake badges up closer to the glass. Knowing the badges weren't real, they quickly flashed them so she could see they were government affiliated.

"Agent Dunlap and Agent Robinson of the F.B.I.," Dunlap said.

"I'm sorry. You must have the wrong address," she said.

"No, Mrs. Jackson, we have the correct address. Could you please open the door, we have a few questions, and some information regarding your daughter, Dominique."

"Dominique isn't here, nor does she live here," she snapped.

"Ma'am, we know she isn't here." Agent Dunlap paused for a second, allowing his words to sink in. "We're so sorry, Mrs. Jackson, but something troubling has happened, and we're here to inform you of the events," he said, with genuine remorse in his voice.

At his last remark, all defenses Cynthia had disappeared. She'd dreaded this day would come. She had been schooled on what to do if the police showed up at her front door, but that was far from her mind. She closed her eyes and mumbled a silent prayer, begging God to let her daughter be alive. Letting her guard down, she opened the door, allowing the two perpretators to step inside, and into her living room.

"Would you like anything to drink?" she asked, trying her best to be courteous, and not appear a nervous wreck.

"Yes, two glasses of water will be fine," Agent Dunlap replied, while closing the door and locking it.

And, as soon as she turned her back to head towards the kitchen, Agent Robinson grabbed her and put her in a sleeper chokehold. She tried to kick and scratch her way out, but the choke hold from a six foot three, two-hundred and twenty-five-pounds man was too much for her five foot two, one-hundred ten pounds frame. Tightening his grip around her neck, he whispered in her ear, "Just relax and obey us, and you will live."

Agent Dunlap walked around to face Cynthia and asked her was there anybody else in the house.

Visibly shaking and losing consciousness, she did her best to shake her head from side to side. Agent Robinson felt her body becoming limp so he loosened the grip on the chokehold.

Agent Dunlap handcuffed her and told Robinson to release his hold on her and sit her on the couch while he did a room by room search. Returning to the family room after confirming she was home alone, he pointed his blue steel 9mm directly at Cynthia's face.

"The last thing I wanna do is use this," he said, taking a step closer toward her. "So far, you've been truthful with us, and I expect you to continue being truthful." Cynthia listened, attentively. Do you know what we're here for?" Dunlap questioned. He stared in her eyes, menacingly.

51

"I-I-umm-real-really-don't-know," she managed to stutter out as she fought the tears back. "Take what. . ."

Slap!!

Agent Robinson hauled off and slapped blood from her mouth. "Bitch, don't lie to us!" he barked.

She let out a loud squeal but it was quickly stifled by a hand around her throat and two more vicious slaps to the face. "The next time you make a loud noise like that, I'ma squeeze the life outta you," Agent Robinson threatened.

"Let her go, she gets the picture," Agent Dunlap ordered his partner. "Your daughter will be back from school around 1:45 p.m. Now, unless you wanna watch us rape and kill her, I suggest you cooperate and get us outta here before she gets home. So, I'ma ask you again, do you know what we're here for?"

"The safe is in my bedroom closet," Cynthia said, feeling defeated.

"Show us," Dunlap demanded.

She led them to her bedroom and opened the closet door, where they found the safe sitting in the corner. Agent Robinson picked it up and placed it on her bed. The safe had a digital keypad and a handle that looked like a small steering wheel. He could tell it was expensive and it resembled a miniature bank vault.

"You sure this safe don't got some type of built in security system that would alert the police?" Agent Dunlap asked, suspiciously.

"No, I'm positive! All you gotta do is press 2 1 4 8 6 and turn the wheel."

"And once I do that, what, exactly, will I find in the safe?" Dunlap inquired.

"Fifty-thousand dollars," she informed him.

"Is that all the money you got?"

"Yeah, except the couple hundred dollars in my purse."

"What about drugs?" Agent Dunlap asked.

"She don't keep drugs here."

"Is that right?" Agent Dunlap smiled. He turned to Agent Robinson and said, "She's lying again."

"No-no… I swear I'm tellin' the truth! Please don't hurt me!" Cynthia pleaded to Agent Robinson, as he loomed over her.

He threw her to the floor and snatched a pillow case off of one of the pillows on the bed. He then placed the pillow case in her mouth and wrapped it around her head, before tying a knot to secure it in her mouth. "Bitch, what I tell you 'bout lyin'!"

Slap! Slap!

Cynthia tried to yell out in fear and pain, but the gag muffled the sounds. He snatched her silk robe open, exposing her bra and panties. Ripping off her bra, he sat down on her stomach, paralyzing her, causing the handcuffs to tighten around her wrists and dig into her lower back. The pain was excruciating. Her small B-cup breasts heaved up and down, up and down, as she struggled for oxygen.

At that very moment, Robinson noticed Cynthia's beautiful face and flawless body. His dick got hard as the tears streamed from her eyes. Unable to control his lust for her, he leaned down and licked her tears. The fear in her eyes excited him, but he knew he had to stick to the script because Dunlap was in the room. Next, he commenced to squeezing her titties, aggressively, with both hands.

Cynthia's eyes grew as big as fifty-cent pieces, and she began to wiggle underneath him, trying to get his attention. "Ugh, umm, uhg," she muttered through the gag, trying to tell him something. But, he was in a trance.

Agent Robinson pulled a lighter out of his pocket and began flicking it on and off. The flame was low, so he turned it off, turned the lighter up, and flicked it back on again. He watched as the flame rose higher. Then he lowered the flame to her left nipple causing her body to wither and contort under his weight. He then repeated this on her right nipple. He was enjoying the torture, and smell of burnt flesh so much, he didn't even notice Dunlap had left the bedroom.

As he was about to repeat the process, Dunlap came back into the bedroom with a pitcher of ice water. "A'ight, that's enough. My turn now," he said in a nonchalant tone. Robinson got up and Dunlap replaced him on top of her. "I see my partner got a thing for you. Personally, I like my women young and tender. Maybe, you'll keep bullshittin' and when your daughter get home we can have ourselves an orgy," Dunlap said, while rubbing ice on her nipples.

"Look, I'm not here 'cause I'm stupid or didn't do my homework. I saw the duffel bag she gave you last night and the grocery bag you gave her in return. Don't insult me with the *"just in case we get robbed, give 'em the $50,000"* story. No more games! I want it all, the money and the drugs!" he demanded.

Cynthia nodded her head up and down. Dunlap eased up off of her, helped her up and removed the gag from her mouth. "Where is the money and dope?" he asked.

"The drugs are downstairs in the basement," Cynthia sadly replied.

Agent Robinson threw her across his shoulder and carried her to the basement. Once inside the basement she directed them to the washer and dryer. Between the washer and dryer was a twenty-gallon tub filled to the top with a strange smelling liquid. She told them it was sulfuric acid, which was there in case the house got raided. All they had to do was dump the drugs in the tub and the acid would dissolve it, leaving no trace of evidence. She then told them the cocaine was inside the washer and the heroin in the dryer.

Dunlap lifted the lid on the washer, removed the articles of clothing, and ten kilos stared him right in the face. He picked up the black gym duffel bag on the floor, in front of the washing machine, and placed the keys inside it. He looked inside the dryer and found four kilos of China White.

"A'ight, this will all be over once you tell us where all the money's at," Dunlap said.

"I swear, she really don't keep money here like that. And when she does, she always returns within a day or two to pick it up."

"Where you keep the money when she drops it off here?" Dunlap probed further.

"Usually, I leave it in the bag she brings it in. Last night she gave me the empty bag you holdin' and I gave her a grocery bag filled with the money she had dropped off earlier."

"See, how hard was that? I believe you. Now, tell me the combination to the safe again."

"2-1-4-8-6," she told him again.

Dunlap looked Cynthia in the eyes and said, "I'm sorry but I can't let you live."

Before she could begin to plead for her life, Agent Robinson began strangling her with a thin wire. She fought for air but with each passing second, her strength and desire to live began to fade.

Her life began to flash before her eyes.   She smiled as she imagined she was standing at the edge of a magnificent waterfall. She gave up on this world and embraced death on her own terms. She jumped head first from the waterfall and into the water.

Agent Robinson felt his legs getting wet, and her body became limp. So, he pushed her down with a forceful shove in the back, causing her skull to crack upon making contact with the concrete floor. It took less than two minutes for Cynthia's life to cease to exist.

Back in her bedroom they opened the safe and retrieved the $50,000. As they were heading to leave out the front door, Robinson abruptly cut in front of Dunlap.   He had a silly smirk on his face and began patting his pockets.

"I think I dropped my wallet in the basement when I pulled the piano string outta my pocket."

Behind squinted eyes, Dunlap sneered, "Hurry the fuck up, nigga! I told you to leave all that shit in the car."

Robinson was an ignorant, diabolical and sociopathic killer with a sick sense of humor. He got off on these types of kills and refused to leave the house without leaving Niq a little something, something. He had spent time considering what to leave her with, and decided on a love letter and two gifts. He raced down to the basement, and placed an eightball of crack, a hundred-dollar bill and a note made from magazine clippings and laid it on Cynthia's lifeless back. I'm not a selfish nigga. Get back on your feet and I'll be back to visit you again. Love always, your secret admirer.

CHAPTER FIVE

Zep had overslept. The blunts and alcohol he'd been consuming over the past few days were taking a toll on his body.

He hated funerals, but the day had arrived for him to pay his last respects to Slickem. The funeral was being held at Calahan & Sons Funeral Home on 70th and Halsted, at 1 p.m. Rome had given everyone orders to be at his apartment by noon, so they could get organized and march up to the funeral together.

Glancing over at his clock, Zep decided to forego a shower and head straight over to the 7000 building.

The walk to the building had been a good thing for Zep. The weather was a blessing in disguise. It was a gray, gloomy day with a little rain, and a cool breeze. The rain and gusty winds felt good on his skin and aided in sobering him up.

Chop immediately scolded Zep when he walked into the apartment. "You fifteen minutes late, 'lil' nigga, and I had just told everybody if you ain't walk through that door in the next minute you was gonna be in violation."

Zep didn't say anything. He just looked at Chop and nodded his head. Chop handed him a T-shirt with a tombstone painted on it, and Slickem's face in the center with the letters R.I.P. Slickem written across the top of the tombstone, and Good Die Young on the bottom.

"Hurry up and put this on then go in Rome's room and holla at 'im, you holdin' everybody up!" Chop spat.

Once in Rome's room, Zep received the news he'd been waiting to hear. "I've been told you want to start hustlin', but you was late for work and B funeral," Rome said.

"Naw, B, I been smokin' and drinkin' too much, and I overslept, but it won't happen again," Zep replied.

"Here's the deal. You, Poopa, Shit-Shit and Tiso gonna be serving on 70th and Emerald. There are 120 bags in each jab. Turn in a stack and keep $200 for ya'self. You down or not?" Rome questioned.

"Yeah, I'm wit it," Zep answered, undoubtedly.

"Okay, but you docked $600.00."

"Docked…what you mean docked?" Zep asked.

"I'm taxin' you $600 fo' bein' late, so the first three jabs you move, you gon' give Chop the whole $3,600. Now, let's get the fuck outta here," Rome stated with authority.

Everyone headed out to the funeral wearing matching T-shirts. Noone had much to say as they walked to the funeral parlor. As usual, blunts and forties were passed around. Occasionally, someone would make a comment about how it was messed up what happened to Slickem or expressed how they were going to get revenge on the GD's for killing Slickem. The overall collective vibe of the gang was somber, to put it mildly.

Once they were in view of the funeral home, it was evident the small place wouldn't be able to accommodate the massive crowd; there were tons of cars, and people were scattered throughout the vicinity.

It was mandatory that all able-bodied BD's be in attendance for the homegoing of a fallen soldier. There were at least 400 people there to pay their respects, all members of the gang from various sections of the city. Members from each set wore articles of clothing to identify their gang affiliation and their location in the city, as a tribute to Slickem, as well as others who were killed from their hood.

Rome was immediattely greeted by the people outside the funeral home, and he introduced all his young thugs to the other high- ranking gang chiefs. Due to the amount of people who had shown up, Rome decided it would be a good idea for Tiso, Zep, Poopa and Shit-Shit to view the body and go straight to serving on the block. Neither young-ster objected to the idea, especially since they didn't want to be bunched up in a funeral home anyway. Besides, they were eager to check some paper since the first day of school was in a couple of days.

Upon entering the funeral home, Zep began to feel nauseous and light-headed. These kinds of feelings always arose in him whenever he attended funerals. The first thing he saw at the end of the long aisle was a baby-blue casket with a wreath on the end of it. In the center of the casket was an assortment of blue carnation flowers arranged in the symbol of the Roman numeral III. On top of the wreath were white carnations arranged to read: 69th with the number *2* on the left side and the number *4* on the right. There was a pulpit directly behind the casket, and a choir stood behind the pulpit softly humming the tune *Precious Lord.*

Two funeral directors were standing at both ends of the casket. They were dressed in black slacks and burgundy blazers with the funeral home's logo patched over the left breast pocket. The organist also worked for the funeral home because he wore the same blazer.

Looking over the rows of pews, Zep noticed they were all empty except for the very first pew. There was a woman dressed in all black, rocking back and forth, sniffling and sobbing.

The whole scene was beginning to become unbearable for Zep. He felt himself about to throw up, but quickly swallowed it back down. He didn't want to appear weak, so he knew he needed to leave before he broke down himself.

"Let's show Slickem some love and bounce," he said, as he leaned over and whispered in Tiso's ear. Tiso shook his head in agreement.

The two of them stood up and made their way from in between the pews. Chop, Poopa and Shit-Shit noticed them and followed them as they walked down the aisle to view the body.

Chop reached his hand inside the casket and formed his fingers in the tray sign then placed them on Slickem's chest. Quitely and just above a whisper, he recited one of the gang's prayers. One by one everybody followed Chop's lead and placed three fingers on Slickem's chest before leaving. *Slickem looks more alive than the funeral directors,* Zep thought. They walked back down the aisle and headed back out on the street, where they rubbed elbows with members from other sets.

Zep's attention was immediately drawn to a group of twenty guys who weren't present before he'd first gone into the funeral home. Each of them was wearing a black T-shirt with the face of a boy centered in the middle. At the top of the T-shirt in big white letters were the words *R.I.P. Yummy,* and directly underneath the picture were the dates *3-12-83/9-1-94.* Zep's eyes were fixated on the picture of Yumny as he thought back to the headlines and all the media attention the boy's murder had received...

"We interrupt your regularly scheduled program to bring you this breaking news. Police have discovered the body of eleven- year-old

Robert 'Yummy' Sandifer underneath a viaduct underpass in the Rose-land area. A source closely connected to the investigation states he was shot two times, execution style, in the back of the head. It has been widely reported on this and other news stations, that Robert 'Yummy' Sandifer was wanted by the Chicago Police Department for the shoot-ings of several people, that accured on August 28th, including fourteen-year-old Shavon Davis, who died from her wounds.

According to reports, Sandifer's actions on August 28th were the results of a gang initiation gone wrong. Whether or not this eleven-year-old boy's murder was a retaliation killing is unknown at this time, however, the same source closely connected to the Shavon Davis, and now Robert Sandifer's homicide, states Sandifer was about to turn him-self in to police and members of the Black Disciple street gang — the

same gang he was reportedly initiating into may be responsible for his murder. Gun violence..."

"Sup B," Big D said, extending his hand to Zep.

"Uhm...nothin'," Zep said, caught off-guard. He quickly cleared his mind of the breaking news report and stared up at the six feet four, four-hundred pound giant towering over him.

"Don't leave him hangin'," Chop snapped, with a scowl on his face. "That's one of the board members," he added, informing Zep of Big D's status in the gang.

"No disrespect, my bad," Zep said, as he performed the gang hand-shake with Big D.

"It ain't no thang," Big D said. "I peeped you starin' at my T-shirt."

"Yeah, I remember some of the guys talkin' 'bout Yummy and watchin' all the news reports about his murder when I was in the third grade. But I don't remember them ever showin' his face on TV.

"I think because Yummy was a minor the news stations couldn't show his face," Big D stated. "But don't believe all the bullshit you heard on the news. Yummy got blessed the same way I did, you did, and every other BD did. So that shit about him doing a shootin' to get initiated was bullshit. The reason I know this is 'cause I was the Min-ister back then and I blessed Yummy myself. And my two young gun-slingers who got locked up for his murder didn't do that shit," Big D said, referring to the two brothers. The brothers were fourteen and sixteen years of age at the time of their arrests, and they were also members of the Black Disciples.

"Well, who did it?" Zep asked.

"I got it, D," Chop said, stepping between Zep and Big D. "I'ma see to it that he get dealt with."

"Naw, B, I got this. Shorty ain't broke no laws. His concerns are genuine and legit. Just look where we at right now." Big D pointed to the funeral home.   "Any time a BD loses his life in the streets, every BD got the right to know what happened to him." Big D gently moved Chop aside. "The same niggas that killed Slickem killed Yummy— them pussy-ass GD's. And, every last one that had something to do with killin' my lil' man is as good as dead. It's yo' job to make sure those responsible for killin' Slickem receive the same fate. Trays!" he said. He turned around and walked into the funeral home without waiting for a response from Zep.

"Trays!" Zep yelled loud enough for Big D to hear him.

Chop took Zep by the shoulders and turned him around so he could face him. "Don't ever question authority again, especially, somebody from another set," Chop threatened. He reached into the sleeve of his jacket and pulled out four jabs. "Find Poopa, Shit-Shit and Tiso, and give them both a jab and y'all go set up shop. I'll be back to check up on y'all after the burial."

***

Once at the crack spot, Poopa instantly tried to establish dominance and make his presence felt. "We gon' rotate servin'. I'ma get my jab off first, then Shit-Shit, then Zep, and then Tiso. Tiso since you got the banger, you gon' work security til we finish, then Zep will hold the banger and work security fo' you.

"Naw, Charlie, I'ma move my jab first, then Zep, Shit-Shit and you," Tiso shot back.

"B, this y'all first day, and I'm tellin' y'all how this shit go out here. Shit-Shit been out here watchin' my back all summer long, and he'll tell you how this shit goes too," Poopa said.

"Yeah, B, Poopa right," Shit-Shit co-signed.

"Nigga fuck you and Poopa!" Tiso growled, "On King David, I'm gettin' my jab off first!"

Zep knew what road this would lead to, so he decided to speak up. "Y'all niggas is trippin'. Poopa, since Tiso got the thumper and gon' work security fo' everybody, let him get his work off first, then you, then Shit-Shit, and I'll go last. It don't make no sense fo' Tiso to be out here holdin' work and a gun too," Zep reasoned.

After taking a few steps away from Tiso, Poopa glared over at Zep. He smacked·his lips and rolled his eyes. "Fuck it," he finally he said.

Poopa was pissed off at Zep for not riding with him. Shit-Shit always had his back but he wasn't the stand-up vocal type. He felt like after giving Zep three-hundered dollars and talking Rome into letting him serve, he should've been showing more loyalty towards him. Poopa hadn't gotten his way this time, but he was determined not to allow this to be an everyday thing. Taking a blunt from behind his ear, he sparked it up and decided he was going to get the last word in one way or another.

"I been out here fo' over a month," he said looking at Zep. "I'm the nigga who talked Rome into lettin' you serve. I know what I'm doin' out here. We can go wit' that rotation fo'now, but tomorrow shit gonna have some order, ya' feel me?" he said, attempting to be the voice of authority.

"Yeah, whatever, B," Zep said, blowing him off. "Pass the ma'fuckin' blunt."

"Yeah, you absolutely right, Poopa," Tiso agreed, as he snatched the blunt out of his mouth and passed it to Zep. "It's gon' be some order out here today startin' wit' you actin' like a real D-boy and not smackin' yo' lips and rollin' yo eyes like a bitch."

"I'm actin' like a bitch?" Poopa replied, as if he couldn't believe what he was hearing. "Nigga, I ain't never actin' like no bitch!" he said, defending himself. "Until Zep came back, you was the one runnin' 'round here wit' ya' head hangin' down, cryin' like a lil' bitch over MiMi," he said, watching Tiso out of the corner of his eyes.

Poopa had struck a nerve, causing Tiso's face to turn blood red. Everyone, except Zep, knew MiMi had Tiso's nose wide open, but they were all too spooked to say something to him about it. Tiso hadn't seen or heard from her since the day her mother caught them having sex. In a fit of rage, she beat MiMi until she blacked out. Then, she put her on punishment and threatened to kill her if she continued to mess around with Tiso. That happened six days prior to Zep returning from Atlanta, and he hadn't been himself during those six days. He barely talked and spent most of his time moping around the house waiting for her to call. It wasn't until Zep came back that he began to turn back into his usual self.

Zep took a long pull off the blunt and passed it to Tiso. "Who the fuck is MiMi?" Zep asked with his lungs filled with smoke.

"Oh, he ain't tell you?" Poopa asked, incredulously. "Ya' man's finally fucks sump'n other than a hype and falls in love with the bitch!"

The statement caused Zep to laugh, choke, and cough uncontrollably.

Tiso had heard and seen enough. Without hesitation, he bum rushed Poopa with a barrage of punches, knocking him clean out. "Talk that shit now, bitch-ass nigga!" Tiso barked, standing over his body. He kicked him in the rib cage, causing him to jerk and groan.

Zep quickly grabbed Tiso and pulled him away before he could do any more damage. Tiso picked up the blunt which had fallen out of his mouth, while Zep and Shit-Shit made sure Poopa was alright. They helped him to his feet and dusted him off.

Embarrassed, Poopa tried to save face. "Sucker punch-he sucker-punched me," he slurred. "I'm bringin' that nigga up on charges at the next meetin'."

Zep put his arm around Poopa and whispered into his ear. "Tiso bogus, but tryna get him violated wouldn't be smart. Think about it. You broke law by callin' his girlfriend a bitch."

After giving it some thought, Poopa realized Zep had a point. "Fuck it, you right," Poopa decided to drop the issue for now. He figured sooner or later he would get his revenge on Tiso, and Zep, if he didn't get with the program.

The four of them walked to the corner of the block, down by the 71st end, and stood silently as they passed the blunt around, waiting for customers to come up. As they got closer, it began to rain lightly.

Almost immediately, the drizzling had stopped and the winds cooled down. The customers began showing up, and Tiso was the first to start moving his work.

Thirty minutes into watching Tiso's back while he served, the monotony within the group began to fade.

Zep was dying to find out exactly who MiMi was, so he approached Tiso with some small talk, as a prelude before grilling him about MiMi. "How much work you got left?" he asked in a casual manner.

"I ain't been keepin' count, but I sold at least half the jab," Tiso replied.

"I was thinkin', if we could get off at least two or three jabs a day, we'd be straight," Zep responded.

"Who you tellin'," Tiso chirped, "I coulda been servin' all summer long but you know I don't fuck with Poopa like that. If you not around, I can't deal with the nigga. His hatin' ass think he tough, and always wanna call the shots. You shoulda seen how he was actin' when you was in Atlanta. I just fell back and let the nigga do him," Tiso ranted.

"Yeah, I can only imagine. He probably jelly you fucked ol'e girl and he didn't," Zep said, using 'jelly' as a slang term for jealous.

"Jelly I fucked who?" Tiso asked.

"MiMi," Zep replied. "Matter fact, who is she? How you meet her?"

"Fam, it's a long story. I'll put you up on everything later," Tiso said, dejected. "But she live on 64th and Lowe in the Englewood Terrace building, and she got a cousin named Capria I'ma hook you up with."

"That's what the fuck I'm talkin''bout," Zep said, satisfied with that bit of information. He balled his fist up and playfully threw a jab at Tiso. "I'ma 'bout to do you the way Poopa wish he could!"

"This ain't what you want!" Tiso threw his guard up, and the two of them began slap-boxing.

CHAPTER SIX

Creeping up the alley in search of a spot for a clear shot of the funeral home entrance, Marco and Toad couldn't believe their eyes.

"Can you believe this shit, G," Marco said, pulling his 16-shot, nine millimeter Ruger from his waist, as he ducked behind a garage.

"Yeah, I see them clown-ass niggas," Toad replied, squatting down to take cover behind a garbage can.

Marco had been on the prowl to kill Tiso, Poopa, Shit-Shit, Zep, and anybody else in his old clique. Ever since he'd become a GD, he felt an overwhelming need to prove his loyalty to the gang, and he'd developed a deep hatred towards the BD's.

After being jumped by his old friends, receiving two broken ribs, he made a vow to kill every last one of them. Since he used to live in the area and hang out with them, he knew all the alleyways, gangways, and dip spots in their territory.

Earlier that week he'd hid in a gangway and waited for hours for Tiso, the BD he hated the most, to emerge from his home. Just as he was about to leave, Slickem came stumbling out of the house of the gangway where he'd been laying low. He called out his name and spit sixteen shots in his direction, hitting him ten times.

Once Marco got word to the location of Slickem's funeral, he decided to shoot up the BD's as they carried the casket out to be placed in the hearse. Although he felt great pride for killing Slickem, he was angry at the fact that some of his guys questioned whether or not he was really responsible for the murder, which is why he brought Toad along with him to hit the funeral. Not once did he think he'd go undetected with a loaded gun, twenty yards from his old clique.

Unable to pass up the opportunity, Marco's attention was shifted to the corner of 70th and Emerald. "G, when them niggas come out the funeral, spray 'em, I'ma air-out these goofy-ass niggas on the corner," Marco told Toad.

Making sure his Tech .22 was properly loaded and ready to fire, Toad took aim and watched the funeral home entrance. He thought about moving closer, because he wouldn't be able to get a clean shot at them from where he stood; the funeral home was on a busy street, and not only was it day light, but heavy traffic was flowing north and south.

He was about to inform Marco of his intentions to find a better position, but the entrance door opened up diverting his train of thought.

A woman dressed in all black rushed out in a hurry. She disregarded her safety as she ran into the ongoing traffic, almost causing an accident. On an emotional rollercoaster, and in need of a great escape, she passed Toad and Marco without even noticing them. She was on a mission, as she quickened her pace, passing Tiso and Zep as they continued slap-boxing.

Locking in on the person she was so desperate to see, she walked straight up to his face. "Poopa, let me get one on credit 'til tonight?" she blurted out without question.

"You know damn well I don't give out no credit!"

"Please, baby," she pleaded, as tears began to well up in her eyes. "You know I'm good for it. I always spend my money with you. I'll pay you back double. I just need sump'n to get me through the burial," she pleaded on, hoping he would show her some sympathy.

"Ain't shit fo' free!" Poopa coldly replied. "You gotta give sump'n to get sump'n."

All too familiar with what he was alluding to, she cleared her throat, wiped her tears, and began the process of numbing her mind. "Baby, we need to do this in a hurry," she said, grabbing his hand, attempting to escort him into the garage they had frequented numerous times.

"Slow ya' roll," Poopa said, refusing to be led into the garage. "I ain't the only nigga out here. Shit-Shit want some head, and I gotta see if folks 'nem wanna do sump'n or not."

"Baby, I just told you I have to get back to attend the burial. I don't got time to take care of all y'all."

Poopa paid her no mind and proceeded to get Zep and Tiso's attention. "B, y'all check it out." He waved them over.

Zep instantly recognized her as the woman sitting in the pew crying, but to her exact identity, he wasn't sure. He thought she looked familiar and tried to get a closer look at her, but she kept her head bowed towards the ground.

"How many she want?" Tiso asked Poopa.

"She ain't got no money but she wanna earn a bag," Poopa informed. "Me and Shit-Shit 'bout to trick off, I'll pay fo' you and Zep if y'all wanna get down too."

"Bet," Tiso said as he shook-up with Poopa.

Feeling hopeless and defeated, the woman didn't protest. They had what she needed and she was willing to do anything to get it. She turned and walked to the abandoned garage with Shit-Shit and Poopa. A few minutes later, the two boys emerged from the garage, and Tiso and Zep entered behind them.

Once inside, they were repulsed by the stench and unsanitary conditions of the garage. Littered throughout were carcasses of dead cats, rats and birds, animal and human feces, rotten wood, old clothes, broken glass, and Hefty Ziplock bags filled with trash. Puddles of bacteria infected water were spread on the floor caused by a leaky roof. Empty crack baggies, used condoms, and syringes, floated around in the water. The garage was so horrendous it should've been quarantined and labeled a health hazard.

One corner of the garage looked as though somebody had swept all the water and trash away, leaving just enough space for a few people to maneuver around without stepping in the filth. It was there the woman was standing with her black lace panties pulled down around her ankles, and a crack pipe made from a car antenna in her hand. Covering his mouth and nose, Zep led the way over toward her, doing his best to avoid stepping in the water and trash.

"Cutie pie, I see you hustlin' now," the woman said, looking Zep in the face, "gimme a light so I can take a quick hit before I take care of y'all."

Only one person called him cutie pie, "Cremey," Zep heard himself speak what he was thinking. He thought he'd recognized her but he had never seen her wearing make-up moderately applied, or a designer dress. Her make-up was always heavy and she dressed in stereotypical prostitution garb.

"Yeah, cutie pie, it's me. I see you gettin' yo' grown man on now. What you do is your bidness, and what I do is mines. You won't never hafta worry 'bout me sayin' a word to Diane and the same goes for you, Tiso."

Tiso dug into his pocket and passed her a cigarette lighter.

She snatched it, ripped open the baggie containing the crack and placed the whole rock on the antenna. A hit is what she wanted but not just any hit, a *godfather blast* is what she was craving. She heated the rock until it disappeared, before placing the other end in her mouth. With her lips wrapped tightly around the makeshift pipe and eyes closed, the crack sizzled as she took a long pull on the antenna, as if she were trying to inhale the fire coming from the lighter.

Cremey was blessed with natural beauty. She used to compete in beauty pageants and was once a lingerie model; that had been many moons ago. She was just getting her feet wet, and in the process of signing a contract with a top modeling agency, when she crossed paths with the man of her dreams, the infamous Magic Don Juan. Two months into their relationship she was out on the track as his top earner. Five years later, she was left on the streets with a crack habit, while he stepped up his pimp game to another level, Bishop Magic Don Juan— *church!*

Unlike most crack addicts, Cremey kept her appearance up. Her butter pecan skin, almond-shaped eyes, and full lips were insinuated by the fire highlighting her feminine features. She looked angelic as a single tear trickled down her cheek. The tear, coupled with her beauty and the euphoria Cremey appeared to be experiencing from the crack, ignited Zep.   This sight, along with her panties down to her ankles got his dick rock hard.

Caught up in the moment, Zep unzipped his pants, freed his erection, and began masturbating as he stared at Cremey with lustful eyes.

Knocking him out of his zone, Tiso bumped Zep as he passed by him to get a better view of Cremey. She blew the smoke up in the air and smiled at them; she was feeling the high. She turned her attention to the task at hand and noticed both of them standing with their dicks in their hands.

All of Zep's sexual fantasies and wet dreams concerning Cremey were about to become a reality. He could thank the crack gods later. He yanked her head down by the nape of her neck, almost forcing his manhood down her throat.

Tiso got behind her, lifted her dress, parted her ass cheeks and decided to play a deadly game of roulette. Without giving it any thought, he shoved his dick in her, raw. Pounding in and out of her doggy style, she threw her ass back at him while skillfully working her tongue and jaw muscles on Zep.

Feeling himself about to cum, Tiso tightened his grip around her waist and began to thrust deeper, harder and faster, causing her to bite down. Zep screamed at the top of his lungs and instinctively pushed her head away.

"Aaaaahh...shit, you bit my dick!'' he yelled, while examining himself for damage.

Tiso mocked him and started laughing. Cremey grabbed Zep's hand. She was about to apologize until she saw the silhouette of an outstretched arm aiming a gun at the back of Zep's head.

POP! POP! POP!

Tiso fired three shots just inches from Zep's face without warning, causing him to fall in the nasty water on the floor.

BOC! BOC! BOC! BOC! BOC!

Marco returned fire, shooting wildly into the garage. Toad's attention was diverted from the funeral home toward the direction of the shots coming from the garage. He left his position and ran towards the garage to make sure Marco was straight.

Poopa ran to the garage door. "Tiso, what the fu--"

TAT! TAT! TAT! TAT!

Toad began busting shots off from the Tech .22 at Shit-Shit and Poopa as they approached the garage door calling out to Tiso. The bullets whizzed past their ears, and they took off running. Toad rounded the gangway to the garage and ran square into Marco, sending him to the pavement.

"Shit, let's go man!'' Marco said, getting up off the ground.

They ran down the alley headed in the direction where Toad had initially posted up.

***

The sidewalk outside was crowded and people were still exiting the funeral home. The hearse was double parked on the busy street. Just as the casket was being placed inside the hearse, the procession came under attack.

TAT! TAT! TAT! BOC! BOC! BOC! TAT! TAT!

The pallbearers dropped the casket in the street and took cover. Cars driving up and down Halsted began beeping their horns and swerving, as one of the cars heading south tried to avoid hitting the casket and crashed into another car in the north lane.   People were in a frenzy knocking and pushing one another down, trying to get back inside the funeral home to safety. Women were yelling and screaming, children were hollering and crying, men cursed and shouted as car alarms sounded off when the bullets struck them. People fished in their pockets for key chains, as survival instincts began to kick in. Trunks to parked cars started popping up.

Just as the shots ended, Tiso came charging down the alley and got his last three rounds off at Marco and Toad as they were fleeing. A bullet hit Toad in the shoulder and he fell, but quickly got back to his feet, leaving his Tech .22 behind. They jumped into their stolen car and sped off.

Zep and Cremey emerged from the garage and hurried down to Tiso.

Running and pointing in the direction where the shots were coming from, Poopa shouted, "The alley, the alley, them bitch ass GD's!" He alerted everybody outside the funeral home. He and Shit-Shit had been yelling and pointing in the direction of the alley, trying to warn their guys where the danger was coming from, but no one paid attention or heard them due to the noise and commotion, and they hadn't quite made it to the funeral home entrance where they'd be able to see the shooters in the alley. Before they could speak another word, two guys got up off the ground.

BOOM! BOOM! BOOM! BOOM!

Both men emptied their clips at the people in the alley. On cue, people began to get up and reach into the trunks of their cars, pulling

out automatic assault weapons. Clips were being loaded in, safeties un-
latched, and rounds entered the chambers of Mack II's, Tech 9's and
AK-47's.

"No, no, don't shoot, that's lil' folks!" Rome yelled, getting up
from behind the casket.

"Stop, stop, put the guns down!" Chop demanded, as he too got up
and began swatting the barrels of the assault weapons towards the
ground.

Then for a moment, it seemed as if time stood still. There was complete silence and nobody made a move. The next sounds was the police
sirens which could be heard from a distance. All hell broke loose as
everyone tried to put as much distance as possible between themselves
and Calahan & Sons Funeral Home.

People were scattering like roaches when the lights came on. The
street was jammed due to the accident, but that didn't stop anybody
from jumping in their vehicles forcing themselves out of the cramped
space, damaging paint jobs and sending door mirrors up into the air.
People stepped on top of the casket, propelling themselves to the hoods
of cars because it was the fastest route to the C.T.A. bus, which was
being held up at gunpoint a half block down.

Miraculously, nobody got shot outside the funeral home. The brunt
of the damage was two totaled cars, a few shattered windows, and a
dented coffin covered in shoe prints. Sadly, the same couldn't be said
for everybody in the alley.

Zep struggled to remain conscious as he tried to make sense of
what was happening, as his body lay sprawled on the concrete. Blood
covered his stomach and head. He tried to lift himself up off of the
ground, but lacked the strength to do so— something was weighing
him down.

"Off," he murmured. "Get off."

In pain, tired and out of breath, Zep's strength began to rapidly
fade. Memories that had been suppressed into the deepest depths of his
mind began to resurface. His mind wandered back to the harmonious
days when he lived with both his parents. Memories of his father teaching him to ride a bike, sitting under the Christmas tree unwrapping
gifts, feeding his sister a bottle, and helping his mother change his

brother's diaper, all danced around in his head. Those pleasant memories eased the physical pain he felt, and the weight that was holding him down was suddenly lifted.

"Zep, look at me!" Tiso's voice was stricken with panic as he held Zep's hand. "Don't die- please- don't- don't- don't die! Look- at- me-" His voice cracked, staring into Zep's eyes.

Those were the last words Zep heard before his eyes rolled into the back of his head and darkness washed over him.

CHAPTER SEVEN

School couldn't end soon enough for Capria. She had been staring at the clock so long, once the bell finally rang, she remained glued to her desk in a hypnotic state. After the teacher called her name twice she snapped back to reality, gathered her books and rushed out the door.

Uninterested in her peers' affairs or feelings, she pushed past the, mostly Caucasian, students, shooting daggers in their direction, daring one of them to get out of pocket. Her mind was fixated on getting with Niq, picking up MiMi, and popping tags at the mall. As she power-walked home, she stopped for nothing and no one.

As soon as Capria made it to her front door, her fast pace came to an abrupt halt; the door was slightly cracked open which was never the case. The family was anal when it came to security measures, ensuring both the windows and doors stayed locked and secured.

She pushed the door open, stepped inside, and called out to her mother. After getting no response, she closed the door, cut off the TV, and called her mother's name a second time, still no answer. The faucet was running in the kitchen so she assumed Cynthia was in there.

On her way to the kitchen she stopped in her tracks when she reached the doorway to her mother's bedroom.

"What-the-fuck," she stammered, as she squinted her eyes and placed her hand over her mouth. Her heart skipped a beat as a twinge of fear rose in her. "Calm down 'Pria, everything is a'ight," she mumbled, trying to ease the tension within herself.

Cynthia was a neat freak, seeing the empty safe on the bed, a pillow case off the pillow, a pitcher of water, and the bra her mother had worn that morning sprawled across the floor, let her know something was wrong. Her survival instincts told her to retrieve the loaded .25 automatic her mother kept underneath her pillow.

Armed with the pistol, Capria searched the first and second floors of the house. She was about to give up on finding her and call Niq, until she thought about the basement.

The basement door was open which was unusual. She cautiously walked down the stairs not knowing what or who was laying in wait. Eerie feelings began to invade her body as she descended each step.

She frowned and wrinkled her nose as a faint musky odor hit her face. She cleared the first couple stairs and her legs began to shake. Next step, her arms trembled. Another stair her stomach started doing flips. The musky odor started to thicken. She took another step, and beads of sweat cascaded down her face, and her heart rate shot through the roof. Her head started spinning and she couldn't stop her eyes from rapidly blinking. She felt herself getting dizzy and stopped. She rest the gun at her side and placed her back up against the wall, in an attempt to regain her composure.

After taking a few deep breaths, she pushed her hair back on her head, wiping sweat away in the process. *Only a couple more stairs,* she thought. She then put both hands on the gun, raised it to the center of her breast, and forged ahead.

Before she made it to the last stair, her mother's legs came into view. Without hesitation she rushed over to her. Standing over her mother's body, it was obvious all the help in the world couldn't save her. She quickly turned her head away from Cynthia's body and vomited on the floor. Her chest started to tighten up and the walls appeared to be closing in.

Breathing heavily, she spoke, winded, "I-I-got-get-ou-out-of-here."

She bolted up the stairs and out the front door like a bat out of hell. She was stricken with a temporary case of schizophrenia as she paced back and forth, brandishing a loaded gun on a residential street in an upscale neighborhood.

***

"What the hell? Is that a gun in her hand?" Special Agent Henry Palko said to his partner, gesturing towards the window.

Agent Jennifer Hoyer scurried to her feet and grabbed her badge and service weapon off the table.

"Where do you think you're going, Jenny?" he asked, in an authoritative tone.

"I'm going to disarm and apprehend the girl before she hurts someone, or herself," she told him.

"And blow our cover, I don't think so, missy! Just sit tight and pass me the damn phone."

"For what?" she huffed.

"Because I said so," he spat arrogantly, "in addition to the fact, the technician unit should be coming around the corner in a minute and I don't want them to get caught up in a situation." He tapped his head with his left index finger, subliminally suggesting, he was thinking, and she wasn't.

The pair was familiar with one another but had never worked together. Special Agent Andy Bochello had originally put together the file on Dominique Jackson, and he'd requested the assistance of Agent Jenny because they had worked well together in the past.

Agent Bochello had been retired for the last three years. In his spare time, he would speak at engagements, law enforcement seminars, and college classrooms where criminology was the subject. He had taken a part-time job for the government training other law enforcement officers who submitted applications with hopes of becoming a Federal Agent.

One of his trainees was ambitious and wanted badly to become an agent, he was a mere narcotics detective. One week into attending class he busted a man with two kilos of coke, and instead of arresting him he flipped him and called Bochello thinking he could gain some points. Bochello had no desire of getting back into the field, but when the detective told him the informant had informed him of his connect's name, who happened to be Niq, it raised his curiosity. The name Niq had rang a bell but he couldn't quite place where he'd heard it before.

So, he decided to have him bring the informant to a secret location while he checked his old files. As soon as he typed the name 'Niq' into his laptop and clicked the search option, Niq's picture popped up on the screen. She was in his personal files as being the live-in girlfriend of David "Bull" Dixon.

The biggest investigation Bochello ever spear-headed was that of the Miguel Carrillo Drug Cartel. Miguel Carrillo was on America's Ten Most Wanted List. He was responsible for countless civilian and law enforcement deaths on both sides of the border, and was estimated to have trafficked over one-hundred-thousand kilos into the U.S. among other crimes.

Special Agent Bochello arrested him, secured his conviction, and was on his way to becoming the next Director, but some kid fresh out of law school derailed his promotion by getting the cartel boss's conviction overturned. That one case was his greatest accomplishment and his biggest failure. He thought he'd never get the chance to catch Miguel Carrillo again until he learned David "Bull" Dixon had ties to the cartel. Just when his hopes started to get high, Bull was killed and the trail went cold— that's when he decided to call it a career. But, the unfinished business with Carrillo haunted him, and any connection to him, regardless how small, had to be investigated, so he got back in the saddle.

As a trained Air Force pilot, Bochello's idea of a good time was taking to the skies. Tragically, two weeks into the investigation, his single engine plane motor failed and crashed in a remote area in Wisconsin, killing him instantly. The lead in the case was reassigned to Special Agent Palko, and Agent Jennifer Hoyer was ordered to stay aboard. However, only a few people were privy to who Bochello's main target was. Those people were the U.S. Attorney handling the case, the FBI Director, and one federal court judge. Even his partner, Agent Hoyer was kept in the dark, for fear of someone tipping Carrillo off and blowing the sting before it got started.

Palko and Hoyer were given a file on Niq, and strict orders to run everything they found on her to the U.S. Attorney General's office, only.

Palko had a reputation within the bureau as being all over the place. At times he would be innovative, intelligent and a consummate professional, closing some of the toughest cases. However, there were also times he would be lackadaisical, over-confident, and sloppy. But, he was consistently arrogant and he'd been working his partner's nerves since day one.

Working on the case for almost two weeks, they moved into a foreclosed property directly across the street from the Jackson's home, posing as a retired married couple with one child off in college. After watching the house for the past week, snapping photos and submitting information obtained by Bochello from his C.I., the federal judge issued sealed subpoenas allowing a wiretap to be placed on Cynthia's home phone, and twenty-four-hour surveillance cameras around her home.

Just as Agent Jenny was preparing to pass the phone to Palko, she turned and looked out of the window. "A day late and a dollar short," she said, returning the phone to the table and pointing out the window at the city maintenance van cruising up the block.

***

Capria was unconscious of her behavior until she saw the van turn up the block. Realizing she didn't want to be seen with a gun on her, she concealed it and rushed back inside the house.   The van kept driving and she breathed a sigh of relief. She snatched the cordless phone off of the sofa, stepped back out of the front door, and dialed Niq's cell phone number, unaware of the Feds' prying ears.

Niq answered on the third ring, "Hel--"

"You gotta come home now!" Capria ranted before Niq could get out the second syllable.

"Damn, girl, calm down. I'ma take you shoppin' tomorrow."

"No, Niq it's important, you gotta come home right now," Capria insisted.

"I'm handlin' some bidness right now. What's so important I gotta come home?"

Capria became silent as she tried to figure out how to formulate her words.

"'Pria, you still there?" Niq asked.

Capria's voice began to crack as she whispered, "I can't say over the phone."

"What do you mean you can't..." Niq stopped herself mid-sentence. "Is everything okay with you and momma?" she asked, with panic in her voice.

Capria began to break down and became hysterical again.

"Naw, it ain't okay, come home, Niq!" she screamed at the top of her lungs, before pressing the off button.

Unsure of how to react to the bizzare phone call, Niq pulled her Benz over and stared at the phone for a minute. She didn't know if her family was in danger or if Capria was overreacting to a minor problem. She contemplated calling up a few of her hired goons to go to the house. However, once that happened she would immediately have to find her family a new place to live. *Please, don't let no niggas be holdin' my family hostage*, she thought to herself. Then, a light bulb turned on in her head. She dialed the house number.

"Hello!" Capria shouted, answering the phone.

"'Pria, do y'all got any company?" Niq questioned.

"No, do we ever have any," she blurted, sarcastically.

"Lemme talk to momma real quick?"

"You can't, that's why you need to get here."

"Okay, I'm on my way, but I'm in a hurry so I ain't comin' in the house, meet me on the corner. I'll be there in thirty minutes." Thinking on her feet, Niq figured this way she wouldn't be walking into a trap.

***

The two agents sat, puzzled, with headphones covering their ears, with their eyes locked on Capria sitting on the edge of her porch, cradling a gun and phone in her lap, as she rocked back and forth.

Palko spoke first. "I hate to assume, because people who assume usually make fools of themselves, so instead, I'll pose a question."

"Lay it on me," Agent Jenny responded.

"Why does she have a gun? What can't she say over the phone? And why can't her mother come to the phone?"

"You said you had a question, that's three, and I don't have a definitive answer to either one," she said, taking the headphones off of her head, placing them next to the computer operating the wiretap. "You know if Ms. Jackson is inside that house injured, precious time is ticking, and if the unthinkable happens and we could've prevented it, how do we explain that to the A.G.?" she added.

"*If the unthinkable happens*," he repeated. Taking his headphones off, he stood up and stared hard at Capria. "The unthinkable already happened and I'm looking at the killer."

"Now you're assuming, but for the sake of argument let's say you're not making a complete fool of yourself. The best move for us is to call the locals as worried civilians and report a teenage girl across the street carrying a firearm, displaying irrational behavior."

"No need to do that!" he quickly shot down that idea. "I'm curious to see how the drug Queenpin handles this situation. I'm wondering if she'll try to conceal the body, or if they'll report it, and what reason the girl will give for murdering her mother. Also, this might be an opportunity for us to get a visual on some of her cohorts. Or…" He turned and locked eyes with his partner.

"Or what?" she asked.

"Or, will she avenge her mother's death and kill her own sister," he said with a sly grin on his face.

She rolled her eyes at him, not sharing in his humor. "This is on you," she pointed her finger directly at him, "if that lady is clinging to life in there and we do nothing…" she paused and threw her hands up in the air and shifted her attention to the computer. "On a positive note, we now have Niq's cell phone number. First thing tomorrow, I'll have the audio recording, transcript, and phone records sent to the A.G.'s office so we can get that wire up A.S.A.P."

Both agents would soon find out tracking Niq's whereabouts and conversations via her cell phone wouldn't be that simple. She used prepaid cell phones and switched them up every week.

***

"Help! Help! Somebody call a ambulance," Tiso yelled, motioning across the street for someone to come over and help his partner in crime. Tears flooded his eyes as he looked down in shock. Zep's shirt was soaked in blood and he had blood dripping from his head.

Rome, Chop, Shit-Shit, Poopa and his off-again on-again girlfriend, Ericka, ran over to see what happened. Everybody stood over Zep with looks of devastation. Tiso was going on a tirade vowing to kill every GD in the city, as well as his own guys who were responsible for, mistakenly, shooting Zep.

Rome tried to console Tiso, while the others bent down to pick Zep up and get him to the street where he'd be more accessible to receive help once it arrived.

They lifted him up into the air. Chop and Shit- Shit held one side of his body up, and Poopa and Ericka held the other. They were just starting to walk to the street when Ericka let out a loud squeal.

"Look," she said, releasing her hand from Zep's body, pointing to the ground.

"Fuck is you doin'?" Chop snapped, as he shifted his body to tighten his grip on Zep, compensating the extra strength needed.

Ericka returned her hand back to its original position. "It's Cremey- she's dead!" She started crying.

Nobody had paid any attention to Cremey who was lying only two feet from Zep. She was barely conscious in a seated position against a gate on the side of a dumpster. When everyone had initially ran over, their focus was on Tiso, and his only concern was Zep. Once they had made it to Zep, their backs had been turned from where Cremey had been lying. Also, it didn't help that she was being camouflaged by the dumpster. Both her feet were sticking straight out for all to see, if they bothered to look down, which Ericka just happened to do.

"Aye! Y'all get over here. Cremey hit behind the dumpster," Poopa called out to Rome and Tiso.

"We gotta get Zep, hold up," Chop said, as he looked at Zep's face. "Let's put him down for a second," he ordered them.

Chop wiped the blood from Zep's head with his bare hands. He then lifted up his shirt to check for any gunshot wounds. He gave Zep two, light slaps across his face and his eyes opened. "Ain't shit wrong with this nigga, he musta' passed out or got the wind knocked out of him," Chop announced as he went over to Cremey.

Cremey had been running alongside Zep when she caught a slug that sent her crashing into him. Her body weight knocked Zep into the dumpster where he hit his head and suffered a mild concussion. She had lain on top of him until Tiso had pushed her off. Clinging to life, she conjured up enough strength to scoot herself into a more comfort- able position. Now, she sat back against a gate, and the right side of her body was leaning on the dumpster with her hand covering her abdomen, as blood leaked out.

The sirens were getting louder by the second, making it evident that the whole vicinity was about to be swarming with the law.

"It's time to get little," Rome announced. "Ericka, stay here and make sure Cremey gets to the hospital, the rest of y'all get Zep and let's bounce."

Making his way across the street, the driver of the hearse yelled, "Where y'all going? What y'all want me to do with the body?"

"Whateva my ten racks paid yo' ass to do," Rome yelled back over his shoulder,

The group never looked back as they fled, stopping only to retrieve the tech .22 lying on the alley ground. By the time the police and ambulances showed up, the only people on the scene were funeral directors, the victims of the car accident, a few on-lookers who'd just walked up, Cremey, and Ericka.

Ericka alerted the paramedics to where Cremey was and they rushed over. They checked her vitals, stabilized her, strapped her to the gurney, and loaded her in the back of the ambulance; Ericka accompanied them to St. Bernard Hospital.

The police taped off the scene, collected shell casings and interviewed everyone there. They left with a bag full of printless shells casings, frustrated, because no one claimed to have heard or seen a thing.

Eddie "Wolf" Lee

CHAPTER EIGHT

Niq pulled her 550 Benz up to the corner of her block, and before she could press the button to unlock the passenger door, Capria was yanking on the handle, anxiously. Barely in the car, she didn't waste time informing Niq about their mother's state.

"Mama dead," she blurted out. "Somebody came in the house, killed Mama, and took the money out the safe!"

"What?" Niq asked in a state of shock. "Are you serious?" She couldn't believe her ears, as tears rained down her face.

Capria wasn't used to seeing her big sister cry, and it caused her to break down again. She leaned over and embraced Niq. The two grief-stricken sisters cried their eyes out in each other's arms. After crying for what seemed like hours, but had actually been only minutes, Niq felt she needed to pull herself together and be strong for her mother, and most importantly, her baby sister.

She grabbed some Kleenex from her purse, flipped down her sun visor, and dried her eyes, as she looked at her reflection in the mirror. She put the car in drive and passed Capria the Kleenex. Niq drove to the front of her house and parked.

She faced Capria. "Don't leave out nothin', tell me everything," she said.

Capria was thorough as she told her about her entire day, beginning at 6:30 a.m. when she'd first woke up for school to returning home from school, searching the house and finding their mother's body, to jumping in the car with her. Niq listened intensively to every word spoken, hoping to find a clue as to whom the perpetrators were. But nothing she said yielded a hint to who could've been responsible. Niq searched her sister's face for more but there was nothing else.

At a loss for words, she said the first thing that came to mind, "Why didn't you call fo' help or sump'n?"

Capria answered. "'Cause I knew she was gone," she explained. "It's real bad, she got handcuffs on, blood comin' out her head and she peed on herself." Swallowing the lump in her throat, she continued, "Plus, I know you got drugs in the house and I didn't want you to go to jail. If something happens to you, I won't have nobody left." She dabbed her eye with the tissue, preventing a tear from falling.

"Nothin's gonna happen to me," Niq assured her.

"Yeah, just like you said nothin' would. . ." Capria stopped speaking when she realized her choice of words were inappropriate. There was an awkward silence between them for a second. "Oh, I forgot to tell you one more thing. Whoever did this left some money, some crack, and a note on mama's back."

"A note… What did it say?" Niq asked, perplexed.

"I dont know, I didn't read it. I just ran out the house."

"You wanna sit here while I go inside?" Niq asked.

'Pria sighed, then replied. "Naw, I'ma go in with you."

Once inside, and down in the basement, the two sisters held hands and wept silently like they didn't want to disturb Cynthia's lifeless body. Niq told Capria to go upstairs in her bedroom and wait for her while she checked her stash spot.

After discovering everything was missing, she picked up the note and read it: I'm not a selfish nigga. Get back on your feet, bitch, and I'll be to visit you again. Love always, your secret admirer.

The note caused misery, confusion and rage to bubble inside of Niq. "Yeah, this bitch gon' find you, torture you, and send you on a permanant visit to hell, muthafucka," she uttered, meaning every word. Walking up the stairs, she pulled out her cell phone and called the one person she knew to give her some much needed counsel.

Ring…Ring… Ring…

"Hello, you have reached the law offices of William Battle and Associates. How may I help you?"

"I need to speak to Bill."

"I'm sorry. Mr. Battle is in a meeting right now. May I take a message or schedule an appointment?"

"This is his wife and it's urgent," Niq said, using the code word 'wife' to let the receptionist know the call was crucial.

"Please hold while I inform Mr. Battle you're on the line."

William Battle was a criminal's dream come true, and a prosecutor's worst nightmare. Since being a youth, his only goal had been to graduate from law school, pass the bar, move to Chicago, and become the best criminal defense attorney in the United States. Thus far, he'd accomplished the first three and was ahead of schedule on the last. He'd been practicing law for the past twelve years and was voted Illinois' best criminal defense attorney by his peers, a record, eight, consecutive years.

Garnering a ninety-percent acquital rate speaks for itself in a city that had an eighty-seven percent conviction rate with the majority of them coming by way of plea deals. His knowledge of the law and gift of persuasion was second to none. When you add these two traits to an individual who's also easy on the eyes, extremely competitive, hates to lose, and will go to the end of the universe to win, you have one hell of a lawyer. John Grisham couldn't have penned a better story than how his career got started.

While attending Northwestern University School of Law, he, along with five other students and two professors, teamed with a legal clinic that represented selected cases pro bono. He single-handedly authored two separate petitions, which were filed in the United States Supreme Court, on behalf of two prisoners on death row. Both times he won 5:2, not only saving their lives, but freeing both inmates. When he wasn't doing pro bono work, he spent the remainder of his free time sitting in courtrooms watching attorneys battle it out.

In his final year of law school he'd been a spectator at what was being called the biggest trial in Chicago since Al Capone. He made sure he sat up front and center.

Miguel Carrillo, head of the Carrillo Drug Cartel had been captured in his hometown of Juarez, Mexico and extradited to the U.S. to stand trial on racketeering charges along side twenty co-defendants.

The indictment listed charges of murder, international drug trafficking, kidnapping, human trafficking for the purpose of slavery and prostitution, extortion, counterfeiting of U.S. currency, and tax evasion.

The who's who of domestic and international attorneys were seated at the tables on both sides of the aisle. His high-powered attorneys fought tooth and nail for him and his co-defendants. But after four days of deliberation the jury came back with a guilty verdict.

Miguel Carrillo was sentenced to life without the possibility of parole and ushered to the Supermax federal prison in Florence, Colorado. The least amount of time any of his co-defendants received was twenty-five years.

William Battle never missed a day in court. He painstakingly followed the trial taking notes and preparing motions, and jotting down questions he believed should've been asked to witnesses, and testimony and evidence he would've attacked more thoroughly than the defense had. He even spent eight hours in front of a mirror rehearsing an elaborate closing argument as if he was first chair for the defense. In his heart, he believed had he represented Miguel Carrillo he would've been acquitted.

So, the day after he passed the bar, instead of meeting with the various law firms that were engaging in an all-out bidding war for his services, he decided to pay the cartel boss a visit. After ten visits and numerous correspondences through mail, he convinced El Guise, Miguel Carillo's moniker, to fire his entire defense team and give him total control.

A year and a half later, El Guise waltzed out the Dirksen building in downtown Chicago a free man, and a friendship was born. As a token of his appreciation he provided him with a blank check to spend whatever he needed to establish his own law firm and an additional five million for his troubles.

As time moved on, the two men developed a strong bond. They accompanied each other on vacations around the world and never missed spending the Christmas holiday together.

William Battle and his team of lawyers began representing and freeing members of Carrillo's organization. It wasn't long before the charismatic Battle began overseeing all of Miguel El Guise Carrillo's business ventures, both legal and illegal.

The receptionist transferred the call to William Battle's line and Niq wasted no time bringing him up to speed.

"I'm very sorry. Cynthia was a beautiful, God-fearing woman who didn't deserve this. My heart, prayers and condolences go out to you and your family," Battle said. "It's a good thing you contacted me before you called the police. Had you called the authorities first, I guarantee they would've launched an investigation into your dealings, giving the items left behind by the savages who committed this atrocity. I just need a few seconds to think."

Close to a minute of silence elapsed before Niq asked, "Are you still there?"

"Yes. Listen carefully. Try not to contaminate the crime scene any further than what you may have already done. We still want the police department to be effective in doing their job but we can't allow them to get the evidence left behind. Here's what I need you to do. Get three clean paper bags and place the cocaine, hundred-dollar bill and note separately, in each bag. Make sure to be careful not to rub off any fingerprints, DNA, or any other traces of evidence that can potentially identify the person who left it there.

Put the bags where the police can't find them and get them to me A.S.A.P. Drain the acid and put the safe and .25 automatic pistol back where they belong. After you've done all that, call the police. Tell them Capria called you after she came home from school and thought nobody was home. Then once you got to the house, the two of you tried to figure out where your mother had gone. After failing to come up with a plausible reason for her sudden disappearance, you decided to search the house yourself for a note she may have left behind. And that's when the two of you went into the basement and found her body. Keep it to the point, and simple. Can you remember all of that?"

"Yeah, I got it," Niq responded.

"Be sure to do everything exactly as I've told you to. And I'll personally show up at the police station once you and Capria are taken in for questioning. Again, I'm so sorry this has happened to you," he said, before ending the call.

Niq sprung into action, completing the tasks instructed by her lawyer. She hid the evidence where she knew the homicide detectives wouldn't find it and coached Capria on the spiel they were going to give the police. Next, she picked up the house phone and dialed 9-1-1.

The dispatcher answered on the first ring, "9-1-1, what's your emergency?"

"Help… I don't know what happened…could you send somebody over pleeease!" Niq said, sounding flustered.

"Calm down, ma'am, and tell me what your problem is."

What started out as an Oscar winning performance, suddenly, turned real as tears began streaming down her face. "Somebody came in our house and killed my mother!"

***

Special Agent Palko removed his headphones and faced his partner as she sat mouth wide-open, dumbfounded.

"Why the look of surprise my sexy wife? I told you that girl killed her mother, and I can't wait to be on the other side of the glass to hear the juicy details when she confesses, but I'm dying to get in that house to take a look at the crime scene. Finally, some action," he added with a sarcastic tone. "The day turned out alright after all, wouldn't you agree?"

Judging by the way Agent Jenny turned her nose up at him, you would've thought he'd shitted on himself. "You disgust me with your shallow and lackluster attempts at humor! It's obvious why no woman will ever marry you."

CHAPTER NINE

The E.M.T. workers were the first to arrive at the Jackson's house. After discovering Cynthia was deceased, they dispatched the police station and homicide investigator Lt. Ralph Patterson was assigned to the case.

When Lt. Patterson showed up at the house, the two detectives assisting him in the investigation were already on location. He ordered the younger, inexperienced detective to escort Niq and Capria down to the precinct and take their official statements. He, then, turned to the other detective and said, "I see the coroner and crime scene investigators are already here. Have you seen the victim yet?"

"No, I haven't," the detective replied, shaking his head. "We were just about to enter the house when the Capt. called me and informed us not to step foot inside the house until you made it here first."

"Those orders didn't come from me, or Captain Wiggins," Lt. Patterson told him. "I don't exactly know what's going on, but I know I don't like it. One minute after I got assigned to this case, Captain Wiggins called me into his office and told me to sit with him until a D.E.A. agent showed up to talk with me. Ten minutes later, the Captain received another call informing him the case may or may not remain under our jurisdiction and for me to get to the crime scene, have the two sisters sent to the station, immediately, and not to enter the house until the agent arrived."

The detective gave Lt. Patterson a confused look. Lt. Patterson shrugged his shoulders and headed into the house.

***

The emergency room at St. Bernard Hospital wasn't bustling with activity until the ambulance arrived with Cremey. The doctors and nurses were on stand-by, and wasted no time getting her into the operating room. En route to the hospital, Cremey began drifting in and out of consciousness, and she was losing blood at an alarming rate. A half-mile from the hospital, she flat-lined, and the paramedics used the defibrillator to revive her.

Ericka was concerned, but before the paramedics could unload Cremey out of the ambulance, she jumped out of the ambulance and sprinted to the restroom to relieve her bladder. She washed her hands and gave herself a quick lookover in the mirror before leaving the ladies room. From there, she went to the cafeteria to feed the cravings she had been experiencing lately for pickles and chocolate. After purchasing the items from a vending machine, she went to the nurse's station and informed them she had come in with Cremey, and they could find her in the waiting room area once she was out of surgery.

Ericka bent the corner and took a step inside the waiting room, but quickly backtracked when she saw Marco and Toad. The two of them were in deep conversation and didn't notice she had stepped in, momentarily. Ericka stood on the opposite side of the wall and listened as they talked.

"Nigga, yo' aim ain't on shit... talkin' 'bout you shot Zep. Look like the only muthafucka you shot was the clucka." Toad continued, "If I woulda been inside that garage, I woulda bodied all three of them bitches."

"Who the fuck you think you talkin' to, G? You had a Tech .22 with a 32-shot clip, and ain't 'nan body came through this muthafucka 'cause of you," Marco retorted. "Instead of you shootin' at them niggas, you shootin' in the air. Nigga, then you ended up gettin' shot ya'self. Then yo' soft ass fell down and left the thumper."

"Tiso wouldn't have been able to shoot me if you woulda handled yo' bidness. And the reason nobody I shot made it to the hospital is-"

"'Cause you ain't shoot nobody!" Marco finished his sentence.

"Naw, 'cause the nigga I shot is dead, and he went straight to the funeral home," Toad retorted, laughing.

"Man, fuck this shit. The nurse said you straight. All you got is a flesh wound. They put bandages on yo' shoulder and gave you a shot. You don't need to see the doctor. Let's be up!"

Ericka made a dash for the ladies room. She waited inside until she thought they were gone, and then she returned back to the waiting room. She hopped on the pay phone and called her sister with the news.

A few minutes later, a man of middle-eastern descent approached her.

"Excuse me young lady, you wouldn't happen to be Ericka would you?"

"Yeah, that's me," she answered.

"You came in with the lady who suffered a gunshot wound, correct?" he inquired.

"Yeah."

"What is your relationship to the woman?" he asked.

"Umm, she ain't no kin to me, I been knowin' her since I was little. She live down the street from me."

"What is her name?" he quizzed her.

"Cremey."

"Cremey," the doctor repeated. "Is that her first or last name?"

"I think that's her nickname but I got her real name right here." Ericka fumbled around in her purse before pulling out Slickem's obituary. "Yeah, right here it say Rhonda "Cremey" James."

"Do you mind if I take a look at that?" the doctor asked, reaching out for the obituary.

He read over the obituary and flipped it over, staring at the picture on the cover. "Did her son's funeral take place today?" he asked.

"Yeah," she said, and proceeded on, giving him a short version of the events which had led to Cremey getting shot.

"That's so sad. I can't recall ever being a part of a more tragic story. I was the doctor who pronounced this young man dead, and I'm sorry to have to inform you that Cremey didn't make it either. We did everything we could, but she had lost too much blood, and her organs sustained too much damage."

Ericka had a blank expression on her face.

"The police have been notified and they're on their way to talk with you. In the meantime, if there is anything I can do to help you, feel free to ask. If you need to make a phone call to your family, or Ms. James's family, you can use the phone in my office."

"I don't know anybody in her family 'cept Slickem and you know where he at," Ericka replied sadly.   She rubbed her stomach and thought about how she had been having unprotected sex with Poopa. "But if you can, I think I need to take a pregnancy test," she added, feeling embarrassed.

***

Special Agent Palko and Agent Jenny slipped out of the back door, went into the garage, and hopped into their back-up vehicle.

Palko drove around the block, parked in the alley of the Jackson home, and hurried inside to prevent the neighbors from seeing their faces.

The two agents entered the home, flashed their shields to the detectives and exchanged pleasantries. Agent Palko explained to them that they were working on a classified case and weren't at liberty to discuss the nature of their investigation.

Lt. Patterson saw their intrusion as disrespectful. However, he didn't pick any bones about displaying his anger over their presence. He voiced his opinion, and added that the very least they could do was be up front with him about why they were there; because after all, they were playing for the same team.

Agent Palko could care less about the detective's bruised ego and it showed in his body language, and the comments he made about him and his partner having even more pressing concerns, aside from this one petty homicide investigation.

Agent Jenny decided to add some estrogen to the rising testosterone levels. She got between them and reiterated that the murder investigation was not their primary concern, and their presence was to remain unknown. She informed them not to mention their involvement to Niq or Capria. She also let them know that once an arrest was made they wouldn't receive any credit. She went on informing them they would also deny knowing anything about Cynthia Jackson in the event one of their names were mentioned.

She then apologized to the detectives and told them the sooner they took a look at the crime scene, the sooner they'd be out of their hair.

Lt. Patterson accepted her apology and led the way to the basement.

In the basement, the coroner snapped pictures of the body while the crime scene investigators were dusting everything for prints.

As soon as Palko saw the state of Cynthia's body, he bent down to Agent Jenny's ear level and whispered. "I told you so. Capria killed her, and Niq came and put handcuffs on her, trying to make it look like a home invasion, or robbery of some sort." He purposely raised his voice a little louder so the coroner could hear him. "Looks like she took a gunshot wound to the head with a small caliber weapon."

Without looking up the coroner replied, "Absolutely not," and continued taking pictures.

"If not, then what is the cause for all the blood loss from her head?" Agent Palko asked the coroner.

"It appears to be from the impact of her head hitting the concrete floor."

"Well, so far what can you tell us?" Agent Jenny asked.

"It's preliminary, but judging by the ligature marks around her neck, it looks like the cause of death could be asphyxiation by strangulation. However, I'd have to conduct a thorough autopsy at the lab to be 100% certain." The coroner looked up at one of the C.S. investigators and asked, "Could you give me a hand turning the body over?"

Once the body was turned face up, everybody moved in to get a closer look. The coroner started taking pictures again.

Agent Jenny tugged at Palko's elbow and whispered in his ear. "You still wanna make a fool of yourself and stick with the assumption that Capria killed her?"

He gave her a disheartened look and bent down to one knee to get a closer look at Cynthia's body. "What are these discoloration marks covering her nipples?" Palko asked.

"Looks like whoever did this tortured her before they killed her. Those are burn marks, and her face has bruising consistent with the shape of a palm, which suggests someone slapped her pretty hard." The coroner placed his hand closer to her face then added, "Someone with hands bigger than mine."

"Around what time would you put the time of death?" Agent Jenny asked.

"Judging by the body temperature, room temperature, and the amount of rigor mortis that has set in, I'd have to put the time of death around 7:30 to 8:30 a.m."

Agent Palko rose up, and without saying a word, high-tailed it up the stairs.

Lt. Patterson called out to him, but he ignored him. Palko's plan to arrest Capria for murder and use that as a bargaining chip to get Niq had gone south. This whole case bored him and he was praying for a quick resolution.

Agent Jenny thanked everybody, wished them good luck catching the killer, and told them they had nothing to add. She stepped out the back door just as Palko was starting up the car. She hastily walked to the passenger door, opened it and sat down.

They rode several miles in silence until they reached a small shopping complex. He brought the car to a stop next to a pay phone and said, "I left my cell at the house. Do you have any change?"

Agent Jenny couldn't wipe the smirk off her face to save her life. She knew he was upset and embarrassed about being wrong on his theory that Capria had killed her mother. Doing her best not to burst out laughing she answered him. "Yes, I have some change, but what you need it for?"

"It's time I meet with the informant. I'm tired of being couped up in a house watching nothing, and I'm fairly certain after what went down today, neither sister will be living there anymore. I seriously doubt what happened was a random act. I think somebody got the drop on Niq, took whatever money and drugs that were in the house, and killed Cynthia."

Agent Jenny finally lost the smirk and replaced it with a look of curiosity. "I'm in total agreement with you, but what does the informant have to do with anything?"

"Shit, probably nothing but I plan to use him to get any info out of Niq in case she mentions anything about it to him. Also, I've been thinking, this pretty drug dealer's file was virtually non-existent. I mean no murders, no mob ties, no gang affiliation, no nothin'. This is a job for a local narcotic's detective, not someone of my caliber."

"Just because we aren't privy to any murders she's involved with doesn't mean there aren't any. No one in her family has a job, yet they live in a half-million dollar home. In less than a week we have estimated she has over a million dollars in property, cars and jewelry, and her sister attends a forty-thousand dollar a year school. I wouldn't classify her as Griselda Blanco, but it's obvious she's operating a very lucrative drug business. And that means she's a part of, or connected to, *something* or *someone* much larger. What do you think, she's growing and manufacturing her own supply?" she asked, rhetorically.

"Ha-ha-ha! Funny, Jenny, but seriously, what if the informant lied to Bochello and he's really her supplier? That would make him, along with who he's involved with a big collar. Whatever deal was promised would be void. I think we're focusing on the wrong person. Check this out-"

"I doubt that very seriously," she cut him off, "Bochello didn't come out of retirement for nothing. The day he called me and asked if I would assist him, he told me this case was potentially a big one, and could define my career. Besides, why do you think it's so sensitive?"

Agent Palko chuckled then said, "Bochello had his time to shine. He scored the game-winning touchdown but under further review he fumbled the ball at the goal line. He was never the same after that. He was training recruits for the Bureau, so when he begged for this job they gave it to him and told him to deal with the U.S. Attorney's office to make him feel important, and to prevent him from wasting man power to assist him on this petty investigation. Since when do two lone people work on a major drug case? And who is Dominique Jackson? You said it yourself, she's certainly not Griselda Blanco," he said, matter of factly.

Agent Jenny threw her hands up in frustration and sighed. "Then why did he bring me on, and why did the Director and A.G. reassign you to the case after he died?"

"You tell me why he brought you on? Because you're easy on the eyes and the case was reassigned. As policy, once we start something, we finish it," he added.

Agent Jenny rolled her eyes at him. "I can hold my own, and my track record will bare that out. And since you've got all the answers, try explaining why or how you missed the person, or people, responsible for murdering Cynthia Jackson?"

Before he could answer, she continuted, "I'll tell you why. Because, instead of us having breakfast at the house, you insisted we go out to breakfast as a couple, and, after three straight days, I repeatedly told you one of us should stay back while the other goes out. But nooooo…" she threw in and paused. "*You* had to walk in the diner and parade me around as if I were *really* your wife," she emphasized and continued, "then you learned the owner had a crush on me," she said, her tone heated.

Knowing every word she spoke was true, he still tried to downplay her accusations. "Oh, please, I didn't know you were so modest! I was just doing my job while remaining in character. We're supposed to be a married couple for God's sake!" he nearly shouted, "and that's what any husband would've done! Like I said, I was tired of being stuck in the house and thought you were too. Anyways, give me some change so I can arrange a meeting with the C.I. and finally steer this investigation in the right direction."

CHAPTER TEN

Following the shoot-out outside of the funeral home, Rome called an emergency meeting for all BD's under his command. The meeting was being held in the private parking lot behind the 7000 building.

Rome stood in the center of the three-sixty, comprised of roughly one-hundred members, capturing their undivided attention.

"The stunt them niggas pulled today just raised the stakes," he spoke with confidence and authority. "Believe me, a hefty price will be paid fo' that shit and I'm takin' full responsibility fo' not havin' security set up around the funeral home." He paused and scanned the crowd until he found Tiso. "B, step up!" he ordered. "Thanks to this lil' nigga right here," he said, looking toward Tiso, "none of the guys got hit. Show 'em the banger, B."

Tiso raised his shirt up and pulled out the Tech .22 from his waistband. He hoisted it up in the air so everybody could view it. Rome stood behind him, placed both hands on his shoulders and said, "Tell 'em where you got that from."

"One of them bitches dropped it when I popped his ass!" Tiso bragged.

"That's what I'm talkin' 'bout!" a seventeen-year-old boy shouted.

"Niggas gon' think twice befo' they try it again!" an older member in his mid-thirties commented.

"A'ight, that's enough!" Rome interjected restoring order. "Poopa, step up and tell 'em what you saw."

"There was two niggas, but the only one I saw was Toad, and he had the Tech .22, but fa'sho, the other nigga was Marco. My bitch, Ericka, seen both of them at St. Benard laughing and talkin' shit 'bout the shootin'," Poopa informed the set.

"Make no mistake 'bout it, we definitely goin' at them two lil' niggas but it's bigger than just them. It's M.A.G.I.C! Murder All Gangsters In Chicago! I'ma appoint certain people to patrol the land twenty-four hours a day. If I find out any nigga is walkin' alone or in a group without a banger, the first time it's an automatic $300.00 fine, the next time it's a $600.00 fine plus a three minute head-to-toe violation. God forbids it happens a third time. All the money will be spent on more guns."

Ring... Ring ... Ring...

In the middle of the speech his cell phone began ringing. He reached in his pocket and pulled out the phone. "Hold up a second. This is an important call from one of the board members," he told the membership. Everybody stood in complete silence. Rome pressed the talk button on his phone and placed one finger in his ear to better hear the caller. "Talk to me," he answered.

"Meet me at the spot in an hour, and don't be late!" the caller spat then hung up the phone.

Rome returned the phone to his pocket then continued addressing the set. "Now, like I was sayin', I'm takin' full responsibility fo' not postin' security up so I'ma fine myself $5,000. Ain't no big I's and little U's in this organization. I already placed the order fo' ten Glocks, two choppers, and a streetsweeper. In a few days, Chop is gon' pass those out to the blocks that need them the most." Rome started walking around the inner perimeter of the circle, making eye contact with the people as he spoke. "We have a duty and an obligation as men and BD's to defend and protect each other, and what's ours. That coulda easily been any one of us in that coffin. We ain't buryin' no more of ours. I refuse to let Slickem die in vain, or let them niggas think it's just sweet to come shoot up his funeral. We don't breed or harbor cowards. So, if any of y'all niggas is scared, this yo' time to leave without any repercussions."

He paused for a few seconds giving anyone who felt the need, time to come forward or forever hold his peace. "That's what I thought," he continued after the brief silence. "As individuals we are strong, but as a nation we are stronger together. I expect every nigga here to play their part, individually, and as a whole. Stand up and be accounted fo' like Tiso did, and you'll be rewarded.

Anybody that catch a case fo' takin' care of nation bidness, I'll personally bond you out and pay yo' legal expenses. If anybody got anything they need to address or any questions, take it up with Chop. Now, let's close this meetin' out 'cause I gotta go attend a heads-only session."

Zep had been paying close attention to the respect and admiration Tiso was receiving. Witnessing Tiso receive praise for his acts caused Zep to feel some type of way; he wasn't hating on Tiso, he just wasn't used to not shining along side of him. They had operated as a team since preschool. Regardless of participation, anything tangible or intangible in value either of them received, they made sure an equal share went to the other person. Zep refused not to be recognized, so he made his move.

"T.P. Folks!" he interjected, before Chop began reciting the prayer to close out the meeting. Although this was Zep's first time attending a meeting, he'd learned through Tiso in order to speak you first had to say 'Thousand Pardons', or 'T.P.' for short, and wait until you were told to speak.

Rome faced Zep, giving him an eye that said, *this better not be no bullshit or else.* "Speak yo' mind and make it quick," he said.

Still wearing the 'R.I.P. Slickem' T-shirt stained with Cremey's blood, Zep strolled out to the center of the three-sixty like he was the H.N.I.C. "I'm feelin' what you sayin' 'bout niggas playin' their part." He made sure he looked Rome directly in the eyes. "I'ma do BD the way you taught me and take care of bidness on the dolo tip," he said, making it known he planned to personally retaliate against the GD's. "But for the set as a whole, here go $300.00 fo' you to put with that five stacks to cop them bangers."

Zep then turned his attention to the membership. "Also, before Chop close this session out, I think every nigga here should contribute sump'n to this kitty, if they can." Light chatter could be heard as everybody started nodding their heads in agreement and digging in their pockets.

Zep walked around and collected the money. He made sure to make eye contact with Rome, seeking his approval. The smile on Rome's face said it all. Chop closed out the meeting and Zep presented Rome with $4,326.00 in cash.

***

Capria folded her arms and slouched back in her chair, refusing to answer another one of the same questions over again. Likewise, in a separate interview room Niq was beyond frustrated and was about to ask for a phone call to her attorney until the door flew open and in walked Battle, Captain Wiggins and Capria. Battle eyed the young detective across the table from Niq, disapprovingly, and spoke his mind.

"These two young ladies have experienced unimaginable pain today. They want nothing more than for whoever committed this horrible crime to be caught and prosecuted to the fullest extent of the law. I'm certain they've both been fully cooperative and forthcoming with all the information they have, and yet, you treat them like they're criminals. If I didn't think it would hamper this investigation, I'd file a formal complaint with internal affairs, followed by a civil suit against this entire police department. These girls are in mourning and should be together with family and friends. Not separated and interrogated like murder suspects. In case it never occurred to either of you, they have to find a suitable place to live, and make funeral arrangements. This interrogation is over; both of them will be leaving with me. If you have any further questions, here is my card, contact me and I'll arrange a date, time and place to meet."

Battle took each of the girls by the hand as he was attempting to exit the room, but he was stopped at the door by Captain Wiggins.

"I'm sorry if either one of you ladies feel like you've been mistreated," he said, apologizing to Niq and Capria. "We were just trying to be sure you girls didn't leave anything out, because what one of you may view as being irrelevant, could actually be pivotal in solving the case. I'm sorry for your loss, and we will do all we can to bring the guilty to justice. If we need to speak with either one of you again, we'll contact Mr. Battle." They accepted his apology and left the precinct.

Once they got in the safe confines of Battle's heavily tinted Executive Edition Excursion, he pulled out a cell phone and dialed a number. After making sure the person he was calling was on the line, he handed the phone to Niq and drove off.

Having a gut feeling as to who was on the line, she spoke tentatively, "Hello."

"Hola, Señorita Dominique. Me get da bad newz and me offer chu deepest condolences and help," Migual Carrillo said, in a thick Spanish accent.

"Thank you. I really appreciate your sympathy and support. Everything has happened so fast and I really don't know what is what right now," Niq responded.

"Me must be honest, chu make big mistake doing bizness from homa, and chu pay huge price. Robbery and murda are jus' two tools dats part of dis bizness. Chu must know when is da right time to use dese tools and how to protect cho'self from having dese tools used on chu. Here in Mexico, we have a sayin, *No cagues donde duermes'* in Ingles means, 'don't shit where chu sleep, comprende señorita?"

"Yes, I completely understand what you are saying," Niq assured him.

"Me tink back when Willie first give me call about chu. Me tink chu no good for bizness but chu prove me wrong. Now chu face wit' big challenge. Now not da time for emotions to get da best of chu. Do chu remember what me tell chu never forget da first time we make bizness?"

"Umm...yes..." she said, recalling his words, "you said this bidness is fo' the strong and not the weak at heart. And your bidness is your bidness, my bidness is your bidness only, and bidness comes first. Never do nothin' to jeopardize your bidness and bidness will take care of itself."

"Si...Si...take some time to bury chu mama, no worry about da debt, it is forgiven. Do as Willie tell chu, and in two weeks chu shipment will be delivered. Last ting, learn from dis, protect cho'self and chu sister, and most of all never jeopardize me bizness again. Me will make sho all who involved wit' chu mama murda die slow and painful."

Click... The line went dead before Niq could respond. She gave the phone back to Battle just as he was turning into the driveway of her house.

Niq and Capria exited the truck, went inside the house, packed a few clothing items, retrieved the items left by the killers and went back out. Niq gave Capria her car keys and told her to go sit in the car while she had a word with Battle. She gave him the evidence and agreed to meet with him the following week. She then hopped in the driver's seat of her car and faced her little sister. After giving the idea a brief thought, she took a deep breath and said, "I guess I'ma take you to stay with your Auntie Carla and MiMi a few nights."

***

With Chop accepting the job as Rome's personal security, law dictated for him to be by Rome's side at all times, or at least, be aware of his whereabouts and in position to assist and protect him as quickly as possible. If any unfortunate events were to happen to him, unbeknownst to the board members, the first person held accountable would be Chop. Therefore, it had taken a lot of persuasion from Rome to convince Chop that the session he'd been called to attend was in a private location, known only to ministers and board members, and no security was allowed.

Reluctantly, Chop allowed him to leave his presence with a promise to call as soon as he got there, and, immediately after the meeting was over. Segments of Rome's life began flashing through his mind as he pushed his brand new platinum colored Lexus LS450 en route to the meeting place.

It seemed like his brain had turned into a projector and his entire life had been dissected and placed on slides for his personal viewing. His inability to control the images, or the random order in which they appeared, caused his emotional responses to change dramatically as new images emerged.

Images of his joyous childhood made him happy, but in the next, instant visuals of his parents' brutal death made him sad. Images of sex, drugs, money, and the power he acquired, got his dick hard and boosted his ego to a God-like status. But before he could get his dick out and relish in his accomplishments, visions of the cutthroat moves and disloyal tactics he employed to get ahead in the game surfaced instantly, altering his feelings of euphoria and invincibility to that of a coward, full of shame and hopelessness.

As the images started to subside, he began focusing on his whereabouts. The last thing he remembered prior to the visions was talking to Chop. Now, he was driving around an industrial area of the city located on the north-west side. He navigated the maze of warehouses and factories until he reached his destination. After finding a parking space, he sat in the car for a couple of minutes, contemplating whether or not he should go through with the meeting.

He knew pulling out wasn't a viable option, and sooner or later he'd have to answer for his indiscretions. He massaged his temples, trying to clear his mind. He checked his appearance in the rearview mirror then got out and went inside a meat packing warehouse. He was met by a lady at the front desk. He told her his government name and let her know he was there to interview for a forklifting job. She gave him a friendly smile, then led him to a small office and instructed him to have a seat. He obliged and was promptly met by DEA Special Agent Henry Palko.

"It's nice to meet you Rome. You don't mind me calling you Rome, do you?" he asked, extending his hand for a formal handshake.

Rome almost fell out of his seat trying to avoid his hand like he had a contagious disease or something. His eyes got buck as if he'd seen a ghost, and beads of sweat formed on his forehead.

"Calm down now, buddy. No need to be scared. I don't bite," Palko said, displaying his badge. "I'm Special Agent Palko and I've been assigned to lead this investigation."

Regaining his composure, Rome cleared his throat and stood up. "Where's Agent Bochello?" he demanded to know. "My agreement was to work with him and nobody else."

"Have a seat," Palko calmly replied, while thumbing through the piles of clutter on his desk. "I'm sorry you didn't get the memo, but Bochello had a fatal plane crash a week or two ago." He found Bochello's obituary and handed it to him.

Rome looked at Bochello's picture on the obituary and thought this was his way out. "I only agreed to cooperate with Agent Bochello. He promised me I only had to deal with him. I was even told I didn't hafta deal with the detective who busted me. So, I damn sho' ain't 'bout to work wit' you," he said, tossing the obituary back on the desk.

Palko stood up and leaned over the desk, meeting Rome nose to nose. "Do I look like a thirteen-year-old, snot nose, wannabe thug in awe of you!" he snarled, through clenched teeth. "You're gonna do exactly as I tell you or I'm gonna lock your fake, wannabe, gang chief ass up for possession with intent to distribute two kilos of cocaine, or maybe I'll save myself the trouble of paperwork and pass along the video recordings of you ratting to Niq and those stupid ass board members you answer to."

"But, Bochello promised-"

"Bochello, Bochello. What? Your dumbass can't read? Didn't you see the date on the obituary?" Agent Palko grabbed the obituary and shoved it in his face. "Three days have passed by and Bochello still hasn't risen which makes me God now, and your salvation is contingent upon how effective of a snitch you are. And since I'm a merciful and compassionate God, I'm going to offer you the opportunity of a lifetime. If you be up front and 100% truthful with me, you'll get to keep all the money you've made once you go to heaven, better known as the witness protection program. Or, you can deny me and start counting the days until Niq or your so-called board members unanimously order one of your underlings to put a bullet between your eyes and off to hell you go. Now, do you accept me as your lord and savior?"

A part of Rome wanted to say, *"Go fuck your self,"* but it was too late for that. He felt the exact same way he did when he was a ten-year-old hiding in the closet, watching his mother and father get raped and tortured to death. He surmised that this wasn't the life he'd chosen, and circumstances far beyond his control had led him down this path, but he would persevere and come out on top like he had always managed to do.

This muthafucka ain't smarter than me. He got me fucked up if he think I'ma spend one day in a witness protection program. Don't none of my guys know Niq, so I can set this bitch up wit' no problem. I'ma tell this cracker what he wanna hear and get back to fuckin' bitches, stackin' paper and runnin' my muthafuckin set, he thought to himself, as he weighed his options. "Cool, what you wanna know?" he asked, dryly.

Agent Palko plopped down in his chair and threw his feet up on the desk. "Everything, beginning with the names of all the BD's in authority and the areas they control."

"What! Hell naw! They ain't got shit to do wit' Niq. They don't even know she exists." Rome couldn't believe what he was being asked to do. "I can't do no shit like that," he said, shaking his head. "Them niggas would kill me! I made it clear to Bochello, and told him up front I wasn't gon' tell on none of my peoples, and he assured me I wouldn't have to. Fuck naw, you just gonna hafta arrest me."

Palko acted as if he didn't hear one word Rome had spoken. He eased his feet down to the floor, swiveled his chair around, and grabbed a peg board that was resting against the wall behind him. He positioned the peg board on the desk so Rome could see the front of it.

"I've already started putting together a chart, outlining the chain of command and the areas in the city under the BD's control. As you can see, I have photos, and under each one is their name and rank, along with the neighborhood they control. I purposely left out some names so you could fill in the blanks. I have some names of sets and I'd like for you to write down the names of the ministers for each one."

"I-I-told y-you, I-I ain't t-t-tellin' on none of th-them," Rome stuttered.

Palko made eye contact with him then looked over at a small monitor on his desk. He turned the monitor around so Rome could see the screen, pressed the rewind button and turned up the volume. Rome appeared on the screen.

"Where's Agent Bochello? My agreement was to work wit' him and nobody else." A hidden camera had been taping everything going on in the office. Palko turned the volume down and returned the monitor back to its original position.   He then took a picture of one of the board members down from the peg board.

"Once Fu-Fu gets a look at this I doubt very seriously he takes your refusal to rat out the gang under consideration. I mean, after all, he is the one who ordered Chop to kill a rising star in the gang because he assumed he was snitching, which for the record wasn't true. I figured you would've wanted him dead since he was from your neck of the woods, and if he was a threat to anybody's status it was yours. But, you had us all surprised when you spoke up on the young fella's behalf," he said, never taking his eyes off the mugshot of Fu-Fu. He then began snapping his fingers rapidly like he was trying to recollect something.

"What's his name? Uhm...damn! What was that boy's name?" he asked himself aloud.

"Ronnie," Rome said, without thinking.

Palko chuckled to himself. "Now that wasn't hard at all. You just gave me a video tape confession. Due to our laws on double jeopardy, Chop is off the hook. However, in addition to the drug charges, I now have enough evidence to arrest you and Fu-Fu for conspiracy to commit first degree murder."

"Conspiracy to commit murder!" he repeated in a baffled tone, "I ain't murdered nobody! You just said yo'self I was against killin' him."

"Maybe you wanted him dead, maybe you didn't, but you just admitted to participating in a premeditated discussion with the highest ranking BD on the streets about murdering Ronnie. The bottom line is the discussion ended with a hit being ordered and was eventually carried out by your cousin and bodyguard, Chop. And you did nothing to prevent it which makes you a participant in the murder conspiracy." Palko stood up, drew his gun, and aimed it at Rome.

"Wait! Hold up!" Rome shouted. Simultaneously, he threw his hands up over his face as if they could protect it from a bullet.

Palko quickly made his way around the desk, blocking off the door in case Rome tried to make a run for it. "Stand up, put your hands in the air, turn around and face the wall," he ordered.

Stunned and confused by the dramatic change of events, Rome slowly complied with his ordered. Once Rome's back was facing him, he put his gun in its holster, pulled out a pair of handcuffs, roughly grabbed his arm, and placed the cuffs on his wrists. "You have the right to remain silent. Anything you say, can, and will be used against you in a court of law. You-"

"C'mon, man! I'm willing to work wit you but-"

"Have the right to an attorney and if you can't afford-"

"Okay, okay, I'll tell you everything 'bout Ronnie's murder, who all the board members and ministers are, and continue to set Niq up. But you gotta promise me you won't let them find out I'm the one tellin'."

"Yeah, whatever," Palko said, turning Rome around and shoving him down in the chair. He pointed his finger at the peg board. "Last chance," he said, knowing Rome would bite, "who is the minister for the Calumet building?"

Rome dropped his head then answered, "Taz."

As much as Rome hated snitching on his own guys, he gave up the names and ranks of members, and even corrected what Palko had wrong on the board. Believing his work for the day was over he got up to leave, but Palko stopped him in his tracks.

"One last thing," Palko said. "You'll be wearing a recording device when you cop from Niq and when you're attending high ranking gang meetings."

CHAPTER ELEVEN

Monday, September 6, 1999
8:03 a.m.

"Wake up, wake up," Kevin coaxed, shaking Zep's right shoulder. Wake up, wake up,'' he repeated.

"Huh," Zep muttered, as he was abruptly awakened out of his slumber. He rolled over onto his back, pushed the sheet covering his body down to his waist, sat up, stretched and rubbed his eyes. "What time is it?" he asked, groggily.

Kevin shrugged his shoulders. "I dunno, Grandma told me to wake you up so you can get ready for school."

"A'ight, you and Sharmaine get ready, then after y'all done using the bathroom, come wake me back up."

"Okay," Kevin replied, exiting the bedroom.

Zep laid back down, pulled the sheet over his head, and drifted back off to Lala-land. He was physically and mentally exhausted. He had spent the entire weekend serving jabs, in an effort to hustle up as much money as possible to buy himself some back-to-school clothing.

Friday had been the first day he'd started selling jabs. Unfortunately, he wasn't able to make any money due to the shoot-out and head injury he'd suffered in the alley at Slickem's funeral. But, he was determined to make up for the lost day of hustling. Saturday and Sunday, he was out of the house before 8 a.m. and didn't return until well after midnight, both days.

However, he did step away from hustling for a few hours Sunday afternoon to get a fresh haircut and to go shopping. Unlike previous school years, Zep was eager for school to start. He couldn't wait to floss and flaunt in the latest name-brand clothing. His grandmother, Mrs. Berry, always made sure he had nice clothes but she refused to over-spend on name brands. No matter how much he begged, she stuck to her tight budget. She would purchase his clothes from Sears and Kmart, but she did allow him to pick out his gym shoes as long as they didn't cost over eighty dollars.

Now that Zep was a corner boy, he planned to dress the part, and department store back-to-school sales wouldn't cut it. He was dead set on rocking nothing but the latest gear, and the most expensive gym shoes for his final year of elementary school. Zep knew his grandmother would never agree to buy him the clothes he wanted, and out of respect for her, he didn't want her to know he was selling drugs. So, he convinced her to give him the money she planned to spend on his clothes so he could purchase them himself.

He happily accepted five-hundred dollars from his grandmother, along with a set of strict instructions. He had to purchase at least ten outfits (pants and shirts), two packs of T-shirts, socks and underwear, all of his school supplies, and he couldn't spend more than one-hundred dollars on a pair of gym shoes.

He left home and returned three hours later with more than double the amount of clothing his grandmother expected him to buy. Zep was well aware of the fact that his grandmother was green when it came to the latest fashions and the price tags associated with them.

All she knew was Sears and Kmart had nice clothes that were much cheaper. Importantly, he also knew she was far from being a fool and he would have to give her a plausible explanation for all the clothes he'd bought.

Before she could question him, Zep admitted all the clothes and gym shoes were name brand and worth more than five-hundred dollars— he lied when he told her the prices had been cut by seventy-five percent because the store had an everything-must-go going-out-of-business clearance sale. And when Mrs. Berry demanded to see the receipts, he pretended to dig in his pockets and fumbled through the bags of clothes, before lying about not being able to find them when he knew he'd purposely thrown them away.

Rocawear, Sean John, Polo and Air Jordan's weren't the only purchases Zep made. He spent $1,800 on a diamond cut, 24 inch, white gold Turkish link chain, with a Roman numeral III charm that had six white diamonds in it. The Roman numeral III was the widely recognized emblem of the Black Disciples. The symbol was spray painted on walls, viaducts and buildings throughout Zep's neighborhood reminding all passerby's "The Black Disciple Nation" controlled the territory they were in. Even Mrs. Berry knew what the Roman numeral three represented, which was why Zep made sure to keep it hidden from her eyesight.

"Zep,'' Kevin yelled, reentering the bedroom they shared, "me and Sharmaine ready."

"Fuck you tryin' to do? Wake the dead?" Zep huffed, poking his head out from underneath the sheet. "What time is it?"

"Eight-forty-six," Kevin replied.

"Shit!" Zep flipped the sheet off of him and scrambled out of bed. He showered and dressed in ten minutes flat, and was off to school with his brother and sister in tow.

***

"Well, well, well, look at who we have here," Mrs. Reid cracked, as Zep entered her classroom, "Mr. Zephaniyah Berry. So glad you decided to grace us with your presence. Boy, aren't you kicking off the new school semester with a blast." She looked him up and down, sarcastically. "Fashionable twenty-two minutes late!"

"Sorry, I overslept," Zep replied, "but I'll be on time tomorrow."

"Tomorrow and every other day after, or you'll find yourself doing extra homework and detention on Friday. You know my rules. Now, close the door and have a seat," Mrs. Reid ordered, pointing her finger at the only available desk in the classroom.

Zep closed the door and glanced around the room. *What the fuck? Same classroom, teacher and students,* he mused to himself. The desks were arranged in six rows with five desks in each row. Zep could feel thirty sets of eyes staring at him as he walked to the sixth row and took a seat at the last desk.

Impatiently, Mrs. Reid folded her arms across her chest and followed Zep with her eyes, giving him time to sit down, before she spoke.

"As I was saying, all of you passed the seventh grade with a GPA of 3.0 or better, justification for your status as gifted students, and proof that when you ten guys and twenty girls apply yourselves, there's nothing you can't accomplish. Our principal decided to keep all thirty of you in the gifted classroom. He also decided that I would repeat being you guys' eighth-grade homeroom teacher, along with also being your math and science teacher too. And, I must say, I feel honored. I promise to do my best to ensure every last one of you graduates with honors."

All this bitch do is run her mouth, Zep thought as he listened to Mrs. Reid babble on and on. *Fuck was I thinking comin' here. I shoulda dropped Kevin and Sharmaine off and went to the block. This school shit is fa' lames... I s'pose to be blowin' 'dro and gettin' money right now.*

Not only was Zep bored, he felt disconnected and out of place. He had known most of his classmates for years and got along with them very well. Half of them had been his classmates since kindergarten. But, things were different now that he was hustling and gang-banging. Flossing and flaunting in name brand clothes at school no longer mattered. In fact, the idea suddenly felt childish and beneath him. He couldn't wait for the bell to ring so he could get on to more important things—like serving jabs.

Zep sighed. "I wish she'd shut the fuck up," he mumbled under his breath. Shaking his head in frustration, he noticed a female student named Jazmina eyeballing him. "Was' up?" he mouthed.

"You," she mouthed back, then, flirtatiously, stuck her tongue out at him.

Jazmina was a five-foot, six-inch redbone with slanted eyes and a head full of jet-black good Indian hair most sista's would kill for. She was one of the girls the old people in the hood pointed to as proof that the government had put something in the baby formula which caused a great deal of 80's and 90's babies to develop at an early age. Her full C-cup breasts, thick thighs, wide hips and phat upside-down heart-shaped booty had all ages of the opposite sex drooling over her, while the same sex hated on her. Simply put, she was a Similac baby—stacked like a video vixen.

However, if you looked beneath her surface, you could clearly see she had jail bait written all over her. Zep shot her a sly grin. *For two years straight yo' stuck up ass played me to the left. Now you see me shinin' an' wanna check fo' a nigga.* Zep kept his thoughts to himself and refocused his attention back on Mrs. Reid.

"To ensure all of you have the necessary educational requirements needed to get into the best high schools this city has to offer, you will be taking Advanced Math, English and Science. However, the textbooks haven't arrived yet. We should be getting them in a day or two. Until then, you won't be switching classes." Mrs. Reid paused to look up at the clock on the wall. "Today is a half day, so school will be dismissed at noon, instead of two-thirty. For the remainder of the day, I'll allow you all to get reacquainted with one another while I step out to have a chat with Mr. Bayliss across the hall. Any questions?" she asked, as she walked over to the door. "I figured there wouldn't be. Don't embarrass me or else!" she warned the entire class.

Mrs. Reid was barely out of the door before all twenty-nine of Zep's classmates hopped out of their seats and huddled up in several small groups. Feeling like he had nothing in common with them, Zep decided to remain at his desk and stare out of the window. He couldn't help but hear his classmates' conversations. They discussed how they'd spent their summer vacations, who had the best back-to-school gear, and who was going to hook up with whom, before the year was out. The more these conversations intensified, the more Zep was convinced of how lame school had become. He tried to block out the chatter around him, but then, someone approached him from behind and covered his eyes with their hands.

"Guess who?" asked a high-pitched feminine voice.

"Whoever it is they betta take their hands offa my face!" Zep threatened.

"And if I don't?" she challenged.

Zep inhaled and exhaled, loudly. "Tahiti," he gritted through clenched teeth. He knew who she was because of her distinct voice. "Quit playin' wit' me. I 'ont know where your hands been!"

"Oh, it's like that, huh?" Tahiti removed her hands and stepped around to the front of his desk. "What's up with the funky attitude?" She placed a hand on her hip and turned up her nose at him.

With a scowl plastered on his face, Zep gave Tahiti a quick once-over. She was petite, weighing about ninety-five pounds, and stood at four-eleven. She had a smooth mocha complexion, a cute little nose, dreamy green-colored eyes, and a baby voice similar to the late eighties/early nineties R&B singer, Michel'le. At first glance, everything about her seemed sweet and innocent. However, she was the epitome of the phrase, 'never judge a book by its cover'; when provoked, she was a firecracker, and it didn't take much provoking to light her fuse. Zep, replaced the scowl on his face with a smile. "I was just messin' wit' you," he replied, pulling her hand into his. Not only did he find her attractive, he also loved her feisty disposition. "You lookin' real good in that all-white DKNY get- up too," he complimented the outfit she was wearing.

"Unt, uh," Tahiti snapped, as she snatched her hand back. "You can run that weak-ass game on the next chick!"

"Look at me," Zep said, gently, grabbing her hand again. "Since when have I ever ran-"

"What's goin' on over here?" Jazmina cut Zep off mid-sentence. She paused, momentarily, and frowned at the sight of the two holding hands. "Well, excuuuse me," she said, boldly separating their hands. "Why you all in his grill anyway? I thought you said you wasn't feelin' him?"

"First off, touch me again an' I'ma touch yo' ass back!" Tahiti spat. "Second, I ain't all up in nobody face. Third, get ya' facts straight; I never told you I wasn't feelin' him.

"You,'' she paused and pointed her finger in Jazmina's face, "told me I shouldn't give him no play because he tried to holla at you first. You said you shot him down because he was a nothin'-ass little boy who wasn't on shit, your words, *not* mines," she emphasized.

"Don't ever put your finger in my face again," Jazmina retorted. "And you need to get yo' facts straight! That's the bullshit you said because you was salty you was his second choice!''

"Second choice to who?" Tahiti fumed, "You? Please," she said, looking Jazmina up and down like she was crazy. "You want facts? These are the facts! You transferred to this school two years ago. Zephaniyah been tryna holla at me since kindergarten. Fuck you thought!"

"Naw, what the fuck *you* thought!" Jazmina hissed. She flipped her curly tresses out of her face, and whipped her head around towards Zep.

"When you tried to come at me last year, I told you, you was cute, but I was in a relationship, didn't I?"

"Lemme think," Zep said, as he tilted his head to the ceiling. He pretended to be in deep contemplation for a few seconds before nodding his head. "Yeah, that's what you told me."

"Ain't you been tryna holla at me every year since kindergarten?" Tahiti asked, refusing to allow Jazmina to one-up her.

Zep's eyebrow furrowed. "Since kindergarten," he repeated. His facial expression and voice was layered with skepticism.

Tahiti rolled her eyes. "Zephaniyah, don't front, keep it real!" She sucked her teeth then added, "actin' like you gotta think about it. Nigga, please!"

"Yeah, I tried to holla at you a few times but I on't know 'bout every year."

"Every year!" Tahiti shouted with conviction.

"Calm down," Zep said in a pleading tone. He began to notice the unwanted attention they were attracting from the other students. "Okay, every year," he admitted.

"That's what I thought!" Tahiti said with a smirk.

Jazmina walked around to the back of Zep's desk, rested her titties on top of his head, and wrapped her arms around his chest and shoulders. She fixed her eyes on Tahiti and said, "You ain't gotta worry about him tryna holla at you this year." She licked her lips, bent down, and whispered in Zep's ear, "Ain't that right?"

The unexpected feeling of Jazmina's moist lips pressed against his earlobe, mixed with the cool sensation of her breath tickling his ear canal, caused Zep to chuckle and wriggle in his seat.

"Girl, you betta quit playin' wit me," he said, as he reached down to his crotch and squeezed his growing erection.

Tahiti had heard and seen enough. "Hmmph... Talkin' 'bout you don't know where my hands been. Well, it ain't no secret where her lips been!" She balled her hand into a fist, put it up to her mouth and started moving it back and forth. Each time her fist touched her lips, she poked the inside of her jaw with her tongue. "Dick-suckin'-ass bitch!"

Last year, Jazmina had been dating an eighth grader, named Antonie, who was the captain of the school basketball team. During one of the home games, which was also the last regular season game, the team needed the win to make the playoffs.

Down two points with four seconds on the game clock, Antonie hit a three-pointer at the buzzer, sending the school to the playoffs. Hyped up, the students rushed the court and lifted Antonie off of his feet and into the air.

Jazmina decided to show Antonie some personal appreciation. After most of the spectators cleared the gymnasium, she lured him into the boy's locker room and was later caught by two members of the basketball team performing oral sex on the star player. After witnessing the deed, both players ran out of the locker room, and, immediately, began reporting what they'd seen to the student body.

The news spread like wildfire, and Jazmina was labeled the school slut. "I got yo' dick-suckin' bitch right here!" Jazmina spat. She took her arms from around Zep and ran to the front of his desk to fight Tahiti.

Zep sprung into action. He grabbed her by her wrists and yanked her back before she could reach Tahiti. "Let me go!" she screamed.

"Yeah, unleash that bitch so I can dog-walk that ass!" Tahiti said, with her guard up in a fighting stance.

"All shit!" yelled Raheem, the class clown. It's about to go down!"

Everybody in the classroom stopped what they were doing and converged around Tahiti, Jazmina, and Zep.

"I know you ain't gon' let her talk to you like that Jazmina," a female student, named Robin, instigated.

"Handle yo' bidness!" someone yelled out.

"Let her go, Zephaniyah," another person said.

"It ain't gon' be no fight," Zep said, with his hand still tightly gripped around Jazmina's wrist. He got up from his desk, positioned Jazmina behind him and stood in between the two angry girls. "Y'all know how Mrs. Reid get down. She will punish all of us if we let them fight, which means she cancellin' all the field trips she got planned for us. And, that's on top of extra classwork and homework."

"He ain't never lyin'!" someone agreed.

"I heard we was goin' to Washington DC," another student said.
"Yeah and y'all suppose to be girls too," Robin said, as she ushered Tahiti away.

"What y'all fighting for, anyway?" Towanda asked Jazmina.

"Why yo' nosy ass wanna know?" Jazmina asked, angrily, "you the police or somthin'?"

"They fightin' over Zephaniyah," Raheem interjected

"You don't know shit!" Jazmina snapped. "You need to speak when-"

"Be cool," Zep cut her off, "you know Raheem just messin' wit' you."

"I knew it was a reason I fuck wit' you," Raheem said, as he stuck his fist out to give Zep some dap, "on the first day of class you got the two baddest chicks in the school fightin' over you. Man, I wish I was you," he said, with his fist still out-stretched. "Don't leave me hangin'!"

"You crazy," Zep replied as he gave Raheem some dap. "It ain't even that."

"I can't tell. You show up late, dressed fresh as hell with yo' pockets on swoll," he pointed to the imprint of money bulging out of both front pockets of Zep's Rocawear denim jeans, "*and*," he emphasized, as if he were in total awe, "you got that Platinum joint shining 'round yo' neck too. Whatever you doin', put me down," Raheem said, jokingly, but was really dead-serious.

"Me too," Calvin chimed in.

"Fuck it, sign me up!" Jimmy added.

One by one, every male, and several female students echoed similar comments to Zep. Although he was getting the attention he desired, it wasn't as fulfilling as he imagined it would be, because he no longer valued their opinions or viewed them as equals. He remained quiet and took in all the gawking and compliments his classmates were throwing his way. *I could never ride the next nigga dick like this,* Zep thought.

"Aye, Zephaniyah," Raheem silenced the crowd. "Why you got the platinum chain tucked? Let us see that joint."

Zep reached for his chain. "This ain't. . ." Zep paused. *Fuck it, if he thinks its platinum then its platinum.* "This ain't nothin' major," he said as he pulled the chain and charm from underneath his Rocawear button-up shirt.

"Trays," Raheem said, with his mouth twisted up.

"Yeah, nigga!" Zep walked up in his face. What, you got a problem wit' it or sump'n?"

Raheem took a step backwards. "Naw, I'm just sayin'."

"You just sayin' what?"

"Nothin'. My whole family GD's, that's all."

Zep walked back up on him. "So you one too?"

"Naw, I ain't shit," Raheem said.

"Well act like it then!" Zep tucked his chain back in. He turned around and nearly bumped into Jazmina who was smiling from ear to ear.

"What's so funny?"

"You checked his punk ass."

"It's all good," Zep replied, looking around at the few students who witnessed the exchange between him and Raheem.

Zep could sense the shock and fear in them, even though they deliberately avoided making eye contact with him. Before he could say a word, each of them went back to doing what they'd been doing before everything kicked off, leaving Zep and Jazmina to themselves.

"Finally," Jazmina breathed a sigh of relief. "'Bout time everybody left us alone and went to minding their own business."

"I feel you," Zep responded, flatly.

"So, you a BD now?"

"Do it matter?"

"Come on now, Zephaniyah." Jazmina batted her eyes at him. "I'm just tryna talk to you and see what's up with us."

"What you want to be up with us?"

With total disregard for her surrounding, Jazmina stood face to face with Zep, with her titties planted firmly against Zep's chest. Then, softly, in her most seductive and flirtatious voice, she purred, "I dreamt about you all summer. I couldn't wait 'til school started back so I could see you again."

Shocked by her closeness, and the boldness of her tactics, Zep took a quick glance around the classroom to see if anybody was paying any attention to them, but no one was watching.

Mrs. Reid had slipped back into the classroom and her face was buried in a book. The other students were huddled around in small groups, conversing amongst themselves.

Zep turned his focus back on Jazmina and looked her directly in the eyes. "You ain't ready fa' a nigga like me," he said, in true playa fashion. "You still a little girl."

Not the one to be outdone, she took a step back, placed one hand on her hip, and the other on the center of his chest. "Baby, you the one that ain't ready," she retorted. She then slid her hand from his chest to his crotch, and gently squeezed his manhood. "What you doin' after school?" she asked.

Before Zep could reply, 12 p.m. hit and the school bell rang.

"All right, class is over," Mrs. Reid said, loudly, over the thirty students stampeding out of the classroom door. "You guys know my rules. Don't be late tomorrow and have a nice day!" she shouted to most of their backs.

Zep was one of the last students to exit the classroom. He weaved his way through the hallway traffic of giggly school kids with Jazmina glued to him at the hip.

CHAPTER TWELVE

Jazmina followed Zep to the doorway of the school library. She, nervously, stood beside him while he bent down and pretended to tie his shoestrings. As soon as the coast was clear, he stood up and twisted the door knob; it was unlocked.

I hope he ain't expectin' me to suck... Jazmina's thoughts were abruptly interrupted when Zep snatched the door open, yanked her inside and closed it with quickness. Once they found a secluded spot, she hugged him and attempted to kiss him on the lips.

"Fuck is you doin'?" Zep spat, as he turned his face, giving her his cheek to kiss. "I ain't come in here to play no K-I-S-S-I-N-G game wit' you!"

He unzipped his pants and pulled out his rock-hard dick. Without uttering a word, Jazmina dropped to her knees, wrapped her hand around his shaft and gasped. She was amazed at the size of his tool. Parting her lips, she inserted the tip of his dick inside her mouth and spent some time sucking on it.

Not satisfied, Zep palmed the back of her head, and tried to force his whole dick down her throat. His dick wasn't even halfway in before she started gagging. She quickly pulled it out of her mouth and slurped up the excess saliva dripping off the tip.

"Your dick too big," she said, stroking his shaft.

"I know, but you're a big girl so handle yo' bidness," Zep replied, with an air of cockiness.

Jazmina cringed and cowered in between his legs as her uncle's voice invaded her mind. *"You can do it, you're a big girl. Just close your eyes and pretend it's your favorite Popsicle."* Her eyes began to pool with tears. She held her breath, peered up, and then, slowly exhaled a sigh of relief. She felt a great deal of comfort knowing she was pleasuring Zep, her soon-to-be- boyfriend, and not her pedophile uncle. Regaining her composure, she blinked away her tears and made eye contact with Zep. "Promise me you not gon' tell nobody."

"Come on now," Zep said, and sighed in frustration. He was so bent on getting a nut he never noticed Jazmina's drastic mood swings.

"You know I wouldn't play you like that," he said, hoping like hell she would finish the job she'd started.

Still holding his throbbing erection in her hand, Jazmina continued to stare at him and debate whether she should stop or continue. "I don't know if I can trust you."

"Really, you can't be serious," Zep said, fearing the worst.

"What you want me to do? Put it on sump'n?" Before she could respond, he continued. "On my mama, on BD, on everything I love!" he swore, holding his right hand up. "Look, I don't put nothin' on my father. But I swear on my father's grave I won't tell nobody.

That's right, keep going, beg some more. Jazmina smiled to keep herself from laughing. She felt a sense of empowerment, as she listened to the desperation in his voice, and gazed into his pleading eyes. "You better keep your mouth shut!" she threatened, then quickly smiled to let him know she was playing with him.

She took a deep breath then started licking around the head of his dick, and up and down the shaft. She made sure every inch was glistening with her tongue juices, before she opened her mouth wide and stuck her tongue out as far as it would go. She re-inserted his dick on a mission. Sucking on his dick, she began making sloppy slurping sounds, mixed in with moans of pleasure.

Zep got light-headed. He had to lean back against a bookshelf for extra support, because his legs could no longer support his body weight. He began combing his fingers through her long, silky hair. She was slurping and slobbing his dick to perfection. With her off-hand, she started to caress his balls. Zep began to lose control. His heart began to pound. His mouth opened for air. His eyes rolled to the back of his head and his fist balled tight with a handful of her hair. His dick started pulsating, causing Jazmina to get more excited. She picked up her pace and began swallowing him whole!

In a coma of ecstasy, Zep moaned. "Oooh…Ooh…Oh my God," and soon after, he busted a nut in her mouth.

"Hmmmmm," was the only sound that escaped Jazmina's lips, as she hungrily swallowed his potential kids.   Then like a starved child with an empty bottle, she feverishly sucked his head while massaging and pulling on his balls, milking him dry of every last drop.

Only after she was sure nothing was left did she come up for air. "Now, what was you sayin' earlier 'bout me not bein' ready to fuck with you?" Jazmina playfully asked Zep, as he was catching his breath. Zep looked down at her and smiled. "I was just tryna see where your head was at. You know I been feelin' you since the first day you transferred to this school." He zipped up his pants.

"Well, I'm feelin' you too," she said, doing her best to make eye contact. "So, am I Mrs. Zephaniyah, or what?"

Zep was feeling her head game so to have her as his girlfriend would surely have its benefits. But, Zep knew why she had a change of heart. He wasn't feeling messing around with no female he felt had her eyes set on his paper. Plus, the idea of claiming the 'school slut' as his girlfriend didn't sit well with him. He had chased her for two years and now the tables had turned. *Girlfriend, I don't think so,* he thought, *but I'll definitely make sure we visit the library as often as possible.*

Opting not to answer her question and avoiding eye contact at all costs, Zep said, "Shit, we gotta hurry up and get outta here, 'cause I need to find my lil' brother and sister."

He rushed out of the library and left Jazmina behind on her knees.

It took Jazmina a few seconds to process what had just happened. *I shouldn't have done that. Now he think I'ma ho and gon' put me on blast. I gotta talk to him before class tomorrow.*

She got up and ran after Zep and spotted him just as he was about to exit the school building. "Zep, Zep!" she frantically called out. "Wait up! Can I get your phone number?"

"I'll give it to you tomorrow," he yelled, never looking back or breaking his stride.

***

Zep bolted out of the school building and made his way to the parking lot where his siblings waited for him, so they could walk home together.

As he entered the parking lot he noticed a brand new, sparkling white Cadillac Escalade approaching him. *Nigga What, Nigga Who* by Jay-Z blared through the Escalade's custom-built sound system. As the

SUV got closer, Zep was able to make out the driver's face. He ran over to the driver's side window and greeted him.

"Was'up, my dude, trays fo' days!" Zep said, sticking his hand through the window to perform the Black Disciples' handshake with him. "Where the fuck you get this whip from?"

"Nigga, while you bullshittin' in school, I'm out here makin' major moves. You ridin' or what?" Tiso asked, with a mischievous grin.

Zep opened up the rear door and instructed his siblings to hop inside. He shut the door then walked around to the passenger side door, opened it and jumped in.

Driving out of the parking lot, Tiso turned down the sounds "You got some ends?" he asked.

"Yeah, why?" Zep replied.

"So we can hit up the 'dro spot and the liquor store, nah'imean."

"A'ight, but first let's drop them off at the crib."

"Zep, we wanna go with you," Kevin said.

"Naw, lil' nigga, not this time, maybe next time, but I'ma give both y'all five dollars a piece so y'all can go down to the Candy Lady. If Grandma ask where I'm at, tell her I walked y'all home and said I was goin' to the playground to play basketball, okay?"

"Okay," Kevin and Sharmaine squealed in unison.

The ride to Zep's house was short. They lived on Lowe Avenue, and their school, Parker Community Academy, was on 68 and Stewart, which was about six or seven blocks away.

After dropping Kevin and Sharmaine off and giving them each five-dollars as promised, Tiso drove to the dro spot on 71st and Green. Zep copped five twenty-dollar bags from one of the older gang members named Mike D. As they were driving away from the dro spot, an unmarked police car pulled up behind them.

"Pull Over!" the narcotic's detective bellowed over the loud speaker.

"Shit!" Zep shouted, looking at the unmarked detective car, through the passenger door mirror. He was trying his best to remain calm and refrain from looking back. "It's the muthafuckin' dick boys, Tiso, you ain't got no guns or work in here, do you?"

"Nope," Tiso replied, with a devilish smirk.

"Cool, pull the fuck over 'cause they ain't gon' trip 'bout this dro or you not havin' no license," Zep said. He knew that unlike uniformed officers, the narcotics detectives wouldn't bother arresting two thirteen-year-old boys for being in possession of a user's amount of high-grade marijuana and joy riding in a brand-new Escalade. They only made arrests for guns, large sums of marijuana and hard drugs such as cocaine, heroin and PCP.

Suddenly, over the loud speaker, the detective ordered, "Make a right at the corner, pull over to the curb and turn off the car.

Once they reached the corner, Tiso made the right turn and brought the Escalade to a stop at the curb. Despite their ages, this wasn't their first run-in with the law. On six separate occasions, over the past three years, the police suspected and questioned them for vandalism, theft and assault and battery.

Luckily, Zep was able to talk their way out of getting arrested each time. But for some reason, he had a funny feeling in his gut that today he wouldn't be so lucky.

The fact that he wasn't in complete control of the situation, coupled with the condescending vibe he was getting from Tiso, had Zep feeling edgy. His heart began to beat rapidly and loudly, so loud, he could hear it. His face, upper body and palms were covered in sweat.

"Turn off the car!" the cop repeated.

"Kill the engine," Zep said. Curiosity got the best of him, so he turned and looked, and the passenger side door of the unmarked car swung open. "They gettin' out the car," Zep blurted, in distress.

For reasons unknown to Zep, Tiso gripped both his hands on the steering wheel, braced his body up straight, and like a villain in a horror movie, let out a sinister laugh. And, just as the detective approached the driver's side door, he leaned back in his seat and faced Zep.

"Fuck these bitches. They gon' hafta catch us," he said. Tiso turned up the sound system and hit the gas!

The Escalade lurched forward, tires squealing and engine roaring, pushing Zep back into his seat. Out of instinct, he grabbed the hand grips to brace himself as the luxury SUV took a sharp left turn into ongoing traffic, sideswiping a minivan driven by a woman travelling with three small children.

"Are you fuckin' crazy?" Zep yelled as Jay-Z rapped over the thunderous bassline of *money, cash, hoes.*

Ignoring Zep's rant, Tiso pushed the Escalade north on Halsted Street, reaching speeds of 80 mph. Fearing for their safety, drivers in, both, the north and south, lanes began pulling over to the curb, virtually allowing Tiso to have the entire street to himself.

Red and blue lights began flashing. Zep dipped his head in between the space dividing the two front seats, to get a look out of the back windshield. He noticed that a strobe light siren had been placed on the passenger side roof of the detective's car. "The Dick Boys on our ass!"

Tiso let out a maniacal laugh then shouted, "No shit, Sherlock! But watch how I shake these bitches!" With the narcotics detectives in hot pursuit, Tiso floored the accelerator.

Fortunately, people driving on Halsted Street had a direct visual of the high-speed chase and were able to get out of harm's way. But, at the intersections, the cars travelling under the green light didn't have the same line of vision.

Approaching 90 mph, Tiso recklessly ran through a red light at the intersection of 69th and Halsted. Caught by surprise, a Dodge Intrepid travelling west on 69th street slammed on the brakes, and at the same time, steered right to avoid crashing into Tiso. The driver rammed into a parked car at the corner of 68th and Halsted, totaling both vehicles.

Tiso was hyped up. "Did you see that shit? he shouted. He yanked on the steering wheel, while bouncing up and down in his seat.

Visibly shaken, Zep wasn't getting any enjoyment or finding anything funny about the situation at hand. And he certainly wasn't about to do or say anything to egg Tiso on more than he already was. He looked out the back windshield a second time and couldn't believe his eyes. Three blue and white Chicago police department patrol cars seemingly appeared out of nowhere, and had joined in on the chase. Zep's heart was beating a mile a minute. Butterflies did flip-flops in his stomach. Sweat poured from every pore in his body as he worked to come up with an escape route. He was doing his best to figure out something…anything.

Drawing a blank, he turned down the music and said, "Ain't no way outta this shit. You either gon' kill us or somebody else. Pull the fuck over!

Tiso shot Zep a look of pure disgust. "Fuck naw," he snarled. "I got this!" He momentarily took his eyes off the road to turn the music back up.

"Watch out! Zep yelled, pointing at a Chevy Cavalier speeding east down the intersection on 67th street.

Instinctively, Tiso mashed down on the brakes, screeching the Escalade's tires to a complete stop. Only inches separated the two vehicles as the Cavalier zoomed past. The near-fatal collision left both of them disoriented. Tiso's hands were trembling as if he were suffering from hypothermia, and Zep was gasping for air as if he'd just run a marathon.

Understanding the enormity of the situation as best as they could they pulled themselves back together. Of all the trouble they'd been in over the span of their young lives, nothing came remotely close to the magnitude of the trouble they now faced. The two best friends sat in silence as they held up traffic, each of them having completely different thoughts about what course of action they should take next.

Outside the confines of the Escalade, loud sirens filled the air. Red and blue strobe lights illuminated the streets. Several more police cars could be seen in the distance, speeding towards the scene. People began to gather along the sidewalks; most of them shouted obscenities at the police officers, and, or, encouraged Tiso and Zep not to give up, but continue to flee. The rest were just thirsty to see some real-life action-packed entertainment— regardless to what expense.

"Driver, kill the engine then slowly stick both your arms out of the window," the narcotics detective ordered over the loud speaker.

Three seconds passed before Zep broke the silence between them. "Tiso, it's over. Do what they say."

With his infamous Cheshire cat grin plastered across his face, Tiso cocked his head towards Zep and replied, "We always follow your plan. Now it's time we follow mines." He reached under his thigh and pulled out a Tech .22; the same Tech .22 he had picked up in the alley following the shoot-out at Slickem's funeral. "Here's the plan…"

Tiso continued to hash out his plan, but Zep couldn't make out a word he was saying. Seeing the gun caused his sense of hearing to fade. When the narcotics detectives first initiated the traffic stop, he'd asked Tiso if he had a gun on him and he had lied. Now Zep was left wondering what else Tiso was lying about or keeping him in the dark on.

Where he get this truck from? Do he got jabs on him? Are more guns in here? These questions ran rampant, weighing heavily in Zep's mind. Not knowing the answers to them infuriated him to a point where he became overwhelmed by a flood of emotions— Pain, shock, fear, hate, anger, and despair. But most of all, worst of all, he felt betrayed by the person he trusted the most, his best friend since kindergarten, Tiso. Slowly, his hearing began to restore itself as he darted his eyes back and forth between the police cars and the gun clutched in Tiso's hand.

"You wit' me, B?" Tiso asked.

Zep's mind was in a fog. "Huh?" was the only response he was able to muster.

"B, I said is you with me or not?"

Zep twisted up his face and narrowed his eyes at Tiso. "I'm here, ain't I?"

"That's what the fuck I'm talkin' 'bout!" Tiso said, mistaking Zep's anger to be towards the police, and not towards him.

"On three," Tiso ordered. Then, "one-two-three!" Tiso aimed the Tech .22 out the window.

"Nooooo!" Zep yelled in vain.

TAT! TAT! TAT!

Tiso sent round after round of bullets into the hood of a police car speeding on 67th street towards them.

BOOM! BOOM! BOOM! POP! POP! BLAKA! BLAKA!

Several police officers returned fire as they pursued the SUV, shattering a tail light.

"Bust back at them bitches!" Tiso frantically ordered. With adrenaline coursing through his veins, Zep gripped the Tech .22 and looked out the back windshield.

BOOM! BOOM! BLAKA! BLAKA! BOOM! BLAKA!

The back windshield shattered. Zep squeezed his eyes shut, as shards of glass peppered his face, and bullets whizzed by his head, shattering the front windshield. Enraged and deranged, Zep slipped into an unconscious state of mind. Unlike his usual conservative and calculating self, he exhibited no regards for his life as he climbed into the back seat and let the Tech .22 spit.

TAT! TAT! TAT! TAT! TAT! TAT! TAT! TAT! All eight rounds found their home in the hood and windshield of the dick boys' car.

"That's right, B!" Tiso shouted, bouncing around in his seat. "Keep airing them bitches out!"

TAT! TAT! TAT! TAT!

The dick boys swerved trying to get out of the line of fire. Two of the shots ricocheted off the ground and struck the dick boys' front tire, causing their vehicle to turn sideways, propel six feet into the air, and perform four 360° flips in the middle of the street, wrecking the other eight police cars as well as four civilian cars. The thirteen car wreckage resembled something straight out of an action movie. But this wasn't Hollywood, and the scene on 66th and Halsted was real!

"BD! BD! BD!" Tiso continuously shouted as he stuck his arm out of the window, flagged the trays, then turned off Halsted, making a clean getaway.

CHAPTER THIRTEEN

Friday, September 10, 1999
3:39 p.m.

"Auaaah... ohhhh... shiit," Jazmina panted. "Right there... yeah... right here... shhhh... ooooooh... Zephaniyah... I'm cummin'."

Jazmina's sugar walls clenched firmly around Zep's condom clad dick, as she released a stream of thick, hot, syrupy, pussy juice. Her pleasure moans and warm tight pussy felt too good for him to hold out any longer, causing him to shoot his load deeply inside her just as she'd achieved her climax.

The two had been sexing each other for five straight days. As soon as school was out, they would sneak in the library and 'fuck like minks'. It was these fifteen minutes of sexual bliss that kept Zep coming to school. Although sex was easy for him to obtain, he would never admit it to Jazmina or himself that he was sprung. Every day, after school, he would hit the block and hustle a few jabs. During that time he would either trick off a bag with a customer, or have sex with one of the many hoodrats that threw themselves at him.

It didn't matter that most of those females were older, and presumably, more experienced than Jazmina; what she was dishing out was unmatched. Her high-intensity sex drive, eagerness to please, and inhibition had him open. Just as open as he was, she was sprung on him times two. Her only problem was, she was wearing her emotions on her sleeve and he was taking full advantage of it.

After catching his breath, he pulled out of her, got himself together, and without saying a word, turned to leave until Jazmina grabbed his arm. "Why you playin' me like that?" she asked.

"C'mon girl, every day we fuck you get on some bullshit. Playin' you like what?" Zep asked frustrated.

"You send me to voicemail when I call you, and you ignore me in class all day. You wait 'til school is almost over before you say sump'n to me, and it's always the same thang, *'Make sure yo' ass is in the library when I get there',* she said, trying her best to sound like him.

"I told you I be hustlin' and by the time I get in the house it be too late fo' me to call you back, and we don't need these nosy ass kids in our bidness. That's why I don't say much to you in class. The minute they think we messin' around, we won't never be able to creep off in here again," Zep informed her.

Jazmina jumped down from the table, pulled her skirt and panties up, and hugged him tightly. She couldn't believe her ears. This was the closest Zep had ever came to acknowledging they were a couple.

Before releasing her embrace, she kissed him on the cheek and looked into his eyes. "So, what you sayin', I'm your woman now?"

Zep lowered his head while he struggled for the right words to say. "Look, we need to get outta here," he said, as he walked to the door. "Gimme some time to think about it over the weekend and Monday, I promise I'll give you an answer. Oh, and make sure you wait a coupla minutes before you leave out behind me," he reminded her.

***

As usual, Zep's brother and sister were waiting for him in the school's parking lot. The trio had walked halfway home when out of nowhere, a blue Astro Van ran a red light at 69th Normal. The van jumped the curb, doing about sixty mph onto the sidewalk, coming within a few feet of running them over, before screeching to a stop.

Zep was startled, and, quickly, ducked out of the way.   It had taken a few seconds before it registered to him to make sure his siblings weren't hurt. Moments later, the driver's side door swung open and Tiso spilled out holding his stomach, laughing so hard he was crying tears. Raging mad, Zep ran over to Tiso.

"Nigga, ain't shit funny! If you woulda hit my brotha or sista, I would've—" He paused mid-sentence to search for better words to express himself because the mere thought of killing Tiso didn't sit too well with him. However, deep down inside, he knew he wouldn't have hesitated putting Tiso six feet deep if would've made such a foolish mistake. "Fam, I love ya' to death," he continued, "but don't get it twisted, my nigga, don't ever do no stupid shit like that again," Zep warned.

Realizing Zep wasn't finding any of his shenanigans amusing, Tiso attempted to cool him off by downplaying what he'd done. "My bad, B, you know can't nobody fuck wit' me on the drivin' tip. I wasn't gonna run y'all over."

He got in the van and drove it back onto the street. "Nigga, you ridin' or what?" he asked, while driving at a turtle's pace in the middle of 69th street.

"Fam, you gots to be jokin' right! After that stunt you pulled Monday in the Escalade, you think I'm rollin' in that hot ass steamer wit' you."

A train of cars began accumulating behind the Astro Van. "Zep, I can't believe you still trippin' off that shit. You knew the truck was stolen. I ain't gettin' that kinda paper to cop no Escalade an' you knew that. C'mon, nigga, hop in. All these muthafucka's beepin' their horns startin' to piss me off."

"Meet me on the block, I'm walkin'. It ain't even 'bout the truck bein' stolen. Nigga I asked you if you was dirty and you said naw. Next thing I know we in a high speed chase, you up and start clappin' at the police then tossed the hanger in my lap."

"Shut da fuck up!" Tiso yelled out of the window at the cars honking their horns behind him. Then he focused his attention back on Zep. "B, how many times I gotta explain this shit. The only way we was gonna get away was to shoot it out with them bitches. Ain't no Escalade out-runnin' a police car. I couldn't drive and shoot, but I knew if I busted at 'em first, they would shoot back, and that was the only way you was gonna air them bitches out. It worked and we got away. Shit... you actin' like you killed 'em. You heard what they been sayin' on the news. 'It's a miracle nobody got seriously injured'! All you did was make 'em crash."

"Nigga, that shit coulda got us killed, or even worse, the death penalty! And I don't like bein' tricked into doin' shit! Meet me on the block," Zep said, as he picked up his stride.

"B, you always gotta spoil shit. We ain't even goin' to the block, 'member I told you I was gon' hook you up wit' my girl cousin? I talked to MiMi last night and she off punishment, and her cousin been stayin' wit' her all week. We goin' over there."

"Cool, nigga, I'm wit' that, just tell me the address and I'll meet you there."

Zep's refusal to get in the van, coupled with the blaring car horns was really starting to get under Tiso's skin. He mashed his foot down on the accelerator, then immediately slammed down on the brakes making the van jerk forward, and the tires screech. He reached under the seat for his Tech .22, looked back at the long train of vehicles he was holding up, and flashed his infamous devilish grin at Zep before speaking again. "On King David, if you leave me hangin' I'ma empty this clip into the car behind me."

Ever since he'd shot Toad, not a day had passed he didn't go searching for a GD to murder. And whenever he wasn't hunting for one to kill, he was talking about killing one. The respect and fear he gained for the shooting bolstered his reputation as a young goon, and rein- forced his callous behavior towards human life, causing him to become trigger-happy. His failed attempts at murdering one of his rivals was eating at him so much, thoughts of killing anybody began to creep into his narrow mind.

Zep knew he was eager to catch a body and he'd seen that sinister look plenty of times, plus, he'd put it on King David, so he knew he wasn't fronting.   Still, Zep didn't care. He was about to tell Tiso to handle his business or accept a violation until he saw the elderly lady behind the steering wheel.

The Astro Van driver's side door slung open. "A'ight, nigga," Zep shouted, "I'm comin' but that's some bitch ass shit you just pulled."

Zep gave his brother and sister a little hush money and made sure they crossed the street safely before getting in the passenger seat. He was heated but Tiso didn't pay him any mind, and all of a sudden, he was in a joyous mood. He blazed up a blunt and passed it to Zep.

"Man, Joe, you gonna thank me fa' this. MiMi cousin bad as hell. If MiMi wasn't wifey status, I'd bust her cousin down wit' you."

"Wifey status," Zep repeated with a bit of sarcasm. "I guess Poopa wasn't lyin', this bitch got you pussy whipped fa' real."

Tiso's body tensed up and the smile on his face was replaced with a frown. "MiMi ain't never no bitch, that's my wife," Tiso said in a tone too firm for Zep's liking.

"B, don't confuse me wit' Poopa. I'm nice wit' mines," Zep retorted, looking at his fist.   "A minute ago you was ready to kill an innocent old lady fa' nothin', now you on some lovey-dovey, catchy-feely type shit, gettin' outta pocket wit' me over a bitch! Oh, excuse my French, young lady."

"All I'm sayin' is, she ain't no bitch, she don't even know you and she made sure her cousin didn't fuck wit' none of these niggas fa' you, least you can do is show her some respect."

"Nigga, what!" Zep said, looking at him sideways. "I'ma pretend I didn't hear that shit. I can't wait to see what this broad look like, or is that disrespectful too?"

Tiso didn't respond, but the look he shot Zep spoke volumes. The tension in the van was thick as they both sat with scowls plastered on their faces. Over the years the two had nearly come to blows on a few occasions but never over something like this.

Neither one of them spoke a word while Tiso made the short drive to the twenty-two story, brown sienna, brick-colored Englewood Terrace Building. On both, the left and right sides of the main entrance, a group of stairs led to several individual townhouses that were built into the exterior of the building.

Each townhouse had its own front and back door, and couldn't be entered from inside the building. An elementary school was located across the street from the building. He drove into the parking lot and parked the van.

"We can't go knock on her door 'cause her hatin'-ass momma don't like me, but she don't live inside the building anyway.

She stay in one of the townhouses attached to the building. She gon' be waiting on the steps fa' me," Tiso said, avoiding eye contact.

Zep didn't reply. He got out of the van and started walking towards the building. Tiso caught up to him, put one hand on his shoulder, and pointed to one of the townhouses. "There she go right there."

As they got closer and Zep was able to make out her facial features, he instantly understood why Tiso was so in love. "Man B, on a scale of one to ten, shorty a dub! I sho' hope her cousin look half as good as she do, then I'll have a dime."

Tiso immediately got in his face. "Muthafucka, if she a dub then MiMi a fifty-cent piece 'cause that ain't MiMi, that's her cousin. Nigga, I told you I had you. "A big smile spread across both of their faces as they shook-up and headed over to Capria, forgetting all about their skirmish in the van.

Zep was truly mesmerized by Capria's beauty, and the closer he drew near, the more captivating she became. Her smooth French vanilla skin tone was blemish-free. She had big hazel-colored eyes and expertly arched eyebrows that set perfectly above a long set of eyelashes. The eyeliner and eye shadow make-up she wore was applied with delicate care, giving her a look of Egyptian heritage. Her full pouty lips sparkled with lip gloss, and her teeth were even and pearly white.

Her hair was simply pulled back into a pony tail that hung down to the center of her back, and on top of her head sat a pair of Chanel shades. The Baby Phat capri pants and matching T-shirt hugged her five-foot four inch, one-hundred and twenty-five pound body just right, showing off her flat stomach, shapely hips, catwalk calves, and palmable derriere. She accessorized with a pair of diamond stud earrings and a thin platinum necklace with a one inch diamond cross that rested just at the crease of her coconut sized breasts. To say she was fine would've been an understatement. Capria was blessed with royal beauty. If a casting director were holding auditions for the part of Egypt's Last Pharaoh, she would definitely land the role to play Queen Cleopatra.

For as beautiful as she looked, upon closer inspection, her body language and demeanor was downright ugly. She was standing on the sidewalk, in front of one of the townhouses attached to the twenty-two story Englewood Terrace Building, with her arms folded around herself. There were hordes of children playing around the building and they may as well not have been there, because she failed to acknowledge their presence until a little boy dribbling a basketball accidentally let it get away from him and hit her on the leg. Instead of passing him the ball back, she picked it up and hurled it into the street, almost hitting Zep in the face. Luckily, he caught the ball and passed it back to the young boy.

Capria's actions caught Zep by surprise and made him apprehensive about approaching her. All indications said she was a high-maintenance, stuck-up chick, at least three or four years his senior. This also intimidated him a little. However, his pride wouldn't allow him to back down from her. He wanted to turn around and leave, but he felt he had to perform for the audience. Albeit, a small audience of just one, Tiso, but a tough one nonetheless.

Disregarding the negative vibe she was emitting, he walked right up on her and gave it his best shot.

"Damn shorty, if I didn't know no betta I'd think you was challenging a nigga to a game of basketball, the way yo' fine ass tossed that rock at me," Zep said spitting game.

Capria looked at him with contempt in her eyes. You would've sworn he let out the loudest, funkiest fart known to man the way she twisted her face up in disgust.

"Lil' boy, who you talkin' to, you betta go play with the rest of these kids before I hurt yo' feelins," she said, rolling her eyes.

"Lil' boy? Bitch you got me fucked up. Tiso, you betta tell this bitch sump'n before I—" His voice trailed off as he looked around for Tiso and noticed he was halfway down the street hugging some girl. Zep returned his focus back on Capria who had already kicked off her sandals and was taking off her earrings.

"Bitch? Yeah, nigga, I got yo' bitch! I'ma 'bout to beat that ass now!"

Zep couldn't believe the way this ordeal was turning out. As salty as he was, the only reason he'd called her a bitch was to save face in front of Tiso. The truth was, Capria was the finest thang he'd ever seen, and as much as he wished it wasn't so, he was finding her more attractive, the feistier she became. Zep had never been in a fight with a female and he certainly didn't plan on making the beauty in front of him the first.

He desperately looked around hoping that Tiso or someone else would step in between them and defuse the situation. Unfortunately, no one did, and before he could react, *BAM!* She landed a straight right to his eye. The punch was so loud it sounded more like a slap, and caused everybody to stop and fix their eyes on the two of them.

"Who the bitch now!" Capria spat venomously as she followed up with more punches.

Zep ducked out of the way then side-stepped her follow-up attempts. He grabbed her by the waist, spun her back to him, and held her close. She clawed into his hands and wiggled her body against his, trying to free herself.

"Let me go and fight!" she ranted, breathing heavily.

He closed his eyes, tightened his grip and deeply inhaled her watermelon-scented lip gloss. Her body felt good up close to him. "Capria, you got your lick off, I 'ont wanna fight you," he whispered in her ear.

Feeling something hard wedged up in the crack of her ass, Capria screamed, "Let me go, you pervert!"

Hearing the comment she made quickly snapped him back to reality. He promptly released her and threw his arms up in surrender. "Capria, I'm sorry for disrespecting, and ummm, I don't know what happened," he said, looking down at his erection.

She threw up her guard inviting him to fight. "Naw nigga, I ain't tryna hear—" She dropped her fists and looked at him curiously. "How yo' nasty ass know my name?"

Just as he was about to answer, Tiso jumped in the middle of them. "What the fuck goin' on?"

"Now you wanna come," Zep replied sarcastically.

"Man, what the fuck!" Tiso said when he noticed the bulge in Zep's pants.

"Beat that nigga ass Tiso!" a female voice yelled, as she was approaching Zep from behind.

Zep turned to see who the voice belonged to and his jaw dropped when he seen who it was. Jazmina!

"Zephaniyah!" Jazmina exclaimed, equally shocked.

138

CHAPTER FOURTEEN

Jazmina couldn't believe her eyes. She leaped into Zep's arms and wrapped her legs around his waist, straddling him as if she hadn't seen him in years. When in actuality, a mere twenty minutes earlier he'd given her an orgasm so intense juices were still dripping from her panties. Jazmina had been on cloud nine as she walked home from school.

Thoughts of Zep consumed her mind and she had convinced herself that come Monday morning, Zep would profess his undying love for her. She was trying to figure out a way to amicably end the relationship with her current boyfriend and officially begin her new one. For a split second, she flirted with the idea of keeping them both but decided she loved Zep too much, and wanted to be loyal to him.

Before Jazmina could peel herself off of Zep, Tiso violently yanked her down. "Get yo' ass off of this nigga's dick!" he ordered, not hiding his jealousy. "How the fuck you know him and who the fuck is *Jazmina?*"

"Boy, I been knowin' him longer than I've known you," she said, watching Zep adjust his hard-on in his pants. "We been in the same classroom since fifth grade, and Jazmina is my real name."

"How come when I told you I was gonna hook Capria up with Zep you ain't tell me you knew him?" Tiso demanded to know. Not waiting for her to respond he turned to Zep. "And that goes fa' you too nigga! Why you acted like you ain't know her?"

Finally hearing the answer to how Zep knew her name, Capria stormed off unnoticed. Zep stared at Tiso in disbelief. He couldn't believe how he was acting. "Fam, this yo' wife?" he asked incredulously. "This the broad you runnin' 'round here fighting the folks over, and gettin' out yo' body wit' me over? Nigga, lemme tell you sump'n!"

Jazmina jumped in front of Zep and silenced him with a glaring stare. She turned to Tiso and said, "What he wanna tell you is he didn't know you was talkin' 'bout me 'cause you called me by my nickname, MiMi. We aren't allowed to call people by their nicknames in our classroom, and you never told me his name was Zephaniyah or even Zep. You always called him folks, my nigga or my cousin. So I think you need to calm down," she intervened giving him the honest to God truth as to why neither of them knew the identity of the other. But most importantly, achieving her main objective which was to stop Zep from telling Tiso how she had been fucking and sucking his dick all week long.

Zep read her mind. And seeing how Tiso was going ape-shit over her, he decided maybe it wasn't a good idea to expose her as the bust down he now knew her to be. Besides, Tiso was so far gone Zep wasn't sure what his reaction might've been if he found out they had a sexual relationship. Then a bulb came on in his head. Zep knew his chances with Capria were all but finished, and divulging the nature of their relationship would certainly be the straw that broke the camel's back. But, the price for keeping Jazmina's secret from Tiso may pay huge dividends, by giving him the pawn he could manipulate into convincing Capria he was the one for her.

"You took the words right outta my mouth," Zep said smiling, lying through his teeth.

"Naw B, I think you was 'bout to say sump'n else. If she fuckin' 'round wit' some nigga up at that school you betta tell me. 'Cause if she is, I'ma fuck her up, and barbecue that nigga!" Tiso declared, lifting up his shirt, revealing the Tech .22.

"Famo, you know if she was hollin' at another nigga I'd tell you."

"A'ight, put it on sump'n then!"

"On my mama, I ain't fuckin'..." Zep paused then quickly swallowed the words he was about to speak. He replaced them with, "I mean, she ain't got no boyfriend at school."

An awkward silence filled the air. He looked at Tiso for a response but got nothing. He turned towards Jazmina, but the cat had her tongue as well. Zep felt as though a spotlight was shining down on him and he needed to disappear like yesterday.

Fuck it. He can't prove I'm lying. He faced Tiso, clenched the gates high to his chest, then announced, "On King David, she don't fuck wit' no nigga at school."

"That's what's up," Tiso said, grinning from ear to ear. "I know my wife ain't fuckin' 'round wit' nobody else." He pulled Jazmina closer to him and stuck his tongue down her throat.

Zep looked over to where Capria was standing and noticed she had disappeared. He walked directly up on the kissing couple and cleared his throat to get their attention. "Jazmina, what's up wit' you, cousin? I tried to holla at shorty but she copped an attitude wit' me. So, I called her a bitch and she sucker-punched a nigga."

Inwardly, Jazmina was beaming after hearing what happened between them, but she kept a poker face. She also had a plan that began with making sure Zep and Capria never got together. Luckily, for her, step one of her plan had taken care of itself, or so she thought. She moved away from Tiso and positioned herself as close to Zep as possible without raising concern from Tiso.

"I don't blame you for callin' her a bitch if she disrespected you. She got a smart ass mouth, and she think she betta than everybody. So forget about her, she ain't nothin'. You already got sump'n betta than her anyway," she stated, referring to herself.

Zep wasn't buying it though. He took what she said with a grain of salt and pushed further. "Yeah maybe so, but I could tell sump'n was bothering her before I even said anything to her. She was mad 'bout sump'n. I don't know what, but I was hoping you could tell me."

"Zephaniyah, I wouldn't lie to you. She ain't worth your time, she was just being herself," Jazmina said, as she touched his hand.

Tiso put his arm around Jazmina's shoulder and pulled her next to him. "MiMi, you did tell me on the phone that her mother got killed, and that's why she was staying with you. Maybe that's why she snapped on B fo' no reason."

"That ain't got shit to do wit' it. That ain't no excuse for nobody to be disrespectful towards you," she said to Zep.

Zep was trying to make some sense out of what happened, and the explanation made perfectly good sense to him. "A'ight Jazmina," he said with a slight chuckle, "We'll be back in a few minutes. C'mon Tiso, I need you to take me to the store."

"Hell naw, B, we just got here, and I ain't seen her in over two weeks," Tiso said, adamantly.

After several failed attempts to pry Tiso away from Jazmina, Zep decided to drive himself to the store. He really didn't like the possibility of being caught driving a stolen vehicle, but desperate times called for desperate measures. "Fuck it, gimme the keys, I'll drive myself."

***

Jazmina was hell-bent on preventing a relationship from materializing between Zep and Capria, and for more than one reason. Yes, she was madly in love with Zep but she hated Capria just as much, if not more than, she loved him. She refused to lose the one person who brought her so much happiness and pleasure to an individual she viewed as a stuck-up, spoiled bitch who was a central figure in a nefarious scheme, conspired against her that had stripped away her innocence.

To the world, Jazmina pretended to love Capria and Niq. She acted as if she was their sister, all the while praying for them to be struck with a more devastating blow than she had received. Her resentment towards her two cousins had started three years prior when Niq asked her if she wanted to spend the entire summer with Capria.

She jumped at the idea but feared her mother wouldn't allow it at the time because they were living in the notorious Village Housing Projects. Words couldn't express the joy Jazmina felt when Niq convinced her mother to let her spend the summer vacation at her house.

Everything was going as planned, until the second week when she woke up to her Uncle Carl's hand fondling her breast. She felt violated and didn't know who to turn to.   She thought about telling her mother but didn't think her mother would believe her own twin brother would do such a thing. She knew telling Cynthia was out of the question, because she worshipped the ground he walked on, and treated him like a king, despite the constant verbal and physical abuse she'd endure from him.

Telling Capria wouldn't help either, because she was just a kid like her. So she turned to the only person who had openly voiced disdain towards Carl which was Niq— little did she know it would be her biggest mistake.

Everybody assumed Niq hated Carl because he wasn't her biological father, and he showed favoritism towards Capria who was his seed, that couldn't have been further from the truth. He had been molesting Niq for six years. Prior to Jazmina's stay, it had been a little over a year since his last failed attempt to have sex with Niq.

Ever since that day Niq had began noticing Carl's behavior around Capria. The looks and comments he began throwing her way sounded eerily familiar to Niq. She couldn't fathom the thought of her baby sister being sexually abused, so she struck a deal with the devil himself in hopes of preventing it.

Niq witnessed how Carl was drooling over Jazmina when she had visited them the week earlier. So she offered up Jazmina on a silver platter in exchange for a hands-off policy on Capria. He eagerly accepted, and Niq made good on getting Jazmina under his roof.

Scared and confused, Jazmina had waited an entire day before confiding in Niq what Carl had done to her. She believed Niq was the only person strong enough to stand up to Carl. The protection, comfort and love she so desperately needed and sought out from Niq proved to be poisonous. Niq was cunning, calculating, and a cold-blooded snake towards Jazmina.

The first thing Niq did was tell her she better not tell anybody because no one would believe her. Next, she assured her that he wasn't hurting her but trying to make her feel good. She then retrieved two popsicles from the freezer and gave her ten one dollar bills. Niq told her it all came courtesy of Uncle Carl.

Then after making Jazmina swear on a Bible she wasn't going to tell anybody else, Niq popped in a porno and explained how sex made women feel good. She proceeded to give Jazmina her first lesson in fellatio using the popsicles for practice. Although Jazmina's gut told her what Niq was teaching her was wrong, her eleven year old mind was easily swayed into believing what eighteen- year-old Niq was telling her was true. Plus, she had seen and heard her mother having sex with various men over the years, and the porno was substantiating everything Niq was saying.

Later that day, after being informed by Niq that Jazmina was good to go, in the wee hours of the night, Carl went in the bedroom Capria and Jazmina shared and quietly snuck Jazmina into the bathroom where she pleasured him orally. Soon, he began fingering her underage virgin womb, and once she started responding positively to his touch, he began having full intercourse with her.

Just as Jazmina was warming up to the incestuous and pedophilic relationship with her Uncle Carl, her initial suspicion that it was all wrong was confirmed, when one night a drunken Carl woke up Capria instead of her. He took Capria in the bathroom, but before he could close the door Niq barged her way inside. She snatched Capria from him and made her go back to bed. Jazmina got up and stood outside the bathroom door and listened to Niq go off on Carl; what she heard she'd never forget or forgive.

"We had a deal, I got MiMi here fo' you to rape, and the little slut actually likes it. Now keep your filthy hands and itty-bitty dick away from Capria like you promised, or I swear to God I'ma call the police and have yo' sick ass arrested," Niq spat, vehemently.

Jazmina crawled back into bed and cried herself to sleep. She felt betrayed, afraid, and abandoned by a person she loved, respected and wanted to emulate. At the time she wasn't sure if Capria or Cynthia had anything to do with Niq and Carl's deal, but she clearly understood the terms of their verbal contract. She was being raped so Capria wouldn't be! She figured since she was the outsider they were all in on it. Instantly, she hated everybody in that house and prayed for every one of them to die.

The next night would be the last time Carl would have his way with her. He was found shot dead in the stairwell of the project building, in what the police called a mistaken identity murder. After hearing the news, Jazmina dropped to her knees and thanked Jesus for answering her prayers. She pretended to be traumatized by his death and asked to be taken home. She kept her pain bottled up and never told a soul what she had suffered. She managed to assuage her pain by praying every night that something ill-fated would happen to Cynthia, Niq and Capria. She wanted nothing to do with that side of her family, and for three months ducked and dodged all Capria's attempts at trying to talk to her.

It wasn't until Niq jumped into the drug game and offered to take her and Capria shopping that she began associating with them again.

Niq made it obvious that she was doing it out of guilt because she spoke little to her, and never made eye contact. Even though, Jazmina could tell Niq regretted what she had done, it still didn't hold any weight.

She continued to pray on their demise, and once again, death came knocking at their front door with the murder of Cynthia. Jazmina was elated. Now, that Capria was living under her roof she planned to get revenge on her any way possible, while milking Niq for every penny she could get in the process.

CHAPTER FIFTEEN

Zep successfully made the round trip back to the Englewood Terrace Building. He parked the van in the same spot it had been parked in before he'd left, and got out carrying a small plush teddy bear, a half dozen of long-stem roses, and a sympathy card he'd purchased from the gift shop. Inside the card he'd added his own personal touch by writing some words of encouragement he'd once read in a card given to one of his cousins after her mother passed away.

Feeling re-energized at the possibility of redeeming himself with Capria, he pimp-strolled his way over to the building. The plan was to reintroduce himself, apologize again, and present her with the gifts. She was by far the prettiest girl he ever laid eyes on, and he'd made up his mind he was willing to go all out to land her. Unlike the first time he'd approached her, this time he felt nothing but positive vibes.

He walked up to the townhouse with high expectations but wasn't the least bit prepared for what was taking place.

"Don't fuckin' lie to me!" Tiso growled with both hands squeezed tightly around Jazmina's neck. "Tell me who the nigga is!" he demanded, spewing spittle on her face.

Tiso was full of rage and didn't realize the damage he was inflicting upon her. "Answer me!" he shouted, as he applied more pressure. "You was sayin' a whole lot, now all uh sudden you can't talk!"

Zep was standing behind Tiso dumbfounded. It wasn't until Jazmina's eyes began to roll to the back of her head that he snapped out of his state of stupor. Dropping the gifts on the ground, he grabbed Tiso by the collar. "Nigga, that's enough! You 'bout to kill her!"

Tiso released his grip on her neck then quickly caught her limp body before she fell to the concrete. Realizing the severity of the situation, he gingerly lay her down on the steps and began pleading over her unconscious body. "MiMi, I'm sorry...wake up...please, MiMi...wake up...I didn't mean it." He was on the brink of tears, as fears that he had unintentionally killed her entered his mind.

"Fuck out the way," Zep ordered as he pushed Tiso to the side and knelt over her. "C'mon, baby girl, open up yo' eyes," Zep said, as he moved her hair out of her face.

Jazmina began showing signs of life. Her eyes started fluttering and she tried to mutter something.

"It's okay, just relax," Zep said, trying to comfort her.

"She woke!" Tiso exclaimed, "Watch out, B, I got her."

Zep looked over his shoulder at him like he was crazy. "Chill the fuck out, and pick up my shit!"

Regaining her strength, Jazmina sat up and stared at Tiso with so much hate and fury, she made Zep give her three feet.

"I'm sorry baby… I didn't mean it... I just don't understand why you don't wanna be wit' me no mo'," Tiso said, searching her face for answers. She just stood quietly and turned towards Zep.

"MiMi, I swear to God I won't never hit you again. Here, I bought you these flowers and teddy bear." He offered her the gifts, hoping that along with his heart-felt apologies, she would forgive him for choking her, and continue on with their relationship as if nothing had ever happened.

"No the fuck you didn't," Zep interjected, "Hand me my shit right now!"

"What?" Tiso shouted in disbelief.

"Nigga, I ain't stutter!"

They exchanged hard looks at one another, but Tiso was the first to retreat. He bowed his head and handed over the items. In all of Tiso's years, he had never felt, or looked, so rejected or defeated. Zep felt bad for him and ordinarily would've done anything to help him out, but this wasn't an ordinary situation. Under no circumstance was he coming up off a single rose. But still, Tiso was like a brother and just like always, he felt obligated to clean up his shit.

Zep gave him a half-hug and whispered in his ear. "You know I got you, just go to the van and wait on me."

Rebuffing his instructions, Tiso took a step forward towards Jazmina and said, "I'm sorry. But-"

"Sorry my ass!" Jazmina screamed, cutting him off. Don't ever say shit else to me."

Tiso stepped back and stared at Zep. His eyes, body language and aura had never begged for Zep's help to the degree as they were doing at this moment. Whenever Tiso backed himself into a no-win situation,

Zep almost always bailed him out. So, he swallowed his pride and went to the van, hoping Zep would come through for the millionth time.

No sooner than Tiso was at a safe distance and out of earshot, Jazmina gave Zep a hug and unsuccessfully tried to kiss his lips.

Zep pushed her back, creating some space between them. "Listen," he stated sternly, "Tiso is like a brotha to me. I been knowin' him my whole life. Had I known you was his girl, I woulda never fucked around wit' you. That crazy nigga loves you to death. All he do is talk about you. On the way over here we damn near got into a fight 'cause I called you a bitch."

"You did what?" she asked in a baffled tone.

Zep sighed. "It ain't what you think. Remember I didn't know who you was at the time. The bottom line is you gotta forgive him and give him a second chance. You see how crazy that nigga is, ain't no tellin' what he might do to yo' ass if you don't take him back."

"Zephaniyah, I love you and I want us to be together. That's why I was tryin' to break up with him and then he went crazy and started choking me," she said teary-eyed.

Zep didn't like the direction this conversation was heading, so he tried taking a different approach. "Don't try to pull that cryin' shit on me. You was fuckin' wit' that nigga first and then you started fuckin' me behind his back. You lucky all he did was choke yo' ass. I oughta be chokin' yo' ass right now, but instead, I'm tryna treat you wit' respect when you ain't shit but a hoodrat-ass bitch."

Jazmina burst out crying. She was hurt to the core by his statement and wanted to explain herself, but she knew there nothing she could say to justify her actions, or change the way he felt about her.

Zep knew he had her exactly where he needed her to be. So, he poured it on thick. "Here I am being disloyal to my nig fo' yo' scandalous ass. I went along wit' what you wanted me to do and all I'm askin' is for you to return the favor. But you know what, fuck it, I'ma just tell 'em the truth."

"Please," Jazmina pleaded. "You can't tell him, he crazy!" she nearly shouted, her voice filled with fear.

Zep figured now was the best time to move in for the kill. He wiped away her tears and gave her a hug. "I didn't really mean to call you a rat but you gotta admit what you did was some foul shit," he said.

Jazmina was too overwhelmed with emotions to talk straight. She shook her head in agreement, blinking back tears.

"You said you love me, right?" Zep continued.

Instantly, she got bushy-tailed and wide-eyed. "Yeah, I love you, and I'm sorry."

"You ain't gotta be sorry, but if you really love me, you gonna hafta prove it."

"Okay, I'll prove it. Just tell me what to do and I'll do it."

Zep couldn't believe how easy this was. He started hatching out his plan. "First, you gon' hafta give Tiso a second chance. Pretend you like him, but because he put his hands on you, make him work hard to get you back. Tell that nigga he owe you big time and tax his pockets. Eventually, he'll think you ain't worth it and dump you himself. That way, you don't hafta worry 'bout him tryna kill you or sump'n nah'imean."

She gave thought to what he was saying then replied, "Yeah, but I really don't want to mess wit' him no more."

"I feel you, but it's the only way you can be sure he won't beat the dog shit outta you, plus, you need to make him pay for chokin' you."

"A'ight, after he dumps me, then what?"

"We'll worry 'bout that once it happens. Now, I need you to convince yo' cousin to holla at me."

"Hell-muthafuckin'-naw!" she said animated. Fa'get that bitch. How that gonna help us out?"

"It's all part of the plan, can't you see? Tiso ain't stupid and he suspects we messin' around. Trust me, I know how this nigga think, but if I holla at Capria, it'll throw him off," he said, running game on Jazmina.

The truth was he was infatuated by Capria's beauty and the challenge she presented him with. And, he knew Tiso didn't suspect the two of them of messing around, because if he did, he wouldn't have hesitated to voice it. "Now you said you would do anything to prove you love me. So go get Capria, tell her you been knowin' me fo' a minute and she should give me a chance. Tell her whatever you gotta tell her to make her holla at me. Be sure to let her know I'm waitin' outside wit' flowers, and a teddy bear too."

"You ain't never bought me nothin'." She sucked her teeth and rolled her eyes at the gifts. "I know I said I would do anything but not that. I can't believe you like her," she said on the brink of tears.

He lifted her chin and pecked her on the lips. "Yes, you will do exactly what I'm tellin' you if you love me. Remember, you created this mess, not me; I'm just tryna fix it. You need to quit workin' wit' feelin's and do what I'm askin' you to do, or I'll just go get Tiso, tell him what the deal is, and whatever happens, happens."

Though every ounce of her wanted to stick to her guns, she began to cave in to the idea. *Zephaniyah right, its all my fault, so I gotta help him fix this. It's a good plan, and in a week or two we'll be together. He didn't tell Tiso 'cause he loves me. I should ask him if he loves me. Yeah, he loves me. Why would he help me break up with Tiso and kiss me if he didn't love me?* Her thoughts and emotions were all over the place as she manipulated herself into going along with Zep's plan.

Jazmina gave him a full-body look over then went inside her house in search for Capria. Minutes later, they came back outside together. Zep met them at the front door and ordered Jazmina to go back inside. He took one look at Capria and stumbled over his words. "I apologize fa' being stupid today. I got you sump'n, and I hope you can find it in your heart to forgive me and maybe we can be friends." He handed her the roses, teddy bear, and card.

Capria reluctantly accepted the gifts while never taking her eyes off of him. He was looking for some kind of response but she offered nothing, and appeared to be unmoved by his gesture. There was an awkward silence between them. She figured he'd said all he'd wanted to say, so she turned to go back inside the apartment.

"Capria," he called out, stopping her in the doorway. She spun on her heels to see what he wanted. "Don't forget to read the card," he said, with a huge smile, admiring her beauty. To his surprise, she took the card out of the envelope and silently read it in his presence.

Sorry for your loss. I know personally what you are going through because I've been there. My dad tragically passed away, and I thought the world had ended. Just know that your mother's memory will live forever through you. You got to hang in there and live your life according to the way that'll make your mother proud because she is in heaven watching down on you. Keep your head up and stay positive. I'm sure that's what your mom would want you to do. Again, I'm sorry for your loss.

Sincerely,
Zephaniyah

Capria's eyes began to water as she placed the card back inside the envelope. She dabbed her finger under her eyes in an effort to save her make-up, and prevent any tears from falling in front of him. "Excuse me," she said, embarrassed by her inability to control her emotions. Somehow she managed to smile at him, and in a low whisper said, "Thank you."

Totally caught up in her rapture, Zep's emotions began to mirror hers. Not wanting to lose any more cool points, he swallowed the lump in his throat. "You don't hafta…" he replied as the door closed in his face… "Thank me." He finished the sentence before taking off to the van.

Tiso was smoking a dro-filled cigarillo when Zep got in. "What she say?" he asked, passing him the blunt.

Zep filled his lungs to capacity with two huge pulls, before replying, "She thanked me fo' the shit I bought her." He relieved his lungs of the potent herb. "She was so happy, she couldn't stop cryin' and thankin' me," he said, exaggerating the truth. "Now, it's just a matter of time before she fall in love wit' a playa, and I'll be tapping that ass on a regular. She felt what a nigga was workin' wit'." He grabbed his dick and hit the blunt again.

"Nigga, I wasn't talkin' 'bout Capria," Tiso said. "'Sup wit' MiMi?"

"Oh yeah, that was some stupid ass shit you did," Zep reprimanded him. "You owe me big time 'cause I had to beg shorty to take you back. Just give her a call tonight and cop her a coupla fits and some shoes. Now, let's hit the block and get this paper 'cause you gon' need it."

***

Zep sold three jabs earning him $600 before he decided to call it a night. It was well after midnight and he was unable to fall asleep. All he could think about was Capria. He kept checking his phone wishing Jazmina would call him like she always did around this time. Finally, after wrestling with the idea for thirty minutes, he dialed her number.

"Hello," Jazmina answered.

"Jazmina," he said, recognizing her voice, "This Zep."

"Hold on, lemme get off the other line." She clicked over. "Tiso, I'ma talk to you tomorrow. Somebody just called for my momma."

"A'ight, I love--" *Click*. The phone went dead on him.

"I'm back. So you finally decided to call," she said excited.

"Yeah, I wanted to check in on you and Capria. How everything go wit' Tiso?"

She exhaled loudly. "I guess it went okay. I did what you asked me to do. He promised to take me to the mall and buy me some outfits and a pair of Jordans."

"That's what's up. I gave you the game and if you work it right, you can get 'way more shit outta him. Trust me, the block startin' to juke harder these last few days. The nigga just made $600, so don't sell yo'self short. Just keep goin' wit' the flow and everything will work itself out. Now, let me holla at Capria."

"Why?" She smacked her lips.

"Don't start wit this dumb-ass emotional shit, put her on the phone," Zep ordered.

As bad as she wanted to hate on Capria, she couldn't because she was staring her straight in the face, curious as to who was on the other line. It killed Jazmina to pass the phone over to her. "Here," she said, tossing the phone in her lap and racing out of the bedroom.

Capria placed the receiver to her ear and listened for a few seconds before asking, "Who is this?"

"Zep," he replied, "I know it's late but I had to call to make sure you was okay."

"Since when it become your business to check up on me?" she asked in a flirty tone.

Hearing the playfulness in her voice was music to his ears. "Since I first seen you, plus I really wanted to hear your voice," he flirted back.

"Is that right?" She giggled. "Well, I'm doing fine and now that you've heard my voice, good night."

"No, don't hang up!" he hastily interjected. "I was thinkin' maybe I could tell you a lil' bit about me, and if you want to, you can tell me a lil' about yourself."

"Hmmmm... Let me think about that," Capria teased. "Okay, but only if you go first."

Things couldn't have gone better. He kicked off the conversation by telling her his birthday, age and that he had a brother and sister. She immediately did the same. Next, he told her he lived with his grandmother and mother, but that his mother was strung out on crack and was rarely ever home— a fact he found extremely embarrassing and never discussed with anybody until now.

She listened without uttering a word. She was so quiet he had to ask her several times if she was still on the phone.   Then he put her up on how he spent his summer in Atlanta, came back home, got blessed BD, and began hustling on the block. He ended by joking about how he didn't have a girlfriend and came to the building to meet her and change that, but blew it.

Capria laughed at his last comment then made it a point to mention she didn't have a boyfriend, and that she was still a virgin. She surprised him with how candidly she spoke. She told him she was born and raised in the Village Projects, and just like him, had lost her father.

Leaving no stone unturned, she revealed that Niq had gotten involved with a big time drug dealer and took over his business after he was murdered. And for Christmas, Niq bought their mother a big house in the suburbs, and enrolled her in a private school. She went on to say everything had been kosher until a week prior when she returned home from school and found her mother dead in the basement. Capria wrapped it up by telling him the reason she had a nasty attitude was because she had just came back from her mother's burial a few hours earlier. She choked up as she explained the only blood relatives she had left were her sister, MiMi, and her aunt, Carla, MiMi's mother.

Zep listened to her story with a heavy heart. He felt genuine sympathy for her and thought she was much stronger than him to have endured so much pain. To not have any parents never entered his mind. He knew first-hand the emotional anguish and harsh realities associated with the tragic death of a father. But the thought of losing his grandmother or mother was hard to digest. Even though he hated the lifestyle his mother lived, he still loved her dearly, and now that he was selling drugs, he was beginning to understand her struggles more clearly. It was his dream that she would overcome that demon and get herself clean.

Although Zep would've talked to Capria until the sun came up, he was getting tired and had heard her yawn at least twice. Before saying good-night, he made sure he let her know how much he enjoyed their conversation, gave her his home and cell phone numbers, and assured her she could talk to him about anything, and not have to worry about it going any further than between them.

Capria expressed how happy she was he'd called, apologized for initially being rude and punching him, and promised to make good use of his numbers.

The conversation ended with both of them feeling good about what their futures may hold.

Zep pulled the covers over his head knowing two things for certain: the library visits with Jazmina were history and never to be brought to the light. And, even though he didn't formally ask Capria to be his girlfriend, as far as he was concerned, they were officially a couple.

As Capria turned off the lamp, she glanced over at Jazmina, who appeared to be sleeping. In the moments it took for her eyes to adjust to the dim light, she thought she saw Jazmina mouth a single word, 'bitch'. Anger swelled and Capria saw red.

"What did you say?!" Capria snapped.

Jazmina, eyes still shut in supposed slumber, provided no response. She merely rolled over beneath the covers, showing Capria her back.

CHAPTER SIXTEEN

Saturday, September 18, 1999
1:13 p.m.

"Damn, a nigga can't get a fader," Poopa issued a challenge for someone to place a bet against him. "Don't tell me I broke y'all niggas," he said, scooping up a pile of money off the floor. I shoot a dub—" he allowed two twenty dollar bills to fall out of his hand— "I hit a dub," he said, wagering twenty dollars as a qualifying bet and another twenty-dollars that whatever number he rolled with the dice, on his first attempt, he'd roll it again before he crapped out.

The dice game had started immediately after literature class ended. Poopa was down on one knee in the corner of Rome's living room surrounded by a group of niggas mad at the fact that fifteen minutes had passed and he hadn't crapped out yet.

"You ain't on shit!" Chop spat, dropping forty dollars on the floor.

"This is where it's at. I'm wastin' time servin' on the block," Poopa said, shaking the dice. "A pimp got six ho's on the stroll...now get money bitches," he said, as he released the dice. One landed on two, while the other spun a few seconds before landing on four.

"You don't six-eight fo' twenty," Yatta said, dropping two ten dollar bills.

"Twenty you don't straight six," Terrence yelled.

"That's all y'all got?" Poopa asked. "I'm takin' all bets 'cause y'all niggas is sweet. Shit-Shit, when I make it, you rake it."

Several more people placed bets varying in amounts, but totaling two hundred and sixty dollars.

"Zep, where you at playboy? I need you to bet 'cause you my personal vic, I mean good luck charm," Poopa said, clowning him. Up until this point, Zep was betting the most aggressively, and had lost well over three hundred dollars to him.

"Niggas always talkin' shit when they winnin'," Zep said, walking away from the crap game.

"Don't run, B, you got the dips next. I'ma personally stain yo' ass and talk Cash Money Baby shit while I'm doin' it."

"I know you ain't gonna let that nigga get away wit' that," Fatz instigated.

"That nigga gotta hit a thousand points in a row to break even wit' me!" Zep fired back.

"That's what I thought, you betta quit—" Poopa said, grabbing his dick— "before I rape yo' ass like a bitch."

Zep did an about-face, darted across the room, and landed a one-two combination to his mouth. Chaos broke out as niggas started shouting, pushing and shoving in an effort to retrieve their money off the floor. Poopa and Zep fell to the floor, knocking over forty-ounce bottles and breaking the arm off the leather couch.

Hearing the commotion, Rome pushed Big Tittie Tina's head up from between his legs, zipped up his pants and bolted into the living room. "You niggas done lost y'all muthafuckin' minds," he barked. "Break this shit up right now!"

Everybody froze except for Zep and Poopa who continued wrestling on the floor. "Y'all ain't hear what the fuck I said?" Rome ranted.

Every nigga in the house rushed over to break up the fight. "Clean this shit up and form a three-sixty 'cause one or both of these niggas finna get a violation," Rome announced.

The floor was quickly cleaned, and a circle was formed around Rome, Poopa and Zep. The prayer was recited and Rome immediately got down to business.

"Poopa, you first, what happened?"

Poopa opened his mouth to explain but got stuck by what he was seeing on the TV. He pointed his finger at the 50 inch flat screen mounted on the wall, prompting everyone to turn their attention towards it. Rome broke through the circle and turned up the volume.

"This is Muriel Clair of WGN Channel 9 news, reporting live on the perilous streets of Chicago. Here on the south side in the Englewood community where a war between rival gangs has taken this area under siege. Less than an hour ago on the 6800 block of South Carpenter, witnesses say a lone gunman shouted, 'BD' then opened fire at the gray house in the middle of the block as 50 or so members of the infamous Gangster Disciple street gang were exiting the home.

As you can see, Chicago P.D. and plain-clothes detectives are canvassing the street for evidence and talking to witnesses. Details are sketchy as to why such a large number of gang members were congregating in that single family home and police aren't releasing any information as of yet. However, there are reports that a uniformed police officer was making a routine traffic stop one block over when he heard the shots and saw the gunman hop in a vehicle and speed off.

He gave chase, causing the assailant to crash three blocks away. It is still unclear whether or not the perpetrator was apprehended or is still at large. Hold on... I'm receiving additional information now," the reporter announced, adjusting her earpiece.

"Okay...I've just been informed that at least five people suffered gunshot wounds and are being treated at St. Benard Hospital. One of the five, an eighteen- year-old black male, is clinging to life and is currently en route by ambulance to Christ Memorial Hospital, which is better equipped and staffed to perform the necessary surgery needed to save his life. This is just the latest in a string of shootings that have been ongoing since the beginning of the year, but rose dramatically since the start of the summer.

Live on the south side...Muriel Clair, WGN News. Back to you, Steve."

"Y'all see that shit! That's the type of shit I'm talkin' 'bout right there," Rome stated, shutting off the television. "Muthafucka's need to be followin' whoever that nigga was example, instead of fightin' amongst each other. Now, tighten up this circle, so I can get to the bottom of why two of my finest soldiers fightin'."

Just as everybody was following his orders to reform the circle, three loud knocks followed by a hard kick to the door put the entire house on alarm. Chop pulled a Glock from his waist, several others followed suit and accompanied him to the front door.

KNOCK! KNOCK! KNOCK! BOOM!

"Quit bangin' on the goddamn door!" Chop shouted. "Who the fuck is it?"

"It's me, Tiso," he yelled at the top of his lungs.

Chop looked through the peephole making sure he was alone before opening the door. "Get yo' ass in here," Chop gritted, grabbing him by the arm and yanking him inside.

"What the fuck is yo' problem? And why you miss a session and lit class?" Rome questioned him.

"I just fanned them niggas on Carpenter, ran from the police and been hidin' in a garbage can fo' 'bout an hour," Tiso informed him, dripping sweat, breathing heavily, and smelling like Oscar the Grouch.

Rome and Chop exchanged devilish smirks, while everybody else had looks of surprise, shock and/or awe plastered across their faces. The three-sixty was reformed, only this time Rome stood alone at the center.

Rome looked around at everyone making sure he had their undivided attention before he spoke. "It ain't by accident each and every one of y'all is standin' here today. I've been groomin' you niggas since y'all first stepped off the porch," Rome said, pointing his finger at everybody except Chop and Fatz. "It's my duty as the minister of this set to recognize problems and fix them. A few months ago we had a problem. And that problem was not enough real niggas to defend and grow this organization into the nation it was birthed to be and will become. My solution to that problem was to turn the future into the present. How did I do that? I did it by turnin' you boys into men, by blessin' y'all into this nation. And I gotta admit, so far I'm pleased with the direction, sacrifice and contributions each one of y'all has made on behalf of this great nation. Another function of mines is to administer punishments and rewards when the situation calls for them. See, you lil' niggas might think I'm in the dark to certain shit but I'm well aware of everything that goes on in my territory. Absolutely nothin' gets past me because I'm Rome and I run this shit. Am I makin' myself clear? I said I'm Rome and I run this shit! Everything begins and ends with me!" he bellowed, as he pounded his fist against his chest for greater effect.

Rome remained silent for a few seconds allowing his words to sink into everybody's head before he began speaking again.

"Fatz," he called out, walking up on the nineteen-year-old, three-hundred pound man-child. "You're a strong nigga. I've seen many niggas fold and bitch up after losin' a close family member. It's fucked up that your mother wasn't as strong and turned to the pipe, but that's the world we live in. Luckily, for you, you took after yo' daddy. Whoever he is," he added as an afterthought, realizing he didn't know who Fatz' father was. "You stood up like a champ after they killed lil' Greg by takin' responsibility fo' yo baby sister, payin' the bills at the house, while at the same time, avengin' lil' Greg's death and representin' BD to the fullest by dumpin' at the GD's every opportunity. That, alone, makes you an outstanding member but you didn't stop there. You helped this nation financially by offerin' up your crib as a crack house. So, I'ma reward you with five stacks to find a safer spot fo' you and yo lil' sister to lay yo' heads at. Also, you ain't gotta sell bags no more. I'm puttin' you in charge of runnin' both my crack spots."

Rome turned from Fatz and began talking to the inner perimeter of the circle, stopping when he reached Yatta, Terrence, Psycho and Krazy. He stared each one of them in the face, silently, making it clear to every one he was about to address them. "In the middle of a war, a block away from the borderline that separates our set from their's, and in less than a month, you niggas got Fatz' house doin' a half-a-brick a day. So, I'm givin' y'all a $1,500 bonus."

Rome walked over to the twins, Psycho and Krazy. Standing six-foot even, he towered over the two fifteen-year-old, five-foot four, one-hundred and ten pound, dark-skinned, cornrow braided hair, over-sized clothes, fearing identical twins. "I gave strict orders fo' everybody in grammar school to attend class every day, and ever since y'all started servin', neither one of you been to school. What y'all thought, I wasn't gon' find out?"

Normally, teens their age were sophomores in high school. However, due to an epidemic prevalent in underprivileged urban communities throughout America known as 'babies raising babies' the twins had yet to graduate out of eighth grade. Tayshawn and Marshawn Beckham's mother, Janay Beckham, gave birth to them at the tender age of fourteen. Their father could've been any one of the five boys her age, or six grown men she slept with during the window of conception. Learning of Janay's pregnancy, not one of them was willing to claim responsibility. As a single mother, Janay dropped out of school, never looked for a job, and spent very little time raising the twins. In fact, she viewed them as an impediment to what she did devote the majority of her time doing: Sex, partying, drinking, smoking weed, and searching for a sponsor.

When the twins turned two, she believed she had landed a sponsor. She moved out of her mother's house and into the home of her thirty-year-old drug dealing boyfriend, Randy. Less than a year later, he was arrested and subsequently sentenced to forty years in prison for murder.

The next ten years of their lives were spent moving from house to house with Janay's poor choices of verbally, and physically, abusive boyfriends. That cycle ended three years ago when she got approved for Section 8 housing and moved into her current home.

But, she continued to neglect her children and date the same types of men. She allowed the twins to come and go as they pleased. Janay's perspective was, the less time they were home, the more time she had to party and chase that elusive sponsor. And, unlike most parents, once they joined the Black Disciples and began selling drugs, she was ecstatic. A blessing in disguise, she called it, because they could finally start helping out financially.

Psycho, being the older twin by twenty minutes and the most vocal, answered Rome. "We stopped goin' to school 'cause all the custies kept sayin' they wished we was open 24/7 'cause they hate to go shop somewhere else when we at school. I told them to go over to Emerald but they said folks 'nem don't always be out there durin' school hours either."

Rome already knew why they weren't going to school and was pleased with their decision not to go. The only reason he brought it up was because their actions went against orders he had laid down and he expected every command that came out of his mouth to be followed to the letter. "That ain't no excuse. That's what Fatz, Yatta and Terrence are there for. They work until y'all get back from school," Rome told him.

Afraid that he and his brother might be subject to a violation, Psycho looked to Fatz hoping he would say something. He didn't and that's when Krazy spoke up. "We had to be the ones that stayed at the house," Krazy said, stepping forward inside the circle. "Yatta and Terrence just started high school, so they be all geeked up to go, and Fatz take his sister to daycare every morning, leaving the house empty. The first day we went to school some custies told us some GD niggas was sellin' dummies in front of the house. So we all agreed not to leave the house unattended again. And we can't leave Fatz there by himself 'cause we done had more than five shoot-outs outside the house already," he explained, then stepped back into his original position.

"Fatz, that's true?" Rome asked, already knowing the answer.

"Yup," he replied.

"From now on, you get the green light from me or Chop before makin' a decision that goes against my orders," Rome told Fatz, then continued, "Education is a must and I'll never promote droppin' outta school. So, Yatta and Terrence I better not never hear 'bout y'all droppin' out of school, or much less, cuttin' class. Or I'ma personally beat both y'all asses myself," Rome threatened then eyed Yatta and Terrence disapprovingly.

"Psycho and Krazy, since y'all did take the initiative to handle the nation bidness, I'm givin' y'all new nines fo' yo' personal use and an A.K. to keep at the spot fo' security, plus another stack."

For the second time a deafening silence swept over the room. All eyes followed Rome as he paraded around the 360° with his hands tucked behind his back and head held up to the ceiling. He relished these moments. Nothing was more satisfying to him than the respect and authority he possessed over killers and drug dealers. He never failed to display his power when the opportunity presented itself. One of the ways he did so was by keeping the focus on his movements and words while instilling a mixture of fear and love any time he held a gang meeting. It wasn't until midway through his third lap when he decided to resume his speech.

"Explain to me why the numbers ain't been comin' back right on Emerald?" Rome asked to no one in particular.

A good ten seconds lapsed before anybody answered him. "I don't understand what you talkin' 'bout," Zep said, just as Rome was approaching him.

"You prolly don't, but Poopa do," Rome said, walking past Zep and stopping directly in front of Poopa. "Ever since you asked me to put Zep and Shit-Shit down, the block been stagnant."

"We out grindin' day and night, but since school started we mostly serve from three o'clock to about one in the mornin'," Poopa replied meekly.

"This shit right here is the main reason why I didn't want none of the lil' folks workin' the joints!" Rome said angrily. "Fatz, if Emerald ain't checkin' at least $30,000 a day by the end of the next month, hire all new workers," he said, sending a mixed message.

Rome had the workers he wanted, they were already proven and under the age of seventeen, which meant if they got busted, they'd only spend a night or two in jail and be released to their parents or guardians without having to post any bail money.

Since school started a few weeks ago, the eight hours they were spending there was hurting his pockets and he was determined to change that today. Rome always preached to the youngest members of the gang the importance of getting an education. And, to drive that point home, made it mandatory for all members not in high school to attend class. Failure to attend class would result in a two-minute head-to-toe violation and revocation of the right to earn a living.

Motivated by greed, Rome's views about education changed; his young workers were highly effective in moving product, elusive enough to not get caught, and most importantly, they were a source of cheap labor. Rome could've easily told them to stop going to school, but since he already told them attendance was mandatory, he didn't want to appear as a hypocrite. Therefore, he opted to use reverse psychology.

Fatz nodded his head, acknowledging that he understood the job he was ordered to do. Rome smiled back at him, clenched the gates and proceeded to take his customary stroll around the circle, only this time as he approached each person, he would either give them a nod of approval or a hard look. Poopa, Yatta, Terrence, Shit-Shit and Zep each received menacing stares.

After finishing that ritual, Rome stepped to the center of the 360° and stood facing Tiso. "Check it out," Rome said, talking to Tiso. "Walk around a coupla times so everybody can get a good look at you."

Tiso began to slowly walk the inner perimeter just as Rome had been doing.

164

"I want all y'all to take a real close look at this nigga right here," Rome said. "Now I need a volunteer to explain why I got everybody lookin' at Tiso."

A few people hunched up their shoulders while others darted their eyes around with puzzled facial expressions. "Oh, can't nobody talk or am I speakin' Japanese or sump'n?" Rome asked, angrily.

"I'll tell you why," Chop blurted out.

"Naw, I know you know. I wanna hear it from somebody else. Shit-Shit, step up and tell everybody why."

"Ummm...what... Tell everybody what?" Shit-Shit stammered.

"What? Tell everybody what!" Rome fumed, mocking him. "You sleepin' in a session? Tiso, wake his ass up wit' a mouth shot!"

Tiso jetted over to Shit-Shit and without warning, punched him in the mouth. Shit-Shit's knees buckled, sending him backwards onto the couch. He quickly sprang back to his feet and resumed his stance in the three-sixty with his mouth bloodied.

"You woke now, nigga?" Rome sneered. "Tiso, go stand next to Zep," he ordered then said, "Zep, I know you pay close attention when I'm addressin' the nation. Answer the question."

Tiso and Zep locked eyes for a split second, both fearing the worst, but letting each other know they understood the situation. Zep jogged his memory, and nervously answered, "I think you want us to look at Tiso 'cause he put that heat on them GD's and we should follow his lead like you said earlier when we saw it on the news."

"That shit made the news!" Tiso shouted, exuberantly, then rapidly fired off a few questions. "What did they say? How many niggas I murked? Did they say I did it?"

"Naw, B, they don't know who done it," Zep informed him. "And five people got shot but nobody died," he added.

"Fuck you mean nobody died?" Tiso asked, as he looked around for somebody to tell him differently.

Everybody started shaking their heads no, causing Tiso's demeanor to drastically change. Almost every day after Slickem's funeral, he went out on a hunt to kill but kept missing his intended targets.

Today, he was certain he had succeeded in his mission to kill not just one, but several GD's. Hearing all he'd done was shoot five left

165

him feeling incompetent and undeserving of all the praise the hood had bestowed upon him as being a 'gunslinger.' At a loss for words, he slid between Zep and Poopa, clenched the gates, and lowered his head to the floor.

"Chop, check this nigga out," Rome laughed. "He salty 'cause he ain't body one of the niggas." Rome walked over to Tiso and pulled him back to the center. "Pick ya'self up. That shit you trippin' on ain't 'bout nothin'. Right now, you puttin' in more work fo' the nation than any other nigga from this set. By you clappin' at them niggas daily, you makin' our presence felt. Not to mention, this makes six of them bitches you done shot and one is in critical condition. The most important thing is you made it back alive and free," Rome explained. "Your motives are good but you going about it the wrong way. To kill a nigga, you need to be more precise and deadlier in your approach. Instead of doin' drive-by's or shootin' wildly into crowds, you need to catch one of them slippin', walk up on him, and put two in his melon. You know where they live, hang out, go to school, sell drugs, party, the corner stores they shop at and the restaurants they eat in. Bein' able to catch one of them snoozin' ain't your problem. The problem is your accuracy, and since you ain't no sharpshooter, get close to your target, cut and dry."

Rome knew every syllable he spoke was absorbed by Tiso as well as everybody else. He was in his element and at the top of his game. New recruits were being blessed into the gang on a weekly basis, increasing the number of soldiers under his count to becoming comparable to the greater number of GD's. He had assembled a bunch of young goons that was making him money faster than he could count it, and ready to bust their guns at the drop of a dime. Life couldn't be sweeter for Rome. His goals of becoming a millionaire, winning the gang war and getting promoted to a board member was fast becoming a reality.

Except, he had a huge dark cloud hovering over his head; he was a confidential informant and if it ever got out, he'd be stripped of everything, including his life. He laiid awake every night wracking his brain, trying to figure a way out of his predicament. He was certain he would, but for now it was business as usual. The business at the moment was to motivate his young soldiers to hustle harder and murder GD's.

"And that goes for each and every one of y'all," Rome continued schooling them. "Zep, you was right about why I wanted y'all to look at Tiso, but it's deeper than just what you said. I wanted everybody to look at lil' folks 'cause he is the definition of what a real Black Disciple should look like. In order for a person to see it, you gotta look past the physical and into his heart and soul. His hunger and thirst to body, any, and all, GD's is unmatched, and we, as a nation, are lucky to have him on our team. So, it's only right I reward you with $3,000 and two brand-new Glock .40's. Now, go take your place in the three-sixty," Rome ordered Tiso, then bowed his head in deep thought.

Rome was contemplating whether or not this was the appropriate time and place to up the ante. He knew the consequences behind the actions he was about to take could be life-altering for these boys and began to waiver. He had known them their whole lives and felt a sense of responsibility for their well-being. *What the fuck... They already knee-deep in this shit anyway*, he concluded.

Rome lifted his head and announced, "I'm puttin' five stacks on the head of every GD one of y'all leave stankin'. Matter fact, I got ten fo' the nigga who drop the first body. Now, Fatz, close out this...oh, yeah, I almost forgot. Zep and Poopa, I'm issuin' a fine of $5,000 a piece for fightin' and breakin' my couch. Y'all got exactly 72 hours to pay that in full, or the fine will increase and a three-minute head-to-toe violation will be tacked on. If either of y'all got a problem wit' that, speak on it now."

"I ain't got no problem," Poopa, immediately, replied.

"Five racks in three days! I guess I'll pay it," Zep said, indirectly, questioning the fine.

"Naw, nigga, don't guess. If you don't wanna pay it, just say so and I'll come up wit' another alternative real quick."

"Nah, I'm cool wit' the fine," Zep said, more convincingly.

"Yeah, that's exactly what I thought," Rome scoffed. "Fatz, close this thing out."

Rome swapped places with Fatz so he could recite the prayer. Practically, no one was listening as the words rolled off his tongue; their minds were someplace else.

I swear to God, I'm killin' a nigga before the week is out or somebody killin' me, Tiso vowed to himself.

Five stacks in three days... Rome must be crazy if he thinks I'm finna bust my ass workin' the joint and give him all the money. Shiiid, this ma'fucka already beatin' us out anyways, sump'n gotta give. Wait... Zep's attention was drawn to Poopa. *I know this pussy-ass nigga ain't mean muggin' me. Yeah, I got you nigga, I'ma give you that ass whoopin' you lookin' fo'. But only after I fuck yo' stankin' ass pregnant bitch,* Zep mused while eyeing Poopa.

Yeah, I'm lookin' at yo' bitch ass. You think you can steal on me and it's over. Yo' ass gon' slip up, and when you do, I'ma make sho' you don't get back up. That's right, keep starin' at me. 'Cause you lookin' at the nigga that's gon' take you and that no-aimin', wanna-be O-dog ass buddy of yours down, Poopa said in his head as if he was talking directly to Zep.

What the fuck was I thinkin'? I should've fined them more money to cover every penny I just pissed away. Fuck it... I'ma make that back a thousand times over now that they gotta quit school in order to check me thirty stacks a day, and Zep too-smart for-his-own-good ass think he ain't like that fine. I wanna see what he gotta say when he finds out I'm only payin' $100 off a jab now. He bet' not say shit if he knows better 'cause I won't hesitate to make an example outta his ass, Rome thought.

Little did they know, all of their thoughts would come to fruition in some form or fashion.

CHAPTER SEVENTEEN

Monday, September 20, 1999

Niq was experiencing the worst month of her life. Seventeen days ago Cynthia was murdered and she couldn't go twenty minutes without being haunted by the sight and smell of Cynthia's body lain out on the basement floor in her own piss and blood. She felt totally responsible for her death. The guilt ran so deep, it was becoming difficult for her to sleep, eat, or look at her sister.

The hurt in Capria's voice, and anguish piercing from her eyes cut into Niq's soul, intensifying her feelings of guilt. After laying their mother to rest, Niq made a vow to herself and Capria to find the person responsible, and make him suffer a more horrific death than he'd put Cynthia through.

Today marked the first day on her quest to make good on her vow. She was scheduled to meet her attorney, and, only link, between her drug supplier to discuss the status of the police investigation, and what turned up on the three items the killers left behind to torment her.

She arrived at his office building fifteen minutes early, checked in at the front desk then headed straight to his office.

William Battle was hanging up the phone with his secretary, who had informed him that Niq was about to barge into his personal office, when the door flew open. "Make yourself comfortable," he said, gesturing to one of the two rust-colored Italian leather chairs in front of his matching cherry and oak desk. "I got some good news and some bad news for you. Which do you wish to hear first?"

Instead of taking a seat, Niq went over to one of the floor- to-celling windows to admire the world renowned Chicago Skyline. William Battle and Associates law firm was located in a high-rise office building in downtown Chicago. The law firm occupied the top three floors of the skyscraper. Battle's personal office sat at the end of the top floor, giving him a spectacular aerial view of downtown Chicago.

"If it wasn't for bad news, I wouldn't have no news," Niq said, never taking her eyes from the window. "I guess you might as well tell me the bad news first."

"You mean if it wasn't for bad luck, you wouldn't have no luck," he corrected. "Now, just come over here and have a seat."

Niq took one last look at the architectural skyline before complying with his request. *I gotta get me a downtown apartment wit' a view this amazing,* she thought.

Battle cleared his throat. "Would you like a snack or something to drink? I could have my secretary grab you anything."

"Nah, I'm straight."

"I'm sorry I couldn't make the funeral. I was held up in court. Did you receive the flowers I sent?"

"Yeah, they were nice. Thank you," she replied dryly, getting agitated by the unnecessary formalities.

"Dominique, my heart and prayers goes out to you, but I know nothing short of turning back the hands of time can assuage your pain. Believe me, if I had the power to do so, I certainly would, but you can rest assured that I have been working meticulously around the clock trying to learn the identity of the person, or people, responsible for this tragedy," he said, then took a drink of water, allowing her time to respond.

Niq remained stolid and didn't utter a word. Sensing that she wanted to get to the heart of the meeting, he jumped straight to business. "Okay, bad news first," he said, placing the glass back on the desk. "The police have gotten nowhere with their investigation and I've had the hundred dollar bill, note and the plastic baggie containing the crack dusted for prints and everything was clean."

"Lemme get this straight!" Niq said, full of attitude. "The police don't know shit and the shit you told me to take from the house that could've helped the police find the muthafucka who did this turned out not to be of any help?"

"That's not what I said," he calmly replied.

"Then please run that by me again, because apparently I didn't understand nothin' you just said."

"Patience is a virtue and you should never jump to any conclusions without hearing all the facts and information first," he said, and then took another sip of water. "I never said the evidence you gave me turned out to be useless. What I did say was that I had good news and bad news. You chose to hear the latter. Now, for the good news, inside the crack we found a single strain of human hair with the root attached. It's being tested for DNA as we speak, and the lab technician conducting the test has assured me that a complete profile will be extracted."

"How is that going to tell us who killed my momma?" she asked, feeling a little bit better with this information.

"Well, I've been thinking, and the only plausible course of action I could come up with is to begin collecting samples of potential suspects DNA, just as any homicide detective would do and send them to the lab until we find a match. Now, I'm willing to bet a million dollars to a bucket of shit that you are connected in some way to the bastard who did this. The note semi-verifies my hunch. All you have to do is bring me DNA samples of the people in your circle or anybody you can think of who might've done this and I'll have them tested. I suggest you start with every man that has hit on you in the last six months, especially if he's of questionable character, like say, a known robber or drug dealer."

"And just how am I s'pose to do that?" Niq asked, throwing her hands up in frustration. "What do you expect me to do, pluck every nigga I know hair out by the roots because they all try to holla at me, and they all have...uhm...what you called it... questionable character?"

"Of course not," he replied, smiling. "But you do have to be extremely careful, discreet and creative," he said seriously. "The last thing we need is for the guilty person to suspect you're rounding up DNA samples in search of your mother's killer. I don't think I need to spell out the potential consequences you could face behind that. Now, getting back on track, there are more ways to get DNA other than from hair samples. Body fluids such as blood, semen, urine and saliva also contain DNA. You can get someone's DNA from something as simple as a cigarette butt. So, my thinking was for you to secretly gather any discarded cigarettes, cups or bottles. Just make sure the person whose DNA you want tested is the only one who drank from it or smoked the cigarette. Then, secure it in a clean bag and get it to me as quickly as possible. Also, make sure you label who each one belongs to."

"Alrighty, I don't think that would be a real hard problem at all," Niq said, ready to leave. "I know this is gonna cost me an arm and a leg, so what do I owe?"

"Wrong again, it's gonna cost two arms and two legs, but lucky for you, Mr. Carrillo will be covering the charges. And, one more bit of news before you leave. I've been instructed to inform you that your shipment will touch down at it's usual time and destination today."

"That's what's up!" Niq said, elated.

She checked the time on her diamond bezel ladies' Cartier watch and realized she had roughly six hours to count out $750,000, gather her mules, and drive 75 miles to Rockford, Illinois. Once there, she'd check her mules into a hotel room, drive herself to a self-storage facility, place the money in a locker, and return to the hotel room.

A member of Miguel Carrillo's drug cartel would retrieve and count the money, then slide an envelope with a key inside it, along with a picture of a car, and the address to where the car is located underneath her hotel room door. Neatly stacked inside the air compressed door paneling of the car, would be fifty keys of coke, and five kilos of China White. In the past, half of the $750,000 would be the debt on the last shipment, and the remaining $375,000 half the payment towards the new shipment. Since the namesake and leader of the drug cartel waived her debt, the money would cover the full payment on this shipment.

With no time to waste, Niq jumped up out of her seat and rushed over to the office door. Right before she let herself out, she turned and apologized for her nasty attitude and thanked her attorney for everything.

CHAPTER EIGHTEEN

Time was dwindling down on the 72 hour deadline Rome had imposed on Poopa and Zep to pay the fine. After listening to Rome's speech at the last meeting, all the jab workers on Emerald decided to ditch school Monday. Instead, they hugged the block hard and made sure at least three of them worked the entire graveyard shift.

Poopa was putting in overtime, and he'd only slept six hours in an all-out effort to earn the $5,000 and get the spot to making $30,000 a day. He was soliciting sales from any and everybody who walked or drove by the block. So far, he'd sold twenty-eight jabs which would've been $600 over the fine, but Rome reduced the amount of money he paid off each jab by $100, making him $2,200 short. To earn the extra cash needed, he convinced Shit-Shit to let him serve his jabs for the day. With less than 24 hours left, he feared the beat down he would receive if he didn't have all the money on time.

"Yo'! Over here!" Poopa yelled across the street to a senior citizen couple. "I got them boulders fo' yo' shoulders!"

They pretended not to hear him and put a little pep into their steps. Upset they weren't shopping, Poopa shouted, "Fuck both you bitches! I hope you two old muthafucka's catch Alzheimer's and die!"

He turned his attention to a middle-aged man dressed in a suit and tie, carrying a briefcase, trying to locate the house that matched the address on a piece of paper he was holding.

"Ay, pimpin' check it out!" Poopa said, shoving a handful of rocks in his face. "I got what you really lookin' fo' right here."

"I beg your pardon," the man said, terrified.

Zep was becoming more and more agitated by the blatant disrespect and ignorance Poopa was displaying. He apologized to the man and assisted him in locating the house.

"Fuck is yo' problem, Poopa?" Zep said, through clenched teeth. "Dude don't look shit like no hype. Yo' stupid ass 'bout to get us all locked up wit' this thirsty-ass shit you doin'."

"Yeah a'ight, you can stand there and front like shit all gravy but I know you only sold twenty jabs. At midnight Rome comin' to collect that paper and I'ma laugh when yo' stupid ass get a PHD (Pumpkin Head Deluxe)." Poopa countered then walked off to make a sale.

It took every ounce of strength Zep had not to lay hands on him. "Pussy-ass nigga," he mumbled as he walked back to the stoop he'd been sitting on and began to weigh his options.

Tiso had watched, and listened, to the exchange between them and knew Poopa wasn't lying. Zep had been quiet and standoffish for the past three days. Tiso figured he was also worried about being able to pay the fine.

"What Poopa saying is right," Tiso said to Zep. "I know you prolly tryna think of a way to talk yo'self outta payin' that fine, but I wouldn't chance that if I was you. You ain't gotta worry 'cause I got that three stacks Rome gave me plus the money I been makin' out here, so whatever you need just let a nigga know."

"B, I don't need yo' money. I need sump'n else."

"If I got it, you got it. What you need?"

"A banger," Zep stated.

"Fuck you need a gun fo'?" Tiso bellowed.

"Fuck is you loud fo'?" Zep gritted. "I don't need Poopa bitch ass or Shit-Shit all in my bidness."

"What the fuck is yo' problem?" Tiso asked with his face twisted up. "I'm only askin' you what you need a gun fo'. What you thinkin' 'bout knockin' off Rome or sump'n?" he asked, lowering the decibels in his voice.

"Hell naw, is you retarded or sump'n? I need it to hit this lick so I can pay the fine."

"You got a lick and you ain't told me about it? Nigga, you bogus as hell," Tiso said, feeling slighted. "Since when we start keepin' shit like that from each other?" He removed a 9mm from his waist and said, "I'll give it to you, but first you gotta put me up on the lick."

Zep snatched the gun and took off running, and Tiso was dead on his heels. He knew if he told Tiso what his true intentions were, he would've never given him the gun, and carried out the mission himself.

Ericka had an older sister named Kathy whose baby daddy was a GD from 69th and Racine. For the past three months, five days a week, at midnight, he would pick Kathy up for work at her backdoor, and drop her back off early in the morning. She lived four houses off the corner. So, he would dip in the alley from 69th street, pick her up at the gate, pull into her garage, back out, and exit the alley the same way he entered it. Using this method, he had been successfully entering BD territory and avoiding detection.

Even though he knew it was risky, he refused to let Kathy take the C.T.A. bus to work when her work hours changed. Her new hours were from 6:00 a.m. to 2:00 p.m. The second day he dropped her off from work, his cover was blown. Zep had come home from school and was walking over to the crack spot when he noticed Kathy getting out of his car. After witnessing it the first time, he made sure to watch for the move and was strongly considering passing the information along to Tiso. But after the last meeting at Rome's apartment, he began to think that rocking Kathy's baby daddy to sleep was something he needed to do.

After running two blocks over to the alley shared by Lowe and Union streets, Zep stopped two houses down from Ericka and Kathy's backyard. He pulled out the 9mm, took it off safety, chambered a round and squatted down between the trash cans. Tiso stood beside him breathing hard with both hands on his knees.

"Duck down before somebody see yo' ass!"

Tiso did the exact opposite and stood straight up. "Nigga, we live on the next block. Everybody know us. So who the fuck you plan on robbin', Mr. and Mrs. Foster, drunk ass Benny, or Ericka and Kathy?" Tiso asked, as he pointed to each of their houses. "'Cause ain't 'nan one of them got no paper and if they did you think they ain't gon' recognize us and call the police?" "Man...I'm startin' to sound like you," he said. "On second thought, fuck it, I'm down wit' whatever."

A freshly painted navy-blue '77 Caprice Classic sitting on thirties and vogues turned into the alley. Instinctively, Tiso ducked out of view.

As the Chevy approached, Kathy's garage door began to rise and the car drove inside. Before the Chevy was fully inside the garage, Zep advanced his position. He darted across the alley and hid behind her trash can, which was right next to the garage.

He began to become a little nervous because this was different from their normal routine. Usually, Kathy got out of the car before he drove inside the garage. He thought about leaving but decided to peek inside first. Kathy's head was bobbing up and down in his lap, so he went back to his position and waited for her to finish sucking him off.

Two minutes later, the side door to the garage opened and closed. Zep stuck his head around the trash can and watched Kathy walk inside her house. No sooner than she shut the door the Chevy began backing out. Zep ran inside the garage with Tiso right behind him.

BOOM! BOOM!

Zep squeezed two rounds into the driver's side window, killing him instantly. Shards of glass, blood and brain matter splattered all over the dashboard and front passenger side window. He didn't wait for his head to hit the steering wheel before he began hauling ass out of the garage. They ran non-stop for three blocks until they reached the 7000 building. They entered the building and took the stairs three at a time to Rome's floor. As soon as they exited the stairwell, they bumped into Chop and Rome.

"Just the man I was goin' to check on. You got what you owe me?" Rome asked, as he patted Zep's pants pockets.

Zep swatted his hand away. "I 'ont got nothin' fo' you. I was comin' to collect what you owe me."

Swiftly, Chop grabbed him by the collar. "Zep, you 'bout to get fucked up, now ain't the time to be playin' games."

"Man, I ain't playin' games, Tiso tell 'em why he owe me $5,000."

"B, I don't know what the hell you talkin'--" Tiso paused mid-sentence. "That was Kathy's baby daddy, that GD ass nigga!" he said aloud, as he began to put together the true motives behind Zep's actions. "You changed that muthafucka, B!" He shook up with Zep. "On King David, you owe my nigga."

Tiso proceeded to explain in dramatic detail how the murder went down. Once he finished with his cinematic rendition, Zep filled in the blanks. He told them how he watched the alley routine for a few days and preplanned the hit. He even took the liberty to apologize to Tiso for keeping him in the dark and explained his reason for doing so. To Rome, the story sounded surreal, and Zep wasn't displaying the body language he believed he should have after killing someone for the first time.

"So, you tellin' me it's a dead GD, right now, in the alley on Union?" Rome quizzed.

"That's exactly what I'm sayin'."

"If you don't believe us, I got five stacks say he ain't lyin'," Tiso said, trying to capitalize as well.

"I know how to settle this," Chop interjected. "What you do wit' the banger?"

"I got it right here," Zep said, reaching in his waistband.

Chop took the gun from him then walked down the hall and knocked on the door next to Rome's apartment. An elderly lady opened the door. "Hold this fo' me 'til I get back." She took the gun and went back inside her apartment without any reservations. Chop walked back to them and said, "We 'bout to take a trip."

They piled into Rome's Lexus and drove over to Union. When they arrived the alley was taped off, and the area was swarming with homicide detectives and uniformed officers. A growing crowd of, at least, seventy-five people stood outside the yellow tape trying to catch a glimpse of the murdered victim.

Rome, Chop, Tiso and Zep wore smiling faces as they sat inside the car and watched the scene unfold before their eyes.

"Noooo… My baby…. They killed my baby!" Kathy screamed at the top of her lungs. "Why… Why… Why? They killed my baby daddy!" she wailed.

Seeing Kathy distressed, family members and friends began trying to calm her down, while she showed her ass throwing the customary over-the-top 'they killed my baby daddy' hoodrat temper tantrum.

"Don't touch me! Don't fuckin' touch me!" she yelled, swinging wildly at any and everybody in her path. "He didn't bother nobody! Why...Why? He never bothered nobody!" She fell to the ground and rolled around while kicking and screaming.

Whatever doubts Rome had quickly disappeared after watching her academy award winning performance.

"Wasn't expecting you to be the one, I thought fo'sho Tiso or one of them retarded ass twins was gonna be the one to cash in," Rome said, looking at Zep through the rearview mirror. He viewed Zep as being mild-mannered and cerebral, not the type to kill in cold blood. "Look, you can keep it real if Tiso actually killed the nigga and you went along wit' him."

"So, what you tryna say, I won't clap a nigga?" Zep said, feeling like Rome was calling him soft and questioning his gunplay. "You owe *me*, not Tiso, Psych or Krazy, five stacks unless you droppin' that bogus ass fine you knew I wasn't gon' be able to pay," he said, with a smug look on his face. "Especially after we only keep a hunnid off a jab!"

"You listenin' to this nigga?" Chop said.

"Yeah, I hear him," Rome replied, laughing. "On some serious shit, I need both of y'all to pay attention. You niggas done stepped ya' game up. Y'all officially playin' in the major leagues, and in this league, ain't no room fa' amateur mistakes. In the murder game, one mistake can cost you a life sentence or the death penalty. Since y'all were shorties, I've been groomin' y'all for this game. Why you think I had y'all scrappin' in the park? It was to weed out the mentally and physically weak from the strong. And you two always fought with heart and never shied away from a challenge, even when you had to fight each other.

What was most impressive about you two was no matter who came out on top, neither of you took it personal and split whatever money the winner made. Over the years, I paid close attention to every one of y'all. I knew all about the little robberies, fights in the parks and school yards, and the knockout games y'all played that terrorized the hood at night. I knew 'bout the little run-ins wit' the law, but what I loved is how y'all kept your mouths closed. Now, that y'all playin' the murder game, keepin' the code of silence is of the utmost importance and the only punishment fo' breakin' that code is death. For the last time, who all know you killed that nigga?"

"Nobody," Zep answered. "'Cept the people in this car."

"And that's the way we gon' keep it," Rome said with authority. "Don't go braggin' to none of the guys. Just 'cause a nigga BD don't mean you can trust him. Take Poopa for example. He fuckin' Ericka, damn near live in the house, so you can't tell me he ain't know that nigga was creepin' through. You definitely can't trust him 'cause when a nigga sprung on some pussy, he subject to do anything. Tiso, I don't wanna hear 'bout you wildin' out. No more runnin' 'round here shootin' up blocks like this the wild wild west or some shit. You ain't gotta prove you'll pop that thang 'cause niggas already know what's up. Take a cue from Zep and be discreet from this point on. I need you out here puttin' in work, not boxed in fo' life. Tomorrow, I'ma have Chop do one on one talks wit' everybody that was at the house the other day when you burst in and stupidly admitted you shot up the house on Carpenter. I gotta find out if anybody said sump'n to somebody else, and if so, who it was to make sho' yo' little ass don't go down fo' murder."

"How I'm goin' down fo' murder when I didn't kill nobody?"

"You must didn't watch the nine o'clock news last night. Dude made it outta surgery but was brain dead. His family decided to pull the plug last night."

"What I tell you Zep? Didn't I tell you niggas wasn't gon' be able to fuck wit' us? We killin' these niggas!" Tiso boasted. "We might as well stop sellin' drugs and get this easy money. I was the first nigga to murk one of them bitches but since I didn't know, I'm cool wit' the $5,000."

"First of all, you need to calm down, and I ain't givin' you shit. I said what I said after you had already shot up that house. Right now, both of y'all just keep servin' and don't run your mouths or do nothin' stupid, Tiso," Rome said, as his phone began ringing.

He pressed the talk button. "Holla at me."

"Hey boo, I'm not sick anymore. So, I'm ready when you're ready to go out on that date you owe me."

"A nigga been missin' you like crazy. Shid, I'm ready like yesterday. How tomorrow sound?"

"Sounds like it's a date. I'll meet you at Houston's downtown at eight o'clock p.m., and don't be late." Niq ended the call.

"A nigga been missin' you like crazy," Chop playfully mocked him. "Don't tell me you done fell in love wit' one of them baller chasin' bitches you be fuckin'."

"Quit playin', since when have I ever been a tender-dick ass nigga? That was the connect callin' to let me know she back in action. I'ma re-up tomorrow at eight."

"Yeah, I was meanin' to ask you when she was gonna get back on. I was gonna suggest you cop a brick or two from Fu-Fu to hold us off. So what you wanna do wit' these two killers in the back seat?" Chop asked, switching gears.

"It's too hot to send them back out on the block," Rome said, as he stopped at a red light. He turned towards the back seat and said, "Y'all rollin' wit' us fo' the rest of the day."

Rome continued to drill into their heads the 'do's and don'ts' of the murder game as he drove around the city to various BD sets. Tiso and Zep soaked up every jewel Rome dropped on them. By the time Rome dropped them off in the hood, they were mentally exhausted, but properly schooled in the art of the Murder Game 101.

***

Zep didn't get both feet through the front door before his grandmother surprised him with a slap across the face. "What job you workin' at where the shift ends at three in the mornin'? You think 'cause I'ma old woman with bad vision I can't see what's goin' on 'round here? Don't think fo' one second you can fool me, an you damn sho' ain't foolin' God," she rattled off accusingly. "I'ma tell ya' just like I told yo momma and my daughter years ago. You betta drop down on ya' knees and repent 'cause the life you livin' is downright ugly. And my sixty-five years of livin' on this earth has taught me, God don't like ugly or much of what you think is pretty," she chastised him then scurried off. "And I can smell them funny cigarettes you been smokin' too. That's that same mess yo' momma started wit', now look at where it got her," she added, before slamming her bedroom door.

Zep was left standing at the front door wondering, *how the fuck she know? Hell naw, she can't possibly know.*

A mere two seconds of contemplating if his grandmother knew about the murder he'd committed was the only credence Zep gave to the words she had spoken. He locked the door and went straight to his bedroom. His brother was sound asleep when he entered the room. Ready to catch some sleep as well, he eased onto his bottom bunk, kicked off his shoes, and dialed Jazmina's home phone number.

"Hello," she answered on the second ring.

"This Zep," he said, yawning, "Put Capria on the phone."

Jazmina sucked her teeth. "Hold on, Tiso on the other line."

"Wait a minute," he said, stopping her from clicking over. "Give Capria the phone, I'm only gon' be a second.''

Jazmina sucked her teeth again. "Okay," she huffed then passed Capria the phone.

"Whatchu' want?" Capria spoke sassily into the receiver.

"Oh, it's like that?" Zep pulled his cellphone away from his ear and stared at it for a second before he placed it back.

Capria smiled, "Nah, I'm just messin' wit' you."

"Okay, 'cause I thought I was gon' hafta get up out this bed and head over to the Englewood Terrace Building," Zep joked.

"And do what?"

"Kiss some sense into you," Zep said. The witty comment caused them both to laugh. "But check it, since you ain't transferred into a new school yet, I'ma come kick it wit' you after I drop my brother and sista off at school if that's cool wit you."

"I'm down," Capria replied.

"A'ight, I'ma see you in the a.m.," Zep said, "but, right now, I'ma finna catch some Zzz's and dream about you."

"Yeah, right." Capria was beaming from ear-to-ear.

"'Fo' real, I dream about you almost every night," Zep said, truthfully.

"I bet you do," Capria replied, not believing one word. "Talk to you later and sweet dreams," she chimed, before ending the call.

No sooner than Zep tossed his cell next to his shoes and pulled the covers over his head, did his grandmother step into his bedroom. "Get up and come with me," she whispered, not wanting to wake Kevin.

Zep followed his grandmother into her bedroom. She closed the door behind him, placed her hands on his shoulders and forced him down on his knees.

"Father God, I come to you as your humble servant, begging you to forgive Zephaniyah for his sins. Father God, I'm asking you to remove the evil spirit of the devil that has corrupted his soul and replace it with the love of Jesus. Father God, you know his heart. You know he's a good boy. And, I'm begging you not to turn your back on him. These, and other blessings I ask, in Jesus' name, I pray, Amen."

"Amen," Zep repeated, getting up off his knees. He hugged and kissed his grandmother then opened up her bedroom door. As he proceeded to leave, her voice stopped him dead in his tracks.

"You need to wash the blood off your hands and throw away them clothes you wearin'. They reek of death," Mrs. Berry said.

Zep looked down at his hands and for the first time noticed he had Kathy's baby's daddy blood on him.

CHAPTER NINETEEN

The next morning Zep woke up feeling like a new man. He had heard stories that once you've killed a person their spirit would haunt you in your dreams. Or, that you wouldn't be able to discard the gruesome images of the deceased person from your mind. Zep feared he would be subjected to these and other forms of mental torture people claimed to have experienced after murdering someone.

However, none of that happened. His night wasn't filled with ghosts, evil spirits, or a zombie GD out to make life miserable for him. Actually, he couldn't have had a better night's rest, or a more pleasant dream, which led him to believe that due to his grandmother forcing him on his knees and praying for forgiveness, he'd literally gotten away with murder.

Suddenly, his conscience began to kick in and he could hear his grandmother's voice echoing *'God don't like ugly or much of what you think is pretty'*.

"Bullshit!" Zep said as he sat up on his bed. It was a fact, last night Zep slept like a baby and had the best dream of his young life, a wet dream. He dreamt of he and Capria engaging in a series of sexcapades. In the first dream, they made love as the sunset on a secluded beach.

As that dream ended, another one came about where they were in a run-down gas station bathroom, and he had Capria bent over the sink, man-handling her doggy-style. The final dream was of him pleasuring her with oral stimulation. Something he swore he'd never do but woke up with a new view on eating pussy. He kind of liked the pleasure he'd seen on her pretty face as his tongue-loving took her to a height of sexual bliss he never knew existed.

"Damn, a nigga just might eat that," he said, smiling to himself, visualizing his dreams while staring down at the crotch of his crusty cum-stained boxers.

Eager to get his day started, Zep took care of his hygiene, put on some clothes, and walked to school with his brother and sister. Only, he had no intentions of attending class. And for the second consecutive day, he didn't. The first day, he'd ditched to serve on the block but today he was cutting class to make good on the promise he'd made over the phone the previous night, to Capria. He trekked over to the Englewood Terrace building and Capria was standing in the exact same spot where he'd first lain eyes on her.

"Heeey you," Capria sang, sporting a smile as big as Lake Michigan. "I see you know how to keep your word unlike somebody else I know."

"Dayummm, you lookin' good today," he said, admiring her beauty, and flashing a smile just as big. Zep opened his arms wide. "Can the kid get a hug or sump'n?"

Capria took one step backwards, crossed her arms, looked him up and down, and with much sarcasm spat, "Fool, you must be crazy. The last time you got that close to me you couldn't control yo'self."

Zep opened his mouth for a comeback line but nothing came out. Their eyes met and for a brief moment they engaged in an awkward silence until Capria bust out laughing.

"Boy, I'm just playin' wit' you," she gushed then rapped her arms around his waist, blessing him with the hug he desired.

He breathed a sigh of relief, then snuggled his body close to hers. They held on to one another for quite some time because neither one wanted to be the first to let go.

Finally, Capria relented and released her embrace. She kissed him on the cheek and whispered in his ear. "So what we gonna do since you ditched school to come kick it with lil' ole me?"

"It all depends," Zep replied.

"Depends on what?"

"Whether you're my woman or not," he said, laying it out there.

She put one hand on her hip and twisted up her face. "Whether I'm your woman or not? Is that how you call yo'self askin' me to be your girlfriend?"

"Naw, it ain't like that. You know I really like you. We talk on the phone every night and I kinda feel like you my girlfriend but I'm tryna find out if you feel the same way. So, now, I'm asking. Will you be my girl?"

"It all depends," she said, giving him a dose of his own medicine.

"Depends on what?" Zep played along.

"First of all, I ain't one of these little hoodrat chicks runnin' 'round here," she said with a straight face, "and if what MiMi been tellin' me about you is true then I'm not so sure if we can be more than just friends."

On King David, if this stupid ass bitch ran her mouth, I'm fuckin' her up, Zep swore to himself. "Whatever Jazmina told you is a lie," he said, defensively.

"How you know it's a lie if you don't know what she said?"

"You right," he conceded. "What she say?"

"Remember we promised not to hold nothin' back from each other. And you told me that no matter what, you'll always keep it real with me, and I said I would do the same. Well, now I want you to keep it real and tell me what you be doin' in the library after school."

"Huh?" Zep couldn't believe his ears. He was stuck between a rock and a hard place. On one hand, he didn't want to lie to her, but on the other hand, he damn sure wasn't about to tell her the truth. So, he did the next best thing, which was stall for time and try to figure out exactly what she knew. "What kinda question is that? We keepin' it real, so whatever she told you, spit it out."

"Okay, MiMi said every day after school, you take this girl name Tahiti in the library and have sex with her."

"Oh really," Zep said, relieved that Jazmina didn't expose their secret. "Truth is, I did take a girl in the library a few times but it wasn't Tahiti. Me and her ain't never got down like that and that was before I knew you. The last time that happened was Friday before last. We met the same day after school. Since then, I barely talk to her or Jazmina at school because I don't want Jazmina tellin' you no bullshit about me. And, so far this week, I cut class every day," he said, telling her the truth but not the whole truth.

Capria knew he wasn't lying because MiMi told her Zep had been acting somewhat shady towards her lately and he admitted to having sex in the library. But, she still had to clear up a few more things with him before she made their relationship official. "So, whoever this library ho is, you dumpin' her, right?"

"She ain't my girl and as long as we together, you ain't gotta worry 'bout her or no other broad."

"You say that now, but I was serious when I told you I was a virgin. I don't run around havin' sex with boys like most these girls do. I'm waitin' until I feel the time is right. I like you a lot and I wouldn't mind bein' your girl, but what if three or four months pass and I still don't feel comfortable about havin' sex? What you gonna do then? Dump me or cheat on me?"

"Neither one," Zep swiftly replied. "We more than just sex. We've only known each other a little over a week and we talk about any and everything. Plus, as good as you look, I'll wait ten years if I have to. Capria, that's my word as long as you my girl and stay real with me, I won't cheat on you or pressure you into doin' somethin' you don't want to do."

Capria felt the exact same way as he did about their brief relation-ship. She looked forward to his call every night. He was a good lis-tener, thoughtful, witty, smart, and not to mention, fine as hell— a male

version of herself. Then, just when she was certain he was going to lie about the library, he stayed true to his word and kept it real. *If he play his cards right, I just might lose my virginity to him,* she thought.

"So, what's up?" Zep asked, breaking her train of thought. "Like I said, ain't no pressure. If you want it to stay like it is, then that's fine too. I'm still gonna wait on you but it would really make me happy to hear you say you're my girl."

How can I tell him no? She thought. Capria didn't hesitate when she spoke the magical words. "I'm your girl," she confessed, then sealed the deal with a kiss.

"That's what I'm talkin' 'bout!" Zep said with a smirk. *Three or four months, my ass, I'ma be hittin' that pussy in no time.*

Seconds turned to minutes, and minutes turned to hours as they sat on the steps conversing a little bit about everything. Religion, music, fashion and food were just some of the topics they discussed. Once the topic of family came up, Capria revealed she could get anything she wanted from Niq because she felt guilty about their mother's death. So, she convinced Niq to let her live with their aunt Carla permanently. She told him how she planned on surprising him by transferring to his school but there wasn't any classroom space. Now, she'd have to attend the school closest to her residence which Walter Reed, since it was directly across the street.

Zep pretended to be upset about it, but he was really relieved. He knew he wouldn't be attending school regularly anymore and he feared she might learn the truth about the library visits from other students at his school.

Like always when they talked, time flew by. It wasn't long before Zep realized he needed to get going in order to make it in time to pick up his siblings. But before he left, he wanted to know if Jazmina was seriously giving Tiso another shot.

"So since Jazmina like runnin' her mouth so much, what she been sayin' 'bout my boy?" he inquired.

"Nothin' much. She said the only reason why she might take him back is because you really want her to," Capria said, then changed the subject. "Sometimes I get the feelin' she likes you. Whenever you call she gets all happy then starts actin' all shady when she hand me the phone. Then soon as I hang up, she either don't wanna talk to me or got somethin' bad to say about you. I don't know if she jealous because you bought me them flowers and that teddy bear on the same day Tiso did her dirty, or if she salty I'm takin' up phone time from her. I told her I could get a cell phone if that's the problem, but she said it wasn't."

"I doubt it's the phone. It's prolly 'cause I don't kick it with her like I used to do at school, and when I call she thinks I'll talk to her then, but I don't. Plus, Tiso did do her dirty but the nigga apologized a thousand times and been breakin' her off money and buyin' her clothes and shit. She gotta get off that bullshit and give my man's a serious shot again. Holla at her on that for me," he said, knowing exactly what her problem was.

"Okay, I gotchu and I'ma let Tiso know he better not put his hands on her again."

"Please do," he said, checking the time on his watch. "I gotta get goin'. It's almost time fo' school to let out."

"Can I get a hug and a kiss before you leave?" she shyly requested.

"Capria, from now on you ain't even gotta ask, just take it whenever you feel the need."

"Boy, you so silly."

They hugged and shared an innocent kiss. "I'ma call you tonight," Zep promised. He took one step then paused. "I almost forgot to ask," he said, as he recalled what she said to him when he first walked up. "Who was you talkin' 'bout when you said I know how to keep my word unlike somebody else?"

"I wasn't talkin' 'bout nobody but Tiso. He promised MiMi something and reneged."

He thought for a second then chuckled. "Trust me, fam ain't gonna go back on nothin' he promised her unless he got a damn good reason."

"Yeah, you right. 'Cause he had a real damn good reason," she said all too convincingly.

Zep became intrigued. "I got a minute. Tell me what he promised her and why he reneged."

Shit, I shouldn't have never opened my big mouth, Capria thought. "I-I can't tell you 'cause I promised MiMi I-I wouldn't tell nobody," she stammered.

He studied her face for a second then said, "I can keep a secret but since you don't trust me, it's cool though." He smiled to let her know it wasn't no big deal before walking off. He didn't get halfway down the block when she began calling his name.

"Zep! Zep, wait up!" she yelled and caught up to him. "I been holdin' something back and this ain't how we get down. But you gotta promise me you won't say nothin' to nobody or get mad over what I'm 'bout to tell you."

Zep gave her a look of curiosity then said, "I ain't gonna get mad."

"Promise me you won't say nothin' either," she asked, staring into his eyes.

"I promise," he assured.

Capria took a deep breath and exhaled before she spoke. "Last night, MiMi was on the phone arguing with Tiso because he promised to bring her some money but didn't come through. She wanted to know what he was doin' all day that he couldn't stop by for a couple minutes. So, he told her everything."

"And," Zep said, impatiently.

"And, when she hung up the phone she told me Tiso told her that he couldn't make it because you killed somebody. At first, I thought she was lyin' until she started goin' into all kinds of details and sayin' she could call Tiso and put him on speaker phone if I didn't believe her."

Zep was livid. "No this nigga didn't!" he huffed. He couldn't believe Tiso put his business out in the streets like that. Especially after Rome repeatedly emphasized how important it was for them to keep their mouths shut. Zep was so heated and ready to confront Tiso that he shoved her aside and stormed off. Capria raced up to him and began blocking his path. "Fuck outta my way," he ordered.

"Please, calm down and listen to me," she said, soft-heartedly.

Capria firmly pressed her body against his and began placing tender kisses around his neck area. Despite never having had sex, she was far from being naive to the power of feminine sexuality. She knew how to use her beauty along with a little seduction to gain control over him. Growing up in the projects taught her how to be calculating, shrewd and a temptress. She also had a very personal and keen understanding as to why he was frustrated.

"I know you mad but I got your back. I'ma make damn sure she don't tell nobody else and I'll get them back together. But you gotta keep your promise to me and not say nothin' to Tiso or MiMi," she pleaded, looking into his eyes.

Zep was spellbound by her display of affection and soft, alluring features.

"Dayumm, you lucky you a cutie. I ain't gon' say nothin'," he promised, ogle eyeing her. "Now, let me get up to this school," he added, before stealing a kiss on the lips.

Love was in full bloom. The chemistry between them was undeniable. Capria couldn't stop blushing to save her life. "I was just thinking, I could go with you and walk back with MiMi."

"You sure, 'cause I don't wanna get you in trouble."

"In trouble? Please... My auntie Carla crackhead ass ain't came out here one time to check on me. She too busy smokin' crack. Niq paying her $2,000 a month to let me live here and she told her as long as I get good grades, I'm straight. And even if I got straight F's, please believe, she wouldn't tell Niq or say nothin' to piss me off, 'cause if I move, that's gonna stop her from gettin' that money."

That was all he needed to hear. Zep put his arm around her waist and led the way. The final bell was ringing as they approached the school building. Zep told her to stand at the main entrance because that's where Jazmina usually came out. He then went around to the side door by the parking lot to grab his brother and sister. When he returned to introduce them to Capria, it was obvious Jazmina was pissed by the way she rolled her eyes at him.

Zep looked at her and shook his head in disgust. Then purposely hugged and kissed Capria on her cheek. "Be safe out on them streets," Capria said, unaware of the tension between them. "And don't forget to call me."

"Do I ever," he said then faced Jazmina. He wanted to say something cordial to her, but he was unable to form the right words. His intentions weren't ever to be cruel or hurtful towards her, he simply wanted her to move on from him and accept the fact that Capria was his girl. But, he could see the pain he'd caused etched all over her face.

Jazmina was holding back tears, and her heart was filled with resentment. As much as she loved Zep, choosing someone other than Capria would've been easier to accept. She was sick and tired of being the sacrificial lamb for Capria. First, she was lured and manipulated by Niq to replace Capria for the role of the eleven-year-old incest rape victim. Now, she was being cast aside to play a supporting role while Capria played Cinderella with her Prince Charming. Only none of this was a movie— this was her reality.

Zep noticed she was getting teary-eyed and gave her a half hug. "Don't cry. It just wasn't mean to be. Tiso is like family to me and I really like Capria. You're still my girl, but it's over. Give Tiso another chance, but if you don't I understand," he whispered in her ear.

Jazmina forced a smile. "It's all good and I'ma do that just fo' you," she said half-heartedly.

Zep introduced his brother and sister to Capria, hugged and kissed her, and the two parted ways. As they walked home, Jazmina chatted with Capria as if they were BFFs, all the while praying and plotting on her demise.

Zep walked home thinking about when, where and how he was going to take Capria's virginity. Fifteen minutes later, after seeing his brother and sister in the house safely, he was posted up against a light pole on Emerald, puffing on a blunt, with two jabs, and a fully loaded 9mm. The euphoric feeling from the marijuana and sense of power the gun gave him took his mind to another place and time. . .

All eyes were on Zep as he stood at the center of the three hundred sixty degree surrounded by Black Disciples. They varied in age, but most were shorties, still green and easy to mold. Tiso was there, mean-mugging anyone who dared to break rank. Zep began to walk the inner perimeter of the circle, just as he'd once seen Rome do with such mastery. He made eye contact with each member as he passed.

This was his set. Tiso was his right-hand man and personal security. Capria was his woman, and the envy of every thorough and wannabe nigga in Chicago. His drugs, and only his drugs, were being sold throughout the neighborhood. His wealth and generosity greatly exceeded his predecessor's. And the lengths his young killers were willing to go for him was unmatched. He felt a surge of power flow through his veins as every member attending the meeting looked at him in admiration, eager to hear and follow his commands.

"We finna take this city," he declared. "I'm puttin' niggas on notice. They got 48 hours to flip BD or--"

"Can I get two?"

"Huh?" Zep was jolted out of his daydream. He reached for the 9mm tucked in his waistline but quickly withdrew his hand once he realized he wasn't in danger.

"You working, right?" asked a skinny, zombie-like looking woman. "I want two." She passed him two crumpled up ten dollar bills.

Zep stuffed the money in his pocket and served her two crack rocks.

"I'll suck yo' dick fo' a bag," she said, smiling a mouth full of rotten, yellow teeth.

"I'm straight," Zep declined.

The crackhead placed a hand on her bony hip, stuck out her flat ass and gave Zep what she thought was a sexy once-over. "What about some of this sweet pussy?"

Zep took a step back from her. "I'll pass," he said, with his face twisted up like he'd just bit into something sour.

"Humph, your loss," she said, then walked off, trying her best to throw what little ass she had side-to-side.

"Bitch prolly got AIDS," Zep mumbled.

Shaking his head, he posted back up on the light pole, closed his eyes and allowed his mind to drift back to that place and time where he was "that nigga".

CHAPTER TWENTY

DEA Special Agent Palko and Agent Jenny remained under-cover, living as a married couple across the street from the Jackson's family home. Activity at the residence had all but ceased after Cynthia's murder. Capria hadn't been back since, and Niq showed up once with two fifteen-foot trailer trucks and a six man moving crew in tow. She supervised the crew as they boxed up every item in the house and placed them, along with all the furniture, in the trailers.

Right before the trucks pulled off, she instructed them to put several suitcases and small boxes in the back seat and trunk of her Benz. Witnessing that, Palko had a highway patrol car pull her over to check the contents of the boxes and suitcases which turned out to be nothing but miscellaneous items, and clothes belonging to Capria.

To make matters worse, the next day a real estate agent entered the property. As the realtor was leaving, the two DEA agents approached her with inquiries of purchasing the house and learned it was available as a rental only. This revelation infuriated Palko, even though he knew the odds were low that Niq would continue to live and/or transport drugs in and out of there. To Palko, the investigation was becoming too much of a nuisance, now that he had to find out where Niq was currently laying her head, and stashing her drugs and money at.

Palko's frustrations didn't end there. It had been over two weeks since he'd had the meeting with Rome. To say he was becoming impatient with him for not providing any solid evidence against Niq or his more pressing target, the BD's, would've been an understatement. He believed Rome was trying to stack as much money as possible then go on the run, something he was determined to not let occur.

Against Agent Jenny's wishes, he was planning to draw up an arrest warrant on Rome with charges of possession with intent to distribute two kilos of cocaine, obstruction of justice, and several other related charges.

Just as he was preparing the paperwork for the warrant, Palko received the call he knew would get the investigation moving towards indictments, arrests and convictions.

Rome surprised him as he spoke with a sense of urgency over the phone. He reported the conversation he'd had with Niq, and informed Palko of his upcoming 8 p.m. meeting with her at a restaurant to cop three keys, and get fronted three keys.

Palko arranged for Rome to meet him at the warehouse at 6:00 p.m. to get wired up to record the drug deal. The clock read 5:30 p.m. when Agent Palko poured himself a cup of coffee, grabbed the daily paper, and kicked his feet up on the desk as he waited for Rome to arrive.

Twenty minutes later, Rome appeared at the receptionist's desk.

"Excuse me. My name is Jerome. A few weeks back, I came here to interview for a job and I received a call-back to re-interview today."

Agent Jenny pretended to be pre-occupied with a magazine. "You remember the office where the interview took place?" she asked, never diverting her eyes from the magazine. "Just go back there. And knock first," she added.

Rome remembered exactly where the office was located and went to it. The door to the office had a glass window that allowed him and Palko to clearly see one another.

Still, Palko waited for him to knock, then only after he sipped his-coffee and finished the article he was reading, did he acknowledge his presence. He tossed the newspaper on the empty chair then motioned for him to come in and have a seat.

Rome picked up the newspaper. "What you want me to do wit this?" he asked, holding it over the waste basket next to Palko's desk.

"The only thing in this office I consider trash is you," Palko sneered, "And I'm the only person with authority to ask questions. You answer questions and do as you're told. Now, park your ass in that chair, turn to page sixty-seven and explain to me what the fuck is going on."

The prideful, egotistical and authoritative swagger Rome possessed vanished while in the presence of Agent Palko. He showed no signs of contempt as he complied with his orders. He turned to the page and immediately knew the article Palko was referring to once he read the caption, 'GANG WAR CLAIMS ANOTHER LIFE' followed by a picture of the victim.

After reading the two paragraphs that stated far less than what he already knew, Rome folded the newspaper and passed it to Palko. "I'm already on top of that," he stated like it was no big deal. "I got wind of it this mornin' but since I had to handle this bidness wit' Niq, I wasn't able to hit the streets and get the full low-down. But as soon as I know sump'n, you'll know sump'n."

Being the seasoned interrogator he was, Palko carefully watched every movement and twitch Rome made when he read the article, and as he spoke. No obvious bells went off alerting him that he was lying, but this new cooperative Rome seemed too good to be true. Years of experience had taught Palko it was normal for a C.I. to be vague, deceitful and in extreme cases, hostile. Especially, once they became fully cognizant to the reality that due to their acts of betrayal, lengthy prison sentences would be given to the people they considered to be friends and family members. Even carrying this guilt, almost all informants stuck to their end of the deal to save their own ass.

However, on the flip side, there were rare cases where once reluctant C.I.'s., turned into overzealous C.I.'s. Usually, their eagerness could be attributed to fear or hatred towards the people they were snitching on, or a strong desire to be freed from the criminal lifestyle they were living. But, the most common reason was due to elevated levels of a morphine-like protein found in the brain called endorphins. The brain automatically releases high doses of endorphins when a person feels physical pain, excitement or euphoria.

Palko knew that covert operations tended to generate excitement and euphoria in most people. And it didn't go unnoticed by him when Rome took over the peg-board and began correcting and volunteering names, ranks and sets of BD's that were incorrect, or not represented at their first meeting. He also heard the enthusiasm in his voice when he called to relay the information about the drug buy. Considering Rome's attitude when they'd first met and his recent behavior, Palko figured this could be the classic case of the reluctant C.I. turned overzealous C.I. But before they went any further, he needed to know exactly what sparked his sudden willingness to cooperate.

"Would you like a cup of coffee or water?" Palko offered.

"Water would be cool," he accepted.

"Be back in a jiffy," Palko said as he rose from his chair and left the room. Two minutes later, he returned. "Just got it out the vending machine, so it's nice and cold," he said, purposely being courteous.

Palko watched as Rome gulped down half the bottle then sat it on his desk. "My fault." Rome apologized. "Lemme get that," he said, as he took the water bottle back.

"Don't worry about it. You can set the bottle there," Palko replied. "Look, we're both men here, so ain't no sense in beating around the bush. I've been doing this a mighty long time and I know bullshit when I see or hear it. In our first meeting, what I saw and heard from you was bullshit, and when you bullshit me, I bullshit you. Today, what I see and hear is somebody that's not about bullshit, and I'm dying to hear from the horse's mouth what happened that got us off the bullshit."

Rome swallowed hard before answering. "If I could do it over again, I would man-up and take the case. I had every intention of doing so until the detective that caught me took me to Agent Bochello. The deal Agent Bochello offered me was too good to turn down. He told me if I gave him the name of the person I cop from, he would instantly make one brick disappear. I agreed and he got excited after he looked her up on his computer and promised me if I delivered Niq to him, I could walk with the two bricks.

He also said I would never have to testify in court, my name wouldn't be associated with the case, and as long as the investigation was pending, I could hustle without worrying about a Fed case. On top of that, he said I could keep all the money I made, and our dealings would stick strictly to Niq and nothing else. I mean, damn, I was just busted with two bricks, so I went along with the deal like any other nigga would've."

Rome drank the rest of the water and tossed the empty bottle in the trash. "Then I got a call thinking its Bochello tellin' me to get to the warehouse and when I get there, it's you. Since Bochello was the only person I was s'pose to work with, as soon as I seen your face, I thought about sayin' fuck it, arrest me for the two bricks, especially since I knew you ain't have the two keys. But--"

"Oh, that's what you thought," Palko interrupted. Bochello kept the two kilos they confiscated from you and gave you two different ones. I ain't mean to cut you off, but thought I'd just let you know that. Now, please continue what you were saying."

Rome resumed. "Once you got me on video implicating Fu-Fu for Ronnie's murder, I pretty much knew I fucked up big time. I violated the most sacred law--the code of silence--and if anybody ever finds out 'bout that, I'ma dead man. Even if I never would've said shit about Fu-Fu or the guys and kept it straight about Niq, they'd still kill me and don't none of them know the bitch. So, I made peace wit' myself and said I gotta do what I gotta do."

Satisfied with his explanation, Agent Palko looked up at the clock on the wall. "You made a wise decision and had you not called me today, you would've been arrested and exposed. The same deal is pretty much in place, but the only difference is you have to hand over the Black Disciple leadership and take the stand against them. Don't feel bad because by the time that happens, you won't be the only one doing it, but you will be the only one walking away completely scot-free with bags full of cash. In the meantime, I want the names of those little gang-bangers responsible for the recent murders in your territory. And we've got fifteen minutes for me to put this wire on you, and for us to go over how you plan to record this drug deal without incident."

Rome was ready, willing, and prepared to take Niq and the leaders of the BD's down; a gang he represented and also held a position of authority in. However, snitching on lil' folks was out of the question as far as he was concerned. He had been grooming them since they were knee-high to obey his every command, and they worshipped the ground he walked on. Any time Rome was in their presence, it was impossible for him not to notice the reverence they bestowed upon him. In a street mentality frame of mind, Rome believed they were his children and it was his job to nurture and protect them against all enemies, including the law. Under no circumstances would he give any of them up, yet he knew he could never let Palko know that.

After spending some time going over what to do in case of emergency, Palko began taping the wire to his body. In the process, Rome assured him that he was a team player and had everything under control before heading out to meet Niq.

***

Forty-five minutes later, Rome was driving 5mph on Ohio Street in downtown Chicago in search of a popular restaurant named Houston's. Niq always picked where and when their drug transactions would take place. She never used the same location more than once within a six month period, and the exchange was handled differently at each location.

Rome had copped from her several times before but this was the first time she had him meet her at this restaurant. After locating the eatery, he noticed they had valet parking and wondered why she would prearrange for the exchange to go down at such a nice establishment. Nevertheless, he drove up to the front entrance and allowed the valet attendant to take possession of his car which held $108,000 in the trunk.

Houston's wasn't packed, but all the patrons were Caucasian and dressed in formal clothing. Rome was wearing blue Pelle-Pelle denim jeans, a black Pelle T-shirt with a lion head stitched onto the front, a Marc Buchannan lambskin jacket, and some all white Nike AirMax sneakers. He felt out of place as the hostess escorted him to the rear of the restaurant where Niq had reserved a booth for them.

Ten minutes later, Niq was ushered to the booth. He stood up and greeted her with a friendly hug and kiss on the cheek.

"I see you lookin' fine as usual," he complimented, while holding her hand up in the air for her to spin around. She obliged, giving him a full three-sixty view of herself.

Niq was wearing a black form-fitting strapless jewel and sequin embellished Prada cocktail dress. Her silky jet-black hair was pinned back and cascaded down to her back. Due to her blemish-free toffee skin complexion, she didn't need to wear make-up. However, the moderately applied eye-shadow and lipstick highlighted her neatly arched eyebrows, doe-eyes, long lashes and full lips. The VVS Tiffany's diamond necklace and dangling earrings she wore sparkled flawlessly, enhancing her beauty. But the jewel-studded Jimmy Choo stilettos and matching bag is what had her looking like she'd been ripped off the cover of Vogue.

"You know how us thoroughbred bitches do it," she bragged, before taking a seat in the booth.

Niq was about to pay him a compliment on his attire until she really noticed what he had on. *Simple-ass nigga! Ain't never been nowhere,* she thought. Niq figured bringing to his attention that he wasn't dressed properly wouldn't have amounted to anything, so she let it be.

The waiter approached, filled their glasses with water and asked if they were ready to order. Niq ordered shrimp scampi and a bottle of Zinfandel. Rome skimmed through the menu and decided to go with the Hawaiian style fillet mignon, medium-well, grilled asparagus topped with parmesan, and a stuffed potato. The waiter jotted down their orders and took off.

"Goddamn, I was happy you got up wit' me when you did," Rome said, as soon as the waiter was out of earshot. "Fo' a second, I thought I was gonna hafta find me a new connect.

"Nah, I just had to tie up a few loose ends and tend to some unexpected family bizness. Everything's in order and I'm back down. So, tell me, what's been up wit' you?"

"Bidness-wise, shit couldn't be betta. I got rid of them six bricks in record time. You gota be gettin' them joints straight off the boat 'cause they ain't been stepped on. I cook up 45 to 50 zones off each one. By next month, I expect to be movin' a brick-a-day in bags, and that's counting the extra zones. Shit been movin' so fast, I wanted to cop two more keys but you rushed a nigga off the phone. So next re-up, I'ma grab five keys and you gon' front me five, right?"

Niq disregarded his business pitch and moved on to an issue she believed he should be directing more attention towards. "What's this war between y'all and the GD's about? The stupid shit is all over the news. Shouldn't yo' number one priority be setting up peace treaty talks?" she said matter-of-factly.

"Yeah, in a perfect world, that would be ideal. But niggas ain't tryna hear that shit. It's only so much I can do and I'm doing all I can," Rome lied.

"Well, Minister Rome, you need to be doin' a helluva lot more. The last thing I need is the Feds to open up an investigation on you 'cause of a stupid ass gang war and end up at my doorsteps. I suggest you do any and everything to squash that shit, or you *will* need to look fo' a new connect," Niq threatened.

Rome noticed the waiter approaching with their food and took that as an opportunity to lighten the mood. "I feel where you comin' from and I promise I'ma be a man and take care of home. I love you wit' all my heart and I don't want our marriage to end over sump'n as petty as that."

"What--" Niq was interrupted by the waiter.

"Shrimp scampi for you, ma'am, and fillet mignon for you, sir," he said, placing their plates on the table. He poured each a glass of wine before departing.

Neither of them spoke on the war or drugs while they ate. They raved about how delicious the food tasted. They discussed which clubs were jumping, what new music was hot, and the type of cars they planned on flossing in the upcoming year. Niq even cracked a few jokes about how he dressed like a thug and offered to help him pick out a more suitable wardrobe the next time he went shopping. Rome knew she had a sense of style and figured spending some quality time with her might land him a shot of pussy, so he accepted.

Just as Niq was fishing through her plate for the last shrimp, her cell phone began ringing. She reached over and retrieved the phone from her purse.

"Everthang's all taken care of," a female voice spoke then hung up.

Niq placed the phone back in her purse and finished off the shrimp. She looked over at his plate and noticed the only thing left was the skins from the potato.

"Damn, nigga, you really ain't been nowhere," Niq said, shaking her head. "Not only do you show up dressed like that, but you licked the plate clean too. You on point as a hustla, but its still a lotta shit you need to learn and experience."

"Whatchu talkin' 'bout?" he asked, clueless.

"Fa'get it," Niq replied. Her eyes drifted to her purse and the White Owl cigar sticking out caught her attention. She scanned the place to make sure nobody was looking then took the cigar out, along with a sandwich bag containing a half-ounce of purple haze." Could you do me a favor and twist me up a blunt?" she asked.

Rome placed the weed on his lap, took the cigar out the plastic wrapper, ran his tongue down the length of it, and began splitting the cigar down the middle, using both his thumbs. He dumped the tobacco on his plate then put the cigar paper in his mouth, getting both sides moist with his saliva. Next, he began filling the center with the high-grade marijuana.

"I been chiefin' my whole life, so I know good shit when I see it," he said, as he lifted the 'purple' to his nose and inhaled. "And this shit fi'yah! I didn't know you was a weed connoisseur."

"Every blue moon, I'll smoke a blunt or two. But I don't make it no habit," she told him.

He made sure a sizeable amount of weed was in the center before spreading it out evenly. Then he folded the cigar paper over and sealed it shut with his mouth. Niq took the plastic wrapper the cigar was in off his plate and stuck the blunt inside it.

"The rest of that be you," Niq said, as she put the blunt in her purse.

"Good lookin'," Rome stuffed the purple haze in his pants pocket. "So, how we s'pose to do this? I don't see you wit' nothin' and I got the paper in my trunk."

"Oh, that's been taken care of. I replaced the money wit' the work," Niq informed him.

"How you do that?"

Before Niq could answer, the waiter reappeared with the bill. Without checking how much she owed, Niq placed ten hundred dollar bills in the binder that held the bill. The waiter cleared the table, thanked Niq and left with the money.

"Like I was sayin', how you--" Rome's sentence was cut short by Niq's hand gesturing for him to drop the question.

"Next time I call you, you should have $144,000. That'll be what you owe me plus the money fo' five bricks. I'ma front you the other five and that'll put you $90,000 in the red.

It's been a pleasure and my treat. Gimme five minutes before you leave," Niq said, as she stood up. She took two steps, turned on her heels and added," I'm dead serious 'bout that peace treaty too. Gang-bangin' and gettin' money don't mix. I'm pretty sure you ain't doin' no shootin', but at the end of the day, you callin' the shots. I would hate fo' us to end up in divorce court or worse, Federal Court, due to some bullshit gang beef."

Niq sauntered out of Houston's with the feeling of sweet success. She had collected over a hundred grand and unloaded six kilo's without touching the money or drugs. Then simply by having Rome roll her a blunt, she secured the final DNA sample she believed needed to be tested. As far as her eyes could see, everything went exactly how she'd planned it. But success couldn't have been further from the truth. What Niq needed was X-ray vision to see the truth concealed beneath Rome's shirt. And the truth would've revealed that, she was officially fucked.

Rome had secretly recorded the first drug transaction the Feds would use to build a case against her. And although she may have gathered DNA samples from everybody who copped from her, as well as a few male admirers, gangbangers, killers and stick-up artists, Niq would soon find out that learning the identity of her mother's killer wouldn't come easy— not one sample would prove to be a match.

CHAPTER TWENTY-ONE

Three months later...
Saturday, January 1, 2000
12:00 a.m.

"5-4-3-2-1 HAPPY NEW YEAR!" Everybody inside the Taste roared joyously. Immediately, the club-goers began to toast and French kiss the closest person of the opposite sex in celebration of the New Year.

The Taste was located on 63rd & Lowe, exactly one block over from the Englewood Terrace building. The one-level club/lounge was a far cry from one of the city's elite night spots, but kept steady clientele because it was a popular hang-out of the BD's. Tonight was proof of that point.

The place was jammed-packed with members of the gang. Rome rented the club and bought out the bar to party with his entire set. All BD's were admitted regardless of age and given a bottle of Moet upon entering the club. The temperature outside was a deep-freezing 20° below zero. But that didn't stop females from lining up around the block to get in, and for good reason too. In addition to the free admission and drinks, Rome gave every female that gained entry inside a crispy hundred dollar bill.

Lost in his own thoughts, Rome stood in the center of the club with two dime-pieces attached to each arm. He couldn't get enough of all the smiling faces cheesing at him. He felt like a king being celebrated by his loyal subjects. And thanks to Niq, he looked the part as well, regal. Rome had on a black two-piece tailored Italian-cut Armani suit, a royal-blue Ferragamo shirt and some black/blue Mauri gators. His ears adorned two golf-ball sized diamond studs and on his left wrist rest a platinum, Presidential Rolex.

Rome's dates were two exotic, multi-racial, scantily clad beauties that looked like they'd walked off a Paris runway, boarded a flight and came straight to the club. They tugged on his arms, snapping him out of his reverie.

Gaining his attention the women engaged him in an overtly sexual three-way kiss. Everybody started applauding and cheering the trio on.

The DJ drew laughter from the crowd when over the mic, he joked, "Fo' Christ's sake! This is a club, not a hotel. Get a room!"

Things had been going great for Rome since he'd recorded the drug deal. Just as he'd planned, all his workers ditched school regularly to meet his quota and bust guns in the frigid cold weather. Together, his rock spots moved over a brick-a-day, he sold another two bricks a week in weight, and he never put forth any effort to get a peace treaty. In fact, he encouraged his set to step up their attacks. Both gangs were experiencing casualties but it didn't faze Rome because none of his main soldiers were killed or arrested.

Contrary to Niq's philosophy, gangbanging and getting money seemed to be working just fine to him. Still, she stayed on his case about ending the war. She seriously considered making good on her threat to end their business relationship but greed wouldn't allow her to. The last time Rome re-upped, he purchased twenty-five kilos.

Agent Palko's patience with Rome was wearing thinner than Niq's. Bodies were piling up on the south side and Rome had yet to name one person responsible. Only when a BD fell victim did he offer up a rival's name, and he still hadn't provided a shred of evidence against the gang's leadership. What was keeping Agent Palko at bay from arresting him was that he was fully cooperating with the investigation against Niq.

Now, armed with more than enough evidence to send Niq to prison for life, he was ready to submit everything to the A.G.'s office and have them both indicted, but he was stopped by his partner, Agent Jenny.

Agent Jenny had finally come around to agreeing with his idea of casting a wider net the moment she realized the amount of drugs Niq was pushing. She suggested that he should make Rome supply high-ranking BD's with keys, record it all on the wire and indict everybody on a CCE (Continuing Criminal Enterprise). Niq would be charged with supplying the gang with hundreds of kilos and have no choice but to roll over on her connect, if she ever wanted to see daylight again.

The problem was everything hinged on Rome's willingness to go against his own, and, thus far, he'd been all talk and little action. So, they agreed that after two weeks, if Rome failed to comply with Palko's orders, they would arrest him and Niq and proceed with plan B, which consisted of making Niq flip on the other people she supplied, and most importantly, her connect.

As soon as Rome broke away from the kiss, the DJ spoke again. "Rome, why don't you bless us wit' a few words."

Flanked by two beautiful women, the crowd parted like the Red Sea as Rome made his way over to the DJ booth. "Y'all muthafuckas know what it is! BD or be dead!" he bellowed into the mic.

That outburst sparked niggas and some women to flag the trays and echo the statement. Close to five minutes lapsed before the frenzy settled.

Rome continued, "I put this together not just to celebrate the new year, but to commend y'all fo' the sacrifice, dedication, and determination each and every one of you niggas put in daily fo' this thang we all love, honor and respect, The Black Disciple Nation. We've made some positive strides over the past year. Our numbers have grown tremendously and I've made it possible fo' everybody to eat. Sadly, we've lost a few soldiers along the way. So, as a nation, our new year's resolution is to continue building on the positive and to remain vigorous in defending the honor of our fallen brethren. Every nigga in here knows exactly what needs to be done in order to fulfill this resolution. Y'all was born and bred fo' this shit. But tonight, let's party 'cause tomorrow its back to bidness. BD!" he shouted.

The DJ dropped the needle on the record and the dance floor came to life as the old house track, *I wanna Fuck U in the Azz* by the Jungle Brothers blared throughout the club. The up-tempo hypnotic beat and sexually charged lyrics had the women bouncing, shaking and winding their hips, titties and asses all over the men. The men matched the women's intensity and rhythm by grinding and thrusting their bodies right back at them. It looked like a synchronized, fast-paced wild orgy was going down on the dance floor!

Rome hadn't completely gotten out of the booth before Chop informed him that Fu-Fu was in the parking lot waiting to speak with him. He left the two women standing there, grabbed a few guys for security and headed out back to holler at the top B.M.

When Rome and his crew got within six feet of Fu-Fu's all black bullet-proof conversion van, Blimp emerged from the driver's seat. The charcoal black, bald-headed, six-foot ten, three-hundred and fifty pound behemoth was Fu-Fu-'s driver and personal security.

"The rest of y'all can hold up right there. He only wanna talk to Rome," he ordered in a husky drawl.

Blimp slid the side door open, allowing Rome to jump in, closed it, and stood guard. Rome took a seat adjacent to Fu-Fu.

Unlike his big status and street rep, Fu-Fu was small in stature, standing just five-foot six and weighing one-hundred thirty pounds. His even brown skin complexion, no facial hair, and one against the grain haircut, made him appear much younger than his forty year age. Wearing dress slacks, a long sleeve shirt and tie, he looked more like he sat on the board of directors for a Fortune 500 company instead of a ruthless street gang.

Never the one to hold his tongue, Fu-Fu spoke his mind. "No need to get comfortable, this will be brief," he said, as he lit fire to a cigar. "You seem to be doin' quite well. So well, you decided to take it upon yourself to end our business arrangement."

"It-it ain't even like-like that. I-I did find somebody wit-uhmmm-wit' cheaper prices- and it was my understanding that it was f-free enterprise fo' everybody wit' authority as long as we paid homage to you. I-I been kickin' up ten-ten stacks to you every week. Don't-uhmm-please don't t-t-tell me you ain't been gettin' it," Rome stuttered.

Fu-Fu took a pull of his cigar then blew three smoke rings. "Yeah, I been gettin' it. But my intel tells me it's short money. So, here's the deal. $25,000 a week," he stated curtly. Next, he tapped on the window, signaling Blimp to open the door, "Oh, I almost forgot," he said as Rome was exiting the van. "Don't party too late 'cause I'm callin' a heads-only session today. Be at my auto shop at 12:00 p.m., sharp."

Needless to say, Rome was hot. Fu-Fu's request was non-negotiable. It was pay up or shut down. *After all the years I done put in fo' this nigga, this is how he treats me. Mutha-fucka, I got a trick fo' yo' ass,* Rome thought to himself.

CHAPTER TWENTY-TWO

Rome had spent the last hour circling Fu-Fu's Auto Body, Sounds and Rims shop in a rented Toyota Camry. He wanted to get a good look at everyone attending the meeting to see if they were being searched. So far, the only people he had seen coming and going were employees and customers. He glanced at the clock on the dashboard and it read 11:55 a.m. Figuring the meeting must have been canceled, he wanted to leave. But since he wasn't informed, had to pay his weekly tax, he decided to dip in. He parked a half-block down, retrieved the manila envelope out of the passenger seat, and headed down to the auto shop.

Nervously, he walked through the front door. As he approached the cashier, Blimp emerged from a door behind the counter and waved him over. They walked down a small hallway to another door which led down to the basement. Voices of several men chatting could be heard as they descended down the stairs. Rome began to sweat, profusely.

He thought about bolting out the way he'd come in, but knew he had zero odds of making it past Blimp. Once his presence came into view of the other men, they simultaneously stopped talking and focused their attention on him.

"Principled, initiative, motivational and punctual are all character-istics of a great leader," Fu-Fu said, as he relieved Rome of the manila envelope containing his $25,000. "It's also an acronym for PIMP, which I just so happen to be," he added, chuckling at his own humor. "But today ain't about me, it's all about you. I don't think nobody here needs an introduction, but just in case, that's Big D, Gene, Craig, Milk-man, and of course, I'm the one and only, Fu-Fu," he said, pointing to each man as he called out their name.

Consumed with fear, Rome stood frozen in the middle of the spa-cious, Chicago sports team decorated, auto shop's basement. He was in the company of the five most powerful BD's on the streets. Each held the rank of Board member and controlled large areas of land that consisted of several different sets and thousands of members.

Born and raised in the Robert Taylor Housing Projects, thirty-two-year-old Gene came from a long line of Black Disciple members. He inherited his position from his father who was serving a life sentence for a triple murder. He ran the section of the city known as the Low-End, which began on 51st & State Street and stretched all the way to downtown Chicago.

Most of the south side projects were under his command: The Robert Taylor's, Hillion's, Ida B. Wells, Stateway, Dearborn's and the Ickies. Geno was beloved by BD's everywhere because he didn't allow his authority to dictate his actions. Since a young teenager, he was a gangbanger and his main target was the GD's. At war time, before and after receiving his BM slot, he would bust his guns right alongside his foot soldiers.

At fifty-five, Craig was the oldest Board member and one of the few relevant members that could honestly make the claim of having personally known King David; he controlled the entire west side, north side and all the surrounding suburbs. Being from the old-school, he didn't agree with the black-on-black violence, drug dealing and overall destruction of the black community, the BD's and other street gangs were responsible for. However, he learned that the ways of the old was dead and people who couldn't accept that fact met the same fate. So, he kept a low profile and allowed the ministers he appointed to pay him taxes and run their sets pretty much as they pleased.

Twenty-three-year-old, ex-collegiate basketball star, and Fu-Fu's nephew, Milkman was the youngest and the most recent Board member. After just one stellar season at the University of Illinois, he lost his scholarship after coming home for summer vacation and catching a gang-related murder charge. A year later, he beat the case but his career was over. Charismatic, book smart, street-smart and driven, Milkman attacked the streets with the same enthusiasm and determination as he did the basketball court.   The fact that he was Fu-Fu's favorite nephew provided him with an unlimited supply of drugs, guns and most importantly, a birth-right entitlement.

In no time, every BD on the east side was singing his praises. Fu-Fu figured there was no sense in delaying the inevitable and used his influence to have Milkman appointed as a Board member, despite his age and never having held a position of authority.

Standing six-foot four and weighing over four-hundred pounds, Big D was the most imposing of them all. He ruled with fear, using intimidation and manipulation tactics, and when that didn't work a bullet to the back of the head. He controlled the Wild Hundreds, which began at the 100th block in Chicago, and reached as far back to the suburbs of Calumet City, Dalton, Harvey, Chicago Heights, and beyond.

"What, you just gon' stand there sweating like a Hebrew slave?" Big D stated. "Show a nigga some love. The last time I seen you, you was hiding behind a casket!"

"Oh, I'm trippin'," Rome said with a weak smile. "I'm just a little shocked to be called to a session wit all B.M.'s."

"Well, you can relax 'cause we got some good news for you. All five of us unanimously voted to promote you to a Board member. Since my job is to oversee the entire organization, I will tender the entire Englewood area over to you. Of course, you'll have to continue paying me $25,000 a week, and as your income increases, so will my cut. Now, the only question is, do you accept?" Fu-Fu asked.

Rome couldn't believe his ears, "I do!"

"We don't need to explain to you how to run your area. You're already doing a fine job at that except for one thing, which we'll get to in a minute. You know law, and as long as you stay within the confines of the law, you will be straight. The seven of us will meet up whenever the situation calls for us to do so. We vote on issues and only I have the power to veto. And that's because I not only speak for myself but for the King as well. Once something is agreed upon or ordered from the top, it becomes law. Today, two important votes took place. The first was to promote you, and the other was concerning the one blip on your resume. Some police officers and city officials on my payroll have been stressing to me that this war needs to end. We're in an election year and the mayor and D.A. are planning on coming down hard on violent crime. So, your first assignment as a B.M. is to orchestrate and maintain a peace treaty with the GD's," Fu-Fu instructed him. "I've already spoken to their top B.M. and he's on the same page as us. The heart of the war is being waged in Englewood and the Low End. So, it's imperative that you sit down with G-Mel, and Gene is gonna do the same with their B.M. for the Low End."

Although Rome wanted to protest, he knew he didn't have any choice but to follow orders. Fu-Fu made him call G-Mel, the B.M. in

Englewood for the GD's, and they arranged to meet at his pool hall on 69ᵗʰ & Racine. After the call ended, Rome assured them that he would get the job done and was escorted out by Blimp.

When Rome stepped foot outside he let out a huge sigh of relief. He couldn't get to the safe confines of his car fast enough. He snatched open the door, hopped in, locked it and checked to make sure he recorded the meeting. "Yeah, betcha won't be pimpin' much longer," Rome said to himself.

As he pulled off into traffic, he called Chop. "What's the bidness, fam?" Chop answered.

"My nigga, you ain't gon' believe this shit. All the B.M.'s voted to strip me of my slot then ordered me to get a peace treaty."

"So who callin' it fo' the set if you ain't, and why they ain't order that nigga to get a peace treaty?" Chop asked heated.

"Shid, the only other nigga qualified got the minno slot and he going wit' me to sit down at the table and holla at them niggas."

"And who the fuck is that?" Chop asked, incredulously.

"You," Rome informed him.

"Says who? Fu? Ain't nobody told me or asked me shit!"

"Nigga, Fu ain't said shit, I said it!"

"A'ight, now you really fuckin' wit' my head. You need to explain what the fuck is goin' on 'cause you trippin' right now."

"Chop, read between the lines. I'm the B.M. for the whole E-dub and I'm givin' you my old slot."

"That's what's up! It's 'bout time they recognized all the contributions you make towards this thang.   You know I'm wit' whatever, and I'ma hold you down to the fullest," Chop pledged. "Now, what's up wit' this peace treaty bullshit?"

Rome inhaled and exhaled deeply. "Ain't no gettin' around it. I already spoke to G-Mel and he waitin' on us to arrive at his pool hall. I'll be pullin' up to the 7000 building to scoop you in a few minutes."

"Like I said, it's whatever. I'll be out front. Trays."

"Trays," Rome reciprocated before ending the call. He dialed another number. The phone barely rang once before it was answered.

"You couldn't have called at a better time. I was just about to touch bases with you. But since you beat me to it, what's on your mind?" Agent Palko asked.

"I got some good news fo' ya," Rome relayed the events leading up to the phone call.   And what he had to say had Agent Palko beyond ecstatic. He was happier than a sissy with a bag of dicks! After listening to the recording over the phone, he realized that what he managed to get wasn't overwhelming evidence. But it was a start, and now that Rome was a B.M. the opportunities to obtain more incriminating evidence was sure to present itself. The added bonus of possibly nabbing crooked police officers and city officials had Palko salivating.

The two kicked it like best friends until Rome pulled up to the curb of the 7000 building. "A'ight, I'ma slide through tonight and holla at ya," Rome said, ending the call as Chop jumped in the passenger seat.

Chop caught his last line and inquired, "Who was that?"

"One of the freak bitches I had at the party last night sweatin' a nigga," Rome lied then pulled off and changed the conversation. "As much as I want to kill every GD in the city, ending this war might not be such a bad idea. We been takin' just as many hits as them, plus we lose money every time somebody get shot 'cause we hafta shut down the spots."

"You right about that," Chop said, nodding his head in agreement.

"But niggas got the game fucked up if they think fo' one second I'ma agree to a peace treaty without the nigga responsible fa' killin' Slickem gettin' touched. That was my nigga and then they further disrespected him, and this mob, by shootin' up his funeral and killin' Cremey," Rome lamented.

"I feel you on that but them niggas ain't gonna hand over one of their own just like that. The minute you start demanding some retribution, they gonna get to bringing up all the shit we did to them and expect some blood as well."

Rome drove into the pool hall's parking lot and was promptly greeted by a group of teenagers who all, but one, shot cold stares at them. As they exited the car, the teen that didn't seem to hold any grudges against them led them inside.

"Congratulations on gettin' bumped up," G-Mel said, as he extended his hand to Rome. The two showed each other some love by mixing their perspective gang's handshakes into one. He then turned to Chop. "I guess it's Minister Chop," he said before shaking up with him. "I don't wanna get down to serious bidness until Spank gets here 'cause he's the Governor for this area. I just hung up wit' him and he's on the way. In the meantime, let's have a few drinks."

G-Mel led them over to the bar where they engaged in small talk over shots of Hennessey. This was the first time in years Rome and G-Mel were in the same room or spoke words directly to one another. Back in the days, they attended Robeson High School together. They laughed about the gang fights they had and reminisced about the females they were both sexing at the time. The alcohol and memories lightened the mood. And when the conversation shifted towards the present, all three men agreed that a peace treaty would be best for both sides.

Just when everything was moving along smoothly, Spank walked in. He shook up with Rome and Chop but it was evident by his gruff demeanor that the gesture was done solely as a formality.

Spank downed the shot of Henny G-Mel poured him and cut straight to the chase. "Personally, I don't give a fuck about no peace treaty. You niggas been creepin' through like a bunch of cowards, shootin' up our blocks and now that we bringin' heat to you niggas, and you realize y'all can't fuck wit' us, you wanna tuck ya' tail. Convince me why I should even consider this bullshit," Spank spat.

"Nigga you must've fa'got who the fuck I am," Chop growled, reaching into his waistband. "I'll leave yo' ass right here," he finished, as he aimed a Glock 9mm in Spank's face.

"Do it, nigga!" Spank challenged. "And I promise, you or this nigga wit' you, won't make it outta here alive!"

"Whoa… Whoa... Everybody just calm down. We're all men here and we came together to iron out our differences through diplomacy. Outta respect and a mutual understanding that we're all on the same page, I made sure y'all had safe passage into my pool hall without getting searched. All this bang, bang, rah, rah shoot 'em up shit ain't gon' happen up in here. This meeting was ordered by people higher up than the four of us, and I'm sure they won't take kindly to this behavior," G-Mel reasoned.

The reality of what G-Mel was saying resonated with Rome. "Put the gun away," he ordered. Chop kept his eyes glued to Spank as he tucked it back in his waistband. "I apologize fo' that but..."

G-Mel waved him off. "No need to apologize, Spank was outta order for that ignorant outburst. Let's fa'get that happened and get to the reason why we're here."

He continued. "Like we were saying before Spank came in with the negative energy, ain't nothin' good comin' from this war. Good niggas dyin' young, innocent bystanders gettin' shot, and we losing money. Here's the bottom line. If y'all can give your word that your guys will stand down, then I can guarantee that we'll do the same. I don't expect these young trigga' happy niggas to be completely on board with a peace treaty after all that's taken place, but if the four of us are united and committed to making this work, then I don't see why it can't happen," G-Mel concluded.

"True dat, true dat," Rome agreed, "But it's gonna take a little bit more to really make this work. Sump'n gonna hafta be agreed upon as far as consequences and repercussions go for anybody who chooses to go against the peace treaty. That way, the four of us know that everybody here is genuine and whatever violations are given to those who choose to be insubordinate, will serve as a deterrent to anybody else that wanna go against the grain."

"So, what are you suggesting?" G-Mel asked.

"I don't know, let's see what they got to say," Rome said, tilting his head in the direction of Chop and Spank, who were still engaged in a stare down.

"A eye fo' a eye," Spank said.

"And a tooth fo' a tooth," Chop finished, neither man looking away from the other.

"Then it's settled. If any of my guys are responsible for any harm to your guys, the four of us will come together, identify the guilty person, and see to it that they get issued the same treatment they issued out and vice-versa," G-Mel said.

Rome nodded his head in agreement. He figured since G-Mel was going along with everything so easily, now was the best time to get what he really wanted.

"I'm wit' it, but before I can take this back to my guys, as a show of good faith, I think it's only right that whoever killed Slickem, shot up his funeral and killed his mother, get his issue."

"You bitch ass nigga!" Spank roared. All hell broke loose as he jumped out his seat and went after Rome. G-Mel dived over the bar and tackled Spank before he could get to him. The loud commotion caused the young goons to burst through the door with guns drawn. Chop immediately pulled out his 9mm.

"Don't shoot!" G-Mel and Rome shouted, simultaneously.

Rome slowly rose from his seat with both arms up in surrender. He positioned himself in front of Chop, blocking his line of fire, which put the young thugs at ease. Several of them rushed over to help G-Mel and Spank to their feet.

"You sho' everything straight up in here?" the youngster who led Chop and Rome inside asked.

"It's just a minor misunderstanding. Y'all can go back outside and post up," G-Mel assured him. "And, Marco, make sure don't nobody come in here unless I say so."

They filed out, and as soon as the door closed, Spank was first to speak his mind. "The nerve of this nigga to come up in here demanding we kill one of ours for some shit that already happened! I done murked niggas fo' way lesser shit than the stunts these niggas pulled in here today."

"Pipe down and let me handle this," G-Mel said in a calm tone.

"I was in the mind frame of letting bygones be bygones, but obviously you feel some kinda way about that situation, and understandably so. I can vividly recall a few months back when I was comin' outta one of my houses, surrounded by thirty of my men and somebody shouted 'BD' then started shooting. In the process, one of my favorite lil' niggas lost his life shielding me from the bullets. I was told a young nigga who works for you named Tiso was the shooter. So, if you're willing to hand him over, then I don't have a problem returning the favor."

That statement caused Chop and Spank to end their stare down and turn it towards their bosses. G-Mel shot an icy glare at Spank, prompting him to keep quiet. At the same time, Rome gave a similar look to Chop.

Complete silence filled the room for what seemed like an eternity, but in reality, was a mere few seconds before Rome spoke, "I don't know where you been gettin' yo' info from but I can assure you Tiso ain't do that shit," he flat-out lied.

G-Mel and Rome spent twenty minutes debating back and forth about whom was responsible for both shootings, before each man was satisfied with who the other claimed pulled the trigger.

Finally, the meeting ended with a deadly handshake agreement between them.

***

Twelve hours later, after smoking a half-ounce of dro and drinking a fifth of Remy to the head, Chop was wasted. High, drunk, sleepy and feeling guilty for the act he was en route to commit, he was in no condition to be driving. The Camry swerved as he pulled up to the alley. "What you just gon' stand there lookin' stupid?" Chop slurred.

"B, you sho' you don't want me to drive?" Fatz asked, as he opened the passenger door.

"Nigga, hurry up an' hop yo' fat ass in befo' somebody spot us!"

Chop floored the gas pedal. He made a sharp right into on-going traffic, prompting Fatz to brace himself by placing both hands on the dashboard. "Fuck!" he cried out. "Before you kill a nigga, can you at least tell me why we secretly meetin' in the alley at two in the morning? Red light!" he shouted, before Chop could answer.

Chop mashed down on the brakes, making the car fishtail before coming to a screeching halt in the middle of the pedestrian walkway. "Nigga, quit bitchin' and smoke sump'n. We gotta go handle some nation bidness."

Three blunts and several near collisions later, Chop exited the expressway in a rural area along the Illinois/Indiana border. He drove a short distance before turning down a backroad and stopped at a small house in a wooded area. "You strapped?" Chop asked.

"And, you know this, maaaan!" Fatz imitated Smokey from the movie Friday, as he patted his waistband, where he had his weapon tucked.

"Lemme get that."

Fatz pulled out his .357 with the intent and purpose of handing it over, then suddenly paused. A cold chill ran down his spine and the hairs on the back of his neck stood up. He surveyed his surroundings and wondered what type of nation business needed to be handled in the middle of the night out in the boondocks.

Sensing his uneasiness, Chop snatched the gun from his hand before he could protest. "Grab the shovel out of the backseat an' let's go," he ordered as he got out of the car. Then, added, "Wit' yo scary ass."

Wit' yo' lazy ass! Got me doin' all the work, Fatz mused. He grabbed the shovel and stepped out of the car. "It's colder than a muthafucka!" Fatz said, trying to coax Chop into a conversation, something he'd been trying to do since he'd first gotten in the car, but to no avail. "Whew, this hawk bitin' ain't it!"

"Man, just follow me," Chop replied, curtly.

Fatz wanted to ask what the shovel was for but decided against it. As they walked around to the back of the house, he couldn't help but notice a familiar looking Lincoln Navigator. He went over to the parked truck to inspect.

"Bring yo ass on, I ain't got all night," Chop huffed.

Fatz hurried up to him. "B, that look like the bitch-nigga, Spank, shit."

Chop's nostrils flared. "Be the fuck quiet and stay close to me," he barked.

Fatz didn't say a word. He just bowed his head and complied. Looking at the snow-covered ground, he saw they were following the same path as two other sets of footprints.

Fifty yards into the woods, he could see a figure keeping warm over a fire burning inside a fifty-five gallon drum. He looked over his shoulder as a voice in his head told him to run. The subtle gesture didn't go unnoticed by Chop. He wrapped his arm around Fatz' shoulders and

216

stared directly in his eyes. "We 'bout to bury a GD," he said with a devilish smirk.

Though something didn't seem right to Fatz, he continued on.

"What took you so long? I been out here damn near an hour!" Spank spat, irritated.

"Who gives a fuck. I'm here now. Where Toad at?" Chop looked around, curiously.

Spank walked about ten steps. "Over here," he said, pointing to the ground.

Toad was lying on his back in a six-foot hole with half his face blown off. Fatz dropped the shovel, leaned over and threw up in the grave.

"This wasn't the agreement. I was s'pose to do the nigga!" Chop said, angrily.

"He was gettin' on my nerves complainin' 'bout it's cold, so I murked him myself. If you got a problem wit' that or you just wanna body a nigga that bad, you can murk him. Either way, it don't matter to me," Spank stated, nonchalantly.

Still hunched over, Fatz turned his head sideways towards Spank, "Murk who?"

BOOM!

Chop fired a round from the .357 into the back of Fatz's head. He fell into the makeshift grave, landing directly on top of Toad. Chop tossed the murder weapon in the grave. "Since you wanna break part of the agreement, I'ma do the same. You can bury them niggas by ya'self." He picked up the shovel Fatz had been carrying and threw it at Spank's feet.

The walk back to the car was long and heavy. If it was up to him, he would've never made such an agreement. If anything, he would've put a bullet in the back of Spank's head, but it wasn't his call to make.

As he drove off, he thought about the explanation Rome gave him for sacrificing Fatz, *'Somebody gotta die fo' killin' Slickem, and if Fatz gotta die in order fo' that to happen, then so be it. The nigga use to be a GD before he moved around here anyway.'*

WHOOP...WHOOP...WHOOOP...

The flashing patrol lights illuminating from the top of the Illinois State Trooper vehicle caused Chop's headache to intensify. He was doing 75 in a 65mph zone. Not feeling up to the task of leading them on a high-speed chase, Chop pulled over to the side of the road. Everything checked out with his license and the rental car, but it was evident by his erratic driving, bloodshot eyes and slurred speech he was under the influence of something. He submitted to a breathalyzer test and failed. To make matters worse, the trooper searched the car and recovered a fully loaded 9mm. Chop was arrested for D.U.I. and unlawful possession of a firearm.

***

Two days later, the headline on the Chicago Tribune newspaper read: FINALLY! TWO RIVAL GANGS AT WAR AGREE TO A TRUCE! WILL THE SENSELESS KILLINGS END?

CHAPTER TWENTY-THREE

A year and a half later...
Monday, June 25, 2001

RING...RING...RING...
The ringing of Zep's cell phone caused him to stir in his sleep. He no longer shared a bedroom with his younger brother, Kevin. As a form of punishment, he was living in the basement of his grandmother's building.

Zep's attendance in eighth grade was sporadic and resulted in a major drop in his grades. However, the D's and few C's he received were just enough for him to graduate on time. Six months into his freshman year of high school, the guidance counselor called Mrs. Berry to inform her that Zep had only attended classes a total of three days, and she believed Zep was a gang member and dealing drugs.

Mrs. Berry was nobody's fool, and her own suspicions started when he began coming in late at night. She hung up the phone, marched into his bedroom and searched every nook and cranny until she found all the proof she needed: a blue-steel 9mm and a little over two-thousand dollars in cash.

Later that night, when Zep came home, she had already packed and moved all of his belongings.

"You ain't fit to live in the house with civilized and God-fearing people. But, because I love you, I can't throw you out on the streets. All your stuff is in the basement. Now take this gun and devil's money back where you got it from, and don't bring it back on my property," she ordered, passing him a towel she had wrapped the gun and money up in.

Mrs. Berry's train of thought was, by banishing Zep to the basement, he would greatly miss the family atmosphere she worked so hard to provide, realize the error in his ways, and transform back into the fun-loving Christian grandson she'd raised him to be— yeah, right!

Had Zep known that getting his own crib was her form of punishment for dropping out of school and stashing guns and money in her house, he would've told her he wasn't going to school and placed the guns, money and drugs on the living room table for everyone to see.

RING...RING...RING...RING

Finally, the constant ringing roused Zep out of his sleep. He reached down to the floor and fished the phone from his pants pocket. There were sixteen missed calls. Ericka had been blowing him up all morning.

"Shit!" Zep exclaimed, as he jumped up and threw on the clothes he'd worn the day before. Without washing his face or brushing his teeth, he dashed out the door. Time was of the essence, and he'd already wasted over an hour.

As soon as he reached Ericka's back yard, the door swung open with her standing in the kitchen wearing only her panties and bra.

"What took you so long?" Ericka asked. "You know my sister will be back from work in ten minutes," she said, with her bottom lip poked out.

Instead of responding, Zep let his actions do the talking. He kicked the door shut, ran his hands down her back, squeezed her voluptuous ass cheeks, and sucked on her protruding lip. Ericka locked her arms around his neck, jumped up, and wrapped her thick legs around his waist.

She rotated her hips in a circular motion while grinding her pussy against his mid-section, as she aggressively snaked her tongue down his throat. Her panties moistened. His dick rocked-up. With not a second to spare, Zep roughly pushed her off of him, spun her around, picked her up by the waist, and laid her flat on her stomach across the kitchen table. Both of Ericka's legs were dangling freely off the table. Zep stepped in between them, dropped his pants, pulled her panties to the side and plunged his dick deeply inside her warm, soaking wet pussy.

Zep's original plan to fuck Ericka one time then clown Poopa about it flew by the wayside. Her pussy was so good he never told anyone and began creeping in and out of her back door, two or three times a week.

Zep knew Ericka had a crush on him but found her to be unattractive. She was about five-feet and weighed around one-hundred forty pounds. Had she lost twenty-five pounds, her body would've been banging, but instead she was on the pudgy-thick side. Plenty of ass, hips and titties, but flabby arms, back rolls, and a muffin top to go along with it. She always kept her short, brittle, nappy hair styled in a wrap with lots of doo-doo brown styling gel caked up around the edges. Her high-yellow skin complexion was marred with scars and red blotches due to bad acne. Zep always wondered why Poopa was so in love with her, and the night of Fatz' memorial service, he got his answer. Ericka was a bonafide nympho!

Approximately one month after Fatz went missing, he was officially presumed dead. Word on the street was he had been kidnapped and killed by some GD's. The BD's wanted revenge but the announcement of a city-wide peace treaty just two days after he went missing, along with the threat of an eye for an eye, tooth for a tooth for anybody who chose not to honor it, prevented any retaliation. The entire neighborhood was grief-stricken behind Fatz's disappearance.

In an effort to boost morale, Chop leaked propaganda that during the peace treaty talks he learned that Toad had killed Slickem, shot up his funeral, and, killed Cremey. So, he personally kidnapped, tortured, and killed him before the official agreement was reached.

On February 5, 2000, the whole hood went to Fatz's memorial service except for Ericka and Zep. At the time, she was five months pregnant with Poopa's son and after what occurred at Slickem's funeral she opted not to attend the services.

The day before the memorial service, Zep overheard Poopa telling Shit-Shit that she wasn't going and later made up a story about having to stay home to look after his sick grandmother. Instead, he went over to Ericka's house, fed her a bunch of lies about how he liked her but didn't know how to show it. He went so far as to say, he wished she was carrying his seed and offered her three-hundred dollars for an abortion. She told him she didn't believe in abortions but he gave her the money to keep for herself. That was all it took. Poopa had never given her that much money at one time. She fell under his spell, gave up the ass, and he had been fucking her ever since.

"Oooh shit...," she moaned. "Fuck this pussy!" Ericka screamed, holding on to the edge of the table.

And, that, he did. Standing on his toes, hunched over her, with his hands gripped tightly on top of hers, he pounded in and out of her mercilessly. Flesh slapping against flesh, animalistic grunts and cries of pain and pleasure echoed throughout the house.

"Aaaaaaahhh...Aaaaaahhh...yes...yeesss!" Ericka shrieked as her orgasm began to near.

Her pussy was hot, dripping wet, and getting tighter around his thickness. Zep felt a tingling sensation in the head of his dick, prompting his assault on her pussy to intensify. He tightened up his hand grip, pumped faster, and rammed into her harder. His heart beat accelerated. His breathing labored. He began to perspire. Beads of sweat rained down on her back with each powerful thrust.

"Arrgh...Arrgh," he grunted.

"Don't stop... Please...Don't stop...I'm cummin'!" she shrilled.

They were so caught up in sexual ecstasy that neither noticed her one-year-old son walk in the kitchen.

"No... Stop... Ma-Ma, stop it," P.J. cried, as he came to his mother's defense and hit Zep on the leg.

"Zep stop, I gotta get my son," she said, breathlessly.

Zep paid her no attention and kept pounding away.

"P.J., its okay, go back in the room. Mommy will be there in a minute."

Ericka was pinned down and couldn't move. She closed her eyes and tried to tune out the sloshing sounds her pussy was making, Zep's grunts, the clashing of flesh and her son's cries. She prayed he would just hurry up. A few seconds later, she got her wish.

"Ooooh...shiiit....bitch," Zep moaned as he came inside of her. Her pussy made a loud *'plop'* sound when he pulled out.

Ericka quickly jumped down off the table and scooped up her son. "Mommy okay, she was just playin'," she cooed, kissing him all over his face. "Now, let's get your diaper changed."

She went into her bedroom, grabbed the items necessary to change his diaper, and came back out. Zep was still standing in the kitchen with his semi-hard penis exposed and glistening.

"My sister will be home in a minute. I gotta go in the bathroom, freshen up and change his Pamper. Here, clean yourself up wit' some of these baby wipes before you leave."

Zep snatched several wipes out of the container and began cleaning himself off. Ericka hurried in the bathroom. He tossed the dirty wipes in the garbage and opened the back door.

"Ericka, I'm up. Get at me tomorrow," he shouted.

"Okay, baby, make sure you lock the door," she yelled back.

As Zep turned to leave, something caught the corner of his eye. She had left her bedroom door halfway open. He thought he'd seen some money sticking out from between her mattresses. He went in the room, lifted the top mattress, and as sure as shit stinks, he was staring at nothing but hundreds, fifties and twenties. Zep locked Ericka's back door $5,500.00 richer.

He hadn't made it completely out of her backyard before his phone began ringing. "What it do," he answered.

"Where you at? I been callin' you all mornin'. I need you at the building not now, right now," Rome ordered.

"I'm on my way."

Fuck is it now, he thought as he headed to the 7000 building.

***

Jazmina was all alone in her bathroom, wallowing in self-pity. "God," she said with her arms stretched towards the ceiling. "What did I do to deserve this?" She had just taken a home pregnancy test. And, the positive results confirmed her gut feeling she was pregnant with Tiso's baby. *What am I gon' do?*

She sat on the toilet, wrapped her arms around herself, and rocked back and forth as she cried her heart out. This was not the life she envisioned for herself. She got back with Tiso simply to please Zep. Never did she expect to be carrying his child. The first few months after reconciling with Tiso, he was good to her. He bought her clothes, jewelry, gave her money and kept his promise not to put his hands on her. She even began to think they could work out as a couple but that idea quickly vanished when Tiso walked up on her having a casual conversation with a boy that lived in her building. She tried to explain to him that the boy was like family to her and she'd known him practically her whole life, but Tiso wasn't trying to hear none of that. He pistol whipped the guy and blacked both her eyes. That was the second time he'd put his hands on her, but it certainly wasn't the last beating she would receive. He would beat her again and again as if she were a nigga in the streets.

Capria, Zep and just about everyone else she knew urged her to leave him. Ever since Carla had caught them having sex, she hated Tiso with a passion. She'd sworn after seeing Jazmina's bruised and battered face, she'd kill Tiso and her, if she continued to pursue a relationship with him.

Then, seemingly out of the blue, Carla became a staunch supporter of Tiso. She began to refer to him as her son-in-law, allowed him in her house, and whenever he kicked Jazmina's ass, she would take his side and tell her she brought it on herself. It wasn't long before Jazmina learned why her own mother had turned against her. The reason was simple, she was a crack addict and he was a crack dealer. Tiso would explain to Carla why he'd beat her, apologize, swear not to do it again, and then, hit her off with a couple of rocks.

For the second time in her young life, Jazmina felt like she didn't have anyone to turn to. Capria was genuinely there for her and went out of her way to prove as much. However, pride, envy and jealousy wouldn't allow Jazmina to completely open up to her.

Occasionally, and when the opportunity presented itself, she would pour her heart out to Zep. He would listen and offer advice, which was mostly to break up with Tiso, or fall all the way in line. She relished those talks and held fast to the belief that Zep would come to his senses and realize they were meant to be together. But as time went on, it became more and more apparent to her that that was probably never going to happen. Zep and Capria's love for one another was undeniable. No matter how much salt she poured into their heads about the other, they remained together. And now that she was pregnant, she was sure a relationship between her and Zep would never be.

Outside the bathroom door, Capria could hear Jazmina's faint cries. She tapped on the door. "Is everything okay in there?" Jazmina opened the door and was immediately hugged by her cousin. "What's the matter?" Capria asked, her voice laced with concern.

Jazmina rolled off some tissue and wiped her teary eyes. "I'm pregnant," she confessed.

"Are you sure?" Capria asked. "How do you know?"

Jazmina pointed to the pregnancy test sitting on the sink. Capria spent several minutes reading the instructions and scrutinizing the test results. "It's not the end of the world, MiMi. We can get through this," she said, sincerely.

Jazmina sucked her teeth. "Humph, that's easy for you to say. *'We'* ain't pregnant by a jealous ass nigga that'll beat the shit outta you if another dude looks your way. *'We'* ain't gotta explain this to my crazy ass momma. *'We'* ain't gon' hafta drop outta school. *'We'* ain't gon' be standin' in them long ass welfare lines beggin' for LINK cards. *'We'* ain't gon' be a strugglin' teenage parent. But guess who is? *'Me'*, that's who!" Jazmina vented.

"Okay, you're right to a certain degree. You talk like I'm gon' leave you hangin'. I'ma be right there every step of the way like I've always been," Capria stated, honestly.

"Puhleeze," Jazmina rolled her eyes. "You ain't always been there for me."

"Since when haven't I been?" Capria asked with much attitude, and one hand on her hip.

When your daddy had me suckin' his dick, Jazmina thought but held her tongue, as images of the sexual abuse she endured played in her head. "You know what, 'Pria, you absolutely right. I'm just upset and takin' it out on you. You probably the only somebody that got my back."

Though Jazmina hated to admit it, she spoke the truth. She knew the grudge she held against Capria was unjustified. Capria wasn't a participant in the conspiracy to have her molested. She was a child on the verge of being a victim too. Capria didn't set out to steal Zep away from her. How could she, when she was none the wiser to them having any type of relationship beyond a platonic friendship. Since moving in, Capria had gone out of her way to bond with her. She treated her more like a sister than a cousin. At times, it would be hard for Jazmina not to return the sisterly love. But when things would get ugly with Tiso and Capria would gush about Zep, or if anything positive happened in Capria's life in which she didn't reap any benefits, Jazmina would revert back into her disingenuous ways.

Capria had caught on to her behavior patterns and as a result, became careful about what she would tell Jazmina when it came to her relationship with Zep. She was aware of the hurt she was experiencing and refused to allow her pettiness to faze her or alter the love she had for her. She just took it all in stride and figured out ways to work around her.

"MiMi, I ain't gon' front like I know what you goin' through right now 'cause I ain't never been in your position. I know you think I got it made 'cause I can call Niq and get whatever I want, and I think I got the perfect boyfriend yadda... yadda...yadda...but shit ain't sweet for me like you think. I listen to you talk crazy about how Auntie Carla is a dick-suckin' crack whore, but at least you got a mother. I'd rather have a crackhead mother than no mother at all.

And don't think for one second me and Zep don't have problems. I just keep my mouth closed 'cause they don't compare to yours. That nigga been fuckin' bitches from day one. He talk that I love you and I'm waitin' on you shit, but I ain't stupid. I know the shit Tiso be tellin' you about the ho's he be fuckin' is true. I choose to say nothin' to him because I don't want to hear him lie or get you beat up for runnin' your mouth. The past few weeks he been talkin' 'bout we need to break up for a little while 'cause he feel like I don't care about him as much as he care about me. When in reality, all he want is some coochie--"

"Who want some coochie?" Carla asked, as she barged in the bathroom, catching them off guard. "What y'all can't speak English, I said who--" Carla spotted the pregnancy test and snatched it off the sink. "Oh, hell nah! I know gotdamn well one of you heifers ain't pregnant!"

Carla scanned her niece's face for an answer before turning to her daughter's. Without either of them saying a word, she knew she'd soon be a grandmother. She snapped!

CHAPTER TWENTY-FOUR

Tiso, Shit-Shit, Yatta, Terrence, Psycho and Krazy were lounging in Rome's living room talking amongst themselves. They wondered why they had been ordered to come to the building so early in the morning. Rome entered the living room and glanced around. "Fuck takin' this nigga Zep so long," he muttered.

He went into his bedroom to grab his cell phone and call Zep again. He dialed his number but hung up after the first ring. He tossed the phone on his bed, went inside the closet and removed a false wall revealing a Nike shoe box. Inside is where he kept the recording device and mini-cassette tapes until he passed them along to Agent Palko.

Late last night, had been the first time in months he'd been able to get some useful audio on Fu-Fu. With this recording, Rome was certain that Fu-Fu's along the other board members and Niq, and even his own reign at the top was nearing its end. It was past 3:00 a.m. when he'd gotten in the house, so he was too tired to check the clarity of the tape. In order to kill time until Zep arrived, he decided to play it back...

"The king approves of the way you been taking care of nation business and so do I. With the exception of a few minor incidents here and there, the peace treaty has held up pretty well. You checkin' plenty paper and breakin' bread with the nation, which is the reason why I haven't raised your weekly tax, even though we both know your profit margins, have, since, increased. The reason I had you meet me privately at the shop on such short notice is because my Connect ain't gettin' back in action, 'til next year. The rest of the B.M.'S, a few Ministers as well as some GD's, Stones and Vice Lords cop from me. I doubled up on my last order, so for the moment, I'm straight. What I need to know from you is can your Connect supply a thousand keys, and if so, at what price."

Tiso pushed the door open and stuck his head in, "You want me--"

"Get the fuck outta here!" Rome yelled, as he shut the recorder off and slid it underneath the pillow.

"My bad, B, I was just askin' if you wanted me to go find Zep," he said, from the other side of the door.

"Yeah, and next time knock before you enter my shit," Rome warned.

Tiso thought he'd heard and seen a tape recorder, but quickly dismissed the notion. His mind shifted to where he would go look for Zep in the event he wasn't at home. At the same time, Tiso opened the front door to go search for him, Zep was about to knock.

"Damn, fam, you on point. Fuck goin' on you can't wait fo a nigga to knock before you snatch the door open?" Zep half-jokingly asked as he and Tiso shook-up.

"We 'bout to find out now. Rome said wasn't shit shakin' 'til you got here. I was leavin' out to go look fo' yo ass."

Zep went into the living room and shook-up with all the guys there while Tiso knocked on Rome's bedroom door to inform him Zep had arrived.

A few minutes later, Rome came into the living room. "Fuck took you so long to get here?"

"That couldn't have been more than five minutes ago when I told you I was on my way," Zep said, taking his phone out of his pocket. "You called me a second time but you hung up before I could get the phone out of my pocket."

"Gimme that," Rome took the phone out of his hand. "I called you three times before you answered." He began scrolling through the numbers looking for the times he'd called. "You see?" he showed Zep all the times he'd missed his calls. "Who number is 9-9-4-"

"Hold up, fam!" Zep said animated, preventing him from reciting Ericka's whole phone number aloud. "I got love fo' the guys but I won't hesitate fuckin' up a nigga 'bout tryna call my girl." Zep grabbed his cell phone from Rome and added, "I overlooked yo' number thinkin' it was Capria. As you can see, she been callin' reckless all mornin'," he lied, after noticing Poopa was sitting on the couch eyeing him suspiciously.

"I know you ain't talkin' 'bout the cutie that was with the lil' chick I had to stop Tiso from slappin' around that day. 'Cause I'll definitely hit shorty back if you don't want to," Rome jived.

"That's the one, but she ain't answerin' no nigga calls 'cept mines," Zep shot back, as he erased all the numbers in his phone and put it back in his pocket.

"A'ight, the rest of y'all sit tight while I holla at Zep in private," Rome announced.

They went inside the bedroom. "'Sup?" Zep nervously asked.

"This morning, Chop went to court expecting to get a continuance but ended up accepting a plea deal for two years. With good conduct, he'll be out in six months. While he gone, I'ma need somebody to step up in his place. To thrive in these streets, you need to be a go getta and a thinker. I see both traits in you. Also, in order to be a great leader, you must first be a good follower. You understand what I'm saying?"

Zep nodded his head, eager to hear what else he had to say. "These last coupla years, I've watched you control a loose cannon like Tiso, settle disputes on the block, and body a nigga. You did all that while servin' every day and you my only worker who ain't caught a case or came back wit' short money. I signaled you out as a leader of men when you was ridin' on Big Wheels, that's why I drilled you harder than everybody else when I blessed you in."

Rome sat down at the edge of his bed and patted a spot next to him for Zep to join him. "What I'm 'bout to tell you is fo' your ears and your ears only. Some serious shit finna hit the fan. Shit that's way above yo' head. It's gonna be a lot of speculation and bullshit said about people, including me. Some of it will be true and some of it won't. Regardless to what a nigga might say or think about me, I got love fo' this mob, and even more love fo' every nigga I brought up in this shit. And when I'm no longer in play, whether it's because I'm dead or behind bars, I plan to leave what I've built in good hands," Rome said, as he pointed to Zep's chest.

Their attention was drawn to the bedroom door as somebody walked past. Rome shut the door completely and sat back down.

"As a leader, sometimes you gotta make tough decisions that might go against law or be unpopular to the masses. But that decision might be fo' the greater good of the mob or yo'self. What do you think happened to Fatz?"

Zep thought about it for a few seconds and replied, "Some GD's kidnapped and killed him. At least that's what the streets was talkin'," he added.

"That's the short version. I'ma tell you what really happened. To make the peace treaty official, both mobs had to show good faith. We wanted them to give us the nigga that killed Slickem and they wanted us to hand over the person who killed Mason. I was stuck between a rock and a hard place. That was the same day I was given the B.M. slot and strict orders to get a peace treaty. So, a sacrifice had to be made and--"

"I 'on't mean to cut you off, but who the fuck is Mason?"

Rome smiled, shaking his head from side to side. "So, you go 'round killin' niggas not knowin' their name. Mason was the nigga you caught slippin' fuckin' wit' Kathy. I personally convinced the GD's Fatz killed him and in return they gave up Toad fo' killin' Slickem and Cremey. That's one of those tough decisions I'm talkin' 'bout. I had to make a judgment call that went against er'thang this nation stands fo' and I hated to do it. But it was either risk my life for not establishing a peace treaty, which wasn't gon' happen, or let them kill you, which damn sho' wasn't gon' happen! Right or wrong, I'ma protect you wit' my life just like I expect you to protect me wit' yours. Had you been in my position, what would you have done?" Rome asked knowing full well at no time during the sit down with G-Mel and Spank did the name Mason or his murder get mentioned.

Zep's level of love and respect he had for Rome went up a notch. "I swear on everything I love, my loyalty to you and this mob is fo' life. That was some real shit you did fa' me and I'll never fa'get that. Had I been in your shoes I woulda did the same thing 'cept gave them somebody else other than Fatz," Zep said.

"Who?"

"Shid...I don't know, let me think about it." Zep faked like he was thinking of a name to tell him but was really trying to figure out a way not to do so.

"You bullshittin' me right now, but that's what I like about you," Rome said seriously. "You can think past go. Poopa is the nigga you woulda blamed the murder on but you got enough sense not to say his name because of the possibility of him finding out which could be a problem for you in the future. That's forward thinking. That's how leaders think," Rome said, wagging his hand back and forth between himself and Zep.

Rome walked over to the closet, took a duffel bag out and tossed it next to Zep's feet. He sat back down and continued, "This conversation stays between me and you. The problem wit' Poopa is he ain't no hitter. Them niggas tried to say Tiso did it. Tiso is my young hitter and second finest turn-out so I ain't gon' let shit happen to him either. I had to give them somebody they felt was a threat, so I gave them a nigga that used to be one of their own. I'm tellin' you this 'cause I trust and believe in you, and I wanna give you some insight into how the politics of this street shit really goes. I'm preparing you to take shit over one day. Right now, I'm not gonna give you a slot. Instead, these next six months I'ma put you in a position of authority to see how you handle it and how these niggas respond to you. I'ma have you delivering messages to the sets in E-dub fo' me, runnin' both crack spots and servin' weight to the guys in the area, almost everything Chop was doing. And, when he comes home, he'll make you co-minister over Englewood, if you prove you can handle it."

"B, I can handle it 'cause I've learned from the best. I been watchin' you my whole life."

"Which is why I hand-picked you. Always remain loyal to the nigga who put you on, but understand that you are the reason why you got put on. Don't get caught up in tryna be me. Do you!"

"I got'cha," Zep said, taking it all in.

"Until your paper straight, I'ma let you drive one of Chop's cars and work off his phone. When a call comes through, serve 'em whatever they want. If you front out any work, that's on you, not me. In that duffel bag is fifty jabs and 1,680 grams of hard bagged up in ounces that sell fo' $700, $350 fo' halfs, $175 fo' quarters, and $90 fo' eightballs. You keep a hunnid off every jab, and 280 grams of weight is yours. Just make sure you turn in my $35,000 first. I'm already a millionaire and now I'm puttin' you in position to become one too."

Instantly, the wheels in Zep's head began to turn. All he could think about was the money he was about to make. The seven-thousand dollars off the weight was good, but he knew from selling jabs on Emerald that he stood to pocket at least two thousand dollars on a slow day, and that's not including what he'd make off the jabs sold at the crack house.

"Ay, you paying attention to what I'm sayin'?" Rome asked a tad bit annoyed.

"Fa'sho, you want me to repeat it?" Zep, replied with assurance in his voice.

"Naw, just when you run outta weight or jabs, go next door to Old Lady Bird's apartment, turn in the money and she'll give you whatever work you need. Tiso is the only nigga allowed to go to her apartment wit' you. It's important that you keep him close and under your control. In the future, he'll be to you what Chop is to me. You can also hire and fire anybody workin' jabs as long as it's for a good reason. Remember, every nigga who say he real, ain't real. Nine outta ten niggas can't be trusted. Those nine niggas are like blades of grass. They move in whatever direction the wind is blowin'. Simply put, they go wit' the flow, whether they agree or disagree, 'cause they're too weak to stand on their own two feet. Don't be one of the many blades of grass. Instead, be one of the few rocks. Stand firm to the code and your core beliefs when the wind blows. My father told me that on my thirteenth birthday. Two days later, he and my mother were killed. I did my best tryna live up to my old man's standards. That's how I got into the position I'm in today. But, I failed him. The City of Wind made a blade of grass outta me," Rome said, becoming emotional. He paused for a few seconds to regain his composure and said, "I believe you are the rock. Chop gave everybody five jabs apiece the other day, so don't fa'get to collect that money. You can keep yours. Now, grab that cell phone and duffel bag and let's go in there and tell these niggas what the bidness is."

Zep understood the metaphoric message concerning the blade of grass and rock. However, Rome referring to himself as a blade of grass threw him for a loop. It was unlike Rome to show emotions or label himself as anything less than 100% thoroughbred, and a stand-up street nigga. Part of Zep wanted to express to Rome that he viewed him as a rock and so did everybody else, but decided to leave it alone. Instead, he grabbed the cell phone off the bed, picked up the duffel bag and remained silent until they entered the living room.

***

Capria stood in the bathroom doorway shocked. She had heard Carla snap on Jazmina plenty of times. Never in a million years did she imagine a day when Jazmina would get equally loud and vulgar to Carla's face.

"Bitch, please! I wish the fuck I would let a crackhead ho decide if I'ma keep my baby or not!" Jazmina twisted her face up.

"You disrespectful slut! I'ma wring yo' neck!" Carla roared as she reached for her daughter's throat. "I'ma choke that bastard outta yo' ungrateful ass!"

"Btich...let...m-me...g...go," Jazmina stammered, gasping for air. She put her hands on both sides of Carla's face and dug her thumb nails into her eyes.

"Aahhh!" Carla screamed. "You dumb whore! How dare you put yo muthafuckin' hands on me!" Carla released her grip around Jazmina's throat, stumbled backwards into Capria and fell to the floor. "Okay, bitch, I get it. You do a dick, get knocked up and think you grown now. I been prayin' fo' this day to come." Carla stood up. "I'ma 'bout to make them ass whoopings Tiso give you look like love taps, and when I'm done you can pack yo' shit and get the fuck outta my house!"

Fearless, Jazmina lunged at her, swinging wildly. She landed several punches to her face and neck area. Carla bent down and drove head-first into Jazmina's stomach. She wrapped her arms around her waist and slammed her into the bathtub. A loud thud sounded as the back of Jazmina's head hit the faucet.

"Stop it, that's enough!" Capria yelled, as she rushed over and pulled Carla off Jazmina before she could do any further damage.

***

Rome entered the living room clearing his throat to gain everybody's attention. "Zep got sump'n to say."

"Chop is goin' to the joint fo' six months. So, I'ma be takin' over in his place. Everything gon' be ran the exact same way 'cept I'ma give a coupla guys that's hurtin' an opportunity to eat too," Zep informed.

"BD!" Tiso shouted, showing his enthusiasm and support for his best friend.

Yatta, Terrence and the twins each flagged the trays. Shit-Shit nodded his head at Zep to let him know he was on board. Zep turned towards Poopa, who had a mean scowl plastered on his face. "Not on Emerald you ain't!" Poopa interjected. "It's been me, Shit, you, and Tiso workin' out there fo' damn near two years. We pumped that muthafuckin' block up so we the only niggas servin' out there 'cept for the few clucka's we let serve a jab or two fo' us when we got some shit to do," Poopa looked to Rome for a co-sign.

Rome smirked, shrugged his shoulders and went into his bedroom without saying another word.

"Nigga, you heard what the fuck I said," Zep sneered. "If you got a problem wit' it, quit and get money somewhere else. Long as it's far away from here ain't nobody gon' give a fuck!"

"Fuck outta here! You talkin' like you in authority or sump'n. Let a nigga pass out a coupla jabs and the shit goes to his head," Poopa spat as he stood up. "This nigga done lost his mind. Y'all can sit here and listen to this shit. C'mon Shitty Boy, we up!"

Zep blocked Poopa's path. "I dare either one of you niggas to leave before I finish sayin' what the fuck I gotta say. Then we gon' see who really lost their mind after you get yo' brains beat out!" Zep threatened.

"You absolutely right! It's whatever you say B.M. Zep!" Poopa replied full of sarcasm.

Everybody except Shit-Shit laughed at the statement trying to instigate a fight. Shit-Shit lowered his head, hoping the whole ordeal ended peacefully. Zep let the backhanded comment slide.

"Chop gave everybody five jabs yesterday. After y'all turn in the fifty-five hunnid, I'ma start passin' out more work. If you ain't finished, just gimme what you got and I'll get at you once you sold out."

Poopa sat and watched as Zep collected money from Terrence, Yatta and the twins first. Neither of them had sold more than three jabs. The four of them left together. Tiso and Shit-Shit, each, gave him thirty-three hundred dollars. "Ain't nobody left but you, playa," Zep said.

"Muthafucka's be killin' me!" Poopa scoffed, as he walked over to Zep. "Niggas claim they 'bout that paper but ain't nobody sell all five jabs 'cept me. I got rid of them shits right after you went home talkin' 'bout I'm sleepy. You prolly sold less than everybody, and Rome got you runnin' the show. Gimme five jabs, I got the money at my baby mama house."

Gotcho bitch ass now, Zep thought and smiled inwardly. "Yeah, well you ain't gettin' shit 'til I get the money, but you can start makin' yo' way over to Ericka's crib while I go holla at Rome. I'll meet you over there in less than ten minutes wit' the work."

CHAPTER TWENTY-FIVE

Zep pressed the button on the key chain, deactivating the car's alarm system and unlocking the doors. He opened the driver's side door, tossed the duffel bag in the back seat, jumped in and brought the engine to life. "Sup, you plan on walkin'?" he asked Tiso.

"Man, I'm trippin' on you," Tiso replied, as he hopped in and closed the door. "I'm tryna figure out why we rollin' in Chop's beat up Celebrity when his brand new Tahoe, 745 and '95 S.S. sittin' on twenty-two's right here in the parkin' lot."

"Fam, we ain't on no joy ridin' tryna bump some bass back, car booty ho's. We on straight bidness," Zep asserted as he drove out of the parking lot, "I gotta prove I can keep both spots jukin', sell weight, and be Rome's eyes, ears and mouthpiece out on these streets fo' the next six months. Then when Chop come home, I'ma get the co-minister slot. I ain't gon' be able to pull this off without your help. So, I'ma need you to stay focused and on point at all times. Startin' today, I'm switchin' shit up to make sure we don't miss out on sellin' a bag. I'ma hire lil' Roadie, J-Doug, Polo, Mousey and Gypsy thick ass. All that allowin' niggas to serve wit' the understandin' that two people gotta be on the block at all times, is over wit'. Tomorrow its gon' be two twelve-hour shifts, three workers on each shift, and the penalty fo' not showing up is a $500 fine, that I'll raise each time after that. But, fo' the next coupla days, I'ma need you to spend a lot of time workin' on both shifts to make sure shit gets ran smoothly. You and Shit-Shit soft ass gotta show the new workers exactly how we do shit out there. Fa' the immediate future--"

"Wait a minute, what about Poopa? Truth be told, that fag spend more time workin' the joint than any of us," Tiso said.

"Dude got a serious problem on his hands, and when we get to Ericka's crib, you gon' see exactly what I'm talkin' 'bout. Like I was saying, in the immediate future, you gon' really hafta hug the block. You know I got you though. Instead of $100 off a jab, you get to keep $200 plus serve on both shifts."

"That's what's up," Tiso said, ecstatic over the pay increase. "Shit finally startin' to fall in our favor. Didn't I tell you the day you got blessed, niggas wasn't gon' be able to fuck wit' us, and one day we was gon' be runnin' shit?"

"Fa'sho, you called that."

Pulling up to the curb in front of his house, Zep reached into his pocket and handed Tiso the money he'd stolen from underneath Ericka's mattress. "Split that in half while I dip in the crib and put this work up."

***

KNOCK KNOCK! KNOCK KNOCK KNOCK!

Poopa banged on the back door. Moments later, Ericka let him in. "Dang, why you always gotta beat on the door like that?" she complained.

"Why the fuck you think?" he retorted. Before she could answer, he said, "'Cause a nigga ain't got no key. So, either gimme a key and some head like you s'pose to be doin', or quit bitchin' and move the fuck outta my way."

Ericka smacked her lips. "Hell, in that case, I guess I'll move then."

Poopa went straight to her bedroom and lifted up the mattress. "Ericka!"

"Goddamn, why you hollerin' an' shit? Kathy in her room sleep and I'm right here in the kitchen!"

"Where my money at?"

"How the fuck I'm s'pose to know? Your stingy ass ain't gave me none," she replied, pouring herself a glass of Kool Aid.

"Fuck I do wit' that money?" Poopa asked himself. He began checking all his hiding spots in her bedroom. After coming up empty-handed, he marched into the kitchen. "Quit playin'and gimme my money before I end up puttin' my foot in yours and Zep's ass!"

"Huh?" she said, startled.

"If you can 'huh', you can hear! This nigga just pissed me off frontin' like he a chief and now you wanna play mind games wit' me."

Ericka let out a huge sigh of relief. For a second, she thought her and Zep's cover had been blown. "Last night when I told you I needed some money for P.J., you said you was broke. Now all of a sudden you got money but can't find it. Well, boo- boo, you can quit lookin' at me 'cause I ain't got it," she said then went to drinking her Kool Aid.

Poopa was heated. He deemed her lack of compassion and smart-aleck remarks as disrespectful. He maliciously stared her down as she drank her Kool Aid, and decided she must be dealt with. He slapped the glass out of her hand, sending it crashing into the wall. Grape Kool Aid and shards of glass splashed all over her face.

"You happy now?" Poopa taunted. "I ain't gon' say it no more. Go get my money!"

"Fuck you and your money!" Ericka shouted, wiping her face with the bottom of her T-shirt.   "Get the fuck out!"

Before Ericka could blink, Poopa punched her in the mouth, knocking her to the floor. He pounced on her, flooding her with punch after kick, after punch, to the body. She cried out, begging him to stop. But her pleas fell on deaf ears. All she could do was curl up in the fetal position to protect herself until he let up.

Kathy hadn't been sleep ten good minutes when Ericka's loud screams woke her up. Immediately, she jumped out of the bed and ran to her sister's defense. "Punk ass nigga," she growled, "get off my sister!"

Kathy jumped on his back, prompting him to end his assault on Ericka and focus on her. While he was struggling to get her off his back, Ericka was able to recover. She grabbed an iron skillet off the stove and attacked him with it. Seconds later, his son joined in on the fray, kicking, screaming and biting him on the leg. Due to all the fighting and yelling, they failed to notice Zep and Tiso standing on the back porch watching them through the kitchen window.

Enough was enough, and Zep decided to go against Tiso's wishes to allow the fight play itself out before making their presence known. He tapped on the window, instantly drawing their attention. Ericka tossed the skillet on the stove, made a bee-line to the door, and opened it.

"Fuck is goin' on up in here?" Zep asked as he entered the kitchen. "You need some A.A. (Aid and Assistance)? 'Cause you know how me and Tiso get down when it comes to any muthafucka puttin' their hands on one of the guys."

"Yeah, bitches and shitty diaper-wearing babies can get it too!" Tiso added, with a devilish smirk.

"Watch yo' mouth, Tiso!" Kathy warned.

"My bad. I meant to say, real pretty ladies and innocent little kids can get it," he sarcastically rephrased.

Embarrassed, and with no idea how to explain to Zep that he didn't have the money, Poopa stood frozen in place, looking like a deer caught in the headlights.

Zep got directly in Poopa's face and he still didn't blink or budge. "What the fuck! You stuck on stupid or sump'n?" He turned towards Ericka and said, "You bogus as hell! Why you ain't tell me you knew that shit. You gotta teach me how to put a nigga on pause. Me and Tiso come in peace, we don't want no trouble. Please, take Poopa off pause so he can fetch Rome's money and we can go about our bidness, Sensei." Zep maintained a poker-face as he clasped his hands together in a praying fashion and bowed his head to her.

Zep couldn't hold it in any longer. He busted out laughing before he raised his head back up. He laughed so hard, tears fell from his eyes. Everybody joined in on the laughter, including Poopa Jr. Everybody except Poopa Sr.

Having been clowned long enough, Poopa finally spoke up. "Lemme holla at you in private fo' a second," he said as he headed into Ericka's bedroom.

"Ain't nothin' to talk about. Just gimme the five and a half racks, I'ma give you five more jabs and get on wit' my bidness," Zep replied.

Realizing Zep wasn't going to grant him the opportunity to talk one-on-one, he came back into the kitchen where everybody was still standing around. "Man, B, I can't find it. Either I misplaced it or somebody stole it." He cut an evil eye at Ericka. "You know how I gets down. Don't nobody hustle harder than me. So lemme work it off, plus I'll hit you wit' a stack fo' yo'self, and if I find the paper before hand, I'ma still bless you wit' the stack on the strength of you lookin' out."

"Fuck outta here wit' that bullshit!" Tiso said in disbelief. "I know damn well you ain't jagged off the B.M.'s money. Nigga quit fuckin' around and go get Rome's money 'fore you get your ears stomped together fo' real."

"Tiso, be cool, I got this. You ain't workin' shit off and I don't need no money from you. I'ma give you three days to find that money before I bring it to Rome's attention. I advise you to find it and hand over every penny 'cause you know what the outcome will be fo' fuckin' up that kinda paper. BD!''

"BD," Tiso repeated, throwing up the trays as he and Zep left out the same way they entered.

Next on their agenda was to find lil' Roadie, J-Doug, Polo, Mousey and Gypsy. But that would have to wait a little while longer. As soon as they got inside the Celebrity, Zep's phone rang. It was Capria telling him to go get Tiso and come over to the building, it was important.

"Check it out," Zep said to Tiso as he ended the call. "We gon' shoot over to Jazmina's crib and see what Capria talkin' 'bout is so important. It's prolly nothin'."

During the drive, Zep spilled the beans to Tiso about how he and Ericka had been creeping since the night of Fatz' memorial service. He spared no details, painting her as a super-freak as he recounted many of their sexual encounters. Turning into the school's parking lot across the street from the Englewood Terrace building, he was finishing up the story of how he'd sexed her this morning, stole Poopa's jab money and split it down the middle with him.

Zep parked the car and waited to hear what Tiso had to say because he kept quiet during the entire ride. "So, what's the deally yo? What! You don't believe me? You think I'm lyin' on my dick?"

"Naw man, I just can't believe you been fuckin' that freak bitch all that time and ain't tell me or put me down wit' a shot of pussy. Who else you fuckin' I don't know about?" Tiso asked, not expecting an answer. "I'm ya boy, ya cousin, the nigga that's gon' ride or die wit' you and you handcuffin' a ho from me. I had a feeling that bitch was a freak, but I ain't know she got down like that, or else I woulda been tried to fuck her. B, put me down."

"You can fuck her. She ain't my woman. Just keep my name out of it. Matter fact, don't tell nobody about this 'cause niggas be runnin' their mouths like bitches and I don't want it to get back to Poopa," Zep said, getting out the car.

Tiso was right behind him. "Fuck Poopa! So what if he finds out, what his ho ass gon' do?"

They were standing at Jazmina's front door when Zep looked his best friend square in the eyes and said, "That nigga still BD, and fuckin' his baby mama while they still together goes against law. I know niggas don't honor that law or enforce it, but it's written and I don't want it out there that I broke the law. That's why I kept the shit a secret, plus, I gave Ericka my word. You the only person I told, and I expect you to keep it that way."

"BD," Tiso replied in a nonchalant tone then knocked on the door.

Seconds later, Capria opened the door and all they heard was Carla cursing up a storm. "Bitch, who the fuck gave you permission to go in my muthafuckin' refrigerator, get my muthafuckin' ice, open my drawer, grab my muthafuckin' towel and put it on your stupid-ass head? Put my muthafuckin' ice back in my gotdamn freezer and my muthafuckin' towel back where the fuck you took it from. Pack all your shit and you bet not leave a muthafuckin' sock, or else it's going in the gotdamn garbage and get the fuck outta my house!"

Tiso squeezed through the doorway around Capria and proceeded to Jazmina's bedroom where Carla's voice was coming from. Zep was on his heels until Capria grabbed his hand, stopping him from going up the stairs. "Bay, let them handle their drama. I need to talk to you about something," she said sweetly.

"Whatever you gotta say can wait. I ain't missin' this shit fo' the world," Zep said before taking the stairs two at a time.

"Hop to it bitch, before I-" Carla cut her sentence short to turn around and see who had the nerves to sneak up behind her. "Don't ever walk up-- Oh, heeey son-in-law," she sang, changing her whole demeanor. "I hope you got a place she can stay at 'cause her triflin' ass can't live here no more."

"Why not?" Tiso asked with his eyes glued to Jazmina. "And who the fuck put their hands on you?" he demanded to know, as he went to her bedside to inspect her wounds.

"She did this to me," Jazmina shouted, pointing a finger at her mother. "She tried to kill me and the baby!" she said being overly dramatic.

"Baby? What baby?" Tiso asked, looking back-and-forth between them.

"Your baby. I'm pregnant," Jazmina announced as she took hold of his hand and placed it on her belly. "Now what you gon' do 'bout it?"

"Yep, that's right, she's pregnant. I beat her ass and he ain't gon' do shit to me if that's what you insinuatin'. Tiso, if you love her, want to be with her and keep that baby, I suggest you take her wit' you."

Without hesitation, Tiso pulled out a knot of money. "What if she paid you rent to stay here?"

Carla's eyes lit up like a Christmas tree. "I want $2,000 a month." She said the first number that came to her mind, which happened to be the amount Niq was paying her to let Capria live there.

"Look, I ain't got it like that but if you promise not to hurt her or my seed, I'll give you five-hunnid— three in cash and twenty bags right now." He stuck his hand in his underwear and pulled out the jab he hadn't finished selling yet.

"Only because it's you," Carla eagerly accepted the cash and tucked it in her bra. "Hurry up now," she said as her body began to tremble in anticipation as he counted out twenty rocks.

"Fam, I'm finna step out front and holla at Capria. Take care of whatever you need to do 'cause we gotta get back to the joint, nah'imean."

Pulling up the front door, in an even tone and straight face, Zep asked, "What the fuck you wanna talk about?"

Capria temporarily lost her thoughts. She didn't know what to make of Zep at the moment. Something seemed a little off about him, plus he never addressed her this harshly before. *Maybe I'm over-reacting,* she thought. "Gimme a hug, I ain't seen or talked to you in two days."

"You serious?" Zep asked. His voice was laced with contempt. "Do me a favor and go tell Tiso I said come on."

"It's like that?" Capria asked. "What have I done to you?"

"You mean, what haven't you done. That's the problem. I ain't been nothin' but good to you and I can't get shit but a hug and a kiss. Fuck is that! Maybe I need to start callin' you bitches and ho's and beat your ass every other day, then I can get some pussy and we can have a baby."

"Oh, that's why you got a little attitude. What happened to 'I can wait ten years' and 'I won't pressure you into doin' nothin' you don't want to.' Huh? And you can quit actin' like you don't be fuckin' other bitches. Did you ever stop to think that I'm still holding out because I don't wanna catch nothing from none of those nasty ass skank bitches you runnin' up in."

"Miss me wit' that bullshit!" Zep said with a look of pure disgust on his face. "Fuck you think they make rubbers fo'?"

Capria's eyes began to water. "So, you admitting you fuck other bitches."

"You damn right. I ain't no virgin, and I ain't practicing celibacy either. If you was on your job, me fuckin' other bitches wouldn't be a problem. I'm done wit' the kiddie games and sugar coatin' shit wit' you. Get up wit' me when you ready to fuck and suck sump'n!" Zep stated bluntly. He walked off, leaving her standing alone and speechless. When he got in the middle of the street, he turned around and added, "Can you tell Tiso I said bring his ass on or is that too much for me to ask from yo' young ass too?"

Tears rolled freely down her cheeks and splashed to the ground as she watched Zep walk across the street and possibly out of her life forever. "And I was ready to give it up to you," she whispered, barely loud enough for herself to hear. After watching Zep get in the car and slam the door shut, she went in the house and delivered his message to Tiso.

CHAPTER TWENTY-SIX

Thursday, June 28, 2001

Three days had passed since Zep had been promoted from pack worker to overseeing and operating two booming crack spots, selling weight, and delivering orders to sets under Rome's authority, and messages to rival gang leaders. He was working tirelessly around the clock to perform those duties. The only sleep he was able to get was power naps a few times each day. If he didn't have Tiso in his corner, he wasn't sure how he would've been able to manage such a demanding schedule.

With Tiso practically running both crack spots, Zep's plan to hire additional workers and implement two twelve-hour shifts was done with ease, and proved to be an effective decision. Zep even hired two more workers to serve out of the crack house to be certain every dime got checked over there as well.

In Zep's mind, the end justified the means. A couple months into selling drugs, he realized he had forgotten about his goal to buy his family a home bigger than the one his paternal grandmother owned in Atlanta. So, for his 2000 New Year's resolution, he decided to save $200 a day.

A year later, he felt so good about the money he was saving, his 2001 resolution was to add another $100. Zep knew he'd have to come up with a clever way to justify purchasing a house with drug money in addition to convincing his grandmother, Mrs. Berry, to move into it. That fact became more apparent when she found his drug money and made him move into the basement.

But, Zep remained steadfast to his resolutions and, as a result, five-hundred and forty-four days later, he had $126,700 stashed in the garage roof.

Zep didn't have a clue as to how much his dream home would cost, but he was sure now that he was running Rome's drug operation, he'd have enough money before the year was over.

Since his promotion, he was on pace to earn more money in three days than he would've made selling dime bags in a month. Together, both crack spots moved one-hundred and four jabs. He made $8,900 because he allowed Tiso to keep his cut off the fifteen jabs he sold. Rome let him keep $6,000 from the five jabs Chop had given him before he went to jail. Plus, he had half the $5,500 he'd stolen from Poopa. That's not to mention what his take for the day was going to be. And he only had nineteen ounces to get rid of before he'd get ten of his own, adding an additional $7,000 to his stash.

Since Tiso was clocking just as many hours, if not more, but making considerably less money, Zep decided to show him a little appreciation. When the 9:00 a.m. shift began, Zep gave him $1,000, drove him to Jazmina's building and told him to get some sleep until 3:00 p.m. At precisely three o'clock on the dot, he was knocking on Jazmina's front door.

He hadn't seen or talked to Capria since he'd broken up with her. She called him several times each day but he'd send her to voicemail each time. He was relieved when Carla answered the door. He told her to tell Tiso he was in the car, waiting.

Two minutes later, Tiso hopped in the passenger seat. All he talked about was how heart-broken Capria was and that he should at least return her phone calls. Zep admitted he still had feelings for her but refused to continue entertaining her or her idea of a sexless relationship. He was done playing house with her.

He double-parked in front of Tiso's house, gave him another $1,000, and a Ziploc bag containing twenty-five jabs. "Fam, I need you to run the spots while I catch up on some sleep. I just hit the workers on both joints wit' a jab a piece, so they straight right now. I'ma holla at you when shift change." They shook-up and Tiso hopped out of the car.

Zep pulled off then suddenly slammed on the brakes. The unexpected sound of screeching tires caused Tiso to swivel his head around. "You gon' meet my new wifey tonight," Zep yelled out the window and sped off.

Truthfully, he had no plans on sleeping just yet, but he did have his eyes set on some one to replace Capria. He circled the block and parked in front of his house with the engine running while he waited on his mother to arrive. He had bumped into her the previous night at the liquor store and told her he wanted to buy a car, but needed her help in order to do so. She agreed and promised to meet him at 3:30 p.m. in front of their house.

To his surprise, she had shown up early. She jumped in the passenger seat. "So, where exactly is this car you tryna buy, or is this it?" Diane asked.

"Nah, this Chop's car; the one I wanna buy is an old-school Chevy Malibu sittin' at a car lot on Seventy-sump'n and Western," Zep replied, not remembering the exact street the car dealership was located on. "I'ma pay you to put it in your name."

"You sure you got that kinda money?" she asked, with a raised eyebrow. Zep opened the glove compartment, took out the $10,000 he had previously placed in there, handed it to her and pulled off.

Caught up in their own thoughts, they rode in silence. Both of them loved each other dearly and had plenty they wanted to verbally express in regards to the lifestyle they'd chosen to lead. Zep wanted to let her know he loved her, but hated she was more devoted to running the streets and smoking crack instead of being a loving, caring and nurturing mother.

However, three facts were preventing him from speaking his mind: One, he cared about her feelings and didn't want to say anything to embarrass, upset, or hurt her. Two, no matter how much of an adult he felt he was, he could never shake off the child-like feelings that overcame him whenever he was in her presence. Lastly, he was well aware that he was living a destructive life as well.

Diane decided to break the ice. "I guess the rumors I've been hearing that my son is next in line to become a major player in these streets are true."

Zep let her comment linger in the air for a few seconds then responded, "Yeah, sump'n like that."

"Son, I know I'm a poor excuse for a mother, but I love you and your brother and sister with all my heart. Not a day goes by that I don't worry about y'all, especially you. There are some things I've been wanting to say to you for a long time but the guilt and shame I harbor because of my addiction has kept me quiet. I'm sorry for--"

"Hold that thought," Zep's voice cracked as he swallowed the lump in his throat. "This the car lot right here." He made a right turn into the dealership.

Based on the direction Diane was steering the conversation, Zep couldn't have pulled into the car dealership at a better time. The last thing he wanted to do was break down and cry in front of her, which was exactly what he was on the verge of doing. He didn't want her to think he was a soft, vulnerable little boy in need of his mother's affection. Plus, he felt she wasn't worthy of his tears, or at least not worthy of seeing him shed tears over her.

They exited the car and were greeted by a well-dressed, middle-aged Caucasian car salesman. "Hello, my name is Paul Wiseman, but you can just call me Paul," he said, as he gave equal eye contact to both of them, because he wasn't sure who he needed to court in order to make the sale.

"I was thinkin' 'bout coppin' that Malibu over there," Zep said, tilting his head in the direction of the car.

"Then let's step right over to it," Paul led the way. "$6,750 for this ugly-ass piece of junk," Diane scoffed at the price tag written on the windshield. "And, it needs a paint job!"

"Not so fast, ma'am! This baby is a beauty in disguise. The previous owner didn't have the funds to complete the restoration he started. However, he did manage to drop a fairly new engine under the hood and fix all the dings and dents. As you can see, the entire car has been resurfaced, primed up and ready to be painted. At $6,750, it's a steal! Want to take it for a test drive?" Paul asked Zep, as he opened the driver's side door.

"Naw, I'm good. I'll drive it when I buy it. I got $5,000 cash right now!" Zep made an offer.

"$6,000!" Paul countered. "Those are low-profile tires you're admiring," he added, as he followed Zep's eyes.

"Six stacks is too steep. Fifty-four hunnid is as high as I can go." Zep extended his hand for a confirmation handshake.

Paul thought about it for a brief second and replied, "Deal!" He made it official with a firm handshake.

"Momma, pay the man."

Diane followed Paul inside the small office to sign the paperwork while Zep took the car for a spin around the block. Paul wasn't lying; the 350 horsepower V8 engine ran with power, speed and authority. On the third trip around the block, he noticed his mother coming out of the office. He pulled up behind the Celebrity and hopped out. "Everythang straight?"

"Yeah, why wouldn't it be? Here's your proof of insurance, registration and the rest of your money."

Zep didn't bother with the paperwork and grabbed the money. "You sure this all of it?" he asked, skeptically, as he did a quick eyeball count.

"Boy, don't ever disrespect me by accusing me of stealing some shit I can take! Insurance, registration, stickers, and stuff cost extra. Just look over the paperwork," she said with indignation in her voice. "Here! Take it! Read it!" She forced the paperwork in his hand. "Wannabe grown ass don't know shit!" she spat.

"Ma, I wasn't accusing you of nothin'," Zep lied. He stuffed the paperwork in his pocket, and handed her the keys to the Celebrity.

Fifteen minutes later, both cars pulled into Fu-Fu's Auto Body, Sounds and Rims Shop. Fu-Fu and Blimp were walking out of the front entrance, as they were driving around looking for a space to park. Zep didn't fully park before he jumped out and approached them.

"Sup B!" Zep greeted. He made sure to keep a safe distance as he clenched the gates to show them he was a BD and that nothing was in his hands. "I just copped that 'Bu' I rolled up in and it's in need of some life support."

Fu-Fu took a hard look at him. "What's your name and where I know you from?" he quizzed.

"My name Zep and I be gettin' money on 70th and Emerald fo'--"

"Blimp, is that you?" Diane yelled over Zep's shoulder. She walked past Zep and stood in Blimp's face.

"Diane," Blimp said more in the form of a question, unsure if his eyes were deceiving him.

"Yeah, it's me in the flesh."

"Wow, it's been a long time. What you been up to?" Blimp asked, staring her up and down. Shock and disappointment were written all over his face.

"Obviously, I've seen better days." Diane kept it real. "I got caught up in these streets but I'm in the process of getting my life back on track. Today, I'm spending time with my oldest son." She stepped back and put her arms around Zep's waist.

"Well, it's good seeing you and if you need any help, here's my number." Blimp reached in his pocket and gave her a business card. "Don't hesitate to call me."

Fu-Fu began singing Reunion by Maxwell, *"So long I've searched for you/So long but now it's true/Diane it's our reunion, reunion/ It's our reunion, reunion."*

When he put Diane's name in the song, everybody started laughing. "I didn't want to be rude and interrupt y'all reunion, so I thought it would be best to blow something for you," Fu-Fu said to Diane. He turned to face Zep. "I recall seeing you on Emerald and you're the one Rome tapped to fill in for Chop while he's on vacation. I gotta go handle some important business. Keep up the good work and I promise you'll go far.

When you go into the shop, ask for Puerto Rican Fred and tell him I said give you a thirty-percent discount on everything you purchase and any work you get on your car." Fu-Fu put up three fingers and repeated, "Thirty-percent discount." He got in the driver's seat of his F-150 and slowly pulled off.

"Good lookin' out, B!" Zep clenched the gates as opposed to flagging the trays because not many regular people knew that gesture was one of their gang signs.

"How you know Blimp?" Zep asked his mother as they entered the auto shop.

"Back in high school we used to date but I dumped him for your father."

Inside the car shop, Zep located Puerto Rican Fred and told him his budget and what he had in mind for his Malibu. With Fred's help and the thirty-percent discount, he was able to get four 12 inch and four 6X9 inch Rockford Fossgate speakers, two 500 watt Punch amps, a

Clarion radio, equalizer, a twenty disc CD changer for his sounds, two 10 inch TVs to go in the driver and passenger seat headrests, and a 7 inch flip-down TV for the dashboard. Last, he chose a wet cranberry-colored paint job and 20 inch chrome Chopper rims. Zep paid $2,500 as a down payment and was told to bring $6,500 in two weeks when his car would be ready.

After they left the auto shop, he drove to McDonald's on 87th and the Dan Ryan to grab them something to eat. "I spent all the money I had on me," he began telling Diane, as soon as they received their orders and sat down. "But once we get back to the hood I'll get some more. How much do I owe you?"

"Son, you don't owe me nothin' but I do have a proposition for you." Diane took a bite of her fish fillet, sipped her milkshake and continued," I signed up for a six month in-patient treatment center a few months ago and got accepted. It's free and a lot of people want to get in, so they're backed up. Today is the day I'm supposed to start the program. I have until seven o'clock tonight to report. It's time for me to get my act together, leave these streets alone, and be a mother to my children. So, I want to make a deal with you. If I complete rehab, come home and not drink or get high, will you stop selling drugs and gang-banging?"

Zep could see the sincerity in her eyes, but this wouldn't be her first rehab stint. The two other times she'd checked into a rehab center, she started back getting high the same day she'd gotten out. Both times he cried for days.

"Ma, I feel you and I want you to get yo'self clean, but every time, you start right back getting high. I'll believe it when I see it."

"Baby, you've got every right to doubt me. I'm serious this time around. Those other times I entered rehab, a judge made me do it. My options were to go to jail for a couple years or a rehab center for thirty days. So I chose the rehab. I wasn't ready, and didn't want to get clean then. This is not court-appointed. This is me signing up on my own. I'm ready! So, do we have a deal or not? Either way, I'm still gonna get clean and be on you every day to get yourself together, too."

Zep looked up at the clock on the wall, which read 5:37 p.m. "You got less than an hour and a half to report. It's a deal under a few conditions."

"What?"

"You let me buy everything you need to take wit' you. I get to drive you there and watch you check in. And, you have to come home and be clean for a month before my end of the bargain kick in."

"Deal!" Diane got up, walked around the table and hugged and kissed him on the cheek. "We need to get going now because if I'm one minute late, they won't admit me. Momma is gon' be so proud of us. She didn't raise us to behave the way we do."

Zep violated several traffic rules on the drive back to their house. He went inside his basement apartment, grabbed a thousand dollars and drove to Walgreens. He purchased over a hundred dollars worth of soap, toothpaste, deodorant, sanitary napkins and other cosmetic items. Then they went to a clothing store where he bought her two-hundred dollars worth of underclothes and spent another five-hundred on two pair of shoes and five casual outfits. It was exactly 6:55 p.m. when Diane checked into the rehabilitation center.

Diane exhaled. "I guess this is it," she said. "I'll be able to get visits in thirty days. In the meantime, keep looking after your brother and sister and think about what we discussed."

"It ain't nothin' to think about. As long as you keep your end of the bargain, I'll keep mines," Zep replied. "And, if you need anything, don't hesitate to let me know."

Diane smiled. "You've given me more than enough. At this point all I need is your love, patience, prayers, and for you to leave the streets alone. Now gimme a hug."

After sharing a brief embrace, Zep stood in the lobby and watched as his mother was escorted down the hall until she disappeared from his view. Despite his promises, Zep remained conflicted. Here he was, on the verge of gaining hood-stardom. And besides, she had failed him too many times in her fight to beat her crack addiction.

Now that I'm finna be a made nigga, she wanna get clean and expect me to leave the streets, Zep mused. *I'll believe it when I see it. But, if she do get her shit together all I agreed to do was stay off the streets. When I make co-minister, I won't hafta be on the streets no more. I could run shit from behind the scenes.*

Zep rationalized that in order for him to keep his end of the bargain he needed to get that co-minister slot. It felt dishonest, but he remembered what Rome had told him. As a leader, sometimes you gotta make tough decisions, but that decision might be fo' the greater good of the mob or yo'self.

He concluded that this was a decision that would benefit his family, the mob, and himself. Comfortable with how he planned to move forward, he exited the rehabilitation center.

Outside, he looked up at the building he hoped his mother would walk out of as a changed woman— this time for good. "Good luck, mama," he whispered with an uneasy feeling that nothing would ever be the same between them again.

CHAPTER TWENTY-SEVEN

70th & Emerald had been dry for over an hour. Four hours ago, Jazmina called Tiso asking him to bring her some Harold's Chicken. Playfully, Tiso made her swear on their unborn child she would suck his dick for a six piece wing and fries dinner. Only he was dead serious! He gave lil' Roadie, Gypsy and J-Doug each a jab, figuring that would last them until he returned. He was wrong. The three of them begrudgingly watched crackhead after crackhead hang around for a couple minutes only to leave and spend their money elsewhere.

J-Doug swore once Tiso returned, he was going to confront him for causing them to lose money. Especially since their shift was about to end in thirty minutes. But he was talking out the side of his neck. As soon as he spotted Tiso, he ran and met him at the opposite end of the block, accepted a jab, shook-up and never voiced his grievance. He happily jogged back down the street and informed everybody out there that shop was back open."

Gypsy got straight into hustle mode. "Listen up 'cause I'm only gonna say this shit once. Everybody make a straight single-file line." She ordered the twenty or so customers who had been waiting to get served. "We ain't accepting no shorts or singles. And this ain't no fuckin' currency exchange either. How much money you got is how many bags you gettin'." Her voice boomed loudly and clearly as she walked up and down the line making eye contact with each customer. "If you got a twenty and only want one bag, get out of line now and come back wit' a ten or two fives. Am I making myself clear?"

Satisfied that her instructions were being followed, she instructed them to get their money out before she stepped back to stand next to lil' Roadie and work security. Both of them watched the line like a hawk as J-Doug began serving the customers.

Shake Bag, a frequent customer standing last in line, got impatient as he watched J-Doug's jabs rapidly dwindle down. Fearing there wouldn't be any work left by the time J-Doug reached him, he spoke up, "Young Blood, dig this here! I'ma take the rest of that jab off yo' hands plus give you a dub if you serve me right now," he proposed, breaking the line, fast approaching J-Doug as he reached into his front pants pocket.

"Bitch, take another step and I'ma leave yo' ass right there!" lil' Roadie barked, aiming a 9mm at his head.

Gypsy quickly looked around for Tiso but he was nowhere in sight. "Muthafucka, didn't I tell you to stay in a single-file line? she sneered. "Slowly take yo' hand outta yo' pocket and put 'em up in the air."

"Who the hell y'all s'pose to be anyway?" Shake Bag asked as he obeyed her orders. "I been coppin' here fo' a year and done sold jabs out here fo' Poopa. Matter fact, where he at? He always let me go ahead of everybody if I buy the rest and give him twenty dollars."

"Shut yo' hype ass up!" Gypsy hissed. "Ain't nobody asked you all that!" She glanced down the block and across the street looking for Tiso to come intervene, but he was nowhere in sight. Thinking on her toes, she took the liberty to pat him down. The only items he had on him was a glass crack pipe made from a single shot grain alcohol bottle, a lighter, wallet and seven-hundred twenty-two dollars in cash. "This is what happens to stupid ass muthafuckas that don't follow instructions," Gypsy bellowed to the customers still waiting in line to shop. "Bust this nigga shit!"

Lil' Roadie cracked Shake Bag upside the head with the nine, opening a huge gash above his left eye.

"Awwww shit, sweet Jesus!" Shake Bag cried out in excruciating pain, as he grabbed his eye and dropped to his knees, with blood gushing from his wound.

Gypsy threw all of his belongings up towards the sky. Bills of all denominations twirled and floated aimlessly in the air. Luckily, for him, the money was new which caused most of it to stick together. A huge wad landed directly in front of him. Shake Bag immediately snatched it up while bedlam was taking place amongst the other customers over the rest of his money.

As he was reaching for his wallet, he noticed Poopa hiding out in the alley. They made eye contact. Poopa put his index finger over his lips and pointed down the alley towards 69th street for them to meet up at.

"A ight, that's enough!" Gypsy shouted in a threatening tone. Order was immediately restored. Lil' Roadie lowered the gun to his side and J-Doug resumed serving the fiends. Gypsy helped Shake Bag to his feet. "How many you want?" she asked him as if nothing ever happened.

Shake Bag jerked away from her, "I'm straight!" he huffed and stormed off.

"I bet you is," Gypsy laughed. She waited until J-Doug served the last customer and asked, "Did you see where Tiso went 'cause I'm next."

J-Doug shrugged. "Yo' guess is good as mines."

"There he go right there," Lil' Roadie pointed across the street.

Tiso was perched at his usual spot on the balcony of a two-flat building a smoker lived in. He acknowledged them and the work they just put in by raising his twin .40 cals up in the air. Seconds later, two customers walked up and Tiso faded back out of sight.

Eddie "Wolf" Lee

CHAPTER TWENTY-EIGHT

Zep sat parked on 69th & Emerald, three car-lengths off the corner of 70th & Emerald, in front of Gypsy's house. Thick clouds of smoke from the blunt he was smoking filled the car's interior, as he thought about the time he'd spent with Diane, and waited for Gypsy's shift to end. Since the first time he'd laid eyes on Gypsy, he was attracted to her. Her hair and facial features closely resembled Tatiana Ali except she was a shade or two darker. However, their bodies were built totally different. Her 32D-25-42 measurements, flat stomach and slim waist, packaged on a five-foot-five frame caused the heads of both sexes to turn when she walked past.

Zep constantly flirted with her and oftentimes she would reciprocate. However, he kept it at just that because he knew getting involved with her would jeopardize his relationship and love for Captia, so he resisted the urge to take it any further. Having casual sex with hoodrats, hypes and prostitutes didn't count as cheating to Zep because he knew that under no circumstances would he ever develop feelings for a female who lacked morals and self-respect. But on her worst day, Gypsy could never be mistaken or classified as a jump-off.

Every thug, drug dealer, player, average Joe or lesbian that crossed paths with Gypsy tried to spit game at her, but came up short, which was a miracle, in, and of, itself, considering the fact she wasn't a virgin and was in dire need of financial assistance. Both her parents were full-blown heroin addicts and provided very little for her aside from the bare necessities: Shelter, food and an outfit here and there.

Seventeen-year-old Gypsy didn't allow the lack of material possessions to lure her into the trap of promiscuity like so many other girls her age in the hood did. Even though she didn't have much, she wasn't void of self-esteem, yet she presented herself as if she didn't know she was a dime. It was her modesty that Zep found most appealing about her.

A few months back, they began to bond on a personal level. It was 3:00 a.m. and Zep was alone hustling on the block. Gypsy couldn't sleep and had stepped outside to get some fresh air, when she peeped the police watching him from a distance.   She alerted him to their presence and ever since then, whenever he served during the night alone, she would keep him company and watch his back. The first night they spent on the block together, Zep bought her something to eat. The second time she stood on the joint with him, he felt bad for not breaking her off some money for the first time, and offered her $300, but she refused to accept it. She told him the next time, just give her a jab and she'd make her own money. Zep respected that and every time after that, he took turns selling jabs with her, as if she was a regular worker on the block.

He was amazed by the way she dealt with the customers. Whenever there was heavy traffic, she made them line up and have their money out before she sold a bag. She never accepted shorts or gave out change. It was then that she told Zep her father used to be a Vice Lord on the west side and once had a heroin spot doing $75,000 a day in a neighborhood known as the 'Holy City'.

Back then, she was ten-years-old and had everything and more, any girl could've dreamed of: Toys, clothes, jewelry, trips to Disney World and her own princess-themed bedroom. She went on to tell him that her father broke the cardinal rule of 'don't get high off your own supply' and ended up a dope fiend himself.

Zep was intrigued and urged her to tell him all she remembered about her father's dope tip. She explained that he had two twelve-hour shifts, and the pack workers would do exactly what she did when she served the crackheads. As Zep's frustrations began to mount with Capria, he started to look forward to those rare occasions when nobody but him was on the block, so he could spend time with Gypsy. Her physical assets, hustler's spirit and down-to-earth-good-girl-with-a-slight-edge persona made Zep view her as wifey material.

Tonight, he planned to test the waters and find out if she was willing to take their flirting to the next level.

Zep took one last pull off the blunt and flicked it in the ashtray. During the time he sat waiting in the car for Gypsy's shift to end, a light drizzle began to fall, and the sun disappeared to be replaced by the moon and dimly lit street lights.

Darkness, coupled with clouds of weed-smoke made it virtually impossible for Zep to see clearly down to the next block. So, he cracked the window to allow the smoke to seep out. Readjusting his gaze back on 70th Street, he noticed a figure quick-stepping towards his way. Thinking it was Gypsy he opened the door, but just as fast, closed it when he realized it was Shake Bag.

Shake Bag stopped before he reached the corner, peered around then sneakily slipped into the gangway of an abandoned building. Seconds later, Zep witnessed Tiso repeat the same inconspicuous behavior. Zep got out of the car and began waving his arms in the air to get his attention. Tiso spotted him, waved him over and ducked down between two parked cars. Zep gently closed the car door and surveyed his surroundings to be sure nobody was watching him. He then sprinted across to 70th street and knelt down next to him.

Tiso never looked Zep directly in the face because he was on constant look-out for any unwanted attention. Before Zep could ask what was going on, Tiso produced his twin .40 cals. "Take this and follow my lead," he whispered.

Tiso sprung to his feet and hastily headed into the gangway. Zep was right behind him. Tiso opted to stop short of exposing himself to anyone that would've been in the abandoned building, backyard, or off in the alley. He pressed his back against the side of the building, put the .40 to his lips, then to his ear, and pointed it towards the alley. The light drizzle began to pick up as they stood silent and listened.

"I tell no lies, these some lil' ass pebbles you got here," Shake Bag complained, as he examined the three rocks Poopa was trying to sell him. "You know my name, lemme see what them shake bags lookin' like."

Poopa fished out three shake bags from his pack. "Hurry up 'cause it's startin' to pour down out here," he said, looking around nervously. "I'm tryna get on my feet, and when I come up I'ma take care of you. These bags might be shorter than what you usta buyin', but it's gonna get greater later, and the yay straight butter," Poopa made his sales pitch and switched bags with him.

"I don't know, nephew," Shake Bag further complained. "I just might hafta swallow my pride and go shop wit' that disrespectful bitch and wannabe gangsta down the street unless you willing to let these go fo' nicks, 'cause they shorter than a mu'fucka, man."

"We don't sell nicks on this block!" Tiso butted in as he walked into the alley, pointing his gun at Poopa.

Zep snatched the pack out of Poopa's hand. "Don't tell me yo' bitch ass is out here double jugglin' on the B.M.'s joint."

"M-man I-I'm j-just tryna c-come up--up wit t'-the f-five f-fifty-five hun-hunnid I owe, B."

"Nigga, lower everything in yo' pockets!" Zep reached in his pockets and took a medium-sized knot of money. "This better be everything!" he gritted.

Poopa turned both his pockets inside-out. "B, you ain't leave me no other choice. How else was I s'pose to come up wit' Rome's paper? Shit-Shit promised to loan me half, and after I hustled up the rest, I was gonna ask you to put me back down."

"Here, man, take this lil' ass shit!" Shake Bag cut in, "I ain't know you was out here sellin' bogus work. I'm finna go shop down the block." He dropped the three bags in Zep's hand.

"Empty yo' pockets too!" Zep demanded, training his gun on Shake Bag.

"Zep, come on man, I always been straight up wit' you. First, some young cunt order a young-punk, still wet behind the ears to split my shit," he pointed to the cut above his eye, "and now you finna rob me. Nephew, you know me. I ain't done nothin' to deserve this, gimme a break," Shake Bag desperately pleaded.

"Yo' hype ass heard what the fuck he said!" Tiso growled, now aiming his gun at Shake Bag as well.

Tiso and Zep's attention was momentarily distracted when an alley cat jumped from one garbage can to another. Shake Bag saw an opportunity and took advantage of it. He pushed Zep into Tiso and took off running. Poopa, Tiso and Zep chased after him. Shake Bag sprinted out the alley, kicking up water. He made a left towards Halsted Street. Shit-Shit was rounding the corner of 69th & Halsted.

"Catch that bitch!" Zep shouted.

Shit-Shit dropped the candy bar he was eating and went after Shake Bag. Shake Bag had to think quickly on his toes because his initial plan to run out on the busy street of Halsted just got foiled. So, he took the next best escape route which was to run in the alley of 69th & Halsted.

Shit-Shit had less than a foot behind him. He swept his foot across Shake Bag's heels, tripping him up. He lost balance and the slippery pavement made it harder for him to regain his footing. He took three long strides before stumbling head-first into a row of commercial dumpsters. As he was attempting to get up, all four of them commenced to beating him back down to the ground.

"Stomp that bitch ears together while I go watch out!" Zep ran to the mouth of the alley and stood vigilant. "Throw his trash ass in the garbage!" he ordered, confident there were no witnesses.

While Tiso and Shit-Shit continued with the beat-down, Poopa lifted up the lid on the first dumpster. It was filled with garbage. He did the same to the second dumpster and it was only half full. "Put him in this one," Poopa said.

Poopa went over to help, and the three of them dragged him over, hoisted him up, and tossed him in with the trash. Zep ran over with murderous intentions. Tiso couldn't hide his excitement when he saw the look in Zep's eyes. Poopa and Shit-Shit stepped out of the way. At the same time, Tiso and Zep pulled out their guns.

CLICK... CLICK...

Lightning flashed, and the rain began to downpour more heavily as they braced themselves up on the dumpster. The city was crying and so was Shake Bag. "Please don't kill me!" he sobbed. "Have mercy on me, Lawd. I don't wanna die! Take all my money, you can have it, just let me live!"

The loud rumbling of thunder deafened his cries and the hail of bullets that rained down from the twin Glock .40's. In just a matter of seconds, Tiso and Zep dumped fourteen hollow point slugs into his face, neck and chest.

Poopa and Shit-Shit were first to run away from the murder scene, followed closely by Zep. Tiso felt obligated to carry out Shake Bag's last wishes. He laid the .40 on Shake Bag's stomach, leaned his entire upper body inside the dumpster, checked all his pockets and took every single penny he had. "'Preciate it, you don't need it anyway," Tiso said to the corpse. He tucked the gun in his waistband, slammed the lid shut, and walked out of the alley, counting up the money.

***

Poopa and Shit-Shit ran non-stop to Ericka's house. They jumped over her front gate and tripped over each other, running up the stairs, leading to her front door.

"Don't ring that bell," Zep yelled as he jumped the fence. "Fuck y'all niggas think y'all goin'?"

They turned around, shocked to see Zep walking up the stairs. "You and Tiso just murked Shake Bag! We gotta lay low fa' a coupla days until shit die down," Poopa said.

"Fuck you just say?" Before Poopa could respond, Zep cocked back and punched him in the mouth. "On King David, you bet' not never come out yo' mouth like that again. And all that layin' low shit ain't gon' happen. Both you niggas workin' the joint tonight. You still owe fifty-five hunnid. I'ma add this lil' shit I took from you towards it and not tell Rome you was serving yo' own shit on his joint."

Zep grabbed Poopa by the collar and shoved him forward down the stairs. "Now let's go!"

With his lip busted and ego bruised, Poopa complied with his orders. He knew he was in no position to put up a fight against Zep. Halfway up the block, they caught up with Tiso. Tiso gave Zep his gun and half the money he'd taken out of Shake Bag's pockets.

"How many jabs you got left?" Zep asked Tiso. "I'ma run the spots fo' the rest of the night. Plus, I need to go holla at Gypsy."

"I just stopped and hollered at her. She mad as fuck 'cause she was next to work a jab and her shift over now. She just went in the crib." Tiso dug in his drawers and pulled out two jabs. "All I got is two left."

"Give 'em to Poopa," Zep said.

Tiso ice-grilled Poopa as he gave him the jabs. "Fuck happened to yo' lip?"

"I hit that nigga in his shit," Zep cut in. "You and Shit-Shit head over to the joint and tell Polo and Mousey I'll be there in a few minutes," he ordered Poopa.

Shaking his head, Tiso said, "Fam, I don't trust 'nan one of them scary ass niggas. We oughta just do both of 'em."

For a brief moment, Zep gave real consideration to his suggestion, but decided against it. "Naw, B, them niggas scary but they ain't crazy. These next few days I'ma play both of 'em close and stand on 'em with an iron fist."

"A'ight, normally you make good decisions. Let's hope this ain't a bad one."

Tiso shook-up with Zep and headed to Jazmina's house.

Zep went home to change into some dry, clean clothes, hide the dirty guns, and figure out his next moves.

"I'ma slide over Gypsy crib after I make sho' these two goofies understand they better keep their fuckin' mouths closed. Man, what the fuck was I thinkin'?" Zep pondered, "That was some dumb-ass, unnecessary shit. I'm s'pose to be movin' like a chief, putting myself in a position of power and authority, settin' an example for these dumb-ass niggas. Instead, I'm out here acting like a young, stupid, trigger-happy nigga myself. Shid... it ain't been thirty minutes since I promised my mama I was gon' leave the streets, and I done killed a nigga fa' nothin'," he muttered, upset with himself as he entered his building.

CHAPTER TWENTY-NINE

Monday, July 2, 2001
9:07 a.m.

Niq was in her Lincoln Navigator driving south on the Dan Ryan expressway near 35th Street when her cell phone began ringing. She retrieved the phone from her purse and answered, "Hello."

"Good morning, Ms. McHenry. The secretary at William Battle and Associates Law Firm greeted. "May I speak with Dominique Curry?"

"Speaking."

"Sorry to call at such an early hour, but Mr. Battle says it's urgent that you come to his office by ten-o'clock today."

"In the morning?"

"Yes ma'am. I know that is in less than an hour, but I called as soon as I was informed to do so."

"Tell him I'll be there," she sighed, ending the call.

It had been over a year since Niq had a face-to-face meeting with her lawyer, and she was on edge wondering what was so important that it couldn't be discussed over the phone. Fortunately, she wasn't too far from his downtown office building when his secretary called. She made it to his office building fifteen minutes ahead of schedule and was pleased when she was escorted directly to his office.

"To what do I owe this pleasure?" Niq asked, entering his private office.

"First, have a seat," William Battle began, "and tell me how life has been treating you."

"I can't complain. I'm still alive, healthy, free as a bird, and business is good."

"How about your family?"

"The only real family I have is Capria and she's doing just fine," Niq sighed heavily. "I know you didn't call me all the way here just for that?

"It's been a long time since I've seen you. What, our relationship is strictly business? I view you as a dear friend. My feelings are hurt," he said, looking away from her.

"You serious?" she asked in a sincere tone.

Battle turned towards her and smiled. "Yes, I do see you as someone more than a client and no, I didn't just call you here for a social meeting. The main reason I called you is because I want to know why you haven't brought me any more DNA samples."

"I've gotten the DNA of every man I associate with and none of them was a match. The only other people I could think of are all females, and you said you're one-hundred percent certain the hair came from a man. Every day I think about my mother and I question whether it was a good decision not to allow the police to get the evidence. Last week, I was thinking about getting samples of DNA from the men that's close to a few women I deal wit'," Niq said.

Battle reached into his desk drawer and pulled out a manila envelope. "No need to do that," he said as he placed the envelope on top of his desk. "Likewise, I was questioning that decision as well. I was trying to figure out a way to move forward with the evidence we already had. And that's when it hit me. A few years back, I was representing the infamous 'Englewood Rapist' and could've beat all twelve rape charges. The police had illegally obtained his DNA and beat a confession out of him. It was a lot of pressure on the state to convict him so the head state's attorney begged me to convince him to take a plea deal for natural life to avoid the death penalty. Being that he was guilty and needed to be off the streets, I agreed, but only if he promised to return the favor."

"So, what, the Englewood Rapist escaped from prison and killed my mother?" she asked.

"Oh, no," he said, as he pulled out the papers inside the envelope. "I decided to call the head D.A. and have him make a down payment towards what he owes me. According to section 730 5/5-4-3 of the Illinois Complied Statutes, all convicted criminals must submit a DNA sample upon entering the department of corrections. I gave him the

DNA profile of the hair sample and told him to run it through the Illinois DNA database and tell me if a match came back. And as sure as shit stinks, a match came back."

He slid the paperwork across the desk to Niq and pointed to the mug shot. "Now, this doesn't mean he's responsible for murdering Cynthia, but it's without question that the hair belonged to this man, Charles Robinson," he stated confidently.

Charles Robinson's face looked familiar to Niq but she couldn't quite place it. "Muthafucka!" she roared as she read his alias, prompting her to recognize his face instantly. "Chop!"

"You know him?" Battle asked.

"Do I know him? He's Rome's right-hand man," she said, heated.

"Who is Rome?" he probed further.

Niq took a deep breath and gathered her thoughts. Suddenly, it all made perfectly good sense to her. "About two years ago, I went clubbin', searchin' fo' some new clientele and met Rome. He was out partying at a strip club wit' Chop and several other members of his gang. I seen the authority he displayed over them gangbangin'-ass niggas he had wit' him, so I asked him out on a date and fronted him a key.

"'Bout a week, week and a half later, he paid me, and paid fo' one up front, so I fronted him one too. The first coupla times I served him, he brought Chop along wit' him but I told him if he wished to continue doin' bizness wit' me, he'd have to come alone. He did, and every month or so he'd buy an extra key until the day somebody hit my house. Right after that, Rome copped two extra keys, and the very next time, he copped twenty-five keys. At first, I was leery, thinking he mighta been workin' wit' the Feds or sump'n, but I knew the blocks he was gettin' money on so I went through and checked them. The nigga was sittin' on a gold mine so I sold him the twenty-five and fronted him another twenty-five. His money always been good, and the only reason I got his DNA was because I made up my mind to get every nigga that cop from me DNA, but I never thought he had nothin' to do wit' it," Niq explained. "He had to have followed me home one day and doubled back. I'm killin' Chop, Rome and his whole little circle," she vowed.

"Not so fast," Battle said. He typed a few keys on his desktop computer and turned the screen around so Niq could see it. "Chop has only been in the system for a week. It says he only has a two-year sentence, but he'll probably do six months with the way the law works. In the meantime, you'll do nothing and--"

"Fuck you mean I'll do nothin'?" Niq said angrily.

"Calm down and listen to what I have to say," he said in a calm, but authoritative manner. "These are direct orders from Mr. Carrillo. After I informed him about Chop, he told me about his connection to Rome and you--"

"That's a goddamn lie! How the fuck he know who I deal wit' when he off livin' in the jungle in a whole 'nother country?"

"Miguel Carrillo is a very, very rich, powerful and extremely well connected man. Not only does he know that you sell to Rome, and that Chop and Rome are blood cousins, he probably knows everybody else you supply as well. He says, and I quote, to tell you to continue doing business with Rome as usual. Find someone to replace him with so that his shipment orders don't decrease, and when Chop is released, he'll personally send his team of sicarios to kill all those that were involved. Now, I'm telling you this myself," Battle said, pointing to his chest. "Mr. Carrillo never gets involved to this magnitude. He usually lets people take care of their own business and when they no longer can, he cuts bait." He made a throat slicing hand-gesture, and continued. "Everything that he's done for you, he's done on account that I personally vouched for you. So, I suggest you do exactly as he says."

"First off, Mr. Miguel Carrillo ain't done shit fo' me!" she said defiantly. "Our relationship is of mutual benefit. He sends me boxes filled with drugs and I send him boxes filled wit' money. And if you're referring to that $375,000 he told me I didn't hafta pay him, he can get that wit' no problem. I'll be damned if I sit back hee-heeing and haw-hawing and sellin' and frontin' keys to a nigga that killed my mama. You and him got me fucked up!" Niq ranted as she got up to leave.

"Niq, this business is for the strong and not the weak at heart. And Mr. Carrillo's business is Mr. Carrillo's business, your business is Mr. Carrillo's business only and business comes first. Never do nothing to jeopardize Mr. Carrillo's business, and business will take care of itself," Battle recited one of The Carrillo Drug Cartel tenets that no member or associate should ever take lightly.

"Whatever," Niq mumbled as she slammed his office door and left the building.

Niq needed someone to confide in, someone she could trust, someone with no ulterior motives, someone who could understand what she was going through and feel her pain. So, before she drove out of the parking garage, she called Capria to do some catching up and to let her know to be on the look-out because she was on the way to pick her up.

Eddie "Wolf" Lee

CHAPTER THIRTY

"Zep, wake up, it's a quarter to eleven," Gypsy said, seductively rubbing her hand up and down his bare chest and stomach. "I s'pose to been gettin' my hustle on two hours ago and we got fifteen minutes to check outta this room."

Zep woke up, grinning from ear-to-ear as the sex-filled night he and Gypsy had replayed in his head. Four days ago when Zep came at Gypsy, she didn't give him the response he had hoped for. Her hesitancy wasn't because she wasn't feeling him. She had the biggest crush on him ever. She was reluctant to commit fully into a relationship with him because she knew how much he cared about Capria and she was privy to his philandering ways.

Initially, she'd told Zep to completely end his relationship with Capria, stop having sex with other females, and she wouldn't have any problem with them being an item. He readily agreed, but the cat was out of the bag, and their once innocent flirting, escalated to a point where they found themselves stripping each other naked in a seedy motel two hours after her shift had ended the night before.

"What's so funny?" Gypsy playfully pinched his nipple. "I need to get home, take a bath, and hit the block."

Zep pulled her on top of him. "I was just thinkin' 'bout them fuck-faces you was makin' last night." He kissed her on the neck and began sucking on her earlobe.

Gypsy slid her hand underneath the sheets and stroked his dick until it was rock-hard, got up off the bed and said, "Don't get ahead of yo'self. This pussy ain't yours yet. I was just sampling the goods." She picked up his clothes, took the keys to the Celebrity, and his cell phone, out of his pockets. "Capria still callin' you like crazy, avoiding her calls ain't manly. I suggest you man up and dead that situation if you wanna hit this pussy again." She tossed his clothes and phone on the bed next to him. "I'll be in the car waitin'," she said, as she strutted out the door, throwing her ass from left to right.

***

"I'm turning down your block," Niq said.

"A'ight, I'm heading out now," Capria hung up the phone. Capria climbed into the passenger seat of Niq's Lincoln Navigator and they hugged and kissed each other on the cheeks. "So, what you need to talk wit' me in private about, sister?"

"While we was talkin' on the phone, I was tryna think of the best way to break this news to you but it's only one way and that's to come straight out wit' it," Niq said as she drove around the neighborhood. "I know who killed mama."

"Who?" Capria asked.

"A nigga name Chop who works fo' this nigga I put on name Rome. I doubt if you know them personally, but you prolly heard their names ringin' 'round here 'cause Rome calls the shots fo' the BD's in this area." Niq looked over at Capria, who was deep in thought. She knew exactly who Rome and Chop were, but more importantly, she knew of Zep's connection to them and wondered if he knew or played a role in her mother's death.

"Capria, the last thing I wanna do is cause hurt and pain in your life by opening up old wounds. In this cruel world, we living in, it's just me and you, we all we got. I risk my life hustlin' in these streets so we don't want fo' nothin' and so you won't ever hafta do what I'm doin' or depend on no nigga to take care of you. I'll admit I didn't struggle at the bottom and work my way up like most people in my position. But that don't mean I didn't come up from the bottom. You know I did because we lived together under the same roof."

"In the short period of time Bull and I were together, he'd taught me a lot about the game. After he was killed, I took the drugs and money he left behind and the knowledge I acquired and made more money than he prolly would have ever made if he hadn't got killed. I played by the rules, I put niggas on; whole hoods eatin' 'cause of me, but that wasn't enough.

A nigga had to get greedy and violate me in the worst way possible. What if you would've been in the house? Not only did I promise my self, I gave mama and you my word that I would find out who killed her and see to it that they meet the same fate. Chop, Rome and any other nigga I find out had sump'n to do wit' that coward ass shit they did, I'ma murk 'em," Niq said with conviction.

"Are you sure they're the ones who did it?" Capria asked as a mixture of emotions and thoughts ran through her mind.

"I not only know fo' a fact they did it, I got proof." Niq steered the Navigator with her left hand as she stretched her body and reached into the back passenger seat with her right one. "Check this out," she said, passing Capria the manila envelope she got from her attorney, William Battle.

As Capria read over the DNA and arrest reports, she listened to Niq explain exactly how she came into possession of the documents. Niq rehashed most of the conversation she had with Battle. The only portion she left out was the strict orders given by Miguel Carrillo for her to stand down until specific conditions were met first. Capria took it all in and was convinced of Chop and Rome's guilt. "So, how you plan on gettin' at them?" she asked.

"That I haven't quite figured out yet, but I do plan on puttin' hits out on all Rome's lil' gang bangin' flunkies first, and then finish him and Chop off myself."

Capria chose her next words carefully. "You can't do that," she said, "what if you end up killin' innocent people?"

"Ain't no innocent people in this game. Every last nigga that cop or serve a bag fo' Rome is benefitin' off our mother's death. Trust and believe, any one of them gang bangin' ass niggas won't hesitate to kill me, you, or anybody else if he gave them orders to do so. That's the same type of mentality I have to have when I come at them."

"Zep won't," Capria mistakenly blurted out.

"Your little boyfriend Zep?" Niq asked as she pulled up to the front of Capria's building and put the truck in park. Niq turned and faced Capria, "What won't he do?"

Capria knew lying wasn't an option, Niq had always been able to read her like a book. First, she explained her and Jazmina's relationships to Zep and Tiso, wishfully thinking that Niq would understand where she was coming from. Then she told her about their ties to Chop and Rome. She even mentioned the murders she knew Zep and Tiso had committed.

"Listen to what you're sayin'," Niq said once Capria finished talking. You're making my point. Zep and Tiso are loyal to two things: gang bangin' and Rome. I'm glad you told me about them 'cause they might be the first two niggas I get murked. I can't allow you to live here anymore, go pack yo' stuff," Niq ordered her.

"You ain't about to touch a hair on Zep's head, much less have him killed. I know you think I'm still a baby, but trust me, I'm not. She was my mother too and I wanna help get revenge."

"Capria, have you lost yo' mind or sump'n?" Niq asked incredulously. "Now do as I said so we can get going. You're moving into my condo downtown."

"Niq, I respect you and love you with all my heart, but you think you know everything and you don't. When I was a little girl, I looked up to you. I wanted to look, walk, talk and dress just like you. And whatever you asked me to do, I did it with no questions asked. Now, I ask you to allow me to do this one thing and you turn me down. You really don't know shit about me 'cause if you did' you would've been put me on the team. Just 'cause you flippin' keys don't make you no killer. I been around Rome and Chop, them niggas killers. It ain't shit to pay somebody to kill a nigga fo' you. What makes you think you got the heart to pull the trigger yo'self?" Capria asked, staring her square in the face.

"And you do?" Niq spat.

"I already have, when you couldn't!" Capria shot back as tears began to fall from her eyes. "I knew my daddy was molesting you all those years. I used to cry myself to sleep. I knew he was doing the same thing to MiMi, too. That night when he came in my room and carried me into the bathroom, I knew he was about to rape me. The funny thing is, even though I knew it wasn't right, a part of me wanted him to do it. I wanted to suffer with you and MiMi. I wanted to feel the same physical, mental and emotional pain y'all felt. I didn't want to be treated any differently. But when you busted in that bathroom and saved me, you just don't know how happy I was to have you as my sister. I went back to bed that night like you told me but I faked like I was sleeping.

276

MiMi got up out the bed and left the room. I got up and stood at the bedroom door. I know MiMi heard every word you said to my daddy because I did. That deal you made to bring MiMi over to the house for the summer so he could rape her in place of me was some foul ass shit on both of y'all parts. I was able to forgive you but what speck of love I had for him on the strength that he was my father died that night. The next day I snuck into his bedroom, stole his gun and waited in the stairwell for him to come home from work. The police said his murder was a mistaken identity but they couldn't have been more wrong 'cause I looked him in the eyes before I shot his ass three times. I dropped the gun down the incinerator, went back in the apartment and watched cartoons. Now, you know why his gun was missing. Now you know why I didn't cry at his funeral. Now you know why I love MiMi so much and put up with her bullshit," Capria said, confessing a dark secret she'd kept to herself for five years.

"I'm sorry, I'm so sorry," Niq sobbed. "I was just trying to protect you at all costs."

Capria wiped away her own tears and said, "You don't owe me no apology. If anything, you owe MiMi one. And it wasn't your job to protect me, it was our parents' job to protect us and they both failed at it. It's our job to protect each other. I'll forever be your lil' sister and follow your lead, but I'm sick and tired of you babying me. Not only am I going to be standing over Rome and Chop's dead bodies, I got a plan on how we can make it happen. And unless you retiring from the drug game, you might as well count me in on that, too," Capria said, matter-of-factly. "Whether it's with you, or on my own, I'm not playing the sideline no more."

"I've always tried to shield you from the street life but considering what I know now, I mean," Niq stumbled over her words, "I guess, uhm...if you got yo' mind made up, well--"

"My mind's made up!"

"Well, I've always told you what's mines is yours. Ultimately, I have the final say on all matters. Now, tell me this plan you got. Partner."

For two hours, Niq listened to Capria plot out a strategy for them to kill Chop and Rome and get away with it. Although Niq had been selling Rome keys for two years, she knew far less about his movements and day-to-day operations than Capria did. Through her dealings with Zep and Tiso running his mouth to Jazmina, she knew specific dates, times and places where both of them would be and where Rome kept large sums of his cocaine and money.

Capria's plan was to kill them both at the same time, but to achieve it she needed to set some things in motion prior to Chop's release from prison. Niq figured six months was just enough time for her to find some new clientele to replace Rome. She agreed to go along with her plan and make her a 50/50 partner in her drug business under one condition. "It ain't no way around it," she asserted, "We gotta kill Zep and Tiso too."

"You got the final say and if that's your call, then that's what it is, boss lady." Capria leaned over and gave her a hug. "Lemme go pack, say good-bye to a few friends and I'ma call you to come get me after I set the first trap."

***

Zep took three long pulls off the blunt and passed it over to Tiso. "Second shift 'bout to start and I'm finna go to sleep," Zep said with his lungs filled with dro.

"Quit playin', you 'bout to creep off wit' Gypsy like you did last night. You a lucky ass nigga, her ass phat as fuck. What's to that shit, B?"

"Shorty still don't wanna let a nigga cuff her."

"What's she trippin' on?"

RING...RING...RING...

Zep flipped his cell phone open. "This right here is what she trippin' about," Zep said, as he showed Tiso the phone number that was calling him.

"B, on some real nigga shit, I think you need to holler at Capria."

"Yeah, you right," Zep said, as he pressed the talk button. "Whatchu want?"

Capria didn't really expect him to answer, but she was glad he did. "Just hear me out," she began, "These last seven days have been terrible for me. I really do miss you and I understand your position now. You said call you when I was ready to fuck and suck. I don't know if I'm ready to suck just yet, but I'm down to fuck if you promise not to hurt me."

"Capria, don't be playin' no games wit' me."

"Baby, I love you and I'm serious. You don't hafta come to me, I'll be at your front door in thirty minutes."

"I'll be waitin'."

"I promise I won't be a second late," Capria ended the call with a kiss through the phone. "MAWH!"

"Fuck is you smilin' about?" Tiso asked as he passed Zep the blunt.

"Change of plans, B. I'm 'bout to creep off wit' Capria tonight."

CHAPTER THIRTY-ONE

Capria stepped back from under the hot water spouting out of the showerhead, and lathered up the sponge with Dove body wash. She scrubbed her entire body, focusing more on her private parts. Then, she squeezed the soapy sponge between her cleavage, allowing soap suds to run down the center of her body. Next, she held the sponge to the back of her neck and squeezed what little soap remained out. She positioned her body back under the showerhead so the hot beads of water rinsed the soap completely off her body.

She turned off the water, pulled the shower curtain back and stepped out of the tub. Using her hand, she wiped the water condensation off the medicine cabinet's mirror and smiled at her reflection. The hot, cozy shower served more than its intended purpose. It was as if all her fears, hidden desires, repressed goals and inhibitions were washed down the drain as well.

Capria felt a sort of rebirth like life was just beginning at this moment. She no longer felt the need or pressure to maintain the image of a sweet, innocent, book smart girl from the hood. Ever since the day she killed her father, she felt incomplete, undervalued, misunderstood and stifled, but not any more. Looking at herself in the mirror, she felt strong, empowered, validated, free and womanly. Now, her body craved to be touched the way she felt— like a woman.

Capria wrapped a huge terry cloth towel around her frame and tiptoed into her and Jazmina's bedroom. Careful not to disturb a sleeping Jazmina, she lotioned her body and put on a white lace panties and bra set she'd purchased specifically for this occasion. She thumbed through a few hangers on her side of the closet looking for the perfect dress but decided not to overdo it. She slipped on a baby-blue North Carolina jersey dress, a pair of all white Air Max sneakers and did a once-over in the full length closet door mirror. She ran her fingers through her hair a few times before heading out the front door.

"Well, well, well... Look at what we have here," Tiso said, shaking his head. "It's damn near eleven o'clock at night. Where you think you goin'?"

"Wherever I'm goin' ain't none of yo' damn business!" Capria snapped.

Tiso stood in her way. "If you plan on goin' to fuck wit' a nigga ain't named Zep it's my bidness!" he shot back. "As far as I'm concerned y'all gotta be broke up at least five years before you can holla at another nigga. And even then, if Zep don't like the clown, I might rock his ass to sleep on G.P."

"Nigga, please!" Capria huffed, brushing past him. "For your information, I'm finna walk over to Zep's house."

"No you not, 'cause he sent me to pick you up and drive you to his house."

***

Zep had just finished tidying up his one-room basement apartment when he heard three light taps on the window. Knowing who it was, he opened up the door.

"Here she go, B— safe and sound," Tiso said. "Now, beat that pussy up fo' me."

Tiso walked off but not before Capria swung at him and missed. "You need to know when to shut the hell up and mind yo' own business," she said, vexed.

"Baby, don't let him get under yo' skin," Zep gave her a hug and a peck on the lips. "That's Tiso being Tiso. That's family right there, you know he'll go all out fo' you if need be."

"Yeah, I know he just get on my damn nerves sometimes with the way he yap off at the mouth," Capria said as she buried her face into his chest and hugged him tighter.

As Capria embraced Zep, she made a conscious decision that no matter what, she wouldn't leave his side until he made her an official woman. Hand in hand, she descended into the darkness of his basement apartment, uncertain of exactly what lie ahead, but ready to give her virginity to the one and only love of her life.

Standing at the foot of his bed, Zep could sense her nervousness. He stared at her with lust-filled eyes and kissed her lovely. "Are you sure you're ready to do this?" His heart still wouldn't allow him to take advantage of her.

"Yes, but please don't hurt me," she replied.

"I'ma try my best not to, but it might hurt a little bit. Just relax and the pain will eventually turn into pleasure."

Capria nodded her head up and down then sat on the bed. She untied her shoe strings and took off her shoes. Then stood back up and pulled off her jersey dress, folded it and placed it neatly on top of her gym shoes. As she was attempting to unfasten her bra, Zep stopped her.

"Ma, leave that on. You look sexy as hell."

In one deft motion, Zep kicked off his shoes and removed his T-shirt.

He began peppering kisses all over her face and neck as he gently laid her down on the bed. Zep took his time, not missing a spot. He slowly worked his way down her body, sucking, nibbling and planting kisses on her exposed breasts and stomach area. Zep had been dreaming for this day to come and he planned to explore and enjoy her body. He spread her legs apart and began to kiss and suck on her inner thighs. He could smell her sweetness and feel the heat permeating through her panties. Capria tilted her head back and let out a sexy moan.

"I-love-you-Capria-and-I'm-about-to-show-you-what-you've-been-missing," he said as he kissed her pussy after he spoke each word.

"Ooooh...Zep...I love you too," Capria crooned as her juices began to flow·.

Zep pulled off her panties and buried his nose in her neatly trimmed soft pubic hairs. He inhaled, deeply filling his nostrils with her womanly scent then traced his tongue along the outer and inner folds of her pussy lips. "Sssssssss..." Capria, hissed as jolts of pleasure shot through her body.

Zep turned his attention to her clitoris. With his thumb and forefinger, he pulled back the hood and exposed her love button. Using the tip of his tongue, he began licking around her clit in a slow, circular motion, gradually picking up speed before rapidly flicking his tongue up and down on it. He slipped his other hand's index finger inside her tightness and within rhythm finger fucked her. Capria's pussy was super-sensitive. His tongue action sent her into frenzy. She squeezed her legs around his neck and placed her hands on top of his head in an unconscious mind struggle to keep him there and push him away. Zep tilted his head up just where he could breathe, eased a second finger inside and sucked on her love button like it was a lemon drop.

"Stop...ooooh....please...ahh...that's enough!" Capria panted as her eyes began to well with tears. She was on the verge of experiencing her first orgasm. Capria put both her hands on the bed and tried to scoot back away from him but Zep refused to allow her to run. He moved along with her inch by inch, two finger fucking her and sucking on her engorged clit until she was trapped against the headboard.

"Ahhhh... ohhh... stop it... shit... please!" Capria arched her back "Oooooooohhhh... yeah... yeah... yes... yesssss... baby... yesssss!" she squealed as cum squirted out of her pussy, coating his fingers, mouth, and chin with her sweet nectar.

Zep pulled his fingers out, licked them and quickly began to lap and slurp her creamy pussy juices. He came up for air and stared at her for a brief moment, totally taking her in. ''I love you, Capria,'' he said once again in a sincere and seductive baritone.

"I love you, too," she said with tears falling from the corners of her eyes. She brought her lips to his mouth and kissed him with more passion than she'd ever done in the past. "I can't wait any longer. I need to feel you inside of me," Capria whispered as she unbuttoned and unzipped his jeans.

She reached inside his boxers and found what she was searching for, Zep's hard dick. She started at the head and gently ran her hand up and down the thickness of his shaft, unintentionally jerking him off. "You better not hurt me," she threatened, feeling his erection grow bigger and harder in her hand.

Zep stood up, took his pants and boxers off and returned back to the missionary position with his feet still touching the floor. He popped her titties out of her bra and sucked her nipples. Capria wrapped her legs around his waist, locking him in place. Zep squeezed his right hand around the base of his shaft and rubbed his dick up and down her moist slit. Each time he reached her small opening, he'd slip a little of the head inside, quickly pull it out, and repeat it again, going a tad bit deeper each time.

A loud hissing sound escaped Capria's lips when his entire head pierced her opening. Her pussy was hot, wet and super-tight. Capria welcomed the mixture of pain and pleasure he was putting on her. "Ooooh... Zep, it feels so good," she whispered in his ear. "This pussy is all yours."

Zep found his rhythm and began stroking her middle. She was taking the three inches of dick he was dishing out like a champ and matched him stroke for stroke with her own pelvic thrusts. She squeezed her legs around his waist and gripped his ass cheeks.

"Fuck me!" Capria commanded. "This is what you wanted, ain't it? Fuck me!" she encouraged, trying to pull him deeper inside of her.

Zep released the hand he had secured at the base of his shaft and shoved the whole nine inches of dick he was packing in her tight virgin womb.

"Awwwh!" Capria cried out. She bit down on his shoulder to ease the pain as he continued to thrust in and out of her pussy like she was a porn star. Capria's body began to squirm and writhe underneath his weight. Zep was rodding and stretching her pussy out. Just when the pain was slowly subsiding and she was beginning to adjust to his size, his strokes became faster and harder.

"Oh... ohhh... ahhhh.... shit, I'm finna cum," Zep said with baited breath. His legs began to tremble. "Oh, Fuck!" he howled as he exploded, then collapsed on top of her.

After catching his breath, he rolled over onto his back. "I'm sorry baby, I didn't mean to hurt you but I couldn't control myself. You got the best pussy I ever had in my life."

Capria rested her head on his chest and replied, "It's okay, 'cause I ain't never had no dick that good either," she joked, "plus I wanted it, and you deserved it."

Exhausted, they fell asleep in each other's arms.

***

"Run! The Dick Boys! Run!" Tiso shouted to the pack workers from the balcony across the street where he was keeping watch over them. He ran into the apartment and disappeared out the back door.

The warning from Tiso didn't come soon enough. Twelve narcotics detectives in eight unmarked cars zooming from four different directions converged on the block. Shit-Shit, Poopa, Polo and Mousey all attempted to flee but none made it more than a block away before getting caught.

Mousey was the only person they found drugs on so he was arrested and taken to 61st & Racine Police Station. Polo was searched and then questioned about the drug activity taking place on the block and the whereabouts of Tiso and Zep. He played dumb and was released on the scene with a warning to stay off the corner of 70th & Emerald. Poopa and Shit-Shit were both handcuffed and handed over to two homicide detectives. They were placed in separate vehicles and taken to 51st & Wentworth Area 2 Homicide Division Police Station for questioning.

***

Just as sure as the sun rises every morning in the east, so does Zep's penis towards the north. Capria took notice and decided to give Zep an extra-special reason to wake up. While Zep was lightly snoring, she spit on his dick. Zep became quiet and moved his arm but was still asleep. She gently grabbed his dick and used her tongue to evenly slather the spit.

"Yeah ... ummm ... uh," Zep groaned as he woke up. He couldn't believe what was happening. He touched her face to confirm if she was real or had he died and went to heaven.   To have sex with Capria was a dream come true, but for her to bless him with some head went beyond his wildest dreams and imagination. "Whatchu doing?"

"I thought you liked for bitches to suck yo' dick," she stated boldly.

"Umm...yeah," he replied, not believing this was the same girl who wouldn't kiss him for longer than a few seconds at a time just days ago, "I do."

Looking into his eyes, Capria filled her mouth with saliva and let it trickle down off her tongue to his hardness. "After you nut in my mouth, I want you to fuck my ass the same way you did my pussy," she said, then wrapped her full succulent lips around his dick.

Capria worked her tongue and jaw muscles like a suction cup. Her head game was nasty and ferocious. She used a whole lot of spit and made loud slurping noises in between savory moans. She bobbed and slobbered on his dick like a woman possessed. In less than two minutes, she had Zep's toes curled up. He balled the sheets with his fists, closed his eyes and tried to make his mind go someplace else. He wanted her to suck his dick for as long as possible but she had other plans.

"Fuck! Bitch, oohhh... Sheeit!" Zep cursed as he nutted down her throat.

KABOOM!

Zep woke up out of his dream as the basement door came crashing down off the hinges. He looked at the spot next to him and realized he was all alone.

"Police! Don't move or I'll shoot!" shouted eight of Chicago's finest trigger-happy gang unit officers as they surrounded him naked in the bed. "Zephaniyah Berry, you're under arrest for first degree murder!"

Eddie "Wolf" Lee

CHAPTER THIRTY-TWO

Immediately after the detectives hit the crack spot, Tiso ran over to the block he lived on to inform Zep about the raid. As soon as he rounded the corner he saw several officers filing out of his house, and Zep being placed in the back of a detective's car. He quickly did an about-face and hid in the gangway. Once the coast was clear, he hopped in the Celebrity, went and bought four bags of dro and a fifth of Remy before he drove to Jazmina's building and scooped her up. He rented a hotel room for them to lay low in for a couple of days until the heat died down. Then he planned to reach out and get word on exactly what was going on.

***

Rome was way beyond pissed at the fact that he was losing money. Due to his C.I. status, he'd been getting money for so long with little to no impunity, he had lost touch with reality. Zep's arrest and Tiso being M.I.A. led to him making a decision to temporarily shut down both his crack spots until he could find a competent person to run them. And to add fuel to the fire, Zep hadn't turned in the jab money from the previous day, plus he'd picked up another 1,680 grams in weight that he had yet to turn in a dime on.

After calling Special Agent Palko to set up a meeting, Rome stormed into his warehouse office, expressing his discontent. "What's the deal wit' my joint gettin' hit? I've done everything you've asked me to and you can't hold up to yo' end of the bargain!"

"First things first. You need to watch the tenor in your voice when you speak to me. Secondly, you haven't done shit yet because no arrests have been made. And third, the reason your block got raided is because those little gangbangers you got selling poison are killing people and terrorizing the community," he stated emphatically.

Special Agent Palko continued, "And how dare you barge in here with an attitude like you deserve some sort of special treatment. Let me be clear when I say that not only are you a disgrace to yourself, you're a disgrace to the human race! You represent all that is wrong with

America today. You're willing to do whatever, whenever, and to whomever, for a couple of dollars then run and tuck your tail like a coward when it comes time to face the music for your indiscretions.

Not once have I heard you express guilt or sympathy for the people in your own community you sell poison to. Never have you truly mourned the death of just one of the many children who have lost their lives fighting gang wars so that you and people like you can reap the spoils. Have you ever stopped to think about the young boys caught up in the criminal justice system for decades upon decades of their lives? I'd bet my life you haven't because you lack morals and integrity. You'd better pray you make this deal go down between Fu-Fu and Niq real soon before I throw your rat-ass in a cage where you belong. Now, get the hell out of my office!"

***

Zep had endured eight grueling hours of non-stop questioning about Shake Bag's murder before the lead homicide detective, Sergeant Graves, decided to give him a little time alone to think. Zep didn't know who, but somebody was talking. Based on the homicide detective's line of questioning, he reasoned the only people that could've given them the specifics they knew, were himself, Tiso, Poopa or Shit-Shit. However, he didn't believe that neither one of them were talking. How they got that information baffled him. Yet, despite the fact that the detective's knew everything, he was sure if the three of them kept their mouths closed they could walk right out of the police station. Mentally and physically exhausted, Zep laid down on the interview room floor and dozed off.

Ten minutes later, Sergeant Graves re-entered the room.

"Get up!" he ordered, "And have a seat. 'Cause where you're going, there'll be plenty of time to sleep if you keep up with this 'I don't know nothin'' facade."

Never taking his eyes off Sergeant Graves, Zep purposely took his time getting up from the floor before sitting down in the chair.

"Tough guy!" Sergeant Graves said with a slight chuckle. "Listen up, killa, remember I said the first person to talk is the one I'm going to work with. Now, I've already told you everything that happened before, during and after you killed Shake Bag. And, I bet you're wondering how I know all of that," he paused to gauge Zep's reaction. Zep didn't blink or budge.

Sergeant Graves continued, "We received an anonymous phone call from an eye-witness who feared for their life if they came forward and pointed y'all out in a line-up. Without the eyewitness I can't charge neither one of you with this murder, however, there's been some new developments. A few hours ago, I asked the three of you to take a lie-detector test since y'all claimed to know nothing about Shake Bag's murder. You refused, but Poopa and Shit-Shit didn't. And, I'm being straight up with you when I say, they both failed."

"So?" Zep spoke for the first time. "What that gotta do with me?"

"Everything," the veteran detective quickly stated. "Now that they failed the lie-detector test, it's only a matter of time before they break. And, when they do, they'll put everything off on you. However, since you were smart enough not to take the test and fail, I'm giving you the opportunity to put this murder off on the two who did fail so you can go home to your family where you belong. So, what do you have to say?"

"Fuck you!" Zep spat.

Shaking his head, Sergeant Graves walked over to the door. "Remember, I gave you the first opportunity," he said before leaving Zep alone in the interview room.

Man, I hope these two niggas stick to the code." Zep closed his eyes, bowed his head and prayed a silent prayer. *Heavenly Father, I never ask you for much, but I need you now. Father God, please deliver me out of here and I promise I'll leave the gang, drugs and streets alone for good.* Before he could end the prayer with an Amen, the interview room door opened and in came the lead detective.

"Looks like the gig's up," Sergeant Graves said as he tossed two signed affidavits on the table. "Your two fellow gang members and drug-dealing cronies are a whole lot smarter than you. They failed the lie-detector test concerning Shake Bag's murder and decided to come clean, well, Poopa decided to come clean," he said on second thought, "and he later convinced Shit-Shit to do the same. The good thing is, they're still claiming they know nothing about who killed Shake Bag but the problem, for you, is, they claim to know who killed Mason. Read over those statements and tell me what you think." He left Zep in the room alone.

Zep shook his head in disgust as he read Poopa's statement. I, Jermaine "Poopa" Barrett, being first duly sworn on oath, deposes and declares that the following facts are true, and if called as a witness, would testify as such: On September 20, 1999, at approximately 2:45p.m., I was selling drugs on the corner of 70th and Emerald along with Peter "Shit-Shit" Michaels, Tiso Unden and Zephaniyah "Zep" Berry, when I overheard Zep ask Tiso for a banger (gun) so that he can go hit a lick (rob someone). I observed Tiso pull a 9mm from his waistline and agree to give Zep the gun only if Zep allowed him to participate with the robbery. But, Zep didn't answer him. Instead, he snatched the gun and took off running with Tiso running right beside him. Me and Shit-Shit waited until they were half-a-block away, and decided to follow them. Me and Shit-Shit kept a safe distance and watched them run into the alley of 69th & Union then duck down next to a garbage can next to my baby-mother's, Ericka Renfro's, garage.

A couple minutes later, a Chevy driven by Mason Larkins, with Kathy Renfro, Ericka's older sister, in the passenger seat pulled into the garage. I watched as Zep pulled out the 9mm he'd snatched from Tiso, and waited until Kathy went inside her house then ran inside the garage along with Tiso by his side.

Next, I heard two gun-shots then seen Zep and Tiso run out the garage, into a gangway then disappeared from my sight.

Signed, Jermaine "Poopa" Barrett.

"Bitch-ass nigga!" Zep grumbled. "I should've listened to Tiso and bodied both them bitches!" He tossed the affidavit back on the table and didn't even bother with reading Shit-Shit's.

Sergeant Graves re-entered the room. "So, are you going to sit back and remain loyal to some bullshit street gang code of silence and spend the rest of your life in prison?" he asked as he gathered the two affidavits, "Or are you going to tell what role they played in each of these murders because I'm not stupid. I know that Poopa has a child with Kathy's younger sister and he probably set the whole murder up;

wouldn't surprise me if he actually pulled the trigger. I also know that him and Shit-Shit are the two that shot up Shake Bag. That's why they refused to admit any knowledge of that murder even after they failed the polygraph. However, I can't do nothing about it without your co-operation. As it stands right now, you're the only person going to jail and that's not fair. Once we arrest Tiso, he's going to point the finger at you. I can guarantee it because I've seen this movie over and over again. Don't be the only one to rot in a jail cell, come clean, and the judge will see that you're just an innocent, naive kid trying to fit in."

Defiantly, Zep looked him in the eyes and recited the last line of prayer he repeated after Rome the day he was blessed into the gang. "I am what I am, a Black Disciple, and that I ain't, I'll never be!" He flagged the trays in the detective's face. "You know the drill. Lawyer!"

"Suit yourself dummy. You're under arrest for the murder of Mason Larkins. You have the right to remain silent..."

***

Capria stood on the balcony of Niq's condo overlooking the city, thinking about Zep and the sex they had last night. Part one of her plan went smoothly. She hated to have been the one to call the police on Zep but Niq left her no choice. Jail was the only place she could think of that could possibly save him from the wrath of her sister. She waited until Zep was in a deep sleep, put on her clothes and searched the basement. Her plan was to take all the money, drugs and cell phones with her to use as a ruse to contact Rome and get close to him. She knew he liked her by the way he undressed her with his eyes every time she had been in his presence. She could remember one time when he winked at her and told Zep he had a cutie on his team. Capria figured with Zep and Tiso in jail, getting Rome to fall under her spell would be a piece of cake.

Also, what she found in Zep's apartment erased any and all doubts as to who was responsible for robbing and killing her mother. The duffel bag containing ten jabs, 1,428 grams of weight and $54,300 in cash she pulled from underneath his bed was the exact same one that went missing from her house on the day Cynthia was murdered. It belonged to her father and had his full name embossed into the leather. Because the bag was so old and worn, unless a person knew where to look, they wouldn't have ever paid the marking any attention.

Niq slid the glass partition open and joined her on the balcony. "Are you sure you're ready to do this?" she asked, handing her Zep's cell phone and a piece of paper with Rome's number written on it.

"Am I? You need to be asking yourself that question," Capria replied as she scrolled through the contacts in the phone. She found a number that matched the one on the peice of paper and pressed the call button. "Now, take notes and watch how easily I play this nigga."

As the phone rang, she glanced over at Niq, who was in her own thoughts admiring the world renowned Chicago skyline. *Poor thing thinks she knows every thing. I can't wait to see her reaction when the time comes to push these niggas shit back!* Capria unconsciously smiled as the gory scene of Rome's and Chop's brains splattered all over the pavement crept into her mind.

"Fuck you at?" Rome spat into the receiver. "Uhm-is-this--uhm-Ro-Rome?" Capria purposely stammered.

She closed her eyes and took herself back to that fateful day her and Niq were standing in their basement looking down at their mother's corpse.

"Who is this?" Rome asked, easing up on his tone.

Tears began to spill from her eyes. "C-Capria I'm-uhm- Zep's-girl-fr-friend,"

"Calm down," Rome said. "It's gonna be okay. Just relax and tell me what's wrong."

Capria began to think about all the joyous occasions she shared with her mother. Knowing those moments would never happen again, she started bawling uncontrollably.

"The police busted into Zep's house," she said, between hiccups and sniffles. "I tried to wake him but he was too drunk and high. So, I took the duffel bag with all the drugs and money and ran out the back door. I didn't want him to go to jail. I tried to call Tiso, but he ain't answer, so I decided to call you."

"Okay, you did a good thing," Rome said, reassuringly. "Just tell me where you're at so I can come pick you up and we can talk about it some more."

"Right now, I'm at my uncle's house. I'll call you back tonight when I get home."

"A'ight, call me as soon as you get in."

"I will," Capria said, ending the call. She turned towards Niq, who had a look of bewilderment etched across her face. "I can see now you ain't built for this shit!" she said, as she switched up her demeanor and began laughing.

To Be Continued...
A Dopeboy's Prayer 2
Coming Soon

A READING GROUP GUIDE
About this guide:

The suggested questions are intended to enhance your group's reading of this book.

Discussion questions:

1) Is Zep a cold-blooded killer or are his actions a result of being a product of his environment? Explain why or why not. The same question applies to Tiso.

2) Zep and Tiso were best friends since birth. Who do you believe had the biggest influence on the other? Why?

3) Do you think Zep was wrong for not telling Tiso that he had a sexual relationship with Jazmina? Based on Tiso's character, what do you think his reaction would have been had Zep told him?

4) Was the agreement Special Agent Palko made with Rome, telling him he could sell drugs, keep the profits, and not do a day in jail as long as he worked as a confidential informant against Niq and the leaders of his gang, fair? Explain why or why not.

5) How do you think Chop, Zep and Tiso would respond to Rome if they were to ever find out he was an informant?

6) As a young girl, Niq was molested by her stepfather. Later, she helped him sexually abuse Jazmina. Neither of them told a responsible adult (i.e. teacher, counselor, relative, neighbor, etc...) or reported it to the police. Why do you think they didn't? How common of an issue is this? What do you think can be done to prevent it and/or encourage young victims to come forward?

7) Do you believe Capria's knowledge of the sexual abuse Niq and Jazmina endured from her father caused her to view sex differently?

8) Knowing all that was written about Niq, Capria and Jazmina, what is your overall view on each of them?

9) Do you know anyone who has been a victim or perpetrator of gang violence? If so, what impact did it have on their life and/or yours?

10) Is there anything family, friends, law-abiding citizens, and/or the government can do to curb gang violence, drug dealing/usage and/or underage sex?

Stay Connected with Us!

Text **LOCKDOWN** to 22828 to stay up-to-date with new releases, sneak peaks, contests and more…

Thank you!

Submission Guideline.

Submit the first three chapters of your completed manuscript to ldpsubmissions@gmail.com, subject line: Your book's title. The manuscript must be in a .doc file and sent as an attachment. Document should be in Times New Roman, double spaced and in size 12 font. Also, provide your synopsis and full contact information. If sending multiple submissions, they must each be in a separate email.

Have a story but no way to send it electronically? You can still submit to LDP/Ca$h Presents. Send in the first three chapters, written or typed, of your completed manuscript to:

LDP: Submissions Dept
Po Box 870494
Mesquite, Tx 75187

DO NOT send original manuscript. Must be a duplicate.

Provide your synopsis and a cover letter containing your full contact information.

Thanks for considering LDP and Ca$h Presents.

Coming Soon from Lock Down Publications/Ca$h Presents

BOW DOWN TO MY GANGSTA

By **Ca$h**

TORN BETWEEN TWO

By **Coffee**

BLOOD STAINS OF A SHOTTA **III**

By **Jamaica**

WHEN THE STREETS CLAP BACK **II**

By **Jibril Williams**

STEADY MOBBIN

By **Marcellus Allen**

BLOOD OF A BOSS **V**

By **Askari**

BRIDE OF A HUSTLA **III**

By **Destiny Skai**

WHEN A GOOD GIRL GOES BAD **II**

By **Adrienne**

THE HEART OF A GANGSTA **III**

By **Jerry Jackson**

LOYAL TO THE GAME **IV**

By **T.J. & Jelissa**

A DOPEBOY'S PRAYER **II**

By **Eddie "Wolf" Lee**

IF LOVING YOU IS WRONG... **III**

A Dopeboy's Prayer

LOVE ME EVEN WHEN IT HURTS

By **Jelissa**

DAUGHTERS SAVAGE

By **Chris Green**

BLOODY COMMAS **III**

SKI MASK CARTEL II

By **T.J. Edwards**

TRAPHOUSE KING

By **Hood Rich**

BLAST FOR ME **II**

RAISED AS A GOON V

BRED BY THE SLUMS

By **Ghost**

A DISTINGUISHED THUG STOLE MY HEART **III**

By **Meesha**

ADDICTIED TO THE DRAMA **II**

By **Jamila Mathis**

LIPSTICK KILLAH II

By **Mimi**

THE BOSSMAN'S DAUGHTERS 4

WHAT BAD BITCHES DO

By **Aryanna**

Available Now

RESTRAINING ORDER I & II

By **CA$H & Coffee**

LOVE KNOWS NO BOUNDARIES **I II & III**

By **Coffee**

RAISED AS A GOON I, II, III & IV

By **Ghost**

LAY IT DOWN **I & II**

LAST OF A DYING BREED

BLOOD STAINS OF A SHOTTA I & II

By **Jamaica**

LOYAL TO THE GAME

LOYAL TO THE GAME II

LOYAL TO THE GAME III

By **TJ & Jelissa**

BLOODY COMMAS I & II

SKI MASK CARTEL

By **T.J. Edwards**

IF LOVING HIM IS WRONG...I & II

By **Jelissa**

WHEN THE STREETS CLAP BACK

By **Jibril Williams**

A DISTINGUISHED THUG STOLE MY HEART I & II

By **Meesha**

PUSH IT TO THE LIMIT

By **Bre' Hayes**

BLOOD OF A BOSS **I, II, III & IV**

A Dopeboy's Prayer

By **Askari**

THE STREETS BLEED MURDER **I, II & III**

THE HEART OF A GANGSTA I & II

By **Jerry Jackson**

CUM FOR ME

CUM FOR ME 2

CUM FOR ME 3

An **LDP Erotica Collaboration**

BRIDE OF A HUSTLA **I & II**

THE FETTI GIRLS **I, II& III**

By **Destiny Skai**

WHEN A GOOD GIRL GOES BAD

By **Adrienne**

A GANGSTER'S REVENGE **I II III & IV**

THE BOSS MAN'S DAUGHTERS

THE BOSS MAN'S DAUGHTERS II

THE BOSSMAN'S DAUGHTERS III

A SAVAGE LOVE **I & II**

BAE BELONGS TO ME

A HUSTLER'S DECEIT I, II

By **Aryanna**

A KINGPIN'S AMBITON

A KINGPIN'S AMBITION **II**

I MURDER FOR THE DOUGH

By **Ambitious**

Eddie "Wolf" Lee

TRUE SAVAGE

TRUE SAVAGE II

TRUE SAVAGE III

By **Chris Green**

A DOPEBOY'S PRAYER

By **Eddie "Wolf" Lee**

THE KING CARTEL **I, II & III**

By **Frank Gresham**

THESE NIGGAS AIN'T LOYAL **I, II & III**

By **Nikki Tee**

GANGSTA SHYT **I II &III**

By **CATO**

THE ULTIMATE BETRAYAL

By **Phoenix**

BOSS'N UP **I , II & III**

By **Royal Nicole**

I LOVE YOU TO DEATH

By Destiny J

I RIDE FOR MY HITTA

I STILL RIDE FOR MY HITTA

By **Misty Holt**

LOVE & CHASIN' PAPER

By **Qay Crockett**

TO DIE IN VAIN

By **ASAD**

A Dopeboy's Prayer

BROOKLYN HUSTLAZ

By **Boogsy Morina**

BROOKLYN ON LOCK I & II

By **Sonovia**

GANGSTA CITY

By **Teddy Duke**

A DRUG KING AND HIS DIAMOND

A DOPEMAN'S RICHES

By Nicole Goosby

BOOKS BY LDP'S CEO, CA$H

TRUST IN NO MAN

TRUST IN NO MAN 2

TRUST IN NO MAN 3

BONDED BY BLOOD

SHORTY GOT A THUG

THUGS CRY

THUGS CRY 2

THUGS CRY 3

TRUST NO BITCH

TRUST NO BITCH 2

TRUST NO BITCH 3

TIL MY CASKET DROPS

RESTRAINING ORDER

RESTRAINING ORDER 2

IN LOVE WITH A CONVICT

Coming Soon

BONDED BY BLOOD 2

BOW DOWN TO MY GANGSTA

A Dopeboy's Prayer